KNIGHT CHOSEN

THE SHACKLED VERITIES

BOOK ONE

TAMMY SALYER

KNIGHT CHOSEN

ALSO BY TAMMY SALYER

SPECTRAS **A**RISE **S**ERIES

When all other options run out, never let go of your gun.

In a few hundred years, the Algol system becomes humanity's new home. The question is: Is it a better one?

THE **S**HACKLED **V**ERITIES **S**ERIES

In a Cosmos-wide war between celestials, humans are as expendable as pawns. Until Ulfric Aldinhuus, leader of the Knights Corporealis, uses the celestials' weapons to fight back.

OTHERWORLD OUTLAWS SERIES

A sawbones fae with a supernatural-sized grudge, a necromancer gnome obsessed with pixie dust, and a hoodoo cowgirl with a Sharps buffalo rifle and damn good aim—the Tuatha Dé Danann will never know what hit 'em.

COLLECTIONS

A Scorpion's Heart: Four Twisted Tales of Love and Lust

SHORT STORIES

Artificial Fate * Creepers * No Suede Soles in Hell

Visit my website to see if anything new has been released since this publication.

www.tammysalyer.com

INTRODUCTION

Hello and thank you for being here! Should you enjoy the words on these pages (and I hope you do!), I encourage you to join my Book Club and visit me at:

www.tammysalyer.com

I occasionally send newsletters to my Book Club with new releases, special offers, and other bits of news. As a special thanks to new members, please enjoy a handful of novellas and short stories from my many and sundry universes FOR FREE.

Dedicated to Liam –
For sharing his brilliant and
boundless imagination with me.

CHAPTER ONE

It could be said that a perk of living for over a thousand turns is that it gives a person plenty of time to think. About everything from oneself to the Cosmos, and all subjects in between—a truly exceptional and marvelous range of ideas to explore. But on this warm morning in the late vernal season, Ulfric Aldinhuus wasn't thinking of anything marvelous or exceptional. He was thinking about his very, very long life, and about whether the reasons he wasn't dead yet were maybe the wrong ones.

Immortal, yes, or close enough not to bother splitting hairs, but there was more to living than not dying, more to *life* than that. Every time his daughter, Isemay, smiled at him or showed him some new and clever trick or trinket she'd created, he no longer wanted to live forever. He just wanted the time he did have to be spent with his family.

But an oath taken one thousand seven hundred and thirty-nine turns ago—by the Verities, he was old!—wasn't easily put aside. Less easily when the one who could release you hadn't graced Vinnr in close to four hundred turns.

And today duty called yet again, and he would not ignore it. Despite his hopes for dismissal from this duty, or curse, he was still devoted to it. An oath was an oath, and the only honorable way to turn from it was with the consent of the one to whom it had been made.

While lost in his thoughts, the scent of Halla-warmed dalla flower petals tickled his nose and he smiled to himself. Isemay, at sixteen turns, still couldn't sneak up on him, though she'd been trying since she'd barely reached his knees. He let her believe it was due to a lack of stealth, keeping it his secret that her beloved scent, as familiar to him as her mum's and his own, was what always gave her away. She was the daughter of two Knights. To not have learned stealth and secrecy by now could only have been due to stubborn resistance. She was sly, no doubt about that, but not against the ways of the Knights Corporealis, whom she aspired to be one day. Her da was Stallari, a role he'd taken reluctantly, and Isemay loved Ulfric and her mother, Symvalline, as a child should love a good mum and da, but she also revered them and all they represented.

"Come here, Crumb," Ulfric said, standing and looking up to the overhanging walkway circling the hall.

He heard her exasperated exhale before she stepped out from behind the thick column hiding her above. She'd dressed in an off-white tunic and wrapped a similar-colored scarf around her head, attempting but failing to hide her dark copper-tinged, slightly untidy waves of hair so she could blend in with the resplendent alabaster hall. "How do you always know, Da? And I really wish you'd stop calling me Crumb. I've told you."

"But you're still no bigger than a crumb, and a name that fits is a name that sticks." He waved her down. "Why aren't you in study at the Conservatum?"

To go with her sigh, she added an exasperated smirk, the same one she seemed to have for all her elders these days. Except for Knight Eisa Nazaria, at whom she didn't dare smirk or do anything else that might be construed as disrespectful. "You know there's no reason to be there today. The whole city of Asteryss will be waiting to catch sight of the entourage from Yor, and the foreigner called His Holiness. I bet even Acolyte Irrick left his lectures today to see them."

Though Isemay was right, it troubled Ulfric how vulnerable the city would be left with such a large part of the population gathered at Aster Keep, distracted. He changed the subject. "I have a gift for you. Quick now, before it's time for me to go."

She chose the shortest route. With a short jump over the walkway banister, she wrapped her arms and legs around an ornamental tapestry hanging next to the shrine and lowered herself with the nimbleness of a creature born in trees rather than an ancient, impregnable stone fortress. The shrine bore a statue representing Vaka Aster and stood twice Ulfric's height: a robed woman wearing a crown of stars, holding out in one hand a globe representing one of the five celestial stones she had gifted to her creations, and in the other was the hilt of a sword that pointed upward and leaned across her chest. Isemay, tapped one foot against the point of this sword on her way down to push herself into a swing over her father's head, then released the tapestry and came to a practiced landing. She spun around flamboyantly and bowed in front of him, a playful grin painted on her face.

"How many times have I told you not to do that, daughter of mine?" He added menace to the timbre of his voice, but it was false. She knew it, and he knew she knew it. He didn't have the heart to fight this morning, as uncertain as the future was. Besides, secretly, he was proud of her talents, as any father would be.

"This thirty-night, or in my life?" she asked innocently.

With a snort, he reached inside the topmost pouch of his bandolier and drew out a copper chain that matched the glints of her hair. Turning his hand over, he dangled the pendant attached to it and watched Isemay's eyes widen as it caught the light from the many illuminate orbs dotting the hall.

"Is it…" she began to ask but lost her breath in surprise.

"Yes, a Mentalios, and more. Of course, you're not a Knight, so you won't be able to use it to speak to the rest of us—yet."

Distracted by her constant ambition to one day join the Order, she smiled broadly. "I can't wait for that! It will be so wonderful to finally know what you and Mum are saying to each other when you don't want me to hear."

"You can wait, Crumb, and you will. Besides, it doesn't work like that. You can't hear anyone's thoughts at any time. And… well, it's not decided yet—*you've* not decided yet if that's the path you want to take." Ulfric delivered these words in his familiar lecturing tone, but inwardly, what he meant was *I've not decided yet if that's the path I want you to take.* He went on aloud, "I designed this pendant especially for you. I call it a memory keeper." He beckoned her to take the jewel.

She reached out slowly, her expression excited and a touch cautious. The overall pendant took the form of a dragørfly carved out of a natural eyestone, its wings just wider than Isemay's palm. Inset beryl-colored gems comprised the creature's eyes, and the center hole in its thorax bulged around a clear circular piece of crystal the size of a sparrow's egg. "It's heavy," she said. "And beautiful."

His lips kinked happily at her joy. "What is the focusing phrase I taught you?"

Without taking her eyes from the pendant, she recited easily, "Cæcra ad resrs, boromcad bea dord. Kucik kea kesrs, emsu kæ lœkra." The words were Elder Veros and meant "cycle of light, balanced by dark, focus my sight, into my heart."

"Good," Ulfric praised. "Now, think back to your fondest memory, perhaps from your childhood. Remember the bird I gave you when you were only five?"

She nodded.

"Think about how much you loved it and focus this memory into the lens there. Speak the phrase to still your thoughts until only that memory remains in your mind."

She pulled the chain free from his hand and held the pendant cupped between both of hers. Staring at the crystal lens, her lips moved soundlessly as she said the Elder Veros phrase. Ulfric, to himself, did the same beside her, wanting to share this moment and this memory with his precious daughter.

The crystal's clarity changed. In its center emerged the hovering image of a wooden bird, painted in bright greens and yellows. She gasped but remained still, her expression now one of pure delight. The image changed, and then Isemay herself, a version of her when she had been small, appeared from within the lens, chasing the bird. Though the vision was soundless, they could both see her as a little girl, giggling and holding the colorful toy, running among the corridors of Vigil Tower and pretending she was flying along with it.

They watched Isemay's memory for a few moments before she tore her eyes free. When she did, the image wavered and vanished. "Thank you, Da. It's the most wonderful thing I've ever seen."

He smiled indulgently, as only a father can. "You're welcome, my daughter." His tone deepened, grew serious. "Anything you ever want to recall, you can see in the pendant. It will always help you remember."

He caught the way her stare lingered, his tone having unnerved her. When he didn't meet her eyes, she lifted the chain over her head and let it fall around her neck. Though Isemay took after Ulfric and her Yorish mother in height, her head still only reached as high as the top of his chest as she wrapped her arms awkwardly around his breastplate and bandolier. He hugged her back, swallowing a knot that suddenly formed in his throat.

From the hall's entryway came the sound of approaching boots. Soon the smoke-roughened voice of Knight Thorvíl called to him. "The skimmer and Mylla are outside, Stallari. We await you in the foyer, we do." He left the way he'd come.

Ulfric released Isemay abruptly. "I will see you this evening."

"Please, Da, let me come to Aster Keep with you. The whole city will be there. Why shouldn't I?"

"For the hundredth time, no. I'm telling you as Stallari, not as your father. You stay here with Stave and Safran and your mother—"

"But—"

"Isemay." Instead of rising angrily, his voice dropped to a menacing note, though it resonated nowhere near as threatening as his enemies knew it could be. "I've forbidden it."

"And so have I." Symvalline entered the hall, dressed in her ceremonial sky-blue cloak in recognition of the day's serious event, though she had opted to remain at Vigil Tower with the other two Knights.

Isemay's eyes bounced between her parents, then she frowned. "So you think I can handle a sword, but not a crowd. I see. You know I'm not a child anymore, don't you?"

Ulfric, sighing inwardly, reached out and gripped her shoulder, pulled her close, and planted a rough kiss on her forehead. "I'll see you tonight, *child*." He strode to the entryway, exchanging a *yes, this again* look with Symvalline, but stopped midway and turned back. "I love you, Crumb."

The words cracked her blustery façade, and for a moment she appeared as she had in the memory keeper, so small, so young and guileless and filled with wonder. Even her voice sounded as it had at five as she said, "I love you, too, Da."

CHAPTER TWO

Knight Mylla Evernal stood outside Vigil Tower with her sister-in-arms Knight Safran Glór at the top of the stairs leading into the tower's main hall, fidgeting with her baldric and sword to make sure they weren't too tight, weren't too loose. Today's planned summit hardly seemed exceptional, but she didn't want to be caught off guard if the visiting dignitary calling himself His Holiness had plans to make it so.

The summit at Aster Keep would include Arch Keeper Beatte of the kingdom of Ivoryss, Stallari Aldinhuus of the Knights Corporealis, and the foreigner coming from the kingdom of Yor, a stranger until recently. Despite the mundanity of kingdom politics, it happened to be the most exciting event she'd been part of since, well, since the day she'd taken her oath to become a Knight Corporealis. Stallari Aldinhuus had prepared them to be ready for anything and shared his suspicions regarding this Holiness Prime. Thus, her struggle to quell her excitement, and a touch of apprehension, wasn't without reason. The other Knights never hesitated to point out that she was the novice among them, to her endless frustration, and today could be her chance to show them she was as capable of fulfilling her duties as any of them.

Worried her fidgeting would be obvious to Safran, or worse, the

Stallari when he emerged, she distracted herself while waiting for him with thoughts of Havelock Rekkr, her paramour, and their conversation the night before. On her way out of the inn they'd tarried in last night, her to return to Vigil Tower, him to his squadron of Dragør Wing Marines to prepare for today's event, she'd warned him that her duties after the summit could call her away from the city of Asteryss for a time, depending on the outcome.

His response, as was typical of him, had been calm and unquestionably accepting of her role. "You don't have to explain anything, Mylla. I'll still be here when your duty is done, whether that's today or tomorrow or a full turn from now. Duty to our maker is your first calling, and mine is to Ivoryss. That's what we stand for, and we stand stronger because of it."

He was so blargin' honorable and reasonable it could, and frequently did, drive her crazy. Especially because he was so blargin' right.

Vaka Aster and each of the five Verities that had created the Cosmos, comprised two forms, one celestial and one physical, a human vessel given in service to the makers. The duty of the Knights Corporealis was to protect and watch over this vessel. Vinnr's was currently an alabaster statue that had long ago been flesh when its maker had still chosen to walk among them. Mylla's term of duty, though short compared to the rest of the Order's, had stretched over the last three hundred and forty-two turns around Halla. Havelock's, of course, was significantly shorter, for he was a commoner and destined to live only a single life span. He and his Marines watched over the rest of the commoners. But she watched over, when it came down to it, the fabric of their world itself, for if the Verity's vessel were destroyed, Vinnr would be as well.

Mylla. Mylla! Safran's voice, sent through a Mentalios lens each of them wore, pulled her from her thoughts back to the present.

"You don't need to shout," she said aloud.

Safran smirked. *I do if I want to be heard through that fog you call Lock.*

"He's spruce, he is, novice, but so young, just a babe yet," Stave Thorvíl added as he returned from fetching the Stallari. "He needs to live a few hundred turns and acquire a few scars before he'll be worth more than a wink and a pat on the head from a warrior like you, he does." The ever-present scent of the lind leaves he constantly rolled and smoked clung to him and gave his voice the same roughness as his features.

"So it's scars that make a man spruce, is it?" she asked, feigning the raptness of an eager pupil. "That must make you the sprucest man alive, then. If by 'spruce,' you mean disheveled, loutish, and often perforated."

"Being the hero of many a battle is what led to these perforations, it is. That smooth-faced pilot of yours doesn't look old enough to know which end of a sword is pointy. And anyway, Safran's is the only opinion of me that matters, and she thinks of my scars as marks of dignity and distinction, she does," he finished, grinning at his mate.

"Safran, is it true?" Mylla asked, enjoying the ribaldry. Among the long-lived Knights, the "youth" of all commoners was simply too easy a mark to ignore. Mylla had learned to laugh along with them instead of taking affront.

Safran's darker-than-coal eyes widened innocently as she turned to face Stave. Though she had lost the ability to speak aloud some turns ago, her voice in the Mentalios link had lost none of its expressiveness, which at the moment, dripped with sarcasm. *I hardly love Stave only for his scars. But I'll grant that leaves very little else to love.*

"What?" Stave argued. "You mean aside from my charm, wit, and great big—"

"Great big what?" Isemay cut in from where she stood behind Ulfric and Symvalline, who'd exited the tower together.

Mylla and Safran tipped their heads and saluted by touching their chin marks, indigo nine-pointed stars, given to them when they'd been ordained Knights. The Stallari returned the gesture, then gave the top of Stave's head a hard stare. Stave had conveniently remembered he needed to tighten his greaves and had leaned down to do so, avoiding Ulfric. After a moment, Ulfric turned back to Isemay.

"I told you—" he began, but she cut in.

"I *know*, Da, but I'm only standing here. I'm staying, I swear!" She waited a beat, but Ulfric's admonition didn't come, so she finished with a mischievous grin, "What was that again, Stave?"

The Knight stood up, cleared his throat. "My collection of axes. All great and big and much-loved by my darling Safran. And sharp as a rook's beak too, they are," he finished proudly.

The six of them broke into laughter, even Ulfric and Symvalline. Safran's amusement was silent but no less animated. Ulfric's was short-lived, though, and Mylla noticed his gaze shift toward the peaks of the Morn Mountains.

Beyond the shadows of the great columns of Vigil Tower, the day was so clear that they could see the distant range fringing the eastern horizon. Mount Omina, nestled among them, would be free of snow now, though the Knights had still been forced to tramp through winter pack a thirty-night ago when they'd secreted the vessel of their maker there. No living commoner had been granted an audience with Vaka Aster since she'd ceased being animated some hundreds of turns prior. Now they simply made due by paying homage to the shrine in Vigil Tower, and few even came to visit that anymore. No one would know the Knights had taken the real vessel away, as Ulfric intended.

To Mylla's surprise, she caught Ulfric's thoughts in their Mentalios link. *Stay vigilant, Eisa, Mallich.*

"They always are," she commented. The two Knights he referred to had stayed with the true vessel at their secret cave in Mount Omina to keep watch.

He turned to look at her, seemingly as surprised as she that she had caught his thought. Much was riding on his shoulders today. She hardly blamed him for this slip in Mentalios discipline. If ever a day or a reason existed when his mind would be scattered, it was this day, this reason.

Because, if Ulfric's suspicions proved true, today brought the unprecedented—and time would tell if also unwelcome—visit by another celestial like their maker. Another Verity, who called himself His Holiness. And with Vaka Aster's celestial presence so long absent, only the Knights were left to protect her inert vessel, if protection was required. Though they'd discussed it at length, none of the Knights could guess why another Verity might visit the realm of Vinnr, and so they had hidden the vessel from the world. Just in case.

We'll know soon if the Stallari is right, Mylla thought and wasn't quite able to stop herself from another reflexive adjustment of her baldric.

Underneath this, she wore her ceremonial breastplate with a dragørfly centered over a nine-pointed star, Vaka Aster's symbol, engraved in the metal. Ulfric's armor sported considerably more dents and scrapes, given its age, though its sheen was prismatic beneath Halla's midmorning rays. All the assembled Knights carried sheathed weapons at their waists, and the crystal Mentalios lenses of their Order hung from copper cuffs around their necks, Mylla's and Ulfric's beneath their armor.

"Anything further from the bruhawks?" Ulfric asked Safran.

Though the Knights could communicate silently with their Mentalios lenses, pendants crafted using a wystic design that channeled their thoughts among each other, they customarily spoke aloud most often, with the exception of Safran.

Safran grew serious again and sent, *It's the same. Ranks of possible fighters, two deep, line the eastern border of the city, a few hundred of them. Some wear Yorish legion uniforms, others the clothing typical of Yorish citizens. A few hundred wear other styles, some look to be uniforms, but not like any I've ever seen.*

"Could they be from Dyrrakium?" Mylla asked.

They could. It's been a long time since we've seen a Dyrrak. They are most certainly different from Ivoryssian and Yorish. That's all I know for certain.

It would be as strange as anything else that might happen this day if the unusually clad entourage that had come with His Holiness were from Dyrrakium. The kingdom had cut itself off from the rest of Vinnr several centuries ago. The word Dyrrakium itself was Elder Veros, meaning "exile." What could it mean if the Dyrraks had abandoned their self-imposed expulsion from the original kingdoms?

"Knight Evernal, say your goodbyes," Ulfric said. "Stave, Safran, Symvalline, remember what we planned. If you see, hear, or sense anything amiss, don't waste your time protecting Vigil Tower. Take the *Vigilance* and rally with us at Mount Omina."

The three nodded and Ulfric turned to Symvalline. As they spoke quietly together, Mylla exchanged a hug with Safran, who clasped her tightly and sent, *I'm looking forward to hearing your stories of the day.* When they separated, the tiny crinkle of concern in Safran's forehead surprised Mylla. She'd never seen her friend anything but composed and confident.

With her lips quirked in a half-grin, she responded, "A day free of Vigil Tower is as much a welcomed adventure as anything. At least one of us will have a story about something more exciting than *axes* to tell tonight."

Her attempt at lightening the mood fell flat. Despite the many turns, most shaded in tedium as the Order had stood watch over the vessel of their maker, the possibility of encountering another Verity had never been an anticipated reason for "adventure." Now that it was, Mylla had to admit she shared more than a little of her friend's worry.

"Novice," Stave said, drawing her attention, "this isn't training. The bruhawks will be watching, they will, but once you enter the keep, you and the Stallari are on your own. Keep your wits as sharp as your weapons, and don't let anything distract you from your duty. A young mind tends to be a wandering mind, it does."

She squashed the urge to roll her eyes. "Understood."

He clapped her on the shoulder as Safran gave a high-pitched whistle. The two silvery bruhawks perched atop the tower leaped clear and dove, streaking downward like stars until the instant before it seemed they would smash into the stone landing. They flared their wings, easily twice as long from tip to tip as an Ivoryssian commoner was in height, and extended their talons just in time to grip the metal perches installed on the landing for them. They came to rest, a few silver feathers alighting and blowing off with the breeze.

Both Mylla and Safran stepped toward them, Mylla with one hand outstretched. The nearest, Yggo, arched her neck forward, inviting Mylla to scratch, which she obliged. Safran bowed her head and began the incantation that would be carried to the hawks by way of the Mentalios link: Vesr sraak aak, sraka aak suu kaa. *With thine eyes, these eyes too see.*

As one, the flying sentries snapped into rigid stances and blinked several times. Mylla withdrew her hand. On the last blink, their bright yellow bird-of-prey irises shifted to a spectrum of color, iridescent greens, blues, yellows, and reds, a swirling mix of hues that mirrored the matching spectrum now swimming in the crystal surface of Safran's Mentalios. What the ordained bruhawks saw, their Knight cohort also now saw, and what she directed, they would carry out. A useful and symbiotic partnership made possible through the wystic gifts of their celestial maker. Today they would fly as sentinels over the keep while Mylla and the Stallari joined the summit inside.

Ulfric and Symvalline stepped apart, and he descended the few steps to the surface skimmer. He didn't beckon Mylla; he didn't need to. The burden of duty pulled her along. Before she sat, she caught the level but stern look Symvalline threw Ulfric and didn't need the Mentalios to know her thoughts. *The fate of this world may rest on our shoulders today.*

⁂

THE SKIMMER, a horseless carriage powered by the harnessed light of Halla, rolled them smoothly over Asteryss's paving-stone streets. Ulfric would have preferred the dignity of arriving at Aster Keep on horseback, but he reminded himself those days were long past. Advancements are aptly named thus, and though he'd lived enough turns to accumulate all the wisdom and prowess of experience that came with long life, he often felt as if his true self, the man inside the warrior, had not advanced with the times. Maybe he *could* not.

He brushed that thought aside and looked to his young protégé. Mylla stared at the passing buildings, her eyes seeing things that lay far beyond the city. He thought he could guess what her thoughts were about: love. She and the young Dragør Wing fighter pilot couldn't hide anything from a man who'd seen as much as Ulfric had. And no sense of duty, no invocation of ambition or honor, no feeling he'd ever experienced held a candle to the overpoweringly potent combination of youth and love. Even the possibility of death fell to a whisper in a mind playing that orchestra. Of all the knowledge he'd accumulated over the millennia, this was a truth he was utterly certain of, which had never changed.

He considered leaving her to her thoughts. Mylla's scant term of service would hardly matter if their visitor turned out to be another Verity. What could one with so little experience, who'd only met the living Vaka Aster on a single occasion, hope to do if this Holiness's intentions were malicious? Of course, he wouldn't, though. Mylla was a Knight first. She'd sacrificed a normal life, as they all had, to get to this station in her life, and in part his own duty was to see to it that she fulfilled hers.

"Mylla," he said lightly, and she faced him. "Beatte's court will demand we meet the Arch Keeper and this visitor unarmed."

Her dark eyes, the irises barely lighter than the pupils, flashed. She had the eyes of a Dyrrak. But when she was alarmed or excited, they stood out strikingly against skin paler than most Dyrraks, more of a Yorish trait. An orphan, no one really knew her lineage. Ulfric had chosen Mylla to fill a gap in the Knight's Order because of her fine scholarship and high marks in the Resplendolent Conservatum, despite many who grumbled about her Dyrrak blood. And Mylla had never made him doubt or question his choice.

"Why would they?" she asked. "Acolyte Irrick and the Conservatum will vouch for us, even if Arch Keeper Beatte has let skepticism make her forget her own lessons."

"Beatte has shown very little favor toward our Order during her reign, and the members of the Conservatum grow less and less true to their first precept with every passing turn. It's a consequence of Vaka Aster no longer walking among us. They no longer think of the creator as their master. They know, or they think they know, where their best interests lie—in the hand that feeds, not the one that travels the stars without a thought for them. Beatte tolerates the Conservatum as long as they don't annoy her with theology. We'll find no allies among Aster Keep, and Acolyte Irrick keeps quiet about his arrangement with us. It's best for him that he does."

Though she kept her expression level, he sensed what she was thinking. If the Resplendolent Conservatum, the proving grounds for all future Knights and senatorial scholars who chose each successive Arch Keeper, no longer served their Verity, what did that mean for the Knights in the long-term? *Does she suspect she's the last Knight?* And on the heels of that: *She may well be.*

"You have your klinkí stones?" he asked.

"I do, Stallari." She placed her left palm against her right vambrace where the secret weapon of the Knights remained in place.

"Good. Keep them concealed. Remember, if this Holiness is the Verity we suspect him to be, he'll be weakened in his sundered form outside of his own realm. Weakened doesn't mean powerless, though. To fight him would be foolish, and if escape is required, follow me to the well. Our intent is not to engage in battle with a foreign Verity or even a foreign invader, only to preserve Vaka Aster's vessel from any, and all, threats."

CHAPTER THREE

A man can live a thousand turns and still have too little time to develop the necessary patience to reason persuasively against the will of a stubborn sixteen-turn-old adolescent. And this was particularly true for Ulfric—because his daughter was exactly like him. Obstinate, intractable, and when pushed downright devilish in her stubbornness. The last thing the leader of the Knights Corporealis of Vinnr needed today was to be upstaged and defied by his copper-ringleted daughter in front of half the realm and its leadership.

But there Isemay was, near the front of the crowd, bearing witness to the proceedings with no regard for her father and mother's instruction to stay away. Her arrival coming so close to his own told him she'd left the tower within moments of his and Mylla's departure. As he made his way to the keep's rampart, he saw the look of surprise on her face when she realized he'd spotted her. Defiantly, she held his eyes until he marched past. *There will be a reckoning when this was over,* Ulfric swore to himself. Daughter or not, he could not protect her if she sought out danger so recklessly. So like her Knight mother. So like her Knight father. Could he even pretend to be surprised?

Once the crowd recognized the Stallari, their rumbling increased, pulling his focus back to the task. Dragør Marine Commander Tannir

Brun, dressed in an elegant tunic of indigo velvet bordered with royal-blue piping, marched one step to the right behind Ulfric past the masses gathered outside Aster Keep, the seat of Ivoryss's leadership. To his left, also one step behind, paced Mylla. The throngs of querying and concerned citizens who'd come to witness this summit hemmed them in from every direction.

Ahead, Ulfric finally spotted the reason for this event: His Holiness. The man stood at least two heads above all others present, though his shoulders were disproportionately narrow, making him look the way a child standing on another's shoulders might. His crimson hair caught the light, its hue and vibrancy like a fuel-oil fire, and cascaded from his head and upper lip in a molten mass, curling here, braided there. Orna-mented epaulets with silver frames polished to a glow sat atop his shoulders and linked in ornate filigrees and decorative scrollwork across his chest to create a ceremonial chain-mail shawl. Near him stood an entourage of six pale soldiers, their uniforms a mix of Yorish and some other design, and three black-robed priests.

It took Ulfric one look at His Holiness and his attending cadre—each priest bearing a mark on his face similar to those carried by Vaka Aster's Knights—to confirm the thing he had worried about since news of Yor had crossed their borders. Worried about and dreaded. His Holiness was the Verity creator of the realm known to the Knights as Battgjald, there could be no doubt now. Having been touched by a Verity himself gave Ulfric the sight to see through His Holiness's façade of being an ordinary man.

The Verity waited at the base of the wide alabaster steps leading over the rampart to the keep's main gate. Lining both sides of the stair-case, Dragør Marines kept watch, each man and woman erect and vigi-lant, their expressions fixed in equal measures of discipline and disdain. The rumors about Yor and how quickly it had come under the sway of this interloper had spread, it seemed, and the small delegation would not leave this place alive if they dared show any aggression here.

The reasons His Holiness had requested this audience had only been explained in vague terms of the usual kind: to discuss diplomacy, trade, borders, contracts, and the like. Arch Keeper Beatte would not suspect another Verity would be walking among them. Yet for Ulfric, why the Verity had also requested Ulfric's attendance was the only question that mattered. What purpose would a sundered Verity, another of the five, have here in Vinnr, and what did it have to do with him?

The Scrylle of Vinnr, a celestial artifact belonging to the Knights that contained the recorded history, lore, and wystic teachings of Vaka Aster, only made sparse mentions of the other Verities and their realms. And why should it? Other realms did not concern the Knights of Vinnr. Their own world was quite enough. Now here the Verity was, calling himself His Holiness, and walking in the body of a man, hiding his true nature. Why the deception?

Ulfric could not stop himself from looking back over his shoulder into the crowd, searching for his daughter's bright hair and beloved face. He could no longer see her. *Isemay, you should have listened to your da, for once,* he thought, unable to hold his growing anxiety in check. He prayed to Vaka Aster that Symvalline would find her in time to get her somewhere safe.

He stopped a stride short of reaching His Holiness, and the intruder spoke.

"Stallari Aldinhuus. Your reputation among the Knights of your Order has reached even me." His voice—deep, rolling, and hard, like kiln-fired bones—held the authority of ages. "A thousand and more years—or, what is it you call them? Turns, I believe—is a long time among your kind. And I can see"—his cheeks wrinkled upward in a ghastly grin—"you also know who I am."

Only the skin of His Holiness's face and hands showed, its striking whiteness even paler than the Yorish. His eyes, blacker than the emptiness between the stars, gleamed in their sunken orbits, the bones of the skull they lay in so sharp and prominent they nearly broke through his crystal-hard flesh. Now that he was closer to the Verity, Ulfric could see that the body he inhabited was not like any of the people of Vinnr. He wondered how long ago this one-time man of Battgjald had lost his body to his maker's vessel.

The first cold tickle of fear, a feeling Ulfric had almost forgotten, whisked over his skin. "Inside," he responded. "We will not begin this meeting until the Arch Keeper attends."

"It is not your kingdom's lowly ruler whom I've come to see."

"And yet," Ulfric said flatly. Perhaps his words were rash, but he was Stallari of the Knights Corporealis, and this being, celestial or not, would not cow him.

The usurper measured him with a steady gaze, and the skin of his pale face tightened further. "It is your time to waste."

As if on command, the gates atop the rampart began their slow, grinding recess into the keep's inner curtain wall, and the keep's receiving horn boomed over the city to beckon them. Ulfric threw a look over his shoulder to Commander Brun, and she nodded that she and her Marines were ready for the procession to proceed. Beyond the wall toward the city's far border, he caught sight of Vigil Tower. The time it would take to climb the forty-four steps to the keep's courtyard would not be enough to begin to measure the depth of danger this Verity's presence signified. Yet it was plenty of time for one fearful thought to ring inside his mind, over, and over. *Will any haven be safe for my family?*

CHAPTER FOUR

Three hundred and forty-two revolutions around Halla had passed since Mylla had last looked into the eyes of a celestial being. Still, her memory of Vaka Aster, brief though their encounter at her oath-taking ordination into the Order had been, did nothing to prepare her for the sight of this other Verity.

Despite her training and her pride, her eyes widened as their groups converged. She knew him for what he was at once. Where Vaka Aster's radiance had seemed bright and enveloping, if not exactly warm, the one calling himself His Holiness seemed to suck the light away from the space surrounding him, leaving a vacuum of chilly emptiness behind. Even through her armor and tunic, Mylla's skin prickled in his presence.

What in the name of a rotting gimgree carcass is another Verity doing in Vinnr? This can only mean... I'm not really sure. But I am sure we'll soon find out.

The receiving horn's low clamor faded, and she followed Stallari Aldinhuus up the rampart steps, the deliberate footfalls of the full procession contrasting loudly, oppressively, in the now still afternoon air. No birds sang, no music wafted from the city's public halls or travelers' inns. The commoners of Ivoryss themselves seemed to hold their collective breath, their cautious silence commanded by the recent gossip and stories about Yor. She could see that more than a few in the crowd had shielded themselves against their fears by downing more lind sap liquor than was strictly necessary. Tension seemed ready to roil into chaos.

Acolyte Irrick says Yor is now under this man's, this being's, control, that he's turned Yor's throne to his ends. The bruhawks saw a small army at the borders. What has Arch Keeper Beatte done to ensure the same kind of takeover can't happen in Ivoryss? Does she even grasp the stakes of this situation?

These thoughts rippled in her mind and faded reluctantly. It was only through her strict discipline as a Knight that Mylla kept herself from turning around to ensure the usurper and his cadre were not drawing furtive weapons or planning an attack at this moment as they trailed along behind. Absurd, naturally, for they'd been stripped of their arms before coming within sight of the keep. Just as she and Ulfric had.

With the exception, naturally, of their klinkí stones, which to commoners would appear to be harmless baubles and bits.

This unwelcome paranoia was new to her, but she supposed seeing a celestial being with the power to create and destroy worlds would have that effect on anyone. In the first and true language of the Verities, Elder Veros, his name was Balavad. Her Knight mentors had taught her about the existence of this Verity and his realm of Battgjald, and she'd read of it in the Scrylle herself. But only cursorily. It had seemed irrelevant, until now.

Her nerves were making her hands want to rub together, so she gripped them into white-knuckled fists. The sun's rays bounced off the Verring Sea to the southwest just beyond Vigil Tower as they climbed, so bright they washed away the water's usual beryl glow. Asteryss itself lay north of the headland on which Vigil Tower stood. It rose from the prow of one hill, Asteryss from another, each overlooking the basin the city was nestled within.

More Halla rays beamed against her breastplate, turning the metal oven-hot around her chest. Sweat leaked from her armpits, her forehead, her neck, made clammy by a lingering dread at this unexpected visit. Would the climb up this staircase ever end? How long could she endure those dark eyes of the foreign Verity flashing like cleavers behind her?

She'd seen young Isemay in the crowd, barely even trying to stay out her father's sight. *He'd never have permitted Isemay to come. Which is probably the main reason she's here. The girl has more of her father in her than he'd probably thank me for mentioning.*

At last they reached the upper courtyard before the keep's inner curtain wall gates. In a show of military might, Commander Brun had ordered a squadron of Dragør Wing fighters to land their single-person aerial combat crafts in the yard. The pilots stood at the ready on either side of the gate, all bearing the same stoic expressions as their ground compatriots below the rampart.

Mylla searched their faces. *There he is.* Dragør Wing Pilot Havelock Rekkr, first to the left of the entryway, the spot chosen specifically because he knew to expect her to be at the Stallari's left side. And because he was a squadron leader, of course. Their eyes found each other.

The procession came to a stop before the massive gates, and Mylla shifted her attention to the elegantly robed Chamberlain Cympher and always numerous courtiers awaiting them. Cympher greeted them with a windy speech that Mylla tuned out immediately. She found life at the keep predictable, if unnecessarily complex. Cympher and courtiers like him were pretentious and pointlessly bureaucratic. Scholars of the Resplendolent Conservatum, like Acolyte Irrick, and warriors, like the Knights, had no time and saw little purpose in pomp.

At last, the chamberlain concluded, "In the name of Arch Keeper Beatte, I bid you follow me." He waved them in and turned in a movement so polished it must have been rehearsed.

As she passed Havelock, he curled the edges of his mouth into a faint smile that did not quite crack his military bearing. *Can he see how nervous I am?* she wondered, feeling as if her anxiety was nearly dripping from her skin. *I hope it isn't obvious. What would he think of a warrior who sweats like a nervous novice at the first sign of a threat?* She nodded back, then saw how sharply his glance strayed to the Verity in her wake. Lock's anxious grimace, like a virus, spread down the line of Marines as they went by.

The Knights and Brun, the foreign visitors, and the chamberlain passed along the hushed inner court of Aster Keep beneath the shadows of spires surrounding the enclosing walls. Green summer grasses and hedges dotted the space with a gaiety none felt. The Stallari had likely warned Beatte of the possibility this visitor could be another Verity. Therefore, Mylla was certain they were being led to the secure throne room below the main court. After descending two stories, she knew she was right, and the cooler air below the courtyard brought some relief from the dank perspiration still clinging to her.

"You seem nervous, Knight," said someone behind her. When she glanced back, one of the foreign black-robed priests was gazing at her. His face and lips were pale, almost translucent, beneath his hood. The man wore the mark of the Battgjald Knights, named Flesh Casters, which the Stallari had once drawn for her: three inverted chevrons rising between his brows to end at his hairline, in a dark indigo color that had faded to sickly green in his colorless flesh. The symbol stood out starkly, and his halting croak made her wonder how frequently he used his voice. "We are all part of the same Order. All unified for the same cause. You have nothing to fear from us," he finished.

Intrigued, she asked, "What cause?"

"To serve the Verities."

"Pretty words coming from a sycophant," Commander Brun broke in, and the foreign Knight's long teeth flashed in a snarl through the gash of his mouth. "Whatever your *Verity* did in Yor will not happen in Ivoryss," Brun continued. "I suggest you think carefully on the limits of your service, such as it is."

She senses the same threat I do, Mylla thought, surprised at the commander's outburst. *Something is amiss. Danger is coming. The Stallari was wise to order the removal of the vessel from Vigil Tower. An army at our gates and a Verity in our midst... the Scrylle has never recorded another Verity trespassing in this realm...*

Even more ill at ease, Mylla considered things. What Balavad's

Flesh Caster said was true enough. The Knights Corporealis had been servants of Verities since almost the beginning of recorded time. Yet, for the first time since she'd felt called to the Order as a child, she wondered what else this service, which had granted her both honor and immortality, might require.

Brun's hostility strangled any further conversation to death. Only their breathing and footfalls made any sound until the hall opened up into an antechamber, large for its subterranean location. The chamberlain finally stopped and thunked the iron knocker against a broad door. Someone slid the peeping port open from the inside, and the chamberlain asked, "Is the Arch Keeper ready?"

A pause, then: "Aye."

One, two, three bolts grated clear, then a brace was unhooked and the door swung open toward them.

The cloister's main room flashed brilliantly from dozens of lens apparatuses adorning the walls, ceiling, and even floor in some places. Much of the kingdom's light and other inventions came from wystic devices that focused and divided radiance into its many forms, a task that fell mostly to the court's scholars, all former students of the Conservatum, and also mastered by Stallari Aldinhuus. Mylla rarely had a reason to visit this chamber, and the round and rectangular, thick and thin lenses meticulously ground and crafted by artisans—and a few by Aldinhuus himself—dazzled her. She was not an inventor, not the way the Stallari was, which made her appreciate his talents even more.

Chamberlain Cympher ushered them to a halt, and Mylla and Brun automatically took several short paces to either side of Ulfric, affording them better views of the chamber and the visitors. Though she knew Brun to be a stalwart if sometimes intemperate leader, Mylla questioned how reliable she was. Then she questioned her own questioning. If, after all, this Verity proved to be a common enemy, even training every weapon in the room on the being would be like trying to hold back a tempest with a neck scarf. Glancing at the Marines ringing the Arch Keeper's throne like a set of sharpened teeth, Mylla thought, *She is right not to trust His Holiness, but does she think swords and soldiers can protect her from a Verity, even a sundered one not at his full power?*

On the other hand, Balavad's Flesh Casters would be little trouble, as frail as they looked. The Stallari could easily dispatch half a dozen foes singlehandedly before pausing to take a breath, and Mylla's close-quarters combat skills were honed, having been drilled into her by the ruthless Knight Eisa Nazaria and the others for many turns. The courtiers and acolytes wouldn't be much use, their attributes being boot-licking and intellect rather than strength or force, but the ten Marines in a semicircle of protection around the Arch Keeper's council table were at least something. Verity or not, Balavad's powers outside his own realm were limited, Mylla reminded herself, an effect of being sundered and split across the Cosmos. And he had only six disarmed soldiers and three of his strange Flesh Casters. As far as she was concerned, aside from Balavad himself, the Knights were the only true threat in the chamber.

Beatte wasted no time getting to the point, without even first inviting anyone to sit. "Your Holiness, I am Arch Keeper Beatte, ruler of Ivoryss. Your message said you claim no land as home, yet many here have heard you took an army into Yor and wreaked havoc. Whether this is true or not is not my concern. Now state your reasons for coming to Ivoryss."

Beatte's diplomatic courtesies had apparently gone on holiday, though her bluntness failed to faze the usurper, who smirked. Disquietingly. "Arch Keeper Beatte, as I told your envoy and Stallari Aldinhuus himself, I am not here to discuss matters of state with you. I merely needed you to agree to this meeting in order to get by your city gates. It is with Aldinhuus I wish to speak. However, since you have insisted on the pomp and circumstance of your kind, I will make clear my intent."

The callow leader didn't like at all what he said. She clutched a heavy gem hanging on a chain around her neck tightly and said, "You brought both a brigade of fighters to our capital of Asteryss and a reputation of dishonorable conduct. Now you insult me in tone, if not words, when I grant an audience—"

"It is you who has been granted an audience with His Holiness," one of the pale Flesh Casters cut in.

The Arch Keeper rose from her seat, and her Marines withdrew their swords. Even standing, she barely reached the Verity's height. Her dark cheeks bloomed rose as she commanded, "Keep your silence, underling, or face the consequences! Yours is not the only Verity in this world."

If the raised eyebrows and looks that passed between the Marines were any indication, Mylla wasn't the only person in the room surprised by Beatte's statement. *So she knows what he is. And claims fealty to Vaka Aster still, even if she doesn't publicly say so. How quickly commoners lose their faith—*

The ghastly smile that curled the lips of the one calling himself His Holiness cut short her thoughts. "Am I not?" he said.

Beatte squinted, her cheeks now practically glowing, and her eyes shifted.

No, don't look at the Stallari, Mylla mentally tried to will her. *The Verity will see it as weakness; he'll know we cannot summon Vaka Aster.*

Too late.

The interloper took advantage of her silence and reached toward the closest of his Flesh Casters, beckoning him forward with a long, thick-jointed finger. The attendant undid the clasp on a leather satchel hanging over one shoulder and reached inside as he stepped up, withdrawing a tied scroll.

Balavad took the scroll and unrolled it. As close as Mylla was, she could see the script written upon it was Yorish.

"A treaty already signed by the Arch Keeper of Yor, declaring a new devotion, kingdom-wide, to me. My Flesh Caster Order," he waved the parchment at another of his Order, who took it and passed it to one of Beatte's guards, who in turn held it before her to read, "will take over all rites and services for your kingdom and the Knights Corporealis of Vaka Aster. Worship of your absent Verity died, as is natural, in the centuries since your creator deserted your world. I have been watching. Vaka Aster has left you behind and left your lost and frail selves to fall into ruin."

The Verity opened his arms in front of him and held his hands out, palms up, in a gesture that seemed a mockery of benevolence. "I have come to fill the void left by your uncaring creator." He stepped forward to tower over the none-too-diminutive Stallari and pointed that bony finger again, this time at him. "And you, Stallari Aldinhuus of the Vaka Aster's Knights Corporealis, will help me."

CHAPTER FIVE

T he moment the words struck his ears, Ulfric knew them for what they were: the end of an age of relative peace—and possibly of his world. He might have laughed at the absurdity of the Verity of Battgjald's words. Ulfric, leader of the Knights Corporealis of Vaka Aster, help a usurper in a takeover of Ivoryss and eventually all of Vinnr? The oath he'd taken was to *serve* his Verity, not become a militant pawn in Verity wars.

None of this mattered, however. Despite his alarm, only two things did: *Protect Isemay and Symvalline. Protect Vaka Aster.* Before his next breath, he calculated that both could only be achieved in one way.

"What is it you want from me?" he asked.

The Verity responded, "Your fealty and that of your Knights, your kingdom under my sway, and above all you are to relinquish both your Scrylle and three Fenestrii to me and take me to the vessel of Vaka Aster. The *true* vessel."

To his left, Knight Evernal twitched as if to attack. Ulfric thrust out his hand in a halting gesture and focused a command through his Mentalios. *Don't.* She settled, grudgingly.

The usurper smiled. "Well done, Stallari. A man with your authority would have a place among my own Order."

He lowered his hand and returned his attention to the towering figure. *Bargain with him, Ulfric. Bargain with the skills of all the centuries you've lived. Bargain for lives more important to you than your own. You can't take him to the vessel.* With this thought came another: *He doesn't know where we've hidden it. Are the Verities blind to each other?* He deposited this thought into his ageless arsenal of wisdom. If true, if the Verities couldn't detect one another, it could be useful someday.

Before he could speak, Arch Keeper Beatte broke in, her voice now cool, on the verge of defeat. "So you've taken Yor. We can only surmise using what guiles. Why Ivoryss too? Why do you want our kingdoms, when you have your own world and a realm of your own creation where you're already the one ruler? Verity or not, this world owes you nothing."

"Keep wagging your tongue," the Flesh Caster with the leather satchel warned her.

Balavad's black eyes lit with some inner flame as he gazed at Ulfric. "Stallari Aldinhuus is the only one among any of you worthy of my attention."

The Arch Keeper, oh so young and hapless, was about to act as anyone as youthful as she might, and Ulfric moved to intervene before she could command her Dragør Marines to attack the Verity, and thus commit suicide. "Arch Keeper—"

Her words froze him before he could finish. "Guards, restrain the turncoat Aldinhuus. Seize this usurper and his entourage. No enemy of Ivoryss will be allowed to walk free another moment."

As a unit, the ten Dragør Marines raised and pointed their swords. Each paced a step forward, and Brun moved in from Ulfric's right. He could almost taste the blood that was about to be spilled. "Stop this madness, Beatte!" he pressed, but his next words—*I would never betray Ivoryss!*—died on his tongue before he could say them. He would betray Ivoryss. He would, if it meant doing his duty. Or saving his family.

Evernal's back pushed against his, ready to defend him. As the Marines moved in, the Verity's forces closed around their leader, forming a circle of defense. Ulfric hesitated to encourage Mylla to withdraw her klinkí stones, or to do so himself. They already had too few secrets or surprises. They needed to wait until the right opportunity struck before revealing them.

The Marines' wariness caused them to crowd in slowly, affording Ulfric time to measure the situation. Yet even a warrior of his long history knew limits. Balavad remained stolid, unconcerned inside his circle of protectors. Ulfric's mind raced with ideas on what to do, what to say to end this certain fate. Why would the Verity want Vaka Aster's vessel? If he destroyed it, he would destroy this world, their entire reality. Why would he have gained the obeisance of Yor, and possibly Dyrakkium, if he simply planned to wipe them from existence?

What am I missing?

"Just relax, Aldinhuus, and we can end this peacefully," Brun said, standing at a sword-length's distance and beckoning toward him with her free hand. "You too, Evernal."

"You and the Arch Keeper are wrong, Brun," Mylla said. "We are not your enemies. That *being* is."

Ulfric kept his eyes fixed on the squad of Marines, mind whirling. *He wants our Scrylle and Fenestrii. He came from Yor. What could I be missing? He is here and needs my aid to find Vaka Aster's vessel. Why? Yor and the Scrylle, the vessel... what is his intention?*

"I have no time for games," the Verity warned.

Then, as if all connected by a common spark, the light reflecting from the chamber's many illuminate orbs suddenly exploded, cutting Ulfric's thoughts short and blinding him. He clutched the Mentalios pendant around his neck with one hand and raised the arm concealing his klinkí stones in front of his face, prepared for battle and death. Mylla pushed harder at his back, using his weight to keep them both upright. As he drew a breath to give her the order to attack, the dazzling light diminished almost as quickly as it had erupted, and Ulfric could see once more.

Balavad still stood between Ulfric and the Arch Keeper, his form a dark shadow in the afterglow. His arms were extended, and between his palms floated a ring of shadow no bigger than a man's head. After blinking rapidly several times, Ulfric realized that every light orb, glass, crystal, and mirror in the chamber had shattered.

The resulting explosion of lethal shards, in the thousands, now hung in midair, motionlessly surrounding the people in the chamber. Glinting sparks flared within the shards, holding the explosion of light the way a mother carries a late-term child, taut and ready to let go. The pieces seemed aimed toward the sphere of blackness between the Verity's palms, being pulled into it, sure to tear through anything and any person that stood between them and the vacuum.

Arch Keeper Beatte sat unmoving and mostly unharmed on her throne, terror and shock frozen on her face. The courtiers and acolytes, however, had not been spared. All lay dead or dying, mutilated by fragments of shards. It had happened soundlessly when the chamber was filled with light, so swiftly that none had even screamed. Only one or two of the Marines still stood, the others having fallen, but they were only stunned and stupefied, not yet suffering the fate of the rest. Commander Brun had stumbled back against the foot of a column and now swiped frantically at her eyes, trying to rid herself of her daze. Behind Ulfric, Mylla remained upright, unflagging in her readiness for battle. As if fighting were a real option against this being.

Reason with him, Ulfric thought. He said aloud, "Verity, there is no need to harm these soldiers or anyone else. They are following orders to protect their ruler. I'm the only one who can take you to Vaka Aster."

"Or her." His Holiness indicated Mylla with a glance over Ulfric's shoulder.

Still just a novice, at least to Ulfric, she wouldn't be a match of either wits or strength against Balavad for long. It was better to keep the Verity focused on him. "If we do take you to the vessel, you could end Vinnr. Is that your aim? You know we will die protecting Vaka Aster."

The usurper's voice burned like oil as it seeped into Ulfric's ears. "But you must understand, Stallari Aldinhuus, I am not ending your world. I have come to save it."

Could Verities cultivate a sense of humor? He thought not. The only thing dangerous enough to threaten their world now stood before him. "Saving Vinnr from yourself, then?" He smirked. "Your trickery is as transparent as water."

"I am not the trickster, Stallari. I'm the savior. See for yourself."

The usurper waved to the Flesh Caster—the title an abomination to Ulfric's ears—carrying the leather satchel. As the warrior-priest withdrew something, his robe shifted open slightly. Ulfric glimpsed a stout chrome chain hanging around his neck bearing a fist-sized crystal sphere: a Fenestros orb, one of Balavad's own five. And in his hand was a Scrylle.

To a commoner, a Scrylle appeared to be a hollow scepter that contained a parchment covered in Elder Veros runes, slightly flared at the ends, and made of a handsome gleaming metal. Only the Knights and a few of the members of the Resplendolent Conservatum could identify the type of metal as having been forged from the stars themselves. The flared ends served two purposes: as a base upon which the Scrylle could be stood upright and as a mount to hold a Fenestros, a celestial orb resembling a smooth gemstone that was in actuality much, much more. The Fenestros orbs served as lenses by which the celestial sparks of Verities traveled and could be harnessed by Knights and others trained in their uses in as many ways as ingenuity and experience could devise. When a Scrylle and Fenestros were joined, a Knight could peer into the barrel of the Scrylle scepter through the celestial orb like a kaleidoscope. But instead of revealing only the Scrylle mount, a gateway between the viewer and the Great Cosmos opened and allowed the viewer access to timeless ideas. Like a library composed of formless but apprehensible thoughts, history, lore, and teachings, the Scrylles contained the accumulated knowledge of millennia, which could only be gleaned by Knights trained in how to read it.

And this Flesh Caster freely brandished the Scrylle and lore of a foreign realm, Battgjald. The realization struck him like a slap. *Looking inside that would be looking inside another reality, another dimension so far removed that, until now, it may as well have not been real.* Being exposed to the usurper's Flesh Casters, taller, thinner, paler than any Vinnric, even the Yorish folk, hadn't brought this fact home to him the way seeing the Scrylle did. His thirst for knowledge suddenly awoke in him, almost edging out his fear.

"Caster Rhafn," the Verity said and gestured for the Flesh Caster to hand the Scrylle to Ulfric. He took it, and was surprised when the Flesh Caster removed his Fenestrii and passed it to him as well. "Look inside," Balavad commanded.

Though now a warrior, Ulfric had been a craftsman and scholar before being called to serve Vaka Aster, and he was not a man who could resist the promise of knowledge, no matter its source. This Verity, it seemed, was intent on hiding nothing if he meant for Ulfric to look into the Scrylle. His curiosity had to be sated.

Holding the artifact close to his chest, he attached the celestial orb, and it stuck in place as if held by a magnetic force. The weight of the joined objects was deceptively light, and with his hands locked around the cylinder, Ulfric focused on moving his mind through the Fenestros until he could "see" what was recorded within the Scrylle.

In a rush no untrained Knight could endure, the annals poured into his mind. All Battgjald's lore buffeted him, drowning his own thoughts to oblivion: a deluge of events and inventions, an influx of knowledge of a world foreign to him, a reality that fit only within vague outlines of his own, peoples and races he could barely comprehend but were similar enough to the Vinnrics to be recognizable. The edges of his mind strained, filled lightning quick to capacity, and he felt it creaking under the force of the tidal wave. *So much to know. So much...* Clenching his jaw, he brought all the strength and discipline of his thousand and more turns into controlling the Scrylle's influx, and with strained yet unbent determination, he began to get a grip, to swim against the flood, slowing the mental invasion and concentrating on what appeared.

Balavad's disembodied voice whispered inside his thoughts: *See the Syzycki Elementum.*

As if commanded, there it was. A myth that Ulfric could not deny, now solidified into fact. A conflux was coming, a gathering of all the Verities into a reunification of their sundered selves into their original singular form. From the five back to the one. But this was not the surprise that turned his marvel to horror.

Ulfric ripped his focus free and staggered against Mylla, the Scrylle falling from his hands. It landed on the alabaster floor, undamaged. Its Flesh Caster keeper hissed as if burned and scrabbled to retrieve it and his Fenestros, throwing a look of hate toward Ulfric that he barely noticed.

"The Verities are…" He couldn't continue, unable to fully believe what he'd read.

"Now do you see, Stallari?" Balavad examined Ulfric's pallor with interest. "Yes, you do. Your kind is coming to an end. We Verities agreed long before we created what you conceive as time, long before we created these realities, that all of these things, and your kind in particular, is merely a… trial. A distraction, an *amusement*. When we once again unify, no longer suffering this fractured and diminished duality of physical and celestial forms, your worlds will end. Your purpose, if you want to call it that, will become fulfilled. Moot, if you will."

The soldiers had begun to stir, though upon spying the suspended shards of shattered glass still filling the air all around them, they chose to remain where they were on the floor, their fear of being skewered winning over duty. Ulfric stared at the Verity, his horror strangled into compliance by the fists of his inner resolve.

"Stallari?" Mylla put a hand on his shoulder, having turned to support him when he'd faltered. "What does he mean?"

Still maintaining the sphere of empty blackness between his open palms, Balavad ignored her interruption and continued. "But *I* will not let this be, Stallari." He drew the word "I" out like a velvet carpet, an invitation to trust. "*I* can stop this foolishness, this absurd waste. I have already begun. *We* are your creators. Weak and frail though you are, so imperfect yet still viable—what is the use in destroying all we Verities have made? *I* can, and will, ensure your continuation and help you flourish."

The words had the cracked melody of a broken and abandoned

child's songbox. Beautiful in intent, haunting in sound. *What does he mean by "viable"?* Ulfric feared the answer.

The Verity waved a hand, and the dark sphere rose toward the chamber's ceiling, growing to the size of a ballroom floor until it loomed over the room like a gateway to oblivion. The legion of suspended shards tilted upward toward the inky corona, like iron filings to a magnet. Balavad stepped forward and reached a white hand toward Ulfric's chest, or, more aptly, toward his Mentalios. Ulfric crushed the instinct to slap it away like he would a cockroach.

He tensed as the Verity swept up the lens, still on its chain, and leaned close. "Your craftsmanship is as commendable as your leadership." He stared into Ulfric's face, and that same oblivion filling Balavad's dark sphere lay in his gleaming eyes. "You have the power to save your world, Stallari." The lens dropped, clanking heavily against Ulfric's breastplate. "Accept my rule, bring me to Vaka Aster, and I will make you the Stallari of not only my Order, but of all the Verity's orders. You will become the most powerful of our creations to have ever lived. And *you*, not *me*, will be the savior of your people."

So that was his design. Power. The Verity wanted power over the realms beyond his own. How simple. How... human. Ulfric's mind had skipped and skidded into many, many things during his brief exposure to the Scrylle, and he knew exactly what the Verity planned to do. He meant to build a cage that would trap Vaka Aster inside her vessel for eternities, leaving Vinnr unprotected and free for the taking by Balavad and his forces. This celestial being wasn't content with his own realm. He wanted those of all the Verities under his sway. Balavad was telling Ulfric that he would be the builder of this cage—if he accepted the role.

But Ulfric wasn't a fool. Once he led Balavad to Vaka Aster, he would most likely be dispatched, and this Flesh Caster Rhafn would be tasked with building the cage. Balavad's pretty words and promises were as empty as the air between them.

"Don't listen, Stallari," Mylla whispered from behind him.

He did not intend to. He stood at the precipice of battle, knowing full well that trying to stop this being would be nothing like stopping a human.

And the first rule of battle was to triage and choose priorities.

Ulfric made a decision. *You claim you're no trickster, Verity, but maybe you've underestimated how cunning I can be.* A deeper voice in his mind warned, *It is insane to think you can match wits with a celestial being.* He ignored this. Straightening to his full height, he stared, unflinching, into the Verity's face. "I'm at your service, Your Holiness. But I require that they," he passed an arm slowly around the room, indicating the Ivoryssians, "be unharmed."

Brun grunted derisively, still pressed cautiously against the column behind her, and Beatte's eyes closed in either acceptance or disgust.

The usurper peered at Ulfric for a moment longer, then smiled. "Very good, Stallari Aldinhuus. Casters, escort these mortals out.

Chancellor Cympher, Commander Brun, and the Marines rallied, showing the hallmarks of protest. Before they got far enough to ensure their own deaths, the Verity waggled the fingers of both hands, and the hovering glass moved inward, like a hive of enraged bees, close enough to press cruelly into any exposed skin. Ulfric watched Brun's eyes widen as one of the longest, wickedest shards floated toward her, and she flattened herself against the column.

"Stop," Ulfric ordered. To his relief, the shards did, and he spoke to the Arch Keeper. "Tell them to leave their weapons where they lay and go. For their lives, Arch Keeper, and your own, command the Marines to disperse."

Beatte's look told Ulfric she had already tried and sentenced him to death as a tyrant in her mind, but she knew better than to sentence the others in the chamber to the same. "Retreat," she ordered.

Mylla stayed put as the reluctant Ivoryssians backed out, and Ulfric turned to her. Accusation and disbelief fought for control of her expression as she stared at him.

"You too, Knight," he said.

With a visible effort to steady her voice, she insisted, "Tell me you're not serious, Stallari."

Using the Mentalios, he sent: *Mylla, do as I say: shield yourself from this being. Warn Symvalline and the other Knights of his intent to ensnare Vaka Aster and rule Vinnr. And on your Knight's honor, swear to me you will help Symvalline protect Isemay.*

She sent: *Ensnare Vaka Aster? How? What are you going to do, Stallari?*

There wasn't time to explain, and he couldn't know if this Verity could sense their Mentalios link and know their thoughts. He could see Mylla struggling between the instinct to trust him and follow his orders and incredulity over his cryptic actions. "Listen to me, Mylla." The command in his voice could wither anyone's will. "*Go.*"

She took a step backward, then another, her eyes pleading for an explanation. Before she finally spun and trudged to the exit, he risked sending once more: *Swear it, Mylla. Protect my daughter, no matter what happens.*

She didn't look back. *On my honor, Stallari.*

When she'd pushed the wooden doors closed behind her, Ulfric stepped to them and threw the thick iron bolts to ensure the Dragør Marine reinforcements, for he knew they'd be coming, would be slowed down.

He doubted he could save all the people of Ivoryss, but if his plan succeeded, he could perhaps save some. "Come with me, Holiness."

CHAPTER SIX

lack. Clack. Clack.

Mylla pressed her back against the door, feeling the heavy thump of the inner bolts slide closed even through the metal of her backplate. *What in Vaka Aster's name is he about to do?*

Brun rattled off orders to her troops, the sound distant beyond Mylla's whirring thoughts. With downcast eyes, she concentrated on reaching the Stallari using the Mentalios, but either he was deliberately blocking her or he was moving out of range.

"The well," she whispered to herself. *The plan had been for us to fight our way to it if need be. What's changed? Why? My duty is to Vaka Aster, not protecting his daughter.* But that had to be it. He was more concerned now with the safety of his family. Which told her just how great the stakes were. He had said Vinnr, not just Ivoryss, was in danger, and they had an invader's army at their borders to prove it.

The tip of a sword beneath her chin changed the direction of her thoughts. Decisively and abruptly.

Commander Brun spoke from the comfortable end of the weapon. "What did he tell you, Knight? I know you use wystic magic to speak through your pendants. Tell me his plans now, or death by beheading for your treasonous conspiring will be the kindest of your punishments."

She decided honesty would be wasted, or worse, get too many killed in this moment. "I swear, Commander, he told me nothing." The entire force of the Dragør Marines wouldn't be able to stop Balavad from doing whatever it was he intended. Better they not be involved. "I know as much about what may be happening right now as you. A Verity not from this world is bent on wrenching Ivoryss from the hands of Arch Keeper Beatte, and—"

"*Pah!* A Verity? Don't spin a myth just to hold my attention, or I'll spin your eyes from their sockets. Verities are an old story, no more likely to show up now than they ever were. The Knights Corporealis keep these fairy tales alive in order to dupe and control simpler minds. It's *your Order* that plotted this takeover, and your accomplice and Stallari have taken the Arch Keeper hostage. Now"—her sword's point pressed harder into the hollow of Mylla's throat—"tell me what Aldinhuus is planning and where they're taking Beatte."

To the fissures of Vaka Aster's ass if you don't start using your brain. With an effort, she kept the desire to speak that thought aloud in check. Brun was clearly too jaded by her fears and prejudices to see the faults in her own theory—such as why Mylla would be standing among a squad of Marines on this side of the chamber door if some conspiracy involving the Knights was at hand on the other—and time was too short to introduce reason.

"Commander, allow me to step aside so you and your soldiers can force open the door. I don't want to cause trouble."

Brun eyed her, then motioned with her chin. "Furthsom, restrain her."

Mylla backed a pace away and extended her left hand, palm out, as if to clasp hands with the approaching Marine and say, *We're all allies here.* Except—

With a twitch of her wrist, three finger-like nine-sided crystals, one for each century she'd served, tumbled from her leather vambrace into her palm. Whip-fast, she flung them outward, mentally channeling them to strike the sword-wielding hands of the three closest Marines, pulled them back, and then hammered the rest. The soldiers cried out in pain as they lost their grips, their hands badly bruised but not broken. At least not intentionally.

"Stay back," she warned. The crystals all aglow with hearts of deep cerulean were now hovering at the tips of her outstretched fingers.

"Flank and charge!" Brun directed.

Reason remained in short supply, and four of the least cowed Marines rushed her in unison. *Remarkably good tactics and training*, she thought. *But poor estimation of the threat, unfortunately.*

In movements akin to a dance, she waved her crystal arm, sending the projectiles to strike the soldiers on the arms, the ankles, the shins. Their cries were as much from surprise as pain and seemed to serve as an invitation to the remaining Marines, who quickly retrieved their weapons, clumsily in their nondominant hands in many cases, and joined the melee. Mylla continued to dance, now wielding Furthsom's dropped sword defensively with one hand, parrying blows and thrusts by the few Marines who managed to penetrate the wall of swirling, abusive crystal menaces. Each time a sword clashed with hers, a projectile found the attacker instantly and dealt another blow to his or her fighting arm, rendering them once again weaponless. In less time than it takes a wave to break over a stranded boulder, the fighters ceased their fruitless and frankly humiliating onslaught and regrouped at a distance.

Mylla wasn't even winded. "So sorry, *friends*." She began sidestepping toward the stairway, leaving the klinkí stones hovering readily between her and the stunned Marines. "But I have a world to save."

Brun remained near the door. "I knew I was right about you." She spit in disgust on the antechamber floor.

It struck Mylla then how similar her own suspended klinkí stones were to the whirlwind of shattered glass and destruction the Verity had created within the council chamber. Nothing she could do about that now though. The heel of her boot struck the bottom of the stairway leading up to the keep's courtyard. "Brun, rally the Marines and prepare to defend Ivoryss. You may not believe our foe is a Verity, but your duty is the same." And because she couldn't think of any meaningful parting words, she said, "Mind the sparkly," and dashed a flashfire petard, pulled from where it was hidden in the leather wrap holding back her hair, against the floor. *Should slow them down a bit.*

CHAPTER SEVEN

I f the fight hadn't winded her, the several sets of stairs nearly did. Brun and her Marines were only moments behind, but she had managed to bar the door at the top of the final flight of steps to hinder them, giving her a few moments to put together a plan. Of sorts.

She sprinted across the shrub-dotted greens, then burst from the massive arched main gate into an awaiting squad of Marines, formed up in ranks and headed by a soldier whose uniform's insignia declared him to be in charge.

Skidding to a stop, she quickly palmed her klinkí stones. "Sergeant" —*gasp*—"the usurper's forces attacked. I'm the first to escape"—*huff*— "tell your troops to get ready! They're coming."

"Where are Commander Brun and the Arch Keeper?" The soldier hadn't yet pulled his sword, but his hand gripped the hilt tightly.

"I told you, under attack. Send reinforcements before it's too late!"

A good soldier takes less time to react to a threat than to take a breath, and these were Ivoryssian Dragør Marines—always ready. Still, their downfall was their discipline, and they would only take a breath when ordered. To Mylla, it felt like days passed before the sergeant made up his mind and gave the command. Of course, reacting without a full debrief of the situation was a bad idea, but Mylla didn't feel the need to point that out before they were on the run toward the inner keep.

She looked to the edges of the rampart. *Thank fate's whimsy.* The Dragør Wing fighter squadron had not been released from their post, and she rushed to Lock's side. If anyone could aid her in this moment of need, he could.

His hands landed on her shoulders as she planted herself, still panting, in front of him. "What in the name of Vaka Aster is going on, Mylla?" he asked.

Before she could respond, from behind her came: "Knight Evernal, where is Stallari Aldinhuus?"

She spun and beheld Symvalline with Isemay beside her, just approaching from the top of the rampart stairs. Unlike an average commoner, Knights, as members of the royal house, still moved mostly freely within the keep. At the moment, Mylla's stomach flipped from relief to distress. *How can I explain to her what I don't understand myself?*

Paralyzed, she merely stared as Symvalline closed the gap. "Mylla, tell me what's happened to Ulfric," her mentor demanded. "What is the foreign Verity's purpose here?" And the unspoken, frantic plea Mylla could almost hear: *For the honor of the Order, tell me Ulfric hasn't been harmed.*

The train of Symvalline's formal sky-blue cloak snapped crisply in a sudden gust, bringing Mylla back to the now. "He's in danger. There isn't time to fully explain, but he and the Arch Keeper are in the hands of the Verity." She felt Havelock's grip on her shoulder tighten. "And I... I think they are using the interrealm well to travel to Mount Omina."

Symvalline's lips drew into a thin line as she regarded Mylla, considering her words.

Mylla addressed Havelock. "I need you to fly me to Omina, the largest peak in the Morn Range. I must try to help the Stallari if I can." She turned. "Symvalline, can you get Safran and Stave and bring them to the mountain? There's no reason to remain at Vigil Tower. Ulfric is going to need us."

Havelock protested, "I have to… Mylla, I can't break ranks from the squadron, not without orders."

"I wouldn't ask if it weren't of the absolute most importance. Of all time," she emphasized. Desperation added its own sharpness to her voice, and she drilled him with her eyes, imploring and commanding with an ageless authority that sprang from her Verity-instilled spark.

Symvalline hadn't said another a word. Her speechlessness, Mylla knew, came not from confusion or a lack of surety, but from the intentionality of a warrior and strategist, and before joining the Knights, a healer and surgeon in the Conservatum. She couldn't be lured into a reflexive, half-baked reaction without a careful consideration of all known angles.

Isemay, however, was still too young for that kind of restraint, and blurted in a fear-tainted squeak, "Mum, we have to help Da."

Mylla. Symvalline's voice came through the Mentalios. *Tell me what occurred. Tell me now.*

Balavad wants Vaka Aster's vessel and the artifacts of Vinnr, all of them I think. He let Ulfric see into Battgjald's Scrylle. Something in it affected him— but I don't know what he saw. He's— we have to get to Mount Omina before the usurper can fulfill his plans, though I don't know what they are exactly. The Stallari made me swear to warn the Knights and sent me and the Marines away. And one more thing: the Verity killed many in attendance before Ulfric got him to stop. She carefully held back the fact that Ulfric had agreed willingly in the end to aid the Verity. Something to consider, but later. Or never. The latter was her preference.

"Battgjald's Scrylle," Symvalline considered aloud.

"Mum!" Isemay cried.

"Mylla?" Havelock said.

"For all the dragørflies in Ivoryss, Havelock, get in that Wing fighter and get me to Omina. Your duty is to the Arch Keeper, and this is your chance to execute it." She had a sudden wish she hadn't chosen that word, *execute.*

The nearest of the other pilots had begun to break ranks and sidle closer, Mylla's disturbance and the rushing away of the officer-in-charge without any contingency directives creating a vacuum in their orders that soon only chaos could fill. "Symvalline, Brun has accused me of treason and must be moments from breaking out of the stairwell I locked her and the Marines in. If we don't act now, we won't be able to." The stunned look in Havelock's eyes made her realize she'd said this aloud.

"Wing Rekkr," Symvalline said, stepping closer to Havelock so that he couldn't look past her, "I knew your great-grandfather, a man of deep courage and irrefutable honor. He served Ivoryss for decades, and every Marine knows him to be a legend. Today you have the chance to prove you are as noble as he was. If you get Knight Evernal to Mount Omina, you could be saving everything this world holds dear." She glanced at Mylla. "Including the woman you love. For life and love, take her."

Mylla looked between Havelock's uncertain face and Symvalline's strained one, counting heartbeats until he decided. Finally, he turned to her and said, "Take the seat behind the pilot bench and strap yourself in."

Releasing a relieved breath, she threw a glance at Symvalline before climbing aboard. The older warrior sent: *I'll warn Stave and Safran and meet you there.*

CHAPTER EIGHT

With the Marines and Mylla clear of the chamber, Balavad pulled the dark wystic circle back to him and closed his hands together in a forceful clap. The empty sphere collapsed between his palms as if it had never been, drawing in and vanquishing the thousands of hovering shards that had filled the air. Not a single ingot of glass or crystal remained in the room, except the Mentalios lens around Ulfric's neck.

"Stallari…" The Verity swept an arm in an expectant gesture.

Ulfric began pacing toward the chamber's far wall, expecting to be followed. "I assume you've sent," *spies* was the word he almost used, "representatives to Vaka Aster's shrine and know neither the vessel or Vaka Aster's artifacts are there."

"Of course. You've been a diligent watcher. It must have seemed wise to move the vessel. My quin chose you well."

"Watcher?" Ulfric mused. *Oh yes, I've seen more than I think you know.*

He reached the chamber's terminus. Built in the shape of an egg, the grand room tapered and ended in a narrow nook of curved space. A convex mirror that helped channel the chamber's illumination had once been fit into it—now gone with all the rest. Behind where it had stood rose the alabaster wall, smooth and white, except for a shallow embedded circle ringed by brass. Below this, a carved series of Elder Veros runes contained the invocation to unlock the doorway, or inter-realm well. Only a few existed in Vinnr. Each one and what they did was a secret the Knights had kept since Ulfric had built them, over a thousand turns ago. To use the well in Aster Keep, all Ulfric needed was his Mentalios lens.

He turned to find Balavad no farther behind him than his arm could reach. The being moved with the soundlessness of passing eternity, though Ulfric wasn't caught off guard. This wasn't his first meeting with a celestial being, having served Vaka Aster for so long. Those who'd served in the Knights for close to as long as he, such as Eisa, so old she and everyone else had nearly forgotten her own ancestor now served as Vaka Aster's vessel, and Mallich Roibeard, whom all but Ulfric called Roi, seemed to even harbor a touch of the divine themselves.

He spoke. "The chamber beyond this wall is older than Aster Keep, though none but our Order knows of its existence. Vaka Aster's vessel and Vinnr's artifacts are safe inside." Which was true, but only partly. He hadn't realized how capable he was of such effortless and quick lies. "I need a moment to unlock the door, and the assistance of your Caster's Fenestros."

Balavad smirked. "Yes, clever indeed. Rhafn." He nodded to the Flesh Caster to step forward.

As the Flesh Caster joined him, Ulfric spared a glance, masked beneath his thick gray-shot eyebrows, at the satchel containing the usurper's Scrylle, still hanging from the foreign priest's shoulder. He didn't need the Caster to help; he just needed him close.

He turned to face him fully and noticed the Arch Keeper, who remained seated in her throne. *You may not survive this, Beatte, but your life is a price I'm willing to pay for the protection of Vaka Aster, and of Ivoryss. You would thank me if you could understand.*

But *he* understood, all too well. If his plan worked and he could dupe the usurper long enough to ensure the vessel's safety, he and his Order would be blamed for any retaliation that would follow. And follow it would. But his duty was to Vaka Aster, in essence, to the entire world, not to this short-lifed, short-sighted ruler of a transient kingdom.

And what of this reunification, the Syzycki Elementum? Why doesn't our own Scrylle say anything about this end of our realm? Or does it, and I simply have not seen it? Will it be possible to reason with Vaka Aster, to plead with her to spare us from this fate?

He would only find out if he survived today.

"The Fenestros," he demanded of the Flesh Caster. When the reluctant man handed it to him, Ulfric pressed, "Concentrate and read this with me."

Without removing the chain from his neck, Ulfric pressed his Mentalios into the brass circle in the wall, and he and the Caster began speaking the Elder Veros words inscribed in the runes. The surface of the Fenestros shimmered, creating an effect like water transforming into light. Slowly, the section of the wall itself, no larger than an ordinary door, took on a glittering sheen. Ulfric channeled an image of Mount Omina, though he labored to keep this hidden.

With a sudden, quiet susurration, the glimmering wall disintegrated, revealing what could have been mistaken as a trick of the mind. It seemed to be a wavering tunnel, deep but hard to focus on, like the dark spots in the eye after staring into light. Instantly, the well passage pulled Ulfric inward. Not into a tunnel to nowhere, but into a portal that would take him to Mount Omina in the blink of an eye.

Just before he slipped inside, he reached for the Caster, gripping him by the arm in hands as strong as iron. As he and the Caster shot through the gateway, Ulfric maintained his focus on Omina, praying to the powers of the Verities that the well would close behind them in time to keep the usurper from following.

In less time than it took to inhale, his backplate clanked against rough stone, and the form of the Caster dropped beside him. Even before rising, Ulfric flung his elbow into the Caster's face, stunning him. In the next instant, he lunged to his feet, facing the now-blank stone wall through which they'd been delivered. As soon as they stopped speaking the incantation the portal closed, but he could not know if the Verity had some wystic artifice that would allow him to follow anyway.

Dozens of glittering dragørflies, disturbed from their rest, had taken to the air the moment he and the Caster emerged. Illumination from their glowing bodies cast enough light for Ulfric to spot a stone-working hammer leaning against the gray rock. He yanked it up and threw all the brute strength in his warrior's frame into one, two, three swings, until he obliterated the matching sigils adorning this side of the portal. The carved runes broke like pottery beneath his blows, and the well was destroyed.

Before he could enjoy the relief of escape, the sound of rock grating under feet caught his ear, and he spun, throwing the hammer up to ward off an oncoming strike from a head-sized stone being wielded like a club by the Caster. It struck the stout wooden handle held horizontally just a fist's width from Ulfric's forehead, sending a tremor into his wrists and elbows. He heaved, shoving the rock and Caster backward.

The Caster regrouped a few paces away as frenzied dragørflies swooped around his and Ulfric's heads. His hood had fallen back, and his eyes flickered against the pale flesh of his face as he sneered, unafraid and undaunted.

Ulfric paid the dragørflies no mind and crouched in readiness, still gripping the sledgehammer. "You fight for the wrong Verity, Caster. I'm offering you a chance to rectify that and reclaim your honor. But this is the only time I will."

The foreigner maintained his gap, disciplined enough to ignore the flitting distractions, and studied Ulfric. He shifted the tote that held the Battgjald Scrylle to his back and vocalized a screeching, high-pitched buzz that was unlike any sound Ulfric had ever heard but was easily identifiable as rage. The dragørflies reacted, becoming, if anything, more discombobulated. They swooped and dove, slamming their fragile forms into the Caster. He slapped against one that had caught a leg inside the fabric of his robe, smashing it and smearing the glistering body against his clothing. "You will die for this, Knight," he said, positioning himself to attack.

"You've chosen your fate," Ulfric snarled.

With a leap backward to gain distance, he extended the hammer with both hands and twisted, winding up like a spring. Throwing his full weight into it, he swung and released the hammer, sending it flying directly into the Flesh Caster's unguarded belly. The man crumpled like watery hash. Ulfric sprang to his side and straddled his fallen body, gripped the hammer, and swung it again, crushing the man's head. It wasn't a beheading, which would ensure the man's permanent death, but it was close enough. If he could recover from such a blow by way of the celestial spark of his Verity, it would take much more time than Ulfric needed.

He dropped the hammer against the cold floor, sending a metallic echo through the grotto. In the stillness, the troupe of dragørflies alighted on the ceiling, calm now that the Caster was, for the moment at least, dead.

Now, Ulfric thought, *to summon Vaka Aster from three centuries of absence and stop her from extinguishing Vinnr from existence.*

Of the many ways he could have imagined this day going, some worse and some better, the task that now lay before him had never once crossed his mind. Not for the first time since joining the Order and becoming its leader, he wondered what his life could have been if he'd simply lived as all common men did. Fallen in love with Symvalline, become a father, grown into dotage, died. That's all he wished for now. But that fate wasn't to be. Not yet. He could not turn away from this task with more than just honor at stake but also the lives of his family and the world itself.

Before he could begin enacting his plan, the door from the outer chamber slammed open and smashed into the wall, the force halfway buckling the hinges from their fasteners.

CHAPTER NINE

"Oh fury of the Verities, I don't think I thought this through enough." Mylla gripped Havelock's Wing fighter seat back so hard her fingers ached. It wasn't that she was afraid of flying, exactly. It was putting her life in someone else's hands, someone who might get them killed in at any second, that gave her second thoughts. But she trusted Lock. Usually.

He responded with something very logical and calming—or would be, if logic could influence fear. "Just hang on and don't look down."

Hang on? If she hung on any tighter she'd start extracting juice from his seat like an ong fruit. The Dragør Wing fighter, hawk-like in shape and size, if said hawk were big enough to swallow a Yorish plains ox, had a clear cockpit that gave them a wide outside view.

Just then, something caught her eye. "Lock, we aren't alone up here."

He looked to his left, then up, and his eyes began tracking whatever it was. He'd said don't look down—*But up is okay. I can look up. There's nothing to get smashed flat by up there.*

She risked it.

Bad idea. Looking up inspired her stomach to begin to spin. But the next thing that caught Mylla's eye froze her guts into stillness. "What…?"

"Must be Dyrrak," he muttered, disbelief plain in his voice. "The Yorish don't have any craft like that."

Above and just off their starboard wing flew a thing that neither of them could think to describe as anything but a flying sickle. The craft seemed made of a single continuous ingot of metal, a featureless U-shaped fuselage as dark as forge-blackened iron. From apex to tip, it was only half as long as the Dragør Wing fighter, and each curved end came to a wicked point, gleaming to Mylla's eyes like a set of terrible black fangs.

"We have to outfly it," she sputtered, just as a pocket of air gave their fighter a jolt that scared a full turn around Halla off her life—or would have, if she aged like a commoner. Wrestling composure she didn't feel into her voice, she tried again, "Well, *you* have to outfly it. I'm just going to hold on and pretend I'm *anywhere* else." She'd have given one of her klinkí stones, maybe even two, to be in the pilot's seat, to be in *control*.

Without turning around, he reached over his shoulder and gave one of her knotted fists a gentle pat. "As you wish," he said, and Mylla knew that tone meant she was about to get exactly what she'd asked for. "This is going to be fun."

The Wing fighter fell into a dive that immediately sent them from falling forward in their seats to being pinned to the backs of them. Much as she tried, she couldn't ignore the way the sky morphed from a blue background, with distant, discrete clouds, to a streaking, amorphous spilled-paint accident. A scream filled her lungs, but the pressure of the dive kept it lodged there, like an anvil in her chest.

"You call this fun?" she whispered.

Ignoring her, Lock muttered, his question not meant for her, "So you know some tricks? Why don't you show me what else you can do…"

"No, no, no, don't ask it to do that—"

The fighter jilted left so hard her head smacked against the cockpit windscreen. *If he does that again, he'll knock me out*, she thought. Great idea, actually. At least she'd be sort of not here. *Do it again, Lock!*

But his plans didn't seem to be taking her wishes into account. With a buzz that could have either inspired, intimidated, or utterly shamed the population of an aviary, the fighter sped toward the foothills marking the beginning of the Morn Range. They grew closer and closer to them and didn't seem to be losing any momentum.

"Lock." Her voice was barely audible, so she tried harder. "Lock!"

It was as if she weren't there. They reached the nearest rise at a nerve-wracking speed and, with the smoothness of rolling waves, skimmed up and over it, then down into the valley behind it, blowing the leaves from the tops of the trees.

His eyes roamed the sky, his neck swiveling. "I think it's gone," he said, and his voice sounded... disappointed?!

What happened next wasn't the worst thing she could have expected, but it was close enough to make it pointless to split hairs. Suddenly, as if flicked by a finger, their Wing fighter changed course, sheering squarely to the west. It was only after this that she heard a small, hollow *tiinggg* and a moment later smelled superheated metal. They'd been hit by some kind of weapon.

She cried again, louder this time, "You call this *fun*?"

"It just got less fun," he mumbled through a clenched jaw. His hands clasped the controls with a bloodlessness that rivaled her own grip, and his feet warred with the pitch and yaw pedals but seemed to be losing. Badly. "Mylla, hold on, we've lost verticality."

Now *that* didn't sound good. And it especially didn't sound fun.

And it wasn't.

The flight took on the hue of nightmares as they begin to zig and zag upward and downward, Havelock barely keeping the fighter's nose from angling either straight into the earth or directly skyward. Fighting lateral forces, she reached out, got a grip on the collar of his leather tunic, pulled herself close to his ear, and groaned, "Maybe we should have walked, Lock."

He strained against the ship's controls, unable to do anything but try to soften the crash they both knew was coming. She almost wished it would come, if only to relieve her of the unbearable anticipation.

"If you think," he wheezed, "all it takes to bring down *my* Wing is a little tap..."

But he didn't finish the sentence, and their speed began to decrease, the fighter's erratic flight staunching it. As the bow rose once more, she saw a second sickle-shaped ship bearing down from above while the first came at them from the side, readying for another shot. *Please let it be quick*, she prayed.

For the first attacker, it probably was.

As she watched, a stream of silvery-white projectiles appeared from nowhere and speared the oncoming ship dead center. Almost too fast for the eye to see, the sickle ship glowed from within like a candle for a moment, then exploded, creating a stream of hundreds of pieces of shrapnel jetting toward them. The resulting force buffeted her and Lock's fighter, jolting them hard into an acute angle that sent them speeding at a tilt to the ground.

Too panicked at the impending crash to feel anything at all, Mylla stared outside the windscreen, wondering where the other sickle ship was and who had caused the first's destruction. The moment of stability provided by their sharp, straight drop of death allowed her to catch a glimpse of the answer. Of all things, another Dragør Wing fighter. It had the first attacker on the run, the two dancing amid the sky together in death waltz that only one partner would survive.

"Come on, come on, old girl. You made it this far," Lock coaxed, speaking to the Wing fighter like a loyal friend.

Mylla realized they were close, so close now, to the Knights' lower landing field on the flank of Mount Omina. Did they actually stand a chance of making it?

Lock slammed the pitch pedal so hard his entire body went rigid, half ripping his pilot's seat from its bolts, and the fighter leveled off languidly, as if giving the position cautious consideration before committing. They hung in nauseating suspension long enough for Mylla to wonder if some wystic force was holding them aloft. The intrepid pilot took full advantage of the momentary equilibrium and gave the controls as much thrust as he could.

They rocketed forward gracelessly and started to spin, having left the other Wing fighter and the second attacker far behind. All Mylla could do was close her eyes and hope for a swift end to what she'd forever remember as a flight worse than death.

CHAPTER TEN

Ulfric faced the door, wiping away a speck of blood near the nine-pointed star marking his chin. "If you'd waited any longer," he said, "I'd've had enough time to cook you supper."

Upon seeing him, Knight Eisa stomped inside, ready to dash any remaining enemies into crushed bone and blood with both her heavy-bladed glaive Fate Forger and her equally perilous tongue. "Stallari, why in Vaka Aster's name are you here?" Spotting the mangled Flesh Caster on the ground, she added, "And who's going to clean that up?"

Knight Roibeard entered with his usual circumspect stride, his greatsword clenched at-the-ready within the knurled ridges of his knuckles. "We were in the antechamber, and by the noise we thought Vaka Aster had returned." He fixed his sanguine golden-brown eyes on Ulfric, his warrior's perception having already measured the danger. "What's happened, Stallari? Why've you come through the well?"

"We're short on time, Knights," Ulfric responded. With the speed of thought rather than words, he explained using their Mentalios link all that had occurred, as he stooped over the Flesh Caster. Careful to avoid the spreading blood and gore, he searched the floor for the usurping Verity's Fenestros and found it near the destroyed well.

Raising it toward the glowing ceiling, lit by dozens of luminous now-calm dragørflies, he said aloud, "Do you know what this is?"

The question was rhetorical, and Eisa and Mallich stepped closer for a better look, their initial surprise at news of a foreign Verity's presence already gone from their faces. Though unprecedented, the Knights had discussed the possibility that the Yorish visitor would turn out to be a Verity, given the rumors, and prepared accordingly. Few other threats, potential or real, could have impelled them to move Vaka Aster's vessel to the obscurity and safety of the Mount Omina sanctuary. Hesitance, fear—Knights shed these qualities like water from oiled canvas, particularly those as hardened by the lessons of longevity as Eisa and Mallich. Eisa had served with Ulfric for fifteen hundred turns and would be the next Stallari if Ulfric ever resigned his service. The ever-stalwart Mallich, at almost twelve hundred turns a Knight, rivaled mountains with his enduring fortitude.

Until looking into the Battgjald Scrylle, Ulfric would have thought handling the celestial stones of a foreign Verity to also be unprecedented—but what he'd seen there disproved this. He marveled at the gleaming ball hanging on its chain from his hand. Its magnificence made his breath catch. Even Eisa grew uncharacteristically quiet. A thing of unparalleled beauty, its core gleamed with a living light, though its color was oblivion black. Between the metal prongs of the pendant's Fenestros setting, Elder Veros runes crusted the surface in swirls of smoke-gray, appearing etched into it. Yet the feel of the oculus itself was teardrop smooth. He lifted it up to catch the dragørflies' glow and noted the way the sigils' patterns changed as he twisted it to and fro. Each flash of light revealed a new message inscribed thereon, their permutations as limitless as light itself. Spells, written by a wystic hand. He could only imagine what uses the Flesh Casters had made of this Fenestros.

Each Verity had their own Order of Knights to protect their vessels, and each had a Scrylle to serve as limitless repositories for their realms' vast history, though Ulfric had never in his long life expected to gaze into the Scrylle of any Verity but his own. The Scrylles' lore was infinite, a history that went back to the first of the first peoples of each realm, filling a space that existed outside of the tangible, which could never be read entirely in one lifetime or even the length of Ulfric's many. But today he had read some, and he had seen more, he thought, than the foreign Verity had anticipated.

I know the usurper's plan, he sent to the Knights. *Balavad spoke the truth. He* can *stop the other Verities from reuniting at this Syzycki Elementum and leading their realities to... whatever the Elementum leads to. He intends to shackle them, all of them, by constructing a cage. To do so, he needs four of Vaka Aster's Fenestrii, and one of his own.* He held the Battgjald Fenestros aloft, for emphasis. *But first, he must recall Vaka Aster, then ensnare her.* He lowered his arm to look fully into their faces, switching to speaking aloud. "And he's already done it at least once, to Mithlí, Verity of Arc Rheunos. Balavad the usurper will overcome Vinnr and control it like it's his own puppet show, and the people here his puppets."

Eisa grunted, the sound a cross between a curse and... just a curse really, and hooked her glaive to its harness on her back. The three stood silently for a moment, contemplating the news.

Some wicked thirst for power had overcome the Verity known as Balavad, a trait so human Ulfric didn't understand how a celestial being, a creator of all things, could succumb to it. His concerns, however, were not why, but how to stop him. And now that they had the usurper's Scrylle and one of his Fenestrii—he made a decision. "We will use his Fenestros and summon Vaka Aster ourselves, before Balavad can set the snare. We need Vaka Aster here, in Vinnr, to banish the usurper. He is sundered, but we are not up to the task of taking on a Verity."

A niggling side issue: he had no idea how to persuade Vaka Aster not to abandon Vinnr to rejoin her kind at the Syzycki Elementum. Balavad had slowed the imminent event by entrapping the other Verity of Arc Rheunos, but that didn't change the fact that their loyalty was to Vaka Aster, and their duty dictated they stop Balavad from usurping her.

"You look to have a plan, Ulfric. Show us what you want to do," Mallich said and thumped Eisa on the back in solidarity.

"Eisa," he responded, "look inside that Caster's tote for Battgjald's Scrylle. Mallich, help me prepare the vessel."

Grim thoughts of what would happen if this plot failed grated the edges of his mind, but he held them at bay and stepped to the rear of the grotto. On a carved stone pedestal stood the statue of the Verity, a human vessel composed of what appeared to be the same white alabaster of much of Ivoryss's stonework. She was an ancestor of Eisa, a woman from the seventh royal bloodline of Dyrrakium who'd given herself to Vaka Aster before any of them had been born. After two thousand turns, the woman's flesh had hardened, her spirit long since departed from the vessel to rejoin the Great Cosmos. The statue tinged the cave in a wavering cerulean color from countless glittering crystalline stones veining the inert form, almost as if the chamber were immersed in water. Before Vaka Aster's celestial form had departed from Vinnr, now more than three hundred turns ago, the statue had been too bright to look upon, seemingly composed not of stone but of celestial light itself.

But now that Vaka Aster had sundered this synthesis, only the vessel remained, a cold reminder of the Verity's lightless side. With the Verity's long absence, the majesty of her role in human affairs had fallen to the fickleness of human memory, and human loyalty, and become an eidolon, an idea with little remaining influence beyond the Knights themselves. The Resplendolent Conservatum continued to teach Verity lore and history and encourage fealty and devotion to their maker, but Ulfric suspected fewer and fewer of the Conservatum acolytes believed these teachings the way they still had when he'd been an acolyte himself. Belief was easier with proof, and Vaka Aster's unsettling absence from Vinnr made proof impossible.

"Got it," Eisa called after retrieving the Caster's satchel. Then she added cryptically, "And more."

Ulfric bridled. "What else?"

She stepped forward with both hands raised, holding two objects.

"Here we have a foreign Scrylle." She opened her right hand to show them. "And here we have…" In her other hand, she brandished another of Vaka Aster's Fenestrii, as well as another of Balavad's.

Ulfric was unsurprised. "So this is the reason for the assault on Yor."

"It would seem," Eisa said. "But why is that Caster carrying two of Balavad's Fenestrii?"

"One to use in the Verity cage, the other to read the incantation from the Scrylle."

She nodded.

Then Mallich voiced what they were each thinking. "And we hold three more here—all the foreign Verity needs to create this cage."

The Fenestrii of Vaka Aster were distributed by agreement among the Knights and Vinnr's two ruling kingdoms. The Knights held three. One was kept in Yor under the protection of their branch of the Resplendolent Conservatum, and the last was retained by the Ivoryssian branch of the Conservatum. Whether the keepers of Yor's Fenestros had given it freely or died trying to protect it, Ulfric couldn't know.

"I'll hold on to that," he said, and Eisa relinquished Yor's Fenestros.

His brief glimpse into Balavad's Scrylle had revealed the incantation for creating the cage and shown him what to do to prepare. Moving quickly, he now arranged the four Fenestrii around the vessel's pedestal, understanding they would both activate the snare and serve as shackles to hold the Verity chained within its corporeal vessel.

"You two," he turned and faced the Knights, "I want you outside the chamber. No one gets in, on your lives. If this fails to recall Vaka Aster, your duty is the same. Protect the vessel. Get it out using the tunnels if you must. Regroup with Symvalline and the rest of the Order. And, Knights, keep faith in our fight."

"And in our Order, Stallari," Mallich responded as he saluted Ulfric.

But Eisa wasn't having it. "Ulfric, let us help. You know what kind of power might be channeled using a foreign Fenestros. It could kill you."

"True. And if it does, you will still be tasked with carrying forth the Order's charge."

"If this Balavad sack of swill wants to fight, we've got to stick together," she continued as if he hadn't spoken. "You can't be martyring yourself… especially if you lack the will to see it through."

Her pause was uncharacteristic, even if her brashness wasn't, and her words snatched his focus like a hawk. "Lack will? A millennium together, and you doubt me?" He stepped close to Eisa and drilled her with his heart-of-a-glacier stare. Though her forehead reached no higher than his cheeks, her bearing was no less firm. She didn't falter, never had. He'd chosen her from among many worthy acolytes at the Conservatum for her iron core, but he'd never expected to have to oppose it. "Are you lacking faith, Knight?"

The defiance in her leaden eyes burned. "You speak of faith, Stallari, but…" And now she faltered, a blink giving away some inner conflict he'd never have suspected. "Is it possible that you've lost it? We know you and Symvalline plan to leave the Order and relinquish your duties. When Vaka Aster returns, you're going to ask for your mortality back so you can raise your daughter in the way of commoners." He voice hardened. "You've lost your faith in Vaka Aster, and in our duty." Another pause. "Do *you* believe you have the conviction it will take to see this through?"

Anger and sadness coursed among his innards in a toxic brew. He'd witnessed many deaths—of foes and of friends. He'd witnessed betrayal and despair. One cannot live for as long as he had and not see these things, not be branded by them. But this loss of trust gutted him almost worse than any of them. Because she was right—he had lost faith, or at least the will to remain faithful.

Regardless, he was their Stallari. "You will follow orders, Eisa, or by Vaka Aster…"

Before he finished the statement, Mallich placed a hand on Eisa's shoulder and gave it a warning nudge. She didn't move but continued to hold Ulfric's stare.

"This fight isn't for now, Eisa," Mallich said. "We have our own duty to see to."

She stood still for another moment, then took a half step back. With a sigh, she relented. "And so we will. Come on."

The two exited through the heavy door, Eisa throwing one last look at Ulfric as she sent, *Don't fail us, Stallari. A life spent unworthy of our maker, mortal or not, isn't worth living.*

CHAPTER ELEVEN

Mylla doubled over beside the Dragør Wing fighter and launched her last meal onto the rocky mountainside. If she weren't thus preoccupied, she would have fallen on her knees and kissed the ground. The prospect of doing so, after painting it with her breakfast, held less appeal now.

Havelock climbed out of the fighter's cockpit beside her. From the corner of her eye, she saw him pat the fuselage gently and murmur something. Then he turned to her and placed a hand on her back. "If I ever doubted the toughness and resolve of the Knights before, I never will again, Mylla. I can't tell you how glad I am you waited until we landed to… let fly."

She knew his tone well enough to know it was accompanied by a smirk, though her eyes were watering too much to see it yet. She couldn't be angry at his gibe. He'd flown with the speed and skill only a true creature born to flight could rival and brought them limping to the landing field in a fighter that shouldn't have been capable of anything but a final fiery explosion after directly darting into unforgiving earth. More than one time up there, she'd wondered if she were going to scream or die, or simply do as she'd just done and reacquaint everything within her to without her.

On the whole, at least she could take comfort in the fact that she hadn't screamed. That would have been irredeemably embarrassing.

They hadn't seen the remaining attacker since its engagement with the second Dragør Wing fighter started, and given the Ivoryssian pilot's tenaciousness, she doubted they would. She straightened, feeling more or less herself again, and wiped her mouth with the back of her hand, then peered far up the mountainside toward the cave leading to Vaka Aster's sanctuary. "It'll take too long to hike up to the main entrance, but a hidden tunnel that leads to it is near. Come on."

Lock remained where he was, staring out over the horizon. "That was Jimp Owers's fighter. I don't know why he would have been up there."

"He saved our rears. Does it matter? Time is short, Lock."

"Mylla, you need to tell me what's going on. Those foreign ships must be part of a fleet. Asteryss City could be under attack right now. I… I should be there."

A worm of guilt writhed its way into her guts. "I understand, but we're here now and that," she pointed to the Dragør Wing fighter, a plume of blue-black smoke still rising from the damaged stern, "isn't taking you anywhere."

He looked at her, his brow deeply wrinkled, his hazel eyes squinted. "I've deserted my post. There will be consequences."

"Trust me, they'd have been much worse if you hadn't helped me get here." She took a step toward the cave entrance, hoping the movement would be enough to entice him along.

It wasn't. "Why?"

"If you come with me, I'll tell you on the way. Now let's—"

Before she finished the statement, a low hum, more pressure than sound against their eardrums, came from above.

Scanning the sky, Lock said, "There he is. Thank Vaka Aster, he made it."

Mylla's instincts were telling her to get inside the mountain before anyone else arrived. Lock was right; the sickle ships they encountered couldn't be the only ones. More could just as likely be approaching.

Then she heard through her Mentalios, *Mylla, we're about to join you.*

Symvalline? Here? It took Mylla another moment to spot the Wing fighter, and then with the nimbleness of a hummingbird and the speed of a diving eagle, the ship settled beside them, its frame easily maneuvering onto the gently pitched mountainside clearing. The area lay within the tree line and had been strategically groomed long ago by the Knights to look as if it were a natural mountain glade. Between the two fighters, the clearing was now full.

The cockpit covering slid back and both Symvalline and Isemay sat inside. Mylla and Havelock exchanged a surprised look.

"What… how… I didn't know you could fly like that," she finally got out.

Symvalline reached the ground and held an arm out. Isemay passed her a burlap bag, then climbed down beside her. "I'm seven hundred and seventy-nine turns old, Knight Evernal," she said. "I've had the time to learn. Don't worry, Wing," she said to Havelock, "this ship's usual pilot wasn't harmed, merely persuaded."

Over her surprise, Mylla said, "You saved our skin, Sym. What happened to the other attacker? Do you know where it came from?"

Symvalline rested the base of the sack against the ground and pulled open its drawstring. She reached inside and withdrew—

"Star Spark!" Mylla said, surprised to see the sword she'd had to relinquish at Aster Keep. More than a mere weapon, it had been hallowed by Vaka Aster, turning it into a weapon powerful enough to destroy not just foes but also the corporeal vessel of any Verity. Balavad's, for example. "How—?"

"Acolyte Irrick retrieved both yours and Ulfric's weapons and gave them to me when I arrived at the keep to collect my daughter." With hard eyes, she stared at Isemay, who looked down with the expression of put-upon shame only half-agers can master. "As for the fighters, they're part of Balavad's forces. They've attacked the city, and soon the rest of Ivoryss, no doubt. I chased your pursuer, but it diverted back to Asteryss. I had to let it go in order to get to Mount Omina as fast as possible." After handing Mylla her sword, she hefted the sack to her back and secured it with a strap across her chest.

"Attacked Ivoryss!" cut in Havelock. "I have to get back there."

"Yes, you should go, Wing," Symvalline said and stepped away from her "borrowed" fighter.

"Wait, Lock…" Mylla reached a hand to stop him, then froze. Who was she to dissuade him from his duty?

He bristled, but only for a moment. "Mylla, it's my city," he said simply.

You could die, she'd almost said. But he was mortal. Of course he could die. She knew it, but it had never hit her in this way before. *He could die, and I will not.* "You're right. Yes, you should go." To hide her pain, she busied herself with buckling Star Spark's scabbard back around her waist.

Before she finished, Havelock drew her into his embrace. "Mylla, we'll see each other soon. I—"

She put a finger against his lips, unwilling to hear promises that neither of them had any power to keep. "Take care of yourself." With a last kiss, she stepped back. Turning to Symvalline, she said, "And Stave and Safran? You warned them…" *through the lens,* she finished using the Mentalios.

Yes, Symvalline responded. "To the tunnel."

Havelock stepped to the Wing fighter. As they took the opposite direction, Mylla felt his eyes on her back, and she turned for a final wave.

At that moment, the dark seeds of a bad dream swarmed up the skin of the mountain, soundless and insidious—a dozen or more of the attack ships.

"LOCK!" she shouted, and the nearest of the ships began strafing the glade with iron projectiles like giant spearheads. They looked almost innocuous as the streamed through the air, but when they struck the earth, the trees, and—oh good Verity!—the two Wing fighters, they exploded in oily crimson fireballs. As Mylla watched, the fighter Havelock was mounting took a projectile near the bow, throwing Lock backward to the ground.

"Come on!" Symvalline yelled, and began tearing down the path, her daughter's arm firmly in her grasp.

Mylla froze as the squadron of attackers shot up the mountainside, then began a wide turn back for another strafing run. *He's not moving.* Her legs made the decision before her mind, and Mylla raced back through the glade to Havelock's inert form. When she reached him, she fell to her knees, skidding along the grass for the final few steps. "Lock, Lock, talk to me."

His eyes opened, unfocused. "Whuh… ?" And he sat up and shook his head as if trying to clear it. "Did that ship just blow up my fighter?"

She didn't know whether to weep or laugh at his sheer incredulity over their attacker's nerve. Reaching out a hand, she demanded, "Can you run?"

He turned his head and tried to focus, his eyeballs still dancing to an internal jig.

Nothing for it. She grabbed him by an arm and hauled his bigger form off the ground with the strength of seven hundred turns as a warrior and a vein-popping dump of adrenaline. "RUN!" she yelled into his face, and this, at least, made it past his fog.

The trees, the trees were their only chance.

The trail led into a forest of straight-trunked pines and aspen. They made it. Just. Mylla felt the breeze from those black darts shooting past her head and back, even after they'd crossed the threshold out of the glade. Despite how shaken up as he was, Havelock's survival instinct kept his footing fast and sure behind her. Branches spread high and wide above them, interlacing densely to create a canopy through which little of the sky could be seen. White and gray lichen-covered boulders and smaller stones dotted the ground, and many turns' worth of dried brown needles lay thickly beneath their feet. A fleeting realization struck her: even if they avoided being skewered or blown to bits, the forest was sure to catch fire, and in the dryness it would spread quickly.

For emphasis, a dart pierced the canopy nearby and impaled an aspen trunk. With a vermillion explosion, the entire tree flared up like a gas-filled hurricane lantern. Glimpses of the speeding attack ships came through the trees as the squadron jetted up the mountainside, still firing darts helter-skelter. Smoke quickly began to limit their sight. But that wasn't the worst part.

"What's that noise?" she managed between gasps.

"Avalanche!" cried Symvalline. "Move!"

No one needed to be told twice.

Ahead, a thin branch split from its tree trunk and crashed down in front of Symvalline and Isemay. They halted in time to avoid it, but Mylla and Lock hurdled it and kept running. Nothing could compel her to look up the slope and watch their own deaths approach. The avalanche may be coming directly at them, but it may just as easily bypass them. No way to tell through the trees, and that was just fine. One thing was sure, it sounded big.

The tunnel's mouth drew near, but she could only see the sigil that marked the keyhole by looking through her Mentalios lens. Scrambling forward wildly, she pulled the pendant free of her armor and placed it against one eye. The rumbling coming from higher up the mountainside worsened, assaulting her inner ear with an ominous base note. What would happen inside the tunnel as the avalanche struck? *Will it collapse and trap us in our own tomb?* A shifting stone tricked her stride and she nearly rolled an ankle but continued to run. *Shut up, Mylla. No more thoughts until we're out of danger.*

She could laugh at her own absurd illogic later, she decided.

"Mylla!" The fear in Isemay's voice brought her up short. "My mum!"

Symvalline had fallen to her hands and knees, looking as if she wouldn't be able to rise on her own. Even as Mylla realized this, a boulder crashed down the mountain's face and caromed into a close-grouped copse of pines, smashing splinters from their trunks before it stopped.

Symvalline commanded, "Take Isemay and get to the tunnel. Go!"

Isemay shot Mylla a desperate glance. Immediately, Mylla raced to Symvalline's side and put a hand beneath one arm. "We're not leaving you, Sym."

"Take my daughter." Symvalline used Mylla's frame to pull herself up. "I'll be right behind."

Mylla spared her another look, then grasped Isemay's hand and tugged her back into motion. Havelock was ahead and she placed

Isemay's hand into one of his so she would be free to take the lead in search of the cave entrance. Focusing too hard on finding the boulder marking the tunnel proved a bad idea when she tripped on an unseen fallen limb. She stumbled to a knee, grunted, and tried to right herself. But Havelock was unprepared for her tumble and came down on top of her, flattening her against the earth, and releasing Isemay, who fell back.

"Oof!" Dirt spattered into her face. Tilting her head to the side, she caught sight of a boulder the size of an unpleasant outcome flying over the top of them, leaving debris to fall in its wake. It landed just beyond their prone forms, then continued down the slopes.

"Close one," Havelock whispered, and she would have kissed him if dirt wasn't coating her lips.

They scrambled up and ran on as she pressed the Mentalios lens back to her eye. *There!* The semirectangular slab she'd been searching for lay just a couple dozen yards away. Risking it, she closed one eye to get a better look through the lens. The Elder Veros rune glowed like blue fire, its middle engraved with a circular keyhole for her lens. "Almost there," she mumbled, saving breath.

"Isemay! Stop!" Havelock yelled.

They were nearly there, and the urgency in Havelock's tone didn't divert her attention. The next moment, she slid the lens home, channeling the sigil's incantation through it, and the stone rumbled into a seam in the slope, revealing a narrow passageway. Jubilant, she turned to usher the other three inside—but only Havelock was there. Peering over his shoulder, she could see Isemay supporting her mother, who hobbled toward the opening with maddening slowness, still many paces distant. Too many.

The ground bucked—it felt as if the entire *mountain* bucked—and a cacophony upslope rent the air with the promise of imminent chaos. She looked upward, then blinked to shake away the sight of half the mountainside sliding toward them. Lunging from the tunnel mouth to help Sym and Isemay, she was brought up short by Havelock grabbed her trailing hand.

"No!" he yelled, and yanked her hard into the tunnel.

Stunned, it took her a moment to react, but his relentless pulling into the dark made it impossible to get her balance.

"What are you doing? They're still out there!" she cried, but his fingers had turned to rods of steel and his grip held. In the next heartbeat, a gust of air smacked into her from behind, sending her flailing, *again*, to her stomach. And the light outside the cave disappeared behind them.

CHAPTER TWELVE

"Faith in the fight," Ulfric muttered to himself as he prepared to call Vaka Aster from her absence elsewhere in the Cosmos. His mind picked up the words and repeated them in a litany. *Faith in the fight, faith-in-the-fight, faithinthefight... inthefight... faith...*

Though empowered by Vaka Aster's celestial spark, which made him practically immortal, he was still just a man, and he knew this summoning would tax him to his limit, maybe beyond.

Positioned on the foundation at the vessel's ankles, the five Fenestrii gleamed—four of Vaka Aster's and one of Balavad's. Ulfric knelt before them and affixed Balavad's other Fenestros to the setting on the Battgjald Scrylle. Before looking into the oculus, he closed his eyes and reflected on what he'd seen in the Scrylle at Aster Keep. It had staggered him, and he wasn't entirely sure it wouldn't again. But if anything could prepare him, his millennia as Knight would have to be it.

He opened his eyes, peered into the Fenestros, and searched for the words to summon Vaka Aster.

Like revisiting the pages of a familiar book, he quickly located the passage, and his mental chorus changed into the language of the Verities as he began the incantation. The words streamed from his lips, part dirge, part melody, vibrating the air with their cadence. As they left his throat, they reached into his spirit and began to drain it. He would weaken, maybe die if too much of his Verity spark was drained, but that wouldn't happen until Vaka Aster's celestial self once more fused with the earthly vessel before him. He wouldn't let it kill him.

The Fenestrii rose into the air and hovered above the vessel. He caught their movement from the corners of his eyes but was unwilling, unable really, to shift his gaze from the Scrylle. Sharp pain tingled in his heels, then shot up his legs and stabbed into his groin, spreading throughout his abdomen, his chest, down his arms. Teeth gritted, focus hardened, he refused to let the pain stop him. It was nothing, a fleeting sensation, only his life being extracted from him like a thorn slowly drawn from a finger. He continued chanting, the incantation growing in strength, and slowly the Scrylle between his hands became all there was, became his thoughts, his mind relinquishing to it, blooming with wystic fire, exploding into a Cosmos of knowledge and wonder and—

A section of the cave's roof shattered as a pillar of liquid blue flame broke through, sending him reeling backward in a fine haze of grit and dust. Slipping in the gore of the dead Caster's body, he crashed hard onto his back and lost his grip on the Scrylle. Panic replaced the pain lancing him, and he tried to grab the cylinder, but a force held him back. Winds like none he'd ever felt buffeted him, pressing him down and swirling chaotically within the chamber. Tiny shards of stone peppered his exposed skin, and the cyclone ripped the air from his mouth and nostrils before he could draw it into his lungs.

Then it stopped.

Coughing, he looked about the chamber. Motes of dust flitted in the air, now lit by outside light spilling through the ceiling's breach. Still daytime. How long ago the morning felt, when he'd climbed Aster Keep's steps and his main worry had been for Isemay's safety. Now he worried about the safety of Vinnr at large. A Knight's duty—his burden—sometimes so very heavy.

Even brighter than the daylight, a corona of blue light encircling the vessel illuminated the chamber: the five Fenestrii, now spinning at an inconceivable speed around its head. He could no longer see the stones individually. They revolved too quickly, creating a vortex of unbroken light on a perfectly level axis. Crackling sparks whipped outward from the halo with furious energy, as if trying to escape the ring. He rose to his feet, unable to believe what his eyes and his mind were telling him. The trap to ensnare Vaka Aster had worked. Their maker was present once more, after almost three centuries. He felt the Verity's power in the acrid sharpness of the air, saw it in those snaps of light shooting from the whirling celestial Fenestrii.

Stones and debris lay strewn throughout the chamber. The force that had collapsed the roof had shaken the walls until they buckled and cracked, and it appeared that the heavy wooden door with iron hinges leading to the sanctuary's antechamber and entry tunnel had taken the most damage. The hinges were warped, and the double-thick pine slats crushed into each other, splintering in places. He wouldn't be leaving that way. He hoped the outer tunnel remained solid and Eisa and Mallich had stayed out of harm's way.

Remembering the Battgjald Scrylle, he quickly inspected the floor around him. It lay nearby, Fenestros still in its setting. *Now what?* He'd imagined that it would be a simple matter to beseech the Verity upon her return to reinstate balance and order and eject the usurper. But now... now he realized he'd been mistaken.

The Scrylle had not shown him how to undo the trap, only how to set it.

As Ulfric stared at the inert vessel washed in radiance by the over-bright halo whirling above, another thought roiled through his mind. *I have overpowered a divine Verity. I, alone, did this.* And for a moment, he wondered what he else he could achieve with Balavad's Scrylle, what other secrets it held. Because of it, he had wielded authority over a *Verity*.

No. He heaved these thoughts away. They were blasphemy, thoughts born of madness. Even at his great age, it seemed he was no more immune from the many absurdities that came from being human as any uninitiated commoner. And blasphemy, the greatest, was also the hardest to root out. *When this task is done,* he vowed to himself, *I will collect and hide all the celestial stones in a place they can never again be found. They hold too much power for people to be trusted with.* Mere mortals, with their many flaws and weaknesses—*Balavad's own words,* Ulfric reflected—couldn't be trusted to handle these relics without havoc and corruption certain to follow. He hardly needed longevity to tell him that.

But you are wrong, Stallari. You are no longer merely human. You have been the pawn of a Verity for far too long not to be changed by us.

The voice came from his own mind, but it didn't belong to him.

"Balavad," he said aloud, his own words too faint for his ears. In fact, he could hear nothing now, no swirl of air from the rent in the roof, nor flutter of dragørfly wings, not even his quickening heartbeat or thump of blood through is veins. He realized his eyes were once more fixed on the Fenestros in the setting of the Battgjald Scrylle, which was once more opened to his mind, his mind opened to it. He had picked it up with nerveless fingers, unwittingly, almost as if it had compelled him to.

You've completed the task, Stallari Aldinhuus, and opened the doorway for me to step forth and replace the lost Verity of Vinnr, your Vaka Aster, who forsook you and all she created. Your service has been exemplary.

Horrified, Ulfric tried to speak, to deny what the Verity said, but his voice had left him. The Scrylle and its ruler held him fixed, entranced. Enslaved.

Didn't you know I would find you as soon as you looked into my Scrylle? Of course you did. Of course. It isn't a mirror, after all, but a lens. When you look through a Scrylle, we Verities look through too.

You're not welcome in my mind, Balavad, Ulfric warned.

Biting frost in the form of a laugh slid over his thoughts. *So much left to learn, Stallari. I am a Verity. I don't require permission. Our creations are always open to our sight.*

But that isn't true, said Ulfric. *If it were, you'd have known my plan.*

The Verity let silence hold sway, giving Ulfric time to grasp the extent of his foolishness. And it hit him. He had been tricked. Balavad had seen, or at least guessed, his plan the moment he'd formed it, maybe even before he had. When Ulfric had stared into the Scrylle in Aster Keep, Balavad had been lurking there, like a malevolent phantasm, reading Ulfric's mind like a book using the medium of the celestial Scrylle. Maybe he'd even planted the seed himself, persuading Ulfric to escape here to Vaka Aster's sanctuary, intent on bringing her back and begging her for aid, caging her if necessary, thus leading Balavad directly to the vessel and doing his dark deed for him. And though the usurping Verity was not here in the flesh, his will was, and his will was now reaching through the Scrylle with an intent to control Ulfric.

Ulfric began to understand the danger his own mind now was to him. He didn't know how much he could hide, but it was clear that as long as he held the Scrylle, his thoughts were laid bare to this being, his mind a battleground and Balavad an invader. Nothing he thought or felt could be guarded from the Verity without, perhaps, a great cost.

And the usurper spoke the truth: Vaka Aster no longer held sway in Vinnr. Ulfric had practically served the world to the usurper on a platter. *What have I done?*

The Verity seemed all too happy to supply him an answer. *You are a young being, yet. As I said, so much to learn. But do not lose faith, creation of Vaka Aster. I am not a monster. I've already told you that I am here to save your world, not destroy it. I see from your thoughts that you have killed Caster Rhafn, but that is well. I told you, I will make you the greatest of your kind to ever live. Now you can join me, replace Rafn as leader of my Order, bring about the resurgence of the Knights Corporealis—call it whatever you wish. And you have made it easy for me. Come and see what Vinnr will be. Let me share with you the beauty of my realm, the splendor and order of Battgjald, what Vinnr may be if we work together. This is the seat of creation, a marvel all other Verities can only admire but haven't the will to achieve themselves.*

At these words, a vision snaked through Ulfric's mind. A vast, far-reaching city, which he somehow knew to be the heart of a massive kingdom, much like Asteryss was the heart of Ivoryss, spread before him. Emerald-flecked graystone towers and buildings spread for miles in every direction, glinting beneath the rays of two suns, one crimson-hued and the other streaked with white and orange belts. People who looked much the same as Vinnrics, perhaps a touch taller on average, dotted the daytime streets, here and there entering and leaving the buildings, carrying totes, accompanying children, all very orderly. Very peaceful. A sea, the waters murky in the diffuse light, lapped at the horizon, with tiny black specks belonging to water vessels bobbing on colorless waves.

The foreign Verity resumed. *Magnificence embodied, more so than your simple realm. I raised this world from nothing, sculpted it from my own divinity, imbued its people with wealth and humility, aware of their station and reason for their very existence. My people, unlike yours, Stallari, appreciate the gifts I have given them. They do not smirk at the sound of my name, nor scoff at the abundance I provide. And they do not pretend I am a myth. Their fealty is total and repaid with all that you see. And there's more.*

A strange feeling of falling, or maybe spinning, overcame Ulfric. The weightlessness took him by surprise, and he sensed himself trying to reach his arms out to regain balance. But the sensation was far away, as if coming from some alien body, not his own. He caught a glimpse of himself for no longer than an eye-blink still standing inside the cave before the whirring corona of blue light above Vaka Aster's vessel, still holding the gleaming metal Scrylle within his hands: motionless, his stare distant, his face a disbelieving rictus. He wasn't sure if he still possessed the body he saw or if he'd somehow become incorporeal. Was he alive? Did he exist in Vinnr at all anymore?

In another blink, the scene surrounding him changed from the vision of Battgjald's great city to a vast sky: Vinnr's sky. The brightness of the daystar Halla surrounded him with a clarity that outshone its usual light. He was airborne, suspended above the planet, yet he felt no fear. But what caught his attention next defied his understanding. Something monstrous and pure black approached him from the air. Some kind of a monolith, a bastion, a…? He didn't have a word for it.

A starship, Stallari. You are looking at the flagship of a great people that takes them beyond Battgjald. With this, I have brought my warriors distances Vaka Aster's creations cannot imagine. This starship brings the bearers of my gift: preservation from needless destruction.

The Verity shifted him again and transported him to the interior of the great ship. He stood on a type of suspended walkway overlooking a chamber below. Hundreds of bodies filled the space, shapes of men and women, tall, thin, clad in black uniforms that clung to their narrow frames like wet parchment. They barely moved and made no noise, seeming to simply be waiting.

For orders, he realized. To be commanded.

No army is a tool of preservation, Ulfric said as black dread squirmed in his guts.

On that, you're wrong. You have served Verities longer than almost any of our creations. You know how slowly your kind accepts change, even when it benefits them, and you are different, greater now than your own kind. For that reason, I would raise you from your humble station and give you the rank you deserve, make you the commander of not only my Flesh Casters but also my army, the Raveners of the Tooth, whom you see before you. You see, your realm is not the only one I will save from the wastage of the Syzycki Elementum. I am dedicated to saving all the realms of my Verity kindred. And you, Stallari, can understand like no Verity what your kind needs, and understand like no human what having the favor of a Verity means. What gifts we can bestow. You are perfect for this task. Lead my Ravener forces to new worlds and help them bring my quins' forgotten people to an everlasting peace and an everlasting order.

No honey could be sweeter, nor poison more lethal. And Ulfric understood at a level deeper than simple thought, through body, mind, and spirit: this flying craft before him was not for exploring new realms and bringing gifts. It was a world conqueror, a war machine for *taking* them. What Balavad offered was neither peace nor freedom. Ulfric's fealty would not be required in exchange for power but for unmitigated servitude. This was slavery.

He strained to hide these thoughts from the usurper, whom he felt like a worm in an apple stealing through his mind, devouring his hopes and reason. Yet he could not conceal them, not all of them. His strength was no match for a celestial's.

Balavad plucked thoughts from his mind like grapes. To Ulfric, it felt as if cold fingers were squeezing inside his head, his concepts, his emotions, his memories. The harder he tried to resist, the colder they became.

The Verity whispered, *Ah. Ah, now I understand. You are not like most of your kind. Power isn't the gift you seek. There are others to whom your fealty is stronger. Their names... their names are Symvalline. A Knight as well. And... Isemay. Your child.*

Gasping, Ulfric fought against the intrusion. Every thought the usurper heard became a liability. Summoning the authority innate to his character, he pushed against Balavad, blanking his mind with an image of gray mist that thickened with each new assault the Verity launched. The surface of his brain crawled with crackling fire and searing bolts of lightning, making him shake and burn, but he held fast —because, despite the usurper's might, Ulfric could feel it working. He swore, *I will never serve you, usurper. If it's my consent you require, then why don't you simply take it?*

In response, Ulfric sensed a strange hesitation from the Verity, a stillness that surprised him. *Can't you force what you want? You are a celestial. Your kind made my kind. Can't you control—*

It felt as if a fist gripped the meat of his brain and squeezed with mighty strength, the sudden pain as acute as all the pain he'd ever known felt in this one instant and then doubled. Screaming, he fell to his knees, the torment spearing him, shattering him.

It stopped on its own. Tears leaked from behind his tightly clamped eyelids and rushed down his cheeks. Ulfric's breath came in gasps as he grappled to regain himself. He opened his eyes and found he was once again in the cave, still in the same place looking upon the swirling Fenestrii over Vaka Aster's vessel, cracking bolts of cerulean light trying to escape the bright corona. He could hear sound normally once more: the dry rustle of the dragørflies' wings as they flittered near the broken ceiling, the pounding on the doors as Eisa and Mallich—still alive, thankfully—beat against it. And then—

Ulfric!

He jumped to his feet. "Symvalline?"

Her voice echoed in his mind, then was replaced by an image, or rather by another shifting of himself to a different place. He, the incorporeal he, stood on the face of Mount Omina, looking across a landscape that was shattered by a recent rockfall. Blasted and scorched trees, many still smoking, lay twisted beneath boulders and stones. Dirt and smoke swirled through the air, ruining the day's clarity. And Symvalline called to him again from somewhere nearby. He gasped. She wasn't supposed to be here.

He turned around and around until he saw her, or rather them. Symvalline and Isemay. They crouched beneath a jagged deadfall of smoldering pine trunks and boulders. He could only see patches of his family amid the debris—Symvalline's raised arms, the white collar of Isemay's tunic—but it took less than a heartbeat to realize the danger they were in. The only thing that had saved his family from being buried beneath the debris were Symvalline's klinkí stones. She wielded them like a shield in suspension over their heads, holding the debris back. A network of wavering and diffuse blue lines of light linked like a cobweb between the stones. He glimpsed Symvalline's knotted face between the lines as she concentrated on holding the debris up, and holding their deaths at bay.

But death approached nonetheless.

From the ruined forest emerged six pale, gangly figures dressed in the black uniforms of Balavad's Ravener army. They approached his family's precarious alcove with drawn swords, their tips bent back in wicked hooks that looked designed to rip the innards from a man.

Battgjald's warriors, Stallari. They were led here by one of your own, the Knight called Mylla. And now they've found your heartmatch and child. But these Raveners can save them. Would you like them to?

He knew the price. *In exchange, I am to be your slave.*

No, Stallari. You will become a leader, savior of your world, as I said, and your family will join you in a future that, together, we will ensure has no end.

It was a lie. He knew it. Everything had an end.

Choose, Aldinhuus. Do they live or die?

He looked closely at the Raveners. Bloodlessly pale and grotesque-looking, their flesh seemed an utter rejection of life. They were taller than he and lanky, almost emaciated, but they walked bowed forward as if hunchbacked. Ulfric's gaze was drawn to their eyes, and he realized with revulsion the soldiers were blind, their sightless yet searching orbs a flat blue-gray swirl in their sockets, like fungus-ridden granite. Even their eyes' natural moistness had dried, adding to the verisimilitude of stone. One spoke, the language sibilant and strange to Ulfric's ears, and their gaunt forms closed in a semicircle around his family.

What unnatural metamorphosis had happened to these people? What future, endless or not, did they represent?

At that moment, Ulfric understood there was no choice. He would not become a slave, nor would he condemn his family to that living death. His ruse has failed, and Vaka Aster's location had been found. His life's purpose lay in waste, and his reason for living was about to be destroyed on the side of this mountain.

… but maybe there was one hope, only one. *I must unbind Vaka Aster. She can save my family.*

He prayed she would.

"Let me look upon Vaka Aster one last time," he said aloud, "and I will serve you."

He stood once more inside his own flesh in the vessel's chamber. *Symvalline, Isemay...* He nearly fell to his knees as the greatest fear he'd ever felt pounded into him—that he may never see their beloved faces again.

The Verity spoke. *You may—*

But whatever the usurper meant to say was cut off abruptly as, without a second thought, Ulfric bounded forward, leaped onto the vessel's dais, and threw his arms into the spinning conflagration of Fenestrii overhead, thrusting the Battgjald Scrylle like a sword into the onrush of Verity stones. Not caring what the usurper could hear, he pleaded with all the force his embattled mind could sustain: *Vaka Aster, protect my family!*

Just before his mind blanked, he heard the usurper's ringing command: *KILL THEM ALL!*

CHAPTER THIRTEEN

Cough, cough, cough. The sound hit Mylla's ears, but seemed to be filtered through wool. It wasn't a sound she could readily ignore, coming as it did from her own throat and lungs. When she realized it was her, she sat up and hacked out a torrent of cave dust and grit.

When her voice worked again, she called, "Havelock? Havelock!"

"Mmpfh."

"Rook's balls, where are you?" Dragging her fingers over the skin of her neck, she traced over her Mentalios chain and followed it down to the lens itself. With a brief chant, she enticed the lens to glow with diffuse light. There he was, lying on his back with a few rocks scattered over his chest and legs, but none large enough to have seriously hurt him. She hoped.

Scrabbling on her knees, she reached him and wiped dirt and small stones from his eyes and nose. When her palm brushed strands of his hair from his forehead, he jerked, and her hand came away bloodied.

"Shh, shh," she soothed as she leaned in and held the lens close to the wound. Tenderly, she pulled more strands free. The gash was the length of her smallest finger but didn't look too deep. The bleeding was already slow and mostly congealed.

He blinked, mumbled again, then sat up abruptly, his hands flying out to grip her arms reflexively.

"It's okay. You're fine," she said, straining to make her voice sound more confident than she felt. "You've been hit in the head, but not seriously. Are you hurt anywhere else?"

He coughed, oddly politely, into his sleeve, considered, then shook his head. Unwilling to accept a simple answer, she pulled her forearms free from his grip and clenched the edge of the Mentalios between her teeth to free her hands. She ran them over his neck, arms, and torso, searching for the odd protrusions of broken bones or more wounds. He remained passive under her ministrations, dazed by the circumstances of their predicament as much as by discomfort. Even as she felt for damage under his thick leather Wing uniform, she scanned the area where the cave entrance… had been.

Finding no other injuries on his body, she gripped the lens once more and stated, "We are trapped." *And Symvalline and Isemay are not here with us.* The thought seemed to rip vitality straight out of her, and she sagged, still perched on her knees. Her Mentalios fell free and dangled against her breastplate. A noise that might have been a sob if she'd not choked most of it back pushed past her lips.

"Mylla, there was nothing you could have done." He seemed to be able to read her mind. "If you'd run back for them, you'd be dead too."

"Don't say that. Don't say they're dead." The anger in the glare she leveled on him seemed to confuse him. She sucked in a breath and calmed herself. Of course, he was a mortal man who saw death more often than the average commoner, given his line of work. She, however, passed most of her days among people who lived for hundreds, even thousands of turns. She'd forgotten what death felt like, not to those who died, but to the living who remained behind and had to accept it, the loss, the inevitability of it. It occurred to her that this was why most of her Knight mentors rarely mingled too closely with commoners. Witnessing another's death was never trivial or painless, especially when you cared for them.

This is a reminder, she told herself. *This is what you'll experience if you continue this tryst with Havelock, eventually. Can you really face this pain, face losing him? Wouldn't it be easier to simply forget him?*

She pushed the thought away. The chaos of their circumstances left no room for her private concerns. "Lock, give me a moment. I'm going to see if I can call to Symvalline. They may have reached safety." Ignoring his obvious doubt, she put her thoughts through the Mentalios. *Symvalline, can you hear me?*

The only consolation she found in the empty silence that returned was that it didn't surprise her. Accepting death, it seemed, could come more easily than she imagined. The thought made her cold.

She pulled herself to her feet and reached a hand to assist Havelock. "Come on. The Stallari will still need our help. If those attackers find the cave—"

The Stallari! She might have slapped herself for not thinking of it sooner and pulled her hand back to reach for the Mentalios, failing to notice Havelock fall back on his hindquarters with the sudden disappearance of her assistance. *Stallari, I'm here to help you. Are you there?* she sent. The vessel's chamber could have suffered damage. Even now, Ulfric, Mallich, and Eisa could be dead or injured. But, again, only silence responded.

They'd tarried too long. They would find torches farther down the tunnel and soon reach the cut-stone stairs leading up—*and up, and up*—to the vessel's sanctuary. If there was any such thing as a Verity's luck to grace them, they'd regroup with the Stallari and the other Knights and devise a plan to keep Vaka Aster from falling prey to the foreign Verity. The Stallari had bought them time at Aster Keep. Now she must face the challenge, show her true worth as a Knight, and ensure her Verity's—and her realm's—continued security.

Havelock fell into step behind her. As they walked, the sound of his breathing brought to mind a new concern. How many air shafts leading from the surface to the bowels of Omina remained? Would their fates be to die from asphyxiation in here, far from light or friends? It would take an untold number of turns of airlessness for death to claim the last of her spark of Verity-given vitality, but Havelock would succumb much quicker. She gripped the thought and strangled it before it could sink cold teeth of fear into her. *One worry at a time, Mylla. Keep your faith in this fight.*

They moved as quickly as the torch's dim light allowed. Once they reached the stairs cut into the mountain's core, their pace slowed even more. The avalanche had vibrated deep, peppering the steep stairs with chunks of slate, just the right size to slip on and with a seemingly personal malice toward them. More than once she braced herself against the chill walls before her feet could slide off a step and send her, and probably Havelock with her, bumping backward into granite-hard, unforgiving darkness. *I would sacrifice a foot if it meant I'd never have to climb another flight of stairs*, she thought, her legs still groaning from her escape up the stairs at Aster Keep.

They couldn't have been trudging up the interior of the mountain for much longer than it would take her to quaff a pint or three—on a slow night, that was—but it felt like half her life. Ahead, finally, she could make out the landing in the glow of her torch, which had not wavered once. They seemed to be doing fine for air.

The landing itself was no wider than her arms could reach to either side of her. An iron ladder, bolted into the stone, led to a Mentalios-locked trap door that opened to the sanctuary chamber above, behind the pedestal where the vessel stood. Just four rungs left before they came to the Stallari's aid.

She pulled herself up the iron rungs and set her Mentalios into the metal circlet forming the trap door's keyhole, then channeled the words to unlock it. Holding the top rung with one hand, she shoved hard against the door, but it wouldn't move. Frustration forced her to speak through gritted teeth. "It's jammed or blocked."

"Let me try."

She hopped down, and he climbed up and pressed his palm into the door and pushed, but still nothing. "Get up here behind me and let me brace against you."

Climbing to the second rung, she traced her arms around either side of his legs in a hug and gripped the top rung, creating an envelope to hold him against the ladder. With her cheek pressed into his midback, she mumbled, "Good?"

"Perfect. I'm going to push hard. Hold on."

She felt the power in his body as he wound up, then released, jamming both palms into the door. It flew upward noiselessly, and Havelock pitched backward at the sudden lack of resistance. She gripped harder, blocking his fall and holding the ladder tight enough that her shoulders ached.

"Okay, let's go," he said.

He climbed over the lip of the opening, and she heard him whisper in amazement, "Clip my wings, what…?"

KILL THEM ALL!

The words stabbed into her mind like a dozen swords at once, causing her to nearly lose her grip. An instant later, the bluest blinding blue she'd ever seen flooded down from the room above and immersed the landing beneath her in overwhelming radiance. With one hand, she shielded her eyes, and with the other held the rung for all her worth as the air lifted in a swirl and blew around her. Then it stopped and the light outside her tightly closed eyelids returned to a mellow dimness.

"Havelock?" she said, dropping her hand and blinking.

No response.

She retrieved her Mentalios and hustled past the trap door, no longer calm or cautious, and entered Vaka Aster's chamber.

CHAPTER FOURTEEN

Brilliant blue light blinded Ulfric and filled the vessel chamber. It thickened and closed around him in a dense blue cocoon, then ripped into him, cleaving more than just his flesh. His bones, his organs, his very being down to the tiniest fragment of corporeality flew apart, shredded and diffused. But he felt nothing, no pain, no heat, no cold, as he turned into formless light, disintegrating and dispersing into waves of phosphorescence that were drawn rapidly up toward the cracked ceiling.

Stripped of sensation, he no longer perceived either the chamber or his body. Something that surpassed both pulled him away. For a moment, he clung to the idea, the *certainty*, that Mount Omina and the world lay below him, familiar landmarks to his unfamiliar self. Then Vinnr itself faded, becoming nothing but a distant phenomenon of air, matter, and dust in an interplay with the light of the Great Cosmos. His world, himself, everything—it all expanded into the immensity of everything that could ever be conceived of and more.

What's happening to me?

He no longer recognized a separation between himself and the Cosmos. And why would he? He *was* the Cosmos. His being had expanded and disintegrated, turning into light and space and energy, both the Cosmos itself and what existed within it. He perceived himself as vastness and potential without limit. He felt himself to be infinite.

Who are you? The voice, was it his? He could not see any others, so it must be him. Who had he directed the question to? Should he answer? Would someone else answer?

Time didn't give him the chance to contemplate these questions before he suddenly started… falling?

And with that thought, whatever was happening to him suddenly stopped. He opened his eyes, which felt bruised and sore, as if he'd been in a boxing match, and saw blue, then gray, then a very hard-looking marble floor. *Not* the floor in Vaka Aster's sanctuary on Mount Omina.

Thuh-clunk!

He hit it, fully splayed out on his torso and face, his armor absorbing some but not all of the impact. His nose splatted like ripe fruit, sending daggers of pain shooting through his face and head. His thoughts grayed out, and he lost track for a moment.

I see. It's you, Stallari. Wake now.

The voice in his head brought his senses back, and with them, the pain. He rolled over and looked around, realizing in an instant that something was wrong. Very, very wrong. He'd hit his head harder than he realized, apparently. Everything in front of his eyes glimmered and glowed. A tiny touch of light coming from somewhere in his periphery turned into an inferno of many dimensions, each familiar color enhanced a hundredfold. Thousands more colors he'd never seen, never knew he *could* see blazed there as well. He squeezed his eyelids shut, and still the interaction of color and light and even a sense of warm and cool, which to his eyes were almost colors of their own, muted but did not leave.

Am I going blind? He didn't care. Only one thing mattered. "Vaka Aster," he whispered, opening his eyes and looking up, "if you're there, please tell me what has become of my family."

A shadow fell over him. Ulfric guessed it was a person by the shadow's shape, but his weirded vision distorted what he saw into shifting hues and depths that revealed more than a physical form. The form spoke, but the words made no sense to his stunned ears.

CHAPTER FIFTEEN

Mylla found Havelock with his back against the vessel chamber wall, his legs splayed out in front of him. He stared at Vaka Aster's pedestal with an expression that told Mylla the light show she'd witnessed from below was a mere shadow to what he'd seen up here. She pulled herself up and hunched over, still keeping the pedestal between herself and the rest of the chamber—who knew who or what else was present?—and peered about.

The cavern's utter stillness rivaled the muted experience of being underwater. Even the usual swarm of dragørflies that lit the interior with an ethereal twinkle was missing, though the gaping rent in the chamber's roof seemed a likely explanation for their absence. The vessel remained on the alabaster dais, unchanged from the last time she'd seen it when they'd brought it to this sanctuary, other than being covered in layers of dirt and grit from whatever had blown out the roof. The outside light was enough to show her no one else but Lock was present.

She turned back to the Dragør Wing pilot. "Lock," she said, "what did you see?"

"I don't even know how to explain it." His voice carried an edge of awe, or disbelief.

"I need to know."

He ran a hand through his hair, usually chestnut colored, now gray-flecked with rock grit. "I saw… Aldinhuus, standing there on the other side of the pedestal. His face was stricken with horror. I've never seen a person look like that. He held something in his hands, it looked like a shaft of some sort. He was staring at it, and a circle of blue lights was spinning above"—he looked up toward the statue, then back to Mylla accusingly—"that."

He didn't know they'd moved the vessel here. No commoner did. And Mylla realized suddenly that he'd perceive it as a betrayal of sorts that the Knights would presume to remove the vessel of their creator from Asteryss, so no commoner could see her if they wished.

She'd deal with that later. Reassured Lock was okay, Mylla scooted aside and peered around the dais to look over the rest of the chamber. "He's not here now," she said. "The Stallari. Did you see where he went? Was there anyone else here?"

His mouth opened, and they both jumped when a heavy thud echoed inside the chamber, followed by several smaller thunks, and then shouting. Mylla realized the noise was coming from the wooden door leading to the antechamber.

"Oh thank the Verities." It had to be Eisa and Roi. "Lock, help me. I think the doorframe's buckled."

They rushed to it and began sweeping rocks and pebbles clear. The iron hinges were indeed twisted and would never move freely. "Roi, Eisa!" she shouted. "Do you hear me? It's Mylla."

Silence fell on the other side. Then: *Mylla?* Eisa spoke through her Mentalios. *How are you here? What's happened?*

I'll show you. But the hinges are destroyed. We'll have to break down the door.

Stand back. This was Mallich.

Mylla pulled Havelock to the side, well clear of any projectiles that might, and soon would, splinter the slats. The thunking came again, increasing in furor and velocity. Soon, chunks of wood began to split off as the force of the Knights' klinkí-stone assault took its inevitable toll. In a matter of moments, they reduced the door to kindling and stepped in.

Mylla greeted them. "Thank Vaka Aster you weren't harmed."

"It was a near thing," Eisa said. "Where's Ulfric?"

"... I hoped you knew."

They all fell silent, looking around the small chamber. There was nowhere to hide, nowhere Ulfric could have gone that they could see. The roof was high enough overhead that it wouldn't have been easy to get out that way, and why would he? Where would he go, with the sky full of attack ships and his companions inside the mountain?

No answers appeared, and as was natural Eisa took command. "Until he's found, I'm Stallari Regent." Her leaden gaze dropped on Havelock. "Why is this commoner here?"

Mylla hesitated. Knight Nazaria was a mentor to her, a paragon of the virtues the Knights represented. Since Mylla had become an acolyte in the Resplendolent Conservatum, she had looked up to the time-hardened, battle-honed warrior. She wouldn't have admitted it aloud, but Eisa always had, and likely always would, intimidate her, probably because it was clear Eisa always had, and likely always would, hate her.

Eisa continued. "Speak up, novice. What is this uninitiated commoner doing in Vaka Aster's sanctuary?" Eisa took a step toward Havelock with her klinkí stones hovering above her palm.

This sight snapped Mylla from her silence. "He brought me here to aid the Stallari after havoc broke out at Aster Keep."

"Ulfric told us what occurred," Roi stated, his eyes journeying around the chamber. "He didn't say what had become of you, though."

Inexplicably, Mylla felt compelled to explain—or rather defend—herself. "Before Lock and I left Aster Keep, the Stallari charged me with warning Symvalline of the usurper's intent, what he knew of it anyway, and... and protecting Isemay." Eisa fastened her with a dead stare at this admission, and Mylla went on. "Symvalline had come to the keep in search of Isemay—pure luck that she was there—and she stayed behind to warn Stave and Safran—"

"Symvalline is dead," Eisa cut in. "You heard the Verity Balavad, yes?"

The words that had thundered through the chamber echoed inside her mind: *KILL THEM ALL!*

She swallowed, looked away. "Yes, I heard him. But that doesn't mean..."

Eisa looked around the chamber suspiciously. "After we heard Balavad's curse, we could no longer link to Symvalline with the Mentalios. She lives no more, and if her daughter was with her, neither does she."

Mylla realized the two Knights thought the usurper had killed them. But she recalled the avalanche that had been heading straight at them, the wall of rock and broken trees pouring from the mountainside like water just before she'd been drawn into the safety of the cave by Lock. What had caused it? She guessed it could have been Balavad.

Regardless, it was she who'd left them behind. Mylla bowed her head to gather her composure. When she looked up, Roi's wandering gaze had finally settled—on her. *Why is he staring?* She feared he could see or glean from her Mentalios what she tried to conceal—the guilt that now rode her shoulders with all the weight of the stones that had buried Symvalline and her daughter. *How could I protect them? The Stallari asked me the impossible: to choose between my duty and his family. How could I not have fulfilled my service to Vaka Aster?* Her stomach knotted, making her breathing shallow.

On a whim, she decided not to tell them about the avalanche or that Symvalline and Isemay had died on the mountainside while she'd run for cover. It was somehow easier if they believed the usurper's forces were responsible. She couldn't face her mentors knowing she'd failed one of their own and worse that she'd been a coward. Letting her eyes hold Havelock's for a moment, she went on, hoping he understood her need to strangle this truth from existence. She dipped her chin toward him. "I think Wing Rekkr can tell us what may have happened to the Stallari."

All eyes on him, the pilot cleared his throat and explained again what he'd told Mylla. He finished the tale with: "Then he leaped onto the pedestal and raised the thing in his hands into the blue circle of light, which then seemed to *burst*. When it did, I stumbled, blinded. When I could see again, the light had disappeared."

"And Ulfric with it?" asked Eisa.

He nodded.

Eisa turned to Mylla. "And where were you?"

"Still below. Lock was able to force the trap door more easily than I and entered first, just as this burst of light happened."

Eisa and Mallich exchanged glances. "The cage," she said.

Mylla asked, "What cage?"

"Ulfric saw something in Balavad's Scrylle," said Roi. "A way to cage a Verity."

She almost snickered but caught herself. Was that what the Stallari had meant while they were still in the keep? He'd sent through the Mentalios: *Warn Symvalline and the other Knights of his intent to ensnare Vaka Aster and rule Vinnr.* "A cage... I don't see how that can be possible."

Eisa's eyes flashed, their lightness almost silver in the cave's diluted sunlight. Her next words illustrated why she was considered to be a woman whose patience gave definition to the word "short." "Doesn't matter if you understand, novice. Our situation is dire. The usurper has a flying army. We saw them from the mountain, dozens. They bombarded the mountainside and started an avalanche."

Mylla had to force herself not to flinch at this.

"You're lucky you survived it. You must have been inside the tunnel already. We know this usurper Balavad controls Yor and now likely Ivoryss as well. The Stallari may or may not be alive, but he's gone, probably dead too. His Mentalios is silent, in any case, and that leaves only us, the five remaining Knights, to hold to our duty. We may not have long before the rest of Balavad's ships arrive. They may never have found us if you hadn't led them here." Eisa stared through Mylla as she spoke the final words, seeming to have already dismissed Mylla from their list of allies.

"I—" Mylla choked, unable to speak. Havelock stepped up beside her, his solidness meant to be reassuring. "I had no intention—"

Eisa cut her off. "Your intentions are another thing that doesn't matter. The vessel is still in danger. We must move it."

"The interrealm well—" she tried.

"—is destroyed. By the Stallari. And the sanctuary itself is blown apart." The tone with which Eisa said the next words could have made ice shiver. "Because of your and Ulfric's actions, there's nothing for us to do but wait for Stave and Safran—if they aren't dead as well—and prepare to see everything we've spent centuries protecting be undone."

The statement hammered Mylla's gut with a physical force. "Eisa, are you implying the Stallari and I are somehow to blame for this?" The words tumbled from her, heavy with disbelief. And worse, a sense of betrayal. "I am a Knight Corporealis, just as you are. I've given everything for this cause, just as you have. Be prepared to back up any further accusations you dare make," she finished.

Eisa took a step toward Mylla, her posture dauntingly rigid. Mylla took a step back and bumped into Havelock. From the corner of her eye, she saw him take a defensive stance. *For his own sake, I wish he weren't here. He doesn't know what she is capable of*, she thought. She raised a palm, anticipating the need to release her klinkí stones in defense. On the heels of that, she thought: *Do I know what she's capable of?*

Roi reached out and placed an implacable hand on the Stallari Regent's shoulder and said, "What kind of fools are we? Are we not Knights? This isn't the time for fear or stupidity. We must warn Safran and Stave, if it isn't already too late."

Hot red blossoms had flared over Eisa's sharp cheekbones, making her gray eyes shine feverishly, and she stood her ground for a moment. Half sneering, showing a hint of her white teeth, she said, "You have no idea what I've given up, novice." Her eyes darted to Havelock, then back to Mylla. "Pray that you never do." Then, as if nothing at all had passed between them, she looked to Roi. "If the *Vigilance* was able to escape Asteryss, it should be here soon." She reached for her Mentalios and pulled it over her head, then held it out. "Join lenses. We'll attempt to warn them. Quickly."

Mylla blinked, feeling like a rug had been ripped out from beneath her. Had she almost come to blows with a fellow Knight? *She's just frazzled. We all are,* she told herself. *She didn't mean what she implied, Mylla. Forget it.*

Roibeard had already followed Eisa's example and removed his Mentalios, and Mylla was next. Piling the three lenses into Roi's wide palm, they wrapped their hands around his, gripping tightly.

Eisa began, *Stave, Safran, take heed. Mount Omina is under attack. Ready the emberflare cannon before reaching us.* Mylla and Roi picked up the thread, combining their thoughts and sending: *Be wary of the danger and get here with all speed...*

CHAPTER SIXTEEN

For a typical pilot, dodging the lightning that filled Himmingaze's tempestuous skies day and night came down to both good instincts and excellent training. For Jaemus Bardgrim, recently-forcibly-retired Glint Engineer in the Glisternaut fleet, it came down to luck. Fortunately, this was coupled with such a healthy infusion of confidence in his own ability to fix anything on his ship that might be hit, the actual piloting part was an afterthought. The marvelous eight-thruster *Octopod*'s sleekness and one-of-a-kind engine, both his own designs, were developed with a plan of making flight less a chore than an event—an event of pure exhilaration. Being a genius and an engineer, after all, had its perks.

Jaemus had nestled the *Octopod* on the flattest part of Isle Stonering he could find and slept for a couple of Glister Cloud cycles. On awakening, he noted with resignation that the current storm hadn't diminished in the slightest, and disembarked with a resigned sigh. The wet, salty air around him whipped him angrily, the wind and water seeming to resent his presence. The Never Sea, its customary purple-black color during Glister Dim, the darker part of the Glister cycle, beat against the island's gray rock as if to punish it. The weather and cheerlessness, however, suited Jaemus perfectly. The grimmer it was, the less likely he'd be found.

"Call me 'broad of ego and lean of wit' all you want, Cote," Jaemus said aloud, still arguing with his recently deserted beloved despite having stomped off without a goodbye nearly three cycles ago. "I got here in one piece. Soon enough I'll prove to you how right I am, and I know I'll enjoy *hearing* you stammer out the apology you'll owe me more than you'll enjoy *making* it."

As he spun around to scan the uninviting area, he reflected that at this point he'd be content to trade up an apology for a simple neck rub. After countless hours of fighting against the storm, Jaemus was still completely exhausted. It felt as if iron rods had replaced his spine.

First things last, he thought and hefted his flight-kit bag over a shoulder, wincing at the tweak in his stiff neck. Picking his way quickly but carefully over the rocky ground, he soon reached the front entryway of the nearby temple, the only structure on this forsaken spit of land. In fact, it was the only structure *and* only spit of land in Himmingaze, as almost the entirety of the world was underwater, its people living in floating habitats. Jaemus couldn't take credit for the habitats, but he did take credit for many of their current amenities and improvements enjoyed by Himmingazians. He was, after all, a fine Glint Engineer, and not many would argue that he wasn't the finest.

The feel of real rock, uneven and random, hostile in a way, jangled his senses. Another positive of living aboard the habitats. Not only were they comfortable, but level footing was always guaranteed.

The goggles he wore kept the rain and wind out of his eyes, but more importantly they enhanced his view of the surroundings. Though it might be ironic if, after getting her in one piece, he were to get swallowed alive by the flying predators that sometimes hunted this shoreline, it would most definitely not be amusing. Wriggly blood-sucking fleeches, three times the length of a person, were transparent except for the greenish globs that made up their internal organs, and his goggles helped illuminate and increase the horizon's contrast enough to spot them should they show up. Another of his designs, the goggles, and very handy, he had to admit.

Hurrying up the crumbling stone steps of the temple, he stepped inside. It had once belonged to the long-dead cult of the Creatress, but was now as abandoned and empty as the island itself. He took a quick look around to make certain he was alone before starting his search for the rest of the Verity stones in earnest.

At least, that *was* the plan—until a strange popping sound coming from the high eaves caught his ear. Jaemus's head jerked up, tweaking his neck *again,* and a flash of light illuminated a falling man, not coming *through* the roof—for no broken plaster or stone showered down—but from just beneath its dark heights inside. The figure splatted in front of him on the crumbling marble floor like an over-sized raindrop made of skin, hair, and… was he wearing a metal shirt?

Jaemus quickly flashed his illuminator on the man and stood in stunned silence as he groaned and grew still.

Did I really just see a man fall from the sky, Jaemus thought, *crash through a roof without breaking it, and drop to his death in front of me?* Chewing his lower lip, he tried to make sense of this. Then instinct added, *Based on the not-breaking-the-roof part, I believe I'll treat the possibility he's dead as a maybe, not a certainty.*

Warily, he looked around, wondering if he were the butt of some hidden prankster's joke. He shined the illuminator into the darkness of the arched ceiling. Immediately, another sharp blue light flashed, then another *pop* sounded and several objects dropped alongside him, thudding heavily on the marble floor. This time he made a little sound that he was not proud of, a cross between a *squeee* and *kaaaa,* as if he were choking on a bone, and fumbled his light. He managed not to drop it and whirled it around the infuriating shadows writhing over the ground, trying to locate what had fallen.

Six faintly glowing stone spheres, amazingly like the Verity stone he already possessed, and a metallic cylinder, also just like the one he carried, lay scattered nearby.

Not a man to trust coincidence without first evaluating the situation, Jaemus took a moment to consider the many possible things that might be about to go wrong—if this wasn't a joke after all. He started with the facts: first he'd defied his commander; then abandoned the

Glisternaut fleet after stealing the *Octopod*; then flown it to a forbidden-by-law Verity temple, just in time to witness an impossible manifestation of a person out of thin air.

But this reflection only took a moment.

"Water and lightning," he whispered, sucking air between his teeth. "What incredible luck. And it isn't even my birthday!" Not trusting coincidence was one thing, but he would never be accused of being one to miss out on an opportunity.

And this was it. Everything he might need to prove he'd been right all along about the latent power in the dead cult's sacred artifacts, and finally get a chance to rub the Glisternauts' and the Himingaze Council of Nine's faces in their idiotic obstinacy, had literally just landed at his feet. He could get back his position as Glint Engineer, get back his respect, and get back in the race to break past the Glister Cloud surrounding Himmingaze before it and the Never Sea swallowed the rest of its inhabitants like fleeches. The people of Himmingaze could, if his luck held, finally find a new home to colonize somewhere beyond this one. And he, Glint Engineer Jaemus Bardgrim, would be the one to thank for it.

With no more hesitation, he quickly gathered the unexpected boon of Verity stones, opened the cylinder to discover, as he suspected he would, a parchment inside covered in strange writing, then tucked all the items into his flight-kit bag.

But what about the unconscious, possibly dead, man? The items must belong to him.

Jaemus stepped nearer the strangely dressed figure, unsure if the tickle at the back of his conscience was guilt, concern, or just hope the man had expired and rendered Jaemus's thievery consequence-free. No luck, the stranger suddenly gulped a breath and rolled over, making Jaemus jump once again. He mumbled something, but Jaemus didn't understand the words.

"Listen, friend," Jaemus started, not quite certain what to say to someone who'd appeared out of the air like an apparition. "Um, you doing all right there?"

The stranger sat up and blinked rapidly, as if dust had blown into his eyes. At the same time, he reached across his body, groping at his side for something he seemed unable to find. Blood leaked from his nose in a slow crimson waterfall, and the bridge of it sported a gash that would leave a heroic scar once it healed.

He was torn. He could sprint out of the temple now, and be back in the *Octopod* and airborne before the man was able to even stand, his boon of Verity stones firmly in hand. Or, he could help the obviously shaken up stranger, and, of course, lose his newfound treasure forever.

Sighing inwardly, *Such a softy, Jaemus,* he reached out and asked, "Can I give you a hand?"

In response, the man homed in on him with a sharp gaze and extended one arm like a whip. From within his metal sleeve flew a glut of small projectiles. Straight toward Jaemus.

He vaulted back and came up hard against a marble column. With an "oof" he dropped the illuminator and threw his arms up protectively, adding a, "Gah!"

Over a dozen crystalline stones, about the size of his thumbnail, stopped short of him and hovered threateningly, giving him an up-close-and-personal. In the middle of each stone, glowing hearts throbbed with a light so blue, so stormy they mirrored the depths of Himmingaze's chaos-tossed sea, seeming to move and flow like miniature oceans themselves. At his wide-eyed stare, strange black marks on the shards' faceted exteriors—exactly the same as the runes on the unreadable parchment he carried—flared with brilliant red, as if alight with flame.

A bubble of glee at recognizing the runes momentarily surfaced, but fear rudely shouldered it back. He didn't have time to be excited, given that he was about to be turned into a walking slurry of holes. "Wait! Can we talk about this? I can explain!"

The man spoke, but the words were incomprehensible at first. Then Jaemus realized he knew the language, or at least he knew a touch of it. Vertasian, a dead tongue taught to him by his gramsirene Vreyja for the fun of it. Gears in his head began clicking into place. Like rust being whacked from an old iron tool, he tried to recall what he'd learned from Gramsirene and said in the old language, "Your speech... Vertasian?"

The figure asked, "You're a Knight? To which Verity are you sworn?"

"Night?" Jaemus said. "Nooo... just a regular guy. Sworn to, er, break beyond the limits of the Glister Cloud using my great intellect and tenacity and bring the people of Himmingaze to a new world." He tended to ramble when he was nervous, and the odd visitor's even odder questions were making him exactly that. His gram had always had a strong spirit, but he wasn't sure her mind had kept up, and this man was starting to remind Jaemus of her.

Still holding his hand out, apparently controlling the hovering stones, the man stood up. "You have a strange way of speaking. What realm is this?"

"This is the southern Never Sea, on Isle Stonering. You're in the old temple of the Creatress." The man stared, his face crinkling into a rictus as if he'd just said they were swimming with sharks while wearing tunafish water shorts. Jaemus tried something else. "Jaemus Bardgrim," he said and gestured, carefully, to himself.

With perfect pronunciation, the man responded in Himm, Jaemus's own language. "If you aren't a Knight, how do you speak Elder Veros?"

Caught off guard, he said, "So you do speak Himm."

The man's face went slack, and Jaemus had a moment to take in an extraordinary marvel he'd missed at first: aside from his odd clothing and dark-brown skin similar in color to Jaemus's morning mug of chuffee—though completely unlike the subtle pale-green bodies of Himmingazians—his eyes were as blue as his hovering stones. They gleamed, pupil-less and prismatic, like light through sapphire. In a monotone, the stranger responded, "He does speak Himm."

Jaemus's eyes darted around for a moment, finding no one else in the temple. "Who?"

"I do."

Well then, he thought. *I am having a conversation with a crazy person.*

Perhaps he'd get along with Gram. He suddenly felt as if he was in over his head. Maybe searching for a dead cult to find its forbidden treasures hadn't been his best idea ever. On the heels of that, he realized maybe stealing Verity stones, or anything for that matter, from a man this confused, and wearing *metal*, was an even worse idea. Giving it one more try, he asked in his own language, "And you are... ?"

With a shake of his head as if to clear it, the stranger said nothing for several moments. Then: "Ulfric Aldinhuus, Stallari of the Knights Corporealis serving Vaka Aster of Vinnr."

"Stallari of the Knights Corporealis. I think I see now, *Knights* not *nights*. So then, Stallari, that must be, what, like a rank? And Vinnr of Vaka Aster? Never heard of it. Where is that?"

"I lead the Knights Corporealis of Vaka Aster, one of the five Verities, the makers of all. Vinnr is the name of my realm, Vaka Aster's realm. Like your Lífs, whom you call Creatress, of Himmingaze, your realm."

Unable to stop himself, Jaemus quirked a skeptical, okay, an *outright disbelieving*, eyebrow. "You're saying you're from another world?"

What this man was implying... well, he was obviously a few stalks short of a kelp forest. Gramsirene Vreyja had often made up stories about Verities, other worlds, and what-not. But they'd just been stories.

Yet Jaemus felt a prickle of excitement, and it was growing...

The man, Ulfric, said, "World, or realm. However you prefer to think of it."

"Five Verities, you say?" he went on. "Friend, you're giving a whole new meaning to the word 'inventive.' The Creatress myth is just that: a myth. Are you ... are you trying to start a new cult? Because if you are, take it from me—and I mean this sincerely—that's the kind of thing that will get your status changed from *important*, which I'm guessing you are based on that fancy title and that peculiar costume, to *imprisoned* faster than a fleech strikes."

The stranger stared wordlessly at him, having grown still as if deep in thought, his attention so acute Jaemus had to suppress the urge to squirm. The floating crystalline projectiles contributed their part to this urge, as well. *Jaemus,* he told himself, *you've never been one to overan-alyze a situation before taking action, but today... today I think you'd better give every thought* and *every action a few more tumbles inside that meat in your head, or they could be your last.*

It only took one look at those unnervingly blue eyes to see the wisdom in that advice.

CHAPTER SEVENTEEN

"Stop shouting, for the love of sanity! We're right here." Stave's unexpected voice boomed from overhead like a frustrated bear, making Mylla squawk.

"Ah!" Her eyes shot toward the breach in the ceiling. The sight of Stave's craggy face leaning over the edge surprised Mylla as much as hearing him had. Safran moved up beside him a second later. There had been no noise from the *Vigilance*'s emberflare cannon firing on the sickle-shaped attack ships, no sound of the ships crashing, just silence and the other Knights appearing with the stealth of specters. "Stave! Safran! How did you...?"

Eisa and Roi managed more decorum and avoided Mylla's unbecoming sound effects. Immediately, Eisa pressed: "The skies were filled with enemy ships. How did you avoid them? Were you seen?"

If you mean those ships that look like burnt moons and shoot exploding spikes, yes, we saw plenty of those, Safran answered. *But not in these skies. The mountainside is littered with their carcasses.* Once her eyes adjusted to the interior gloom, she drew in a short breath. *By Vaka Aster, what happened here? Is everyone all right?*

Eisa responded, "We're alive, which is as good as can be hoped for. Wait on the ship for us. We have a great deal to fill you in on. Mylla,"

Eisa continued, wielding her authority like a whip, "gather the Scrylle and the Fenestrii. We need to leave the mountain immediately."

But Mylla hesitated a moment. "You said the mountain was littered with enemy ships?" she asked Stave and Safran.

"Aye, a couple dozen, there were," Stave said.

"But we didn't bring them down. Which means…" She trailed off, looking at the others to fill her in on what she must have been missing.

Yet the rest were quiet, no one seeming to have an answer. Finally, Eisa said, "We have allies, then. They must have defeated the enemy here and have already gone back to Asteryss."

No one had a better idea and chose to accept her statement without further scrutiny. There were more important issues to attend.

As Mylla was about to turn and begin searching for the Verity artifacts, Stave lifted an eyebrow and said, "We thought Symvalline and Ulfric were here, we did. Where've they gone, then?"

"That's part of what we have to fill you in on," Eisa stated. "For now, I'm Stallari Regent."

Silence struck a jagged note, as if time and action were out of sync, then Safran's voice came to Mylla: *Mylla, what's going on?*

We've lost the Stallari and Symvalline, Isemay too. There's much to tell, but it's too dangerous here now. Eisa is right, we have to get away from Omina, the sooner the better.

Stave and Safran disappeared from the gap, needing no further prompting. Mylla wanted to hurry for more reasons than to escape the immediate threat. She wanted to know what was happening in Asteryss. How bad was it?

Following Eisa's directive, she turned back to the vessel's podium to collect the celestial artifacts. Vaka Aster's Scrylle, which had been stored in a depression in the dais, lay beneath a chunk of rock, and she tucked it inside a bandolier pouch. The Fenestrii that should have been with it were not as readily visible. She walked around the pedestal, kicking the larger chunks of debris out of the way as the others Knights cleared rocks from the vessel itself.

Eisa wasted no time in doling out more directions. "Knights, we'll link our klinkís to secure the vessel and lift it aboard the *Vigilance*.

Commoner…" She paused, considering what they were to do with him, then decided: "Come aboard with us. Once the vessel is safe, we need to take stock of the *Vigilance*'s stores. Find out what we have available and see what we need to resupply."

"Eisa—" Mylla began, and Eisa looked to her. "The Fenestrii aren't here."

Both Eisa and Roi shuffled around the podium as well, finally fanning out to search the full chamber. Mylla shifted her hunt toward the far wall where the interrealm well had been. Passing the body of the Flesh Caster, she carefully avoided the congealed, dirt spattered puddle of his blood. *Poor bastirt. The Stallari showed you no mercy at all. Good.* The dead man's satchel lay nearby under a mound of rubble. She pulled it free by its strap and searched the contents. The only thing remaining inside was the parchment decreeing the kingdom of Yor to be under His Holiness's dominion, signed by Yor's Arch Keepers. Folding this, she deposited it in the same pouch as the Scrylle. Swallowing her disgust, she also rifled through the Caster's clothing, finding nothing useful.

In a few moments, Eisa stated, "Every one of the damn things is gone. Along with Ulfric."

"This man must have come by way of the well with the Stallari," Mylla said, waving a hand at the corpse. "I saw him at the keep. He was part of the usurper's Flesh Caster Order."

"When you're ready to tell us what's going on, we're listening. All ears, I say," prompted Stave, still waiting above.

"We're coming up," said Eisa, nodding at the others to join her.

Gathering in a circle around the dais, the three Knights turned their backs to the vessel and pulled free their klinkí stones. Mylla ushered Havelock to stand behind her so he was within the circle, then each channeled their stones into a ring encircling them. As a group, the Knights channeled a command using their Mentalios lenses. The hearts of the klinkí stones began to glow the deep cerulean of Vaka Aster's spark, which blossomed and began to spread, covering the Knights like a cloud until they stood within its bubble. They began to ascend through the gap in the cave roof and into the hold of the *Vigi-*

lance hovering above. The vessel and Lock, in the midst of this bubble of light, rose with them. Mylla heard his breathing change to shortened bursts, no doubt rattled by what he must think was wystic conjury, but he said nothing.

Once inside the ship, they hurriedly placed the celestial vessel safely in its alcove in the main hold, unmoored the *Vigilance*, and began a hasty search of the area. From the observation deck on the *Vigilance*, Mylla looked out over the blasted carapace of Mount Omina, looking for any sign of Ulfric. Just as Safran had described, dozens of the black ships she and Lock had barely escaped lay in scattered, smoking ruins amid the carnage they, the fires, and the avalanche had caused. But what had destroyed them? She couldn't guess. If Ulfric had escaped the sanctuary, he couldn't have gone far, but they saw nothing to indicate he had. He had simply vanished.

As they scouted, the Knights briefly speculated about this, but no easy answers came. *Did Vaka Aster return?* thought Mylla. *That other-worldly light... but where is she now? Have she and Ulfric gone somewhere?*

The mystery made them all uneasy, but at the moment the immediate threat seemed to by stanched. With Stave at the helm, they made a pass at the hidden meadow where the Dragør Wing fighters had landed, explaining to Stave and Safran all that had occurred at the same time. As with the sickle-shaped ships, the two Wing fighters were now blackened, useless husks. Mylla scanned the mountainside fervently where she and Lock had last seen Symvalline and Isemay. There was no sign of them, either. Nothing could have survived the wasteland that Omina had become.

The *Vigilance* served the Knights as a means of travel and transportation, primarily for the purpose of moving the Verity's vessel when necessary. Ulfric had shared key elements of the ship's design with the commoners some turns ago, which had given rise to the Dragør Wing ships. Yet, he'd not shared all his secrets, and the *Vigilance* was unique in Vinnr—though, as it was cloaked from commoners' sight, none knew *how* unique. The inner hold was the size of a modest ballroom, serving as both a strategy room and safe quarters for the Knights. Spacious and silent, the airship's shape resembled a spade, and it flew fast enough to cover the distance between Asteryss and the Morn Range in the time between Halla's rising and setting. With the daystar already lowering, Mylla's mind pondered morbidly: *This day's deeds deserve the requiem of a dark night.*

For its many attributes, however, the *Vigilance* could not outfly a Dragør Wing fighter, nor, it was obvious, one of the usurper's attack ships. And it didn't need to. Rare Vinnric flint glass, ground down to fine powder and painted on in a film so thin it was nearly weightless, coated the ship's metal hull and wings. After architecting the craft itself, the Stallari used wystic alchemy to infuse the protective layer with the ability to cloak the ship from all eyes, night and day. By design, no one in the world besides the Knights, and now one Dragør Marine, even knew the *Vigilance* existed. As stealthy as an eel in dark water, the Knights could traverse the globe unceasingly using the endless power of Halla, except for one thing—

"Three days, we have food for only three days. Why are we so unprepared for catastrophe?" Eisa wondered aloud, not hiding her frustration. The Knights could, of course, linger on indefinitely without food, but their strength would wane until they became withered husks. Food sustained them still, despite the Verity spark, though in a slightly different way from commoners.

That's if we were at our full complement, Safran pointed out. *With the Stallari missing, and Symvalline...* She didn't finish the statement, and each one aboard except Havelock pressed the fingertip of their primary weapon hand against the nine-pointed star marking their chin, then to their heart, and lowered their eyes in grief and tribute to their fallen sister and missing Stallari.

Mylla was sitting next to Havelock at the hold's rectangular meeting table. He must have sensed the somberness, and he softly placed a hand on the small of her back, giving what comfort he could. Inexplicably, she felt tears threatening. She would not give them a chance to fall.

This isn't his sadness, and I shouldn't have made it so. How can a common man—a good man, but a commoner—be expected to join us, or even understand what we must do? It would cost him too much. Without me and my debt to duty, his life could be so much richer. And he deserves it, a full life. All I have is this duty, with nothing more to offer. It's selfish of me to wish him to shoulder it too. Even Stave and Safran found their promise with each other, not with commoners. Even Ulfric and Symvalline... I should have known better than to fall in love with a commoner.

With a resolve that impaled her like a cold sword, she decided that whatever the Knights did next, those plans would not include the Wing fighter. He had to be sent back to his home and his squadron as soon as Mylla could find a way. He deserved the freedom to fight for his family and his people. *I must make him forget about me. It's the only right thing to do. For him.*

Breaking into these thoughts, Eisa spoke up and pointed to Havelock. "We have *him* to feed, now, too. So we need to resupply. But first, you two, tell us of Asteryss. What was happening there when you departed? What are we dealing with?"

Mylla considered arguing there was no need to resupply for Lock's sake, that he should be returned to the nearest Marine unit they could find. But she held her tongue. There would be a better time to push for his release. Or maybe she wasn't ready to face it herself.

In turns, Stave and Safran described the fall of Asteryss. *When Symvalline warned us of Balavad, Safran began. We scrambled the* Vigilance *at once and launched. And then came the most... extraordinary sight I've ever seen. A flying vessel, at least as large as Aster Keep, descended from high in the sky like a comet. It was all black, shaped like a fang, but the size of—*

Stave interrupted, "It was the size of my worst nightmare. The thing gave off fumes that tasted like poison, it did."

Yes, exactly as he says. Safran nodded. *But not fumes you could see. It was more like a... feeling. As if a dawning awareness of a storm cloud just outside your range of vision, and getting closer...* She trailed off as her fingers rose to her Mentalios and idly traced its circular frame. As a prominent political peace broker and border dispute judge between Ivoryss and Yor before joining the Knights Corporealis, she'd faced down war chiefs and faction leaders alike without ever flinching. A vengeful attack by the loser of a land dispute had left Safran with a wounded throat and inability to speak, but her spirit was too strong to let that thwart her. She'd turned from serving Ivoryss to serving Vaka Aster instead. With such a background, it took more than a little squall to ruffle her.

Thus her hesitance now made Mylla breathe shallowly until Safran went on. *The bruhawks were still on sentry, and I sightlinked with them once we were airborne. The chaos throughout the city as the people saw that massive vessel—their raw fear—was beyond measure. We saw no weapons on the monolith, but it looked dense and strong, like granite. Perhaps the ember-flare cannon could penetrate it, but one hit would hardly have made a differ-ence in something that size, and our two dragørfly scouts would be like pebbles flung at a mountain against it.* She paused to look around at each of them somberly, her dark eyes marking her point. *Then hundreds of those cres-cent-shaped ships began to flow from ports along its flanks, like black tears. They filled the sky and surrounded Asteryss.*

"Did any see you? Follow you?" asked Eisa.

Stave shook his head. "The *Vigilance's* cloak is effective, it is, even against the lackeys of another Verity. A few flew near as we cleared out, but we weren't detected, that we could tell. Just before we got out of range, we saw squadrons of Dragør Wings engage them, we did." He looked toward Havelock and said in a tone that conveyed his condo-lences, "But their counterattack was outnumbered."

Saying nothing, Havelock rose and paced toward the edge of the hold, his shoulders rigid and tight, his head erect. It was Mylla's turn to suffer on his behalf. Each of the Knights had experienced the same ache over a fallen comrade, the same questions: Why hadn't they been there? Why hadn't they done more to aid their friends? For Mylla, the pain was doubled. She'd been the one to cause him to leave his post and be no help in the defense of his city and fellow Marines.

She rose and stepped over to him, taking his hand. "Lock, I'm sorry."

"You probably saved my life by leading me here," he said shortly. His response surprised her, both in sentiment and the bitterness with which he said it. "And I don't know whether to be sorry that I wasn't there, or *grateful* I wasn't."

"You've been spared. Maybe it means you'll be better placed to help later." She wished he would look at her instead of staring at the floor.

"Or deemed a coward for running. For not being there to defend Asteryss with my squadron."

More like with your corpse. She would never say something like that aloud. The best she could answer was: "Many days may lie ahead for you to seek the redemption you crave."

At the table, Eisa brought the conversation back around. "We'll head to Dyrrakium once we've resupplied."

Stave tipped his chair back and remarked, "You think we need to go the exiled empire, take refuge in their treacherous arms, Eisa? As Stallari Regent, that's your recommendation?" His wooly eyebrows, easily mistakable for the vacation homes of small birds, had a way of saying quietly more than he said aloud. Which was saying something, as the Knight wasn't known for his shy and withdrawing personality.

The poisonous fumes Stave had mentioned coming from the usurper's massive vessel now had a rival in the fumes of mutual dislike billowing between him and Eisa. The two had never mixed half as well as fire and water.

She stepped back to the table and leaned in. "If I may make a point—"

Having none of it, Eisa cut to the quick. "When did you start questioning your betters, Stave? Was it when you realized you'd never be a match?"

"If by 'better' you mean better at pretending your head's big enough to wear a leader's crown, then I've questioned *you* from day one, I have. On second thought, maybe your head is *too* big for any crown, except perhaps one of shame."

Both Knights pushed away from the table and rose to their feet, nostrils flaring like rams about to lock horns. Before either launched another volley, Roibeard smacked a flat palm against the surface hard enough to make it, and everyone in the hold, jump. He stated evenly, if a touch testily, "An army of flying attack ships, but merely six of us. Seven if we count the Wing."

After several heartbeats of silence in which Stave and Eisa

exchanged rancid gazes, Eisa recovered with the same swiftness as when she and Mylla had argued. "Five," she stated. "We can't expect Ulfric's return."

Havelock, having rejoined the group, interjected, "You should include the remaining Dragør Wings and Marines. If this marauder intends to subjugate Ivoryss, the rest of our fighting force will soon be summoned from Magdaster and other forts around the kingdom. And this time, they won't be caught by surprise."

"And do you recall hearing about the takeover of Yor?" asked Eisa, her tone the lying sweetness of trap bait.

Havelock opened his mouth but wisely closed it without a word. Mylla had a moment of insight about how Eisa must look to him, and how different. Tall, head shorn except for black banding in the center ending in a braid that fell down her back to her waist, and tattooed features that appeared hewn from heartwood, Eisa had been born into Dyrrakium's most revered family and didn't bother to conceal the harshness their warrior-priest culture had bred into her. Mylla shared Eisa's coloring, her own hair shoulder-length and woven in braids, and nothing else, despite being born, it was assumed, a Dyrrak. Eisa *was* authority, where Mylla was just an outcast orphan rejected by their shared empire.

She knew what Eisa had meant. There had been no news of a battle for rule of Yor, because none had occurred. The foreign Verity had taken control quietly, insidiously, according to the scant reports that had made it to Ivoryss.

"A coup, commoner," the Stallari Regent went on acidly. "Mylla already told us Balavad the usurper has taken Arch Keeper Beatte hostage, or simply killed her. He's already achieved his goals: subdue the Arch Keeper, subdue the Marines, subdue the city. And finally, subdue the kingdom. The Verity doesn't need to fight a battle. He merely needs to cripple Ivoryss with fear. If Beatte's alive, he'll bend her to her knees with the kingdom watching and bleed resistance dry by making her swear fealty to him publicly. And your Dragør forces, whatever remains of them"—she stared at Havelock, the gray of her eyes glinting—"will follow their Arch Keeper's orders to stand down."

The room grew silent as they all considered her dark words.

"Eisa," Mylla said after a pause, "there's no precedent for this, is there? You've read deeper into the Scrylle than anyone except the Stallari. Why would a Verity from another realm do such a thing?"

Eisa eyed her, seeming to consider if Mylla was up to knowing the answer. "Power is a living thing, novice. It needs to feed and it grows. Its ultimate end is more power. Why would a Verity be any different? A being of *all* power. What's left for it to gain but *more*, and what's left for it to become but not just *a* being of power but *the* all powerful."

She ambled from the group toward the vessel and swept at the dust still powdering it. "Balavad's power is diminished outside his own realm, but that doesn't mean he'll stop coveting it. As for what occurred in Yor, deceit is always easier to wield than swords and wars. But once he finds the vessel, I doubt he'll wait for deceit and manipulation to bring Ivoryss to heel. He'll subdue, and as the commoner said, *subjugate* it with all his force. And we know there's a countdown. This Syzyckí Elementum Ulfric spoke of—Balavad's countdown. *Our* countdown—" She stopped brushing away the grit suddenly and murmured, "Something has changed."

"What was that, Eisa?" asked Roibeard.

She turned back to the group and went on without answering him. "It's the Fenestrii Balavad seeks, a crucial element of this cage he wants to create. For all we know, Ulfric took Vaka Aster's away to hide them. But without all of them in our possession, the only thing we can do is remain true to our primary duty and protect the vessel. We need to keep it concealed here on the *Vigilance*. And go as far as we can from where we know our enemy to be. So, to Dyrrakium"—she sent Stave a withering look—"it is.

"The Scrylle, Mylla," she finished, and beckoned Mylla.

Mylla, having doffed her armor and now wearing only her bandolier over her tunic, pulled the wystic cylinder free and passed it to her. Eisa took it wordlessly and opened it. With a gentle tilt, she slid free the parchment inside and placed it flat against the table.

Mylla watched Lock lean in to get a closer look. He had, she suspected, never seen either the artifact or what it contained. "Are those… I don't recognize the writing. It's strangely fuzzy," he said quietly.

"Elder Veros runes," Mylla explained. "But different from commoner writing in that they are transmutable."

He looked at her quizzically.

"They change, according to what they say. It's hard to understand without the proper training."

He nodded, not needing to be told in plainer terms that he was out of his depth. A quick learner—Mylla had always liked that about him.

Eisa, leaning over the parchment, raised her head abruptly. Her eyebrows arched, and she and the other Knights could only look at each other, wonder mixing with confusion in their expressions.

Where are they? said Safran.

"With Ulfric, like I thought." Eisa said the Stallari's name like a curse.

Lock continued to whisper. "I don't understand."

Mylla took a moment to absorb what she was seeing, as unbelievable and unprecedented as it was, like so many of the day's happenings. "The Fenestrii—they're gone. They've just disappeared. The runes are a map, they tell us where the celestial stones are at all times. For them to be missing from the map means—"

"It means Ulfric has taken them," Eisa stated again.

Why would he? Safran said. *And to where?*

Eisa gazed at him for a moment, weighing the likelihood, then gave a short nod and began to re-roll the parchment. "If the Fenestrii are gone with him, and they aren't on the map, that must mean he's left Vinnr," she said.

"Could he do that?" Mylla asked, surprised.

For the first time, Eisa appeared pensive, worried. "He could have used the Scrylle to open a starpath well. It's been done before."

This was news to Mylla, and she had many questions, but now was not the time. She settled for: "If he did that, why didn't he take the Scrylle?"

"He did," Roi stated matter-of-factly.

"But…" Mylla's eyes dropped to the table, where Vaka Aster's Scrylle remained in plain sight.

"Why would he need Vaka Aster's Scrylle, when it seems he has another one?" Eisa looked around the table. "The usurper's. We can't even guess what lore it may contain, or what Ulfric intends to do with both our own and our enemy's artifacts."

Mylla didn't like the implication in her tone. "Perhaps he knows what happened to Symvalline and Isemay and intends to get revenge," she suggested, grasping for possibilities.

"Then he has forsaken his duty, and there's nothing we can do for him now," Eisa said with finality. "There is only one Fenestros remaining, protected by the Conservatum. We have to get that one before Balavad finds it. We cannot let him acquire the means to create this cage. And we'll need it to access the Scrylle."

So you suspect Ulfric collected Vaka Aster's Fenestrii, along with those belonging to Balavad and the Battgjald Scrylle, Safran broke in, unwilling to leave off the issue of their Stallari. *Perhaps he's going to try creating this cage himself to capture Balavad.*

"Of course," Mylla said. "That would be the best way to stop the Verity."

"But he'd need Balavad's vessel," said Stave.

"So it's possible he's gone to Battgjald," mused Mylla. "But would he do that, with Ivoryss and Vaka Aster in danger? And by himself?"

That still supposes the Stallari left of his own free will, Safran said. *And we have no way of knowing if that is so. No way at all.*

In the rising uncertainty, the Knights began speaking over each other, their statements slowly spiraling from hypotheses to suspicions to ever more ominous accusations.

At last, Roi said solemnly, "Too many questions and tis late. We have been drifting west toward Ivoryss since leaving Omina, and so must continue until we acquire the last Fenestros from the Conservatum." He scratched his neck through his shaggy blond beard. "I think it time to start watch rotation, rest, and regroup when we are fresher and less… dismal." He held Eisa's eyes steadily as he spoke, deferring to her for final orders.

The Stallari Regent nodded once. "We'll hover for the night without landing. We must be ready to move quickly if necessary."

She ordered each of them to stations and set the watch rotation. Mylla and Havelock left the hold to be first on bridge watch, where the night air fed the blooms of her dark thoughts. It felt like admitting defeat, but Mylla knew they had no other choice, not with a massive foreign force out there and only the few of them in here. *We didn't even try to recover Symvalline's and Isemay's bodies,* she thought. *We left them behind. If the Stallari is still alive, will he ever forgive us?*

Roi had called them "dismal," and the word certainly fit. She couldn't recall a time in her three hundred and some turns around the daystar that she'd felt less... well, *less.* Small, mean, and very, very dismal. From the observation deck, she watched the black sky around them flare in familiar patterns with the lights of all the other stars that brightened Vinnr, and she recalled the words the usurper had spoken to Aldinhuus underneath the keep, the ones she'd heard but not understood. *Your kind is coming to an end. We Verities agreed long before we created what you conceive as time, long before we created these realities, that all of these things, and your kind in particular, is merely a... trial. A distraction, an amusement.*

If it's true, she thought, *and we* are *merely playthings for our creators, then we Knights protect the being who has already sentenced us to doom.*

If any duty could be more dismal than that, Mylla couldn't think what it might be. Nor could she blame Ulfric if he had realized the same—and had chosen to renounce his oath.

CHAPTER EIGHTEEN

If fear had a flavor, it would be the bitter spice of the long-dead Reaper's Breath flower. Warm and cloying, raw and syrupy, fear would be a taste that drowned its victims as it slid down their throats. Fear is a fate worse than death.

Regardless, a quick, simple death was all Acolyte Irrick of the Resplendolent Conservatum wished for as he waited in a vast chamber aboard the sky fortress called the *Primator*. Yet based on the strange artifacts placed around the chamber he and the other Ivoryssian prisoners now occupied, he feared a simple death wasn't their destiny.

After the attack on Asteryss and their transport to this immense vessel, Irrick and the prisoners had been positioned in eight lines behind eight alabaster navel-high pedestals. Atop the pedestals rested alabaster bowls, each as flawless and gleaming as a new tooth and filled with clear liquid. They'd been waiting for so long that their initial tears and shrieks and yowls for freedom had died away, leaving the prisoners mute and exhausted. The current of dread had vibrated almost visibly between them as they pondered the reasons for their being here and the meaning of these stone altars. Now, though, Irrick's only thoughts were of the horror who had just entered and stood towering over them. Standing at an inhuman height at least two heads taller than the tallest man, the desecrator of both Ivoryss and Yor, the Verity known as Balavad stared down at the assembly as if expecting all to cringe like rats at his feet.

Irrick refused, staring at their captor with as much courage as he could muster. The hours of waiting with no food or water since the campaign against Asteryss had not weakened him so much that his powers of observation failed. Only the skin of the Verity's face and hands showed, its striking whiteness more like cold stone than the pale dermis of the ill or malnourished. His eyes, all pupil and blacker than the emptiness between the stars, gleamed in their sunken orbits, the bones of the skull they lay in so sharp and prominent they nearly broke through his hard flesh. Crimson hair the hue and vibrancy of a fuel-oil fire cascaded from his head and upper lip in a molten mass, curling here, braided there. An ochre cape of some rough material dragged along the floor behind him in an uneven hem.

As Irrick took this sight in, the retinue of crimson-robed Flesh Casters trailing slowly in the wake of the Verity like drugged flies dispersed and fanned out beside the prisoners. Once positioned, they turned to give Balavad their full attention.

The Verity spoke, and his words confirmed at least part of Irrick's fears. "You are all forsaken by your maker. And today, you will all die."

Renewed wails and cries for mercy washed through the chamber. Irrick maintained his calm. If their deaths were inevitable, he reasoned, then he had nothing to lose. "To rot with your gimmicks and games, monster," he cried. "Just make our ends swift."

Balavad's head ticked a few degrees to the side. He smiled a bloated corpse's humorless smirk. "A brave spirit. A fighting spirit. A Knight Corporealis in training, if I'm not mistaken," he crooned. "I want to keep this one."

His last words were directed at the Flesh Caster next to Irrick, who turned to look at the priest and then back at the usurper. Fear ran amok inside him, but he would not show it.

The desecrator continued speaking to the congregation as if Irrick hadn't interrupted. "Your deaths are yours to choose. You can be dead for the rest of eternity, as you call it, by having your throats opened..."

He paused, allowing time for each of the Flesh Casters to reach inside their robe and withdraw ceremonial daggers the length of candlesticks, no wider than a finger in breadth. The priests held the blades in extended arms, decorated hilts in one hand and tips lying across the knuckles of their opposite hands. "Or you may choose to be consecrated in a new unlife as a soldier among the Raveners of the Tooth, and become one of my own people."

The roomful of prisoners gaped, eyes wide and many glistening with fresh tears. Irrick struggled to hold a mindful calm and control his shaking limbs.

"You will die and be remade, and you will serve me. But I promise, you will rejoice at the things I'll show you, the worlds you cannot yet imagine, which I will take you to. Your sacrifice of the life given to you by your Verity will be repaid in something more wondrous than life, something only *I* can give you." The Verity stared into the room, wearing the passionless grin once more, then gestured toward one of the liquid-filled bowls. "My tears, shed to mourn your mortal weakness and collected within these vessels, will be your resurrection. You will become part of me, and I of you.

"And now, you must choose."

Stallari Aldinhuus's face came to Irrick's mind, the stern lines that sank to black cracks in his oak-brown skin, his glacial eyes always steady, always certain. He drew strength from the lessons of the leader he had hoped someday to follow. "No Vinnric will ever bow to a fiend like you," he spat at Balavad.

This time the desecrator did not look at him but focused his attention on the sound of someone weeping, then glided forward to seek her out.

A young woman with skin mottled by goose bumps covered her mouth with one hand as Balavad approached. Her wide eyes took over her face. The desecrator stopped beside her and looked at the top of her head. She would not raise her face to his.

"Why do you cry?" he asked.

"I'm scared," she said simply.

"Of death? Your kind only fears what it doesn't know, but I have told you all you need to know. You are going to die. What else is there to dread?"

She sniffled as more tears overtook her, unable to answer.

The Verity looked over the crowd, and when he spoke next, his voice sounded nearly human, nearly compassionate. "What does anyone here have to fear? You don't have to be lost to your deaths, a timeless oblivion with no meaning. You can choose the rewards I offer. An *easy* choice. Its simplicity is merely clouded by your illusions and inability to see the truth as I've described it. Your kind is so limited in its grasp, but I assure you, you have *nothing* to fear. You have only to make the right choice."

He looked back to the weeping woman. "Now, creature of Vaka Aster, a maker who has never cared for you, is the matter less frightening?" He reached out and cupped her chin in his bowl-sized palm, the tips of his long fingers caressing her temple, pulling her head up so she couldn't refuse to stare into his face.

"Leave her alone!" Irrick cried, this time in pure reflex, and jerked forward to try to come to her aid.

As he did, the shadows surrounding the far walls inside the cavernous chamber began to dance and writhe, and the shapes of bodies distilled from what had seemed to be empty space: the soldiers who had so easily overcome the city's defenses and brought them all to this cursed place. Like Balavad and the Flesh Casters, their skin was as white as the light of distant stars. Their bloodless lips peeled away from mouths filled with dagger-like teeth, the points protruding and gleaming. Each was as different from the other as the prisoners were different from each other. There were women and men. Red-haired, black-haired, sable-haired; younger, older; thicker, thinner; all carrying vicious blades that were *not* ceremonial. Dozens of them suddenly populated the space, threatening and ready, and Irrick stopped cold in his steps.

"The brave one," the Verity said, and with a speed too fast to see he stood before Irrick.

His hands wrapped Irrick's head between them, the palms covering his ears, the fingers linking in the back. Irrick started to struggle, but the Verity leaned forward and tilted Irrick's neck backward until their gazes met.

Balavad's inky eyes began to change.

Instead of bottomless black pits, Irrick was staring into aquamarine pools as clear as crystal, the color so vibrant he gasped. A memory from childhood filled his mind, when his parents had taken him to Kolga, an Ivoryssian city surrounded by lakes. There were salt-rich lagoons in Kolga where visitors could swim. He'd been almost twelve, just shy of entering the Conservatum, and had since thought back to the feeling of silky weightlessness while swimming in those heavily mineralized pools, of his body gliding amid the emulsion like a fish, as if he'd been born with wings that only unfurled when submerged. It had been sublime, the greatest joy of his childhood, and the memory of that day had brought him moments of peace in an oftentimes hectic, sometimes hard life ever since. Looking into the Verity's eyes made him feel as if he were back in that enchanted pool. If fear had a flavor, the bliss of that joyous time in childhood had a color, and it was the warmly inviting azure of Balavad's improbable eyes.

Distantly, Irrick was aware he should fight against this mesmerism, yet he did not have the will. The Verity, hands still circling Irrick's head, drew him toward the front of the line. They stood before one of the pedestals holding the alabaster bowls, and Irrick's eyes stayed fixed, his thoughts lost in his childhood. The Verity released him, reached out, and grasped the hilt of the dagger held by the nearest priest. Fingers suddenly penetrated his lips and pushed inside, seizing his tongue between them. They yanked, and Irrick felt someone else's hands on either side of his head, keeping it from being drawn forward as his tongue was drawn out. From somewhere behind the bliss, his mind screamed in alarm, and he knew that he should fight whatever was about to happen. But the Verity's unwavering gaze was peace, and Irrick did not want to fight.

The dagger was lifted, and it reflected from his hazel eyes in a piercing flicker that caused him to blink. Then it fell, stabbing straight down into the center of his distended tongue, cleaving into its thick meat. His blink broke the trance he was snared in, and pain rocketed all the way to his spine. He shrieked, the movement so involuntary and sudden that his tongue ripped itself from the fingers grasping it. The narrow dagger sliced through its center smoothly, splitting it in two like a snake's. Blood quickly filled his mouth, and he shrieked again, vaguely aware of other howls of fright and horror rising around him.

His head was still being held, and Balavad grasped his chin, drawing Irrick's gaze once more. But his eyes no longer held the lovely blue of Irrick's memories. They were obsidian. The Verity spoke, and his voice was shattered glass. "Now drink."

The white bowl was placed at his lips, his head was pulled back, and the clear blue liquid joined the blood in his mouth. He had to swallow or choke. His throat convulsed and the mixture squirmed into his stomach. Gagging, he swallowed once more.

And then he was released.

Nothing supported him, and his body rebelled, spilling him bone-lessly to the cold chamber floor. He noted that it felt like steel, and he suddenly remembered where he was. On a ship, flying through the Vinnric sky. This was not a nightmare, not some strange and morbid fantasy of immortal imps from some other world, though that's what it felt like.

Moments passed and the chamber fell mute. His violated tongue throbbed with agony. No one came to his aid. Warm blood ran down his chin, and he gingerly pulled himself from the floor until he rested on one hip, his arms stretched out stiffly to hold him up. He looked around.

Is that all there is? he tried to say, but splintering pain from his tongue dissuaded him. Instead, he questioned with raised brows, his stare on the desecrator.

"No, that is not all there is," the Verity said, as if he knew Irrick's intended question.

And then new pain exploded from everywhere in him at once, growing to the size of worlds and ripping through his body like a tempest.

He shrieked, and shrieked some more, so shrilly it seemed to split his throat. His body convulsed and his back arched wickedly, threatening to break him in two. Blood began to pour from his eyes, his ears, his mouth, slicking the floor. His skin faded into the white pallor of the desecrator's minions. His bifurcated tongue, no longer bleeding, flailed like a lizard's, a pathway for his continuous, echoing screams to follow from him ravaged throat. In a moment that felt like lifetimes, the seizure ceased and he went utterly limp. Nothing moved, not even breath in his lungs.

One of the Flesh Casters came forward, carrying a black tunic. She stopped before the lifeless, drenched body of Irrick lying in a bloody pool, and her black boots squished in the liquid. With one toe, she nudged his feet. Irrick's eyes shot open, now as dull and sightless as the Raveners'. The Caster beckoned with her empty hand, and Irrick stood, docile and obedient. She dropped the tunic over him, and together they waited for their next command.

"New life!" Balavad intoned, his voice echoing as loudly as Irrick's shrieks had. All the prisoners jumped, startled, and many whimpered or gasped. The desecrator's voice lowered. "Now all of you, choose."

Irrick stood silently, no longer a man or an acolyte but a Ravener of the Tooth, one of Balavad's legions of realm-crossing soldiers. His thoughts drained with the color of his skin until only one voice remained in his head. Balavad's, a whisper like a spider's legs on stone: *Welcome to new unlife, Ravener. You are no longer a creature of Vaka Aster. You are one of mine now.*

With the Flesh Casters as their aides, one by one the prisoners chose their fates. The deck of the ritual chamber grew slick with gore. By the ritual's end, Balavad's retinue of Raveners had swelled by hundreds. As the desecrator grinned the grimace of the dead, Irrick's mind filled with his glee. *My legions are growing.*

CHAPTER NINETEEN

If the mind were parchment, Ulfric's was being ripped in half. Everything from his eyesight to his own thoughts seemed to be twisting and doubling up in a way that made him wonder if he'd fallen into madness. A distant voice spoke: *I have interfered.* And then answered itself: *If I hadn't, Vinnr would be lost*, and he didn't know if the voice came from inside or outside his head.

What had he meant when he'd told the Himmingazian "She speaks Himm"? Who was she? *He* wasn't *she*. The voice had said it in his head, and his mouth had repeated it—all happening as if he weren't present. Yet here he was, in a strange place, the smell of a strange sea in his nose, and a stranger speaking a strange language to him. And how did he know this language, anyway? He had never heard it until now. Perhaps it was an artifact of transporting along the celestial paths of Verities?

This fact was the one clear thing: when he'd broken the corona of Fenestrii caging Vaka Aster, either he or Vaka Aster had triggered a starpath portal, a well between realms. He couldn't guess how he'd done it, if it was him—mysteries he'd eventually need to solve. Did Vaka Aster send him here for a reason? Had she been present, or was she still caged? All he knew was that he was no longer in Vinnr but in a realm called Himmingaze. He didn't need to be told this. When this man had said this was the Creatress's shrine, it all became… well, not clear, but somewhat less foggy.

A Knight's mind could rarely, maybe never, become unhinged. The fortifications that gave them limitless longevity, accelerated healing of wounds, and immunity to disease also made their wits more resilient to things that would scramble any commoner's (otherwise, their cognition could never withstand the trials and taxations of their overlong duties). And he didn't *feel* as if he'd gone insane. At least not in any way he imagined it might feel. He simply felt his ordinary clarity one moment, but distracted the next. He quickly realized this muddling that both made his vision abnormal and twisted his thoughts cleared when he closed his eyes. But he could hardly keep his eyes shut now that he was in an entirely new reality.

Still holding the Himmingazian back with his klinkí stones, he turned his thoughts inward. If he'd created the interrealm well once, he could do it again, he just had to read the incantation from the—wait… the Scrylle, the stones, where were they?

Swiveling his head around, he searched the room. His strange vision cast everything in wavering, luminescent lines, but he saw nothing that suggested the artifacts had made it through the well with him. *What has happened?* Guilt knifed into him, chased by despair. *What have I done? What has become of Symvalline and Isemay?*

They must be dead.

No, they weren't. He wouldn't believe that. He had to cut through this lowering despair immediately and think clearly. If unable to open another starpath and return to Vinnr, what other options did he have? During his brief exchange with the foreigner (*But I'm the foreigner now,* he thought absently), he clung to what little he knew. He had entered the realm of Lífs, a Verity mentioned in the Scrylle. Beyond that, he knew nothing of this world or its people. More importantly, he didn't know what had happened, was still happening, in Vinnr. Mount Omina may as well have ceased to exist for him.

He had one other potentially useful fact at hand: this man before him knew of the Knights. Perhaps he knew more.

His vision swam and pulsed in colors and shades. His damaged, traitorous eyes had become a hated distraction. If he moved, he wasn't sure he would be able to keep his balance while at the mercy of the chromatic morass the world now swam in. So he stayed put. "Tell me your name again," he said.

"I'm Jaemus Bardgrim, Glint Engineer, at your service. *Disgraced* Glint Engineer, actually, but whatever. Cake and eating it too and all that."

"I don't want any cake. Can you tell me where the Mystae of Lífs reside?"

Confusion danced across the Himmingazian's face. "I'm not offering you any..." He trailed off, then said, "Say, would you mind with these... rocks?"

Ulfric scoffed. "Rocks? These are klinkí stones, lit by the wystic spark of Vaka Aster. Perhaps your realm doesn't have them."

"K—... kinky stones?"

The Himmingazian's dimwittedness would destroy his patience quickly, but perhaps the man would be more forthcoming if he felt less threatened. "I see you're unarmed," Ulfric said, then twisted his outstretched hand and closed it slowly. The stones pulled away and retracted back inside his vambrace. "Don't make the mistake of testing me."

Bardgrim's posture relaxed a bit. "Oh, I wouldn't dream of it. It looks to me like we're both a little out of our element, wouldn't you say, and I'd like to know more about that thing you mentioned, the five Verities. Maybe we can try this: you ask me a question. After I answer, I get to ask you one. Sound good to you?"

Ulfric swiped the back of his hand across his top lip, the stickiness of the blood telling him it was already drying, his nose already healing. "The Mystae, Himmingaze's own order of Knights Corporealis. Do you know where they reside?"

"Look, as far as I know, you're the only, er, Knight in Himmingaze.

But look, this place we're at, the Creatress's shrine, people aren't supposed to come here. I had to stop for… repairs to my ship and just happened to find you. Actually, I can't tell you how lucky you are I came across you. No one comes here anymore. You could have been stranded. But if someone *did* find us here, we could be in the proverbial boiling eel pot. We should maybe both be on our way." The Himmingazian paused again, seemed to calculate, then prompted: "So you must have a ship outside?"

Lífs, my quin, is leading her creations to oblivion.

Ulfric wasn't listening to this damnable voice anymore. At least he was trying not to. He didn't even have a twin, much less a quin, and Bardgrim talked too much. The last words that mattered were Bardgrim's statement: there were no Knights, which meant no allies, and maybe no way for Ulfric to find this realm's Scrylle and at least one of its Fenestrii—his only way home, and his only way to learn Symvalline and Isemay's fate.

Face the truth. They're dead, he told himself, his own voice clear in his mind. *Murdered by that corruption of power, Balavad. That monster. And Vaka Aster did not save them, did she?*

How can I know? How can I live not knowing? They *were my life.*

As if in response, a leaden certainty came to him: *They are not dead, Stallari.*

He feared this was a lie he wanted to tell himself, but he wouldn't, *couldn't,* allow himself such a luxury as hope. How could they possibly have survived? He had caged his own celestial maker. He had brought Vaka Aster to heel, then released her, and now, apparently this was his penance. Balavad showed him what Verities were capable of: the maliciousness, the darkness. Wasn't it obvious that they were likely to mete out punishments? And who deserved to be punished more than he?

"Sir? Knight?" The Himmingazian broke into his spiraling thoughts. "Did you fly here? Do you have a ship?"

Ulfric's gaze had wandered, but he now brought it back to bear on Bardgrim. The figure wavered and coalesced into glints and streams of light of every hue, barely a solid shadow to be found in the prism. "Do you know where the Scrylle of Lífs's Order is kept?" he asked.

"So—no quid pro quo, then?"

"The Scrylle, where can I find it?" Ulfric raised his klinkí stone arm menacingly.

"Okay, calm down. I don't know what you're talking about. What's a Scrylle?"

He would not play games with a commoner, even if the commoner belonged to another realm. With a twitch of his pointer finger, a single stone rolled from his vambrace and perched just above the fingertip. He longed for his sword. In Ulfric's lengthy experience, a hostage's fear of being chopped into pieces often took hold faster and resulted in compliance sooner than the fear of being struck by a klinkí stone. The sword should have been hanging at his side, but it had been taken at Aster Keep by Arch Keeper Beatte's guards. "You are in the shrine of Lífs, you speak Elder Veros, and you know of my Order. You expect me to believe you don't know what a Scrylle is?" he accused. "And Lífs's Fenestrii? I've already told you once not to test me, so I'm going to ask only once more. Where do I find them?"

To his own warped vision, the stone hovering at his fingertip was a tear of vibrant blue in a fabric of shifting radiance, but the Himmingazian's wide-eyed and immediate focus on it indicated the fear Ulfric anticipated. Still, he felt a shade of regret. His nature wasn't inclined toward cruelty. He simply needed answers. With a casual flick of the finger, he sent the stone shooting toward Bardgrim's throat.

To what seemed to be their mutual surprise, Bardgrim flinched at first, but then he straightened defiantly and said, "Can you maybe give the I'm-going-to-turn-your-skin-into-bleeding-polka-dots thing a rest?" He raised a hand to bat the stone away, now close enough to his throat to force his eyes to cross to look at it, then thought better of it. "Haven't you ever heard of catching more phanks with sugar than darts? I can help you, but you need to recognize that I'm a citizen of Himmingaze, and we've outlawed worship of the Creatress, this Lífs, before my mother's great-great-gramsirene was born. We may both be speaking Himm right now, friend, but sure as the Glister Cloud glows, we aren't speaking the same language."

The Himmingazian had a fair point, and after a moment of consideration, Ulfric beckoned the stone back, stowed it in his palm, and stared at the stranger expectantly.

Bardgrim let out a breath, relieved. "Good, thank you. That's what I call crossing the cultural divide. So now we can talk. Tell me about this Scrylle. What does it look like?"

CHAPTER TWENTY

Dawn hit Mylla with an impact that could have dislodged a gimgree swamp sloth from its tree: sudden, hard, and paralyzingly bright. She woke as the merciless Halla beams plunged through a porthole along the *Vigilance*'s hull and struck her in the face. *Teach me to sleep in the top bunk*, she thought, stretching and sitting up to escape the blinding glare.

Mylla and Lock had spoken little during their watch on the bridge. He'd tried a couple of times to entice her to share details about the situation he knew he was missing but had given up when it was clear she was either too tired or too troubled to illuminate him any further. It hadn't taken her much effort to dissuade him. He, too, had his worries to fester on.

She listened to Lock's breathing from the bunk below her for a moment, the sound much loved and intimately familiar. Almost ten turns now they'd been together. His youth had hardened a bit to a nobility she found more handsome every season, while hers... well, she changed much more slowly.

A memory of a conversation she'd had with Symvalline five or six turns ago came to mind. They'd been dining together at the Conservatum, and she'd asked Symvalline why she and Ulfric had never thrown a nuptial feast and made their union official.

Bemused, Symvalline had said, "Did you know that in Ivoryss four hundred turns ago, newly joined couples had to sleep in their betrothal gowns for a thirty-night before they could consummate their marriage?"

"Verity's eyes," Mylla had proclaimed. "Why?"

The older Knight shrugged. "And in the Dastrart Age, prior to Ulfric's birth, a couple couldn't refer to themselves as 'married' until they had children and those children were old enough to give *their* consent to the union."

Mylla had grown silent, marveling.

"That's right. The opinions of children were deemed the superlative judgment on a couple's compatibility... a custom I can't say I completely disagree with, in truth. But my point is this, Mylla. Customs and habits all die or change with the passage of time. Why would Ulfric and I define our union by one such practice when our own time is unlimited? Our bond is to each other, not to transient ideas."

Mylla had understood her point, but something about the conversation now unnerved her. Symvalline and Ulfric would outlive any notions of formality or custom, just as Safran and Stave would, even Mylla. But Havelock, a commoner and mortal, was himself utterly and irrevocably bound by limitations. How much longer would he accept their different fates and still love her? And how much longer would she? She'd believed when she'd taken her oath that time would no longer hold meaning for her. Yet now she found that it meant more than ever.

The sleeping berth held fourteen bunks, and she guessed by the room's quietness that she and Lock were the only people there. She climbed down and looked around, just to be sure. Shafts of direct light coming in portholes made the contrast of shadows within the sleeping spaces that much darker, but she could tell by the sheen of his opened eyes that Lock was also awake.

"How did you sleep?" she asked, resisting the urge to sit beside him and run her fingers down his arm.

"Like a bird in its nest. Must be the pilot in me. I can't believe you never told me about this incredible ship." The wonder in his voice bordered on delight. To the sky born, indeed. He sat up and reached for her, but she abruptly turned away. After a moment of silence, he asked, "And you?"

She turned back, fiddling with the neck strings on her tunic to avoid his eyes. "Lock, I'm going to have to insist you remain in Asteryss once we've returned to the city. You aren't"—she swallowed—"you aren't a Knight. Protecting the vessel isn't your duty."

There, she said it. Among all the vagaries and uncertainties of the past day's events and conversations, one thing was crystal clear. Lock had to go home. He could not remain among the Knights, with danger and death and uncertainty the only things he could look forward to. She refused to think about whether sending him away would reduce his troubles or worsen them.

From his carefully controlled expression, she couldn't tell whether he detected her true meaning or not. But his calculated response made it clear he had no intention of making shunning him any easier for her. "I'll find my squadron and assess its strength. If the Marines are as overrun and outnumbered as Knights Glór and Thorvíl believe, I may be able to do more good among the Knights. And I would rather stay by your side."

"No, that isn't possible. Go back to your family, help them."

"They know I'm a soldier. I won't quit the fight. My father may be retired from military service, but he can still wield a sword. And my mother and sisters are more than capable of protecting themselves,. They'd want me to stay true to my service. And to you, Mylla."

At his mention of his five sisters—from ten-turn-old Lizet to twenty-turn-old Hilla—the hollow space forming inside Mylla's heart expanded. Her fondness for them made her almost think of them as her own sisters. Orphaned when her own Dyrrak parents had been exiled from the shunned empire and then slain by strangers from Yor who were never found, she'd been raised with the children of the other acolytes in the Conservatum. But being a Dyrrak, they had not accepted her, and in many ways she'd grown up alone in the shadows of the great halls and pillars of the Resplendolent Conservatum. Lock's sisters, who never cared about her heritage, were the first people outside the Knights she'd become attached to in a very, very long time. She hadn't foreseen the pain she'd feel at the idea of losing them too.

But what choice did she have? She wasn't out there, protecting them. She was here, fulfilling her duty, and they were too far away to reach now. Pain was inevitable at this point. Better to get it over with. "I was groomed for this life, Lock. It's all I know. All I need."

His response was, as usual, much too reasonable. "I've never asked you to give it up for me. I only ask that you include me."

"But you don't belong," she said, struggling to keep her voice steady.

"I do. I belong both by your side and where I can most aid Ivoryss. From my vantage, those two places are the same at the moment. If a Verity is threatening us, who but another Verity is left to stop him? That's where your Order and my duty fit together."

He paused and stretched his legs to the floor. While she locked down her chaos of emotions—growing grief at knowing she would lose him, anger that he made it so hard to let go—he put on his boots.

Finally, he broke the silence. "But you seem to want to be rid of me."

"It's… it's for the best. You know why."

As she stood to leave, he took her hand. "What is it you're afraid of, Mylla?"

She couldn't say it, to herself or to him: she didn't have the courage to face the day that would inevitably come when he would die—and she would not.

Before she could respond, Eisa's curt voice came from the hatch. "Fear is a luxury for hedonists and commoners, not Knights. Don't forget what you are, Mylla."

Mylla turned quickly to the Stallari Regent, who still wore her armor and looked as if she hadn't slept. *How long was she eavesdropping?*

Eisa ignored her questioning stare. "Come to the hold. Both of you. We've decided our next course of action. Commoner," for the first time, her tone held no mockery, "you're right about one thing: you aren't rejoining the Dragør Marines anytime soon. We have a use for you."

AS THEY FOLLOWED EISA, excuse after excuse for refusing to include Lock in their plans rushed through Mylla's mind. Not because she didn't think he was up to the task, but because Eisa could not be trusted to care about the dangers faced by a commoner, even those the older Knight herself put him in. Perhaps *especially* those she put him in. Eisa thought of anyone who wasn't a Knight as unworthy, as *less than*, just like she thought any Dyrrak who'd been ejected from Dyrrakium was unworthy. Their children, too, and Eisa had fought against letting Mylla into the Order because of her parents' unworthiness. The idea of putting Lock at her mercy dredged up an image of a meat grinder—with Eisa's hand at the crank.

But the Knights had a hierarchy, and she couldn't say no to whatever Eisa may have cooked up without risking another confrontation like yesterday's. *I'm stuck between a Lock and hard case,* she thought acidly.

Upon entering the hold, she automatically dipped her head slightly toward the vessel and touched her chin star in deference. The statue, still covered with a heavy layer of dirt, disturbed her for reasons she couldn't put her finger on, and she recalled Eisa's unexplained statement from last night: *Something has changed.*

A new worry bristled inside her. Had the Stallari's cage worked after all?

Safran waved at her and Lock from the table, beckoning them over. Roibeard, still on watch, was absent, which only increased Mylla's worry. The stoic Knight's unsung talent seemed to be the ability to throw a bucket of cold reason on Eisa's oft-fiery ire.

As they chose seats at the great wooden table, Lock asked Mylla, "Do you know where we're heading?"

She hadn't noticed it, but his query made her realize the *Vigilance* was once more on the move. She shrugged, about to speak, but Eisa beat her to it.

"Sit, novice," Eisa said. "You too," she added, nodding at Lock. "We're returning to Asteryss. Or rather, you are, commoner. You're going to become our spy, eyes and ears on the ground, and help us recover the final Fenestros from the Conservatum. If you can retrieve it, we'll need your help to resupply. If not..." Eisa's explanation ebbed, and her expression made it clear she saw no need to explain the *if*.

So, Mylla thought, *this is a fragment of a plan, not a plan itself.* That wouldn't do. "We shouldn't use a"—she glanced at Lock, apology in her eyes, before continuing—"commoner to do the Knights' work."

"We can, and we will," Eisa said. "The usurper's spies will know us on sight, and we can't move through the city without risking being recognized."

"Spies," Mylla mumbled to herself. "That must be how Balavad knew the vessel wasn't at Vigil Tower."

"But a commoner?" Eisa continued. "There are enough of them that the usurper's forces won't know one from the next."

Scrambling for a reason not to send Lock into needless danger, Mylla said, "But wouldn't it be better to search for the Stallari than go to Asteryss? He knows more than any of us what's going on. If we—"

"And where, Evernal, should we look?" Eisa said.

Mylla sat quietly, trying not to visibly seethe at being overruled. Again. *Safran,* she sent, *has this already been discussed and decided? Without me?*

Safran replied, *Action has to be taken swiftly, Mylla. We didn't think it necessary to wake you.*

It was a sucker punch. Her closest friend... to treat her like a, a *novice.* What would she have to do to prove herself to her Order?

Stung, she looked to Stave and, without thinking, carelessly pressed the sore spot she knew would draw a reaction from him. *Stave, how much of this is the Knights' decision, and how much is it Eisa's alone?* she sent.

"I can see your doubt, novice," Eisa said. "We have nothing to hide from each other. Speak openly."

For once, Stave showed some diplomacy, but only a dash. "Mylla thinks it's unwise to rely on someone who isn't tested, for something so important," he stated. "Can't disagree with that, I can't." Before his bait could lure Eisa into another argument, he continued, "But this time it's no small matter, it isn't. Mylla, you can't argue with the wisdom. We Knights can't move freely in the Conservatum. A nameless Marine, though, he can. As far as we know, leastways."

"I am glad to help, but what exactly can I do?" Havelock asked. "It's been a few turns since I left acolyte training. I'm not as familiar with the layout as I once was."

"Don't worry, we have someone on the inside who can assist you," Eisa said. "An acolyte we can trust."

They spoke of Irrick. "And if Irrick isn't there?" Mylla asked.

Eisa's eyes glittered with a challenge as she spoke. "*You* trust the commoner, novice, and think him smart and capable of noble deeds. Why shouldn't we?"

"He has a name, Eisa," she spat.

The Stallari Regent leaned toward her, her eyes narrowed. "And if he dies," she promised, "be content knowing that neither you nor history will soon forget it."

CHAPTER TWENTY-ONE

Jaemus knew he was gambling with his life, but sometime during this bizarre exchange he became aware of two things. The first gave him hope, the second made him feel like he might whizz in his flightsuit.

One, chances were good that the errant foreigner's "Scrylle" was the same thing as the metal scepter and the parchment contained within it that Jaemus now carried. Rather, the *two* he now carried after bagging the one that had arrived just after the Knight had. And if the Knight knew what they were, then he must know how to read the parchments. *Read* them. This was the key Jaemus desperately needed to assist him in proving to the Glisternauts that the old cult's secrets offered possibilities for aiding them in the quest to save their future—setting aside the mythology of the Creatress and foretelling of their world's doom. And that they had an obligation, an *imperative*, to explore it. And of course, it was the key to helping him earn back his stripped prestige. If there was one thing he couldn't abide for long, it was being considered a superstitious idiot.

Two, the foreigner was asking for the *Creatress's* Scrylle, *not* the one that had fallen from the eaves with him, and these things he called Fenestrii, which Jaemus suspected were the Verity spheres of Creatress lore—and apparently the lore of *many* Verities. The implication being that the Knight didn't know the items were here. If true, this had the nice side effect of blunting Jaemus's guilty conscience a smidge. However, the moment the Knight found out he had them, he was pretty sure he would never have to worry about whizz stains in his flightsuit again.

Thus, his gamble. Persuade the foreigner to tell him what the Scrylle said, the one belonging to the Creatress cult that Jaemus had come across legitimately—sort of. And if it was a map, as he speculated, the Knight could illuminate the locations of the other four of the Creatress's spheres, these things called Fenestrii, for him. In exchange? Jaemus would have to work on that, starting with finding out what Aldinhuus wanted them for. Perhaps he could offer to split the stones with him—at least, after he'd distilled and replicated the process that made them tick and gave them the ability to produce what seemed to be endless power. This could take anni-cycles. And judging by the intensity of the Knight's... well, *everything,* Jaemus wasn't sure how that barter would go. That was something to worry about later.

And he'd better be very crafty if he wanted to ensure there would be a later.

Regardless, he was accustomed to taking gambles. It was half of what being a Glisternaut was about. And since he'd been, in his roundabout logic, *bestowed* the first sphere and the parchment, or Scrylle, he'd pushed more boundaries with the 'Nauts, with his inventions, even with his own beliefs than he'd even known he was capable of. The way he'd come across these artifacts in the first place had been the catalyst.

As he did often, he'd gone to visit his gramsirene one Glister Dim. She lived in the remotest part of the Dryside Quarter, where the plantlife of the Never Sea had encroached and grown to cover many of the buildings, turning them into unhospitable, decrepit structures. But Vreyja refused Jaemus's requests that she move somewhere less *ancient* feeling, so he checked in on her when he could.

Voices from inside had made him hesitate before going in. He recognized her guest: that strange hermit was visiting her, the sickly-looking man named Griggory. Though he was an old friend of Gram's, Jaemus found more than his pale skin and unidentifiable accent odd, and he preferred to avoid him. He'd been considering coming back another time, but a brilliant flash of light beneath the jamb had stoked his curiosity. He'd snuck inside and witnessed Griggory giving Vreyja the metal cylinder and a single stone-like orb, about the size of his fist, that seemed to be glowing with an inner light. Griggory was explaining how these artifacts related to the old Creatress cult, requesting that she keep and hide them until he returned, and Vreyja had willingly agreed.

Jaemus's gramsirene was superstitious to the point of being considered unhinged by many Himmingazians. It was only her age that kept her from being apprehended for dabbling in the old forbidden cult. But Jaemus got a good look at those artifacts, and he knew then and there that there was much more to the dead beliefs than simply ideas that threatened Himmingaze's orderly and strict laws. That stone looked as if it was a fallen piece of the Glister Cloud. And it looked... powerful. The engineer in him couldn't see something like it and not want, *need*, to know its capabilities. Not too long afterward, he'd borrowed the artifacts—without asking, but... he'd get around to that part later.

So now here he was, with a crazy man and more of these powerful cult artifacts. And though Aldinhuus may have withdrawn his flying stones at Jaemus's insistence, he still apparently had no qualms about skewering him with that harsh blue gaze.

"You're right, Himmingazian," the Knight said. "I shouldn't expect you to know such things. You seem to be merely a commoner."

Was that an insult?

"Forgive my impatience. So much has happened..." The Knight trailed off, his expression hardening into a grimace. Whatever had happened to him, it obviously pained him to think about it. "The Scrylles are records, of a sort, kept by each individual Order of the Knights Corporealis. They appear to be cylinders, made of metal or stone, about this long"—he held his hands apart about the length of Jaemus's forearm—"and adorned by Verity runes. To a commoner, they would seem like—"

Too excited to let him finish, Jaemus cut in, "Yes! I know exactly what you're talking about."

"And you know where to find it?"

"As a matter of fact, I have one aboard the *Octopod*. Just outside. What do you need it for?"

For the first time since he'd arrived, Aldinhuus's expression shifted to something a shade lighter than bleak. Yet somehow the look unsettled Jaemus just the same. "Show me," the Knight said, taking a step toward him. Like a man walking ashore after many cycles at sea, his legs seemed uncertain of the ground. He lurched slightly and spread his arms to help him rebalance.

Jaemus said, "Looks like that knock on the head hasn't quite worn off."

"I'm fine." The Knight placed the back of each of his wrists against his eyes and rubbed. "It's just this… never mind. The Scrylle, take me to it."

The moment to bargain had come, and Jaemus quickly gagged the little voice in his head telling him not to antagonize this man. He argued back that this might be his only chance to help not only himself, but also (and here he took liberties with hyperinflating the importance of his role in the grand scheme of things) *all* of Himmingaze. *I have to persuade him to help me, even at the risk of a shard of rock going through my liver.*

Adjusting his shoulders and lifting his chin, he said, "Perhaps you'd be open to discussing terms first?" The way Aldinhuus's expression didn't seem to change yet still shot him full of icy daggers impressed Jaemus. "And before you pull out the kinky stones again," he added hurriedly, "hear me out."

"I don't have time for troghopping schemes," Aldinhuus growled.

"Do you have time to consider the fate of the world?" Hyperbole rarely worked on rational people, of course, but the way it seemed to catch the Knight's attention prompted Jaemus to run with it. "I mean, the people of Himmingaze need someone of your great wisdom," and flattery, yes, flattery, always a good tactic, "to help us survive the stranglehold of the Glister Cloud."

And then it hit him, and he couldn't believe he hadn't realized it sooner. If Aldinhuus had appeared out of thin air, he might know something about off-world travel that even Jaemus's studies in celestial transport hadn't yet uncovered. And those hovering stones, which seemed to be mind-controlled, what advancements in material methods led to the invention of such a thing? Could it be that he needed Aldinhuus more than he'd initially realized? Maybe the foreigner *was* the answer to the Glister Cloud. Maybe he *was* in direct service to a Verity. And maybe, just maybe, the Creatress *was* real, and Jaemus, a man of science and technology, who laughed at the idea of magic and the arcane, a man who believed intellect trumped unchallenged belief, might truly be face-to-face with a chance to witness something… divine? A superstition that maybe wasn't? He had to make a decision: to let go of reason and just believe, or to forever cling exclusively to what he could explain with logic and study.

Or maybe he was just exhausted, hungry, and not thinking clearly. It was the obvious answer, and ninety-nine times out of one hundred, the correct one.

He'd start with showing Aldinhuus the Scrylle and see what the foreigner knew, then take things from there. He was nowhere near ready to accept the many-Verities, multiple-realms business, and never would be. But this strange man believed in them, obviously, and between the two of them, only the stranger had ever defied the Great Cosmic laws governing how solid-state objects worked. Jaemus was willing to go along with what he said, at least until a better explanation could be found.

As he deliberated, he watched Aldinhuus, waiting for the man to either take the bait or take Jaemus's life. And finally, the Knight said, "Explain yourself, Bardgrim. Sharpish."

CHAPTER TWENTY-TWO

Mylla had sat silently in the common room as Eisa instructed her and Lock on the remainder of the mission plan, unable to mount any more protests after the Stallari Regent's chilling statement: *Be content knowing that neither you nor history will soon forget it.*

His name, Havelock Rekkr, her own Lock, of course she'd never forget it. That's what gutted her. And she'd realized there was one thing worse than someday witnessing her beloved die. And that was *not* witnessing it—but knowing it had happened. If Lock failed to return from Asteryss and meet at the rendezvous point with the *Vigilance*, all aboard could and would assume he was dead. She didn't have it in her to live with that uncertainty. She had to go with him.

They stood now on the launch deck as Stave revealed one of the two dragørfly scouts—slightly modified Dragør Wing scouts—that the Knight kept on hand for emergencies, which Lock would be taking to Asteryss.

Upon seeing it, Lock crowed, "I'd fly *that* into battle!"

His enthusiasm was the precise opposite of the dread that had taken up full-time residence in Mylla's gut. The Wing crafts were "scout" ships in the same way swords are good tools for buttering bread.

Essentially winged cannons, the ships comprised a pilot's seat wedged inside a fuselage and a rear cargo compartment that one could describe as big enough to hold a passenger—if the passenger in question was either a child or else comfortable being folded in half like a shirt—directly over an emberspark heavy gun, a diminished version of the *Vigilance*'s emberflare cannon. If you wanted something condensed to formless burnt rubble, and didn't have the means to haul around a volcano, the emberflare and emberspark were your best solutions, and were far more powerful than the regular Dragør Wing petard launchers, which could damage an enemy's craft but wasn't powerful enough to obliterate one. With two thrusters per side and a comparatively massive engine in the aft, the scout was as fast and nimble as the dragørflies that were their namesake, and a flint glass coating rounded out their deadly design. Lock's reaction to such a superior fighting ship was one part combat soldier, one part boy at his birthday celebration.

The issue of Mylla's dread, simply put, was the entire plan from this point forward. Initially, she'd assumed the Knights would fly the *Vigilance* as close to Asteryss as they could get before engaging the enemy's ships and leave Lock to enter the city by foot or whatever other means of locomotion he could find. Yet, perhaps not unforeseeably, his flying mastery led to this outcome, which she would much have preferred to avoid. Lock was skilled enough to manage a dragørfly scout, so why not let him?

It made the most sense. The scouts were quiet, lightweight, invisible, agile as insects, and could take him quickly and directly to the Conservatum's inner courtyard with none the wiser. In theory, he could slip in, find the celestial stone, and slip back out without alerting even the most vigilant of sentries—provided he was as fleet of foot and stealthy of approach as Eisa credited him to be. But this meant Mylla would be riding in the cramped cargo space.

Not that she'd been tasked with accompanying him on this mission… In fact, in the discussion, Eisa had made it clear he was to go to Asteryss alone. Mylla didn't care. She would face the Stallari Regent's wrath when, and if, the time came. It wouldn't be the first time.

Lost in these thoughts, she now stood in the hold while Stave acquainted Lock with the specifics of flying the dragørfly scout.

"… and of course, your engine is primed with this," the ruddy Knight was saying as he stood atop the fuselage and pointed out the acceleration controls inside the cockpit. "Keep that pressed to the floor and you'll go so fast even your thoughts will have to take another ship to keep up."

Lock's legs dangled over the side of the fuselage while his upper half appeared to be caught in the cockpit mid-swallow. His muffled voice came from inside. "Not too different from my own ship. And this is the cannon trigger?"

"Right, takes two fingers so you don't accidentally fire it. But you won't be needing it, you won't. The name of your game is stealth for the foreseeable. You start plugging up the sky with crispy enemies, it won't take them long to figure out *that* you are if not *where* you are. And that will compromise the mission, it will."

Lock retreated from the cockpit and stood on the deck. "It'll be just as compromised if I can't defend myself," he argued. "I'm no help to anyone dead. Trust me, I'm capable of handling any ship and any weapon you give me."

Mylla, as always, marveled at his confidence. What she'd give for a fraction of it right now.

"So you think you can take on the might of an entire hostile army, a *Verity's* hostile army, do you?" Stave's grizzly eyebrows steepled in mock appreciation. Then he snorted, rooted in his bandolier for one of his choice stubby cigars, lit it with a match, and puffed satisfyingly, giving Lock a penetrating stare through the thick blue smoke. He finally continued as if Lock had never spoken. "You won't want to be diving too hard when you land. Gently ease the engine down while manipulating the thrusters to bump you into line. The wings will guide you, but don't push them if they resist too much. These little dragørfly ships are sensitive. They know the skies as well as a bird; you just have to listen." Stave spoke affectionately of the ships, having himself forged and worked most of the metal they were made of and crafted the finer controls by hand. To him, they were as much an art and symbol of his pride as they were a tool, a quality about him Mylla found ironic when contrasted with his coarse exterior.

Lock seemed to understand the Knight's attachment and said, "Don't worry, Master Knight. I'll bring your ship back safely."

With a smirk that was not unkind, Stave continued the end of the lesson, both men too absorbed to pay attention to Mylla nearby.

Safran entered the launch bay with a sack and handed it up to Stave. *Provisions. In case he needs to stay longer than a day,* she sent. Stave shoved the sack unceremoniously into a space behind the pilot's seat. *And these to accompany your sword,* she finished and passed a set of daggers to Lock, who couldn't hear her but guessed her meaning.

She looked to Mylla. *He'll be off soon. You two should say whatever you need to now. C'mon, love,* she finished, gesturing at Stave.

Stave jumped from the fuselage and landed beside Lock. He put his hand, cigar extending between his fingers, on the pilot's shoulder and smiled. "I know a good combination when I see one, I do. I've a feeling you'll do mighty fine, and I know Mylla's confidence in you is deserved. They call you flying Marines Wings, right?"

Lock nodded, waving smoke from his face.

"Then fly like you've got some of your own, pilot. Like a bruhawk feather, you are. Remember." He reached for Safran's hand, and the two Knights exited.

Lock fumbled the daggers for a moment, having no sheath of his own to place them in, then dropped them into the scout's cockpit and turned back to regard Mylla, who'd walked up beside him. "I'll be back soon. Shouldn't take me—"

She cut him off: "I'm not letting you go alone."

Surprise danced across his features. "But your duty... Knight Nazaria..."

"I know. But she can't stop me. Only Vaka Aster herself can release me from the Knights' oath. I'm coming."

"Mylla if this is about thinking I can't manage—"

She reached for his hands. "I already told you, this isn't *your* duty. And I know you can do it, but... I just don't think you should have to. Not alone, at least. I'll ride in the rear."

She supposed the incredulity in his expression was deserved. "After last time," he said, "you're sure you can handle it?"

"I can. With extreme reluctance."

"This morning you were trying to get rid of me. Now you're coming with me. What's changed?"

"I've had time to do some reflecting."

He eyed her with one part gratitude, one part suspicion. "Time to reflect? The daystar hasn't passed through a quarter of the sky since we awoke."

"I was sprint reflecting. Do you want me to come or don't you?"

"Yes, of course I do."

The sound of the launch bay hatch opening alerted her, and she dropped his hands. "We have to go now."

Wait.

Relieved, yet still wounded from Safran's earlier willingness to leave her out of the planning, Mylla turned to her friend—and found that it was her turn to be surprised. "What's that?"

Safran held out a sheath for Lock in one hand—and in the other, another set of daggers for Mylla. *What's it look like? You may be a Knight, but you still need as many weapons as you can carry. Take them.* She pressed the dagger hilts into Mylla's palms. *I'll send the bruhawks to watch over you. If you need the* Vigilance, *we'll come to your aid. There's no need to lose more Knights, or allies. Not at a time like this.*

Mylla's tongue needed coaxing before she could speak. "You knew I'd go with Lock?"

The age wrinkles around Safran's eyes—she'd been fifty-five turns before taking her oath—deepened as a shrewd smile spread across her lips. *Of course. Mylla, you're the sister I never had, like my twin. I know you as well as I know myself. You're in love, and love will always be your first duty. Even if—*she gave Lock a knowing look—*you sometimes lose sight of it.*

Mute with gratitude, Mylla let Safran pull her into a short but solid embrace.

Hurry. Eisa is on her way to see him off. Trust Havelock to get you there safely, but you know the Conservatum. You'll find the Fenestros faster than he could. If you also find Irrick, tell him to head to the tower, and we'll try to retrieve him if we can. Now go, and hasten back.

CHAPTER TWENTY-THREE

Ulfric listened closely as Bardgrim explained how he'd acquired Lífs's Scrylle and, as impossible as it sounded, a single Fenestros.

Griggory Dondrin, you old wanderer, he thought, *so now I finally know what became of you. Hard to believe you live still, after all of these turns.*

Yet the discovery of the long-lost Knight—missing from Vinnr for over seven hundred turns—only held his attention for a moment. Potentially everything he needed to secure his return to Vinnr lay nearly at his fingertips, and he could barely force himself to hear the Himmingazian out. He needed those artifacts.

"So, if you could perhaps read me the Scrylle," Bardgrim was saying, "and tell me what it says and if it is a map as I believe, maybe it can help me find the other four Verity stones, or Fenestrii—that's what they're called, right?"

"Map?" Ulfric asked. Of course, this commoner of the Creatress's realm had learned to open the Scrylle and found the Fenestros parchment tucked within. It seemed he thought the parchment was the Scrylle and not the metal scepter itself. It was clever of him to have learned how to open it, but he still had no idea, it seemed, what the Scrylle itself could do or what knowledge it contained. "Yes. Fenestrii.

They're spheres made from the elements of the Verities that hold a spark of power, an energy of a kind. They can be used by Knights for... many things."

"Exactly! When Griggory gave them to my gram—"

"A Knight Corporealis," Ulfric stated.

Bardgrim looked almost startled, then continued, "Of course! He must be. Or was. Anyway, the sphere isn't made of anything I recognized and it intrigued me, so I tested its components and came up with... well, you must know. Nothing I've ever seen before. And the energy it put off—remarkable."

"Where is Griggory now?"

"No idea. Haven't seen him." Bardgrim, for as much as he talked—and talked, and talked—could not be diverted from his topic it seemed. "I built a power siphoning harness for the Fenestros and use it in the *Octopod*. If I can locate the rest of them, I may be able to use them to build the ship the Glisternauts need to explore beyond the Glister Cloud. We can find a new home, a place where the people of Himmingaze can relocate, before it's swallowed up completely by the Never Sea."

"You intend to use the Fenestrii as fuel?" The question was rhetorical. The celestial spheres had incalculable uses, which is what made their bestowal to humans "remarkable," as Bardgrim had just put it. The Himmingazian's discovery of how to use one to power a ship was clever indeed. "What is this Glister Cloud?" he asked.

"You don't know what the Glister Cloud is? How is that even possible?"

"We've nothing called that in Vinnr."

Ulfric sensed the Himmingazian now fought an internal struggle, and he guessed who knew over what. Was Ulfric crazy or lying? For his own part, the thread of his patience frayed more with each syllable the man uttered. Bardgrim struck him as intelligent, but no warrior. Even a bit like Acolyte Irrick, one of the few remaining scholars in the Resplendolent Conservatum still wholly devoted to Vaka Aster. But concealed beneath the craftiness ran a kind of cunning, as well. He could trust this Bardgrim to give him only enough information to string him along, the aim always to achieve a purpose he may not fully reveal. Perhaps he was more like a politician than an acolyte. For now, Ulfric's restraint depended as much on what Bardgrim didn't say as what he did, but of course, he couldn't very well kill the man without first acquiring the Scrylle and Verity stone.

Maiming him, on the other hand, was becoming more of an option moment by interminable moment.

Bardgrim went on. "Well, in layman's terms, the Cloud is the end of the world as we know it." At the scowl Ulfric gave him, he cleared his throat, then carefully reworded his response. "Though you're no layman, naturally, Master Knight. It's an atmospheric anomaly that's turned us Himmingazian into squatters in our own world. Exploration has uncovered a bit. It appears to be an envelope of Cosmos detritus: rocks, metals, gasses, and ice. It has a radiant rhythm and waxes and wanes to illuminate Himmingaze—more or less. Are you familiar with a kaleidoscope?"

He waited for Ulfric's response, but Ulfric remained silent, likely appearing to Bardgrim to be waiting for the story's end. In fact, he was calculating which finger to break first to speed up the man's rambling.

"Maybe?" Bardgrim continued. "Okay, basically, we're inside one, a cosmic kaleidoscope. The Cloud has been closing us in for hundreds of cycles, like a noose cutting us off from the rest of the Great Cosmos as it tightens. As it gets bigger and closer, Himmingaze grows wetter, colder, more hostile to life. And we are not equipped to do much more than watch it come."

Ulfric could easily guess the cause of this world-ending "anomaly." He didn't have to guess, though, did he? The voice in his head had said: *Lifs, my quin, is leading her creations to oblivion.* He shook his head, confused by the thoughts that didn't seem to be his own, the strangeness of the entire experience. But, he concluded, this wasn't his world, and it wasn't his duty to change its fate.

"Take me to the Scrylle," he pressed, "and I'll... *read* you its contents." He chose the word "read" to aid Bardgrim's understanding, though reading wasn't strictly how one gleaned the Scrylles' content. He didn't think this Himmingazian could grasp this, though, despite his cleverness. Untrained commoners could be quite dim, though it wasn't their fault.

Bardgrim's tense expression spoke clearly of his uncertainty. He had no alternative, and he knew it. And it was likely dawning on him that Ulfric could take Lífs's artifacts any moment he chose to, *if* he chose to. The Himmingazian obviously thought himself smart, but his self-assuredness had failed him this time.

"You know, on second thought, let's look at it in here. The *Octopod* isn't terribly roomy, and the weather, well, it's always blustery. No reason we should both get wet. Heh. We have more room in the temple to really give the moment its proper, er, I guess 'ceremony' is the right word. I'll be back in just a moment."

Ulfric released a caustic laugh. "Temple? You call this ruin a temple?" Like a whip crack, .his demeanor sharpened again. "If you think to test me for a fool, Bardgrim, you will lose."

With his klinkí stone arm still at his side, he balled his hand into a fist, watching as Bardgrim picked up to the gesture. The Himmingazian didn't have to see the stones themselves to feel their threat. He sighed with exasperation, and with a nod spun on a heel and began walking toward the chamber's wide doors.

"You forgot your bag," Ulfric commented.

Without turning, Bardgrim said, "I'll come back for it later," and pushed the doors open.

Despite the aged, cracked plaster inside the building, the immediate cold of the gust that blew inward told Ulfric the dilapidated temple still retained enough integrity to shield them from this world's weather, which he hadn't guessed would be quite so turbulent. The light coming through seemed tinged by lavender, but a living lavender, dotted and speckled with iridescent raindrops, at least they appeared so to his enchanted eyes. Nothing disturbed the retreating horizon, but the far-off sky exploded in glittering lights and pirouetting hues of every color real or imagined. *The Glister Cloud,* he realized. It was awesome, a sky so profoundly different from any he'd ever seen.

Immediate problems quickly surfaced and took his mind off the sight. The challenge of stepping into that pulsing glow might be beyond him. He could barely focus inside the crumbling temple. How was he to see anything in this radiant miasma?

Bardgrim, it seemed, had an advantage after all: the Himmingazian might pick up on Ulfric's affliction. And outside, it could be worse. Did he have no choice but to trust Bardgrim? No. The instinct of millennia told him he couldn't, and the desperation of his plight told him trust was another luxury, like hope, he could not for a moment expect. He'd simply have to strangle the hindrance into submission and carry on till he was back in Vinnr, back on Mount Omina with his Knights and—

—and what? What had he done? Where now were Vaka Aster, and her realm's nemesis, Balavad?

"Coming?" Bardgrim had turned and now watched him keenly, perhaps sensing a hesitation Ulfric hadn't meant to show.

With legs that felt as lumbering as tree stumps, he stepped forward, again with a lurch and fumble, his body feeling unfamiliar and disjointed, as if it weren't his own. Seventeen hundred turns he'd walked in this flesh, and now it betrayed him. Like his Verity had. Like, the Glister Cloud seemed to prove, all Verities did.

"Need a hand?"

The Himmingazian's attentiveness—or was it vigilance?—irritated him. They were not allies, so why did he pretend to be one? By fate's fickle whimsy, Ulfric could use an ally…

He ignored the question and continued his forward momentum, gracelessly, though with each step it became easier. When he reached the door, Bardgrim turned back outside and continued down a short flight of stone steps. The biting chill scoured the skin of Ulfric's face and lifted his tangled hair from his brow. His breastplate guarded him against the worst, but he noted Bardgrim closing the oddly high collar of his one-piece uniform more firmly over his chin and lower part of his ears. The unfamiliar material looked thin, but Bardgrim seemed more comfortable in the squall than Ulfric was.

The Himmingazian hooked left around the building, throwing over his shoulder: "I'm docked out back."

The ground's slick and uneven rocks and his hindered eyesight seemed to be teaming against him. Between moments of watching the earth to pick sound footing, he scanned the area. As Bardgrim had said, they were on an island, a small one at that, with waves smashing fiercely against the stony shore like gnashing, foamy teeth. How could any boat dock in this? In every way, the surroundings were opposite of his beloved home of Ivoryss, with its white sand beaches, limpid beryl ocean, weathered wooden piers reaching far into the bays until the water was deep enough to dive into and spear-hunt the shoals of maggies and bewlies amid the red and green corals of the reefs. He had no doubt this island's reef's only bounty was a quick, airless, pummeling death. At least for commoners. Knights weren't easily drowned.

The answer to what kind of boat the Himmingazian captained came as they turned the corner at the temple's end—but it was not the answer he expected. A bulbous, inelegant craft stood on a tripod, but it bore thruster-like units on its flanks that made it appear capable of flying, not bouncing along a sea. For the first time, a sense of foreign-ness so complete it threatened his equilibrium (again) hit Ulfric. This was what another reality looked like, felt like. Himmingaze was not his home.

Recovering, he paced behind Bardgrim beneath the *Octopod*'s hull, gaining respite from the heavy rain. The craft's stilts reached high enough that neither of them had to stoop. Bardgrim climbed a short ladder and peered into an unobtrusive half-spherical bulb depending from the metal, and as he did so, a hatch slid open above him. Without a word, he climbed inside. Warm light—Ulfric's new vision seemed to transform light and color to sensation, the lambency literally warming him—emitted from within, beckoning Ulfric to follow.

The interior spread out in a cabin designed to be living quarters, with the necessities of daily life dotting the area: seating and a table, containers for sundries, mechanisms and devices he didn't recognize but likely had equivalencies in his own realm. It reminded him of the *Vigilance* but specific to its own time and place. The contrast between the very familiar and very foreign continued to strike Ulfric unexpect-edly. He imagined he'd get used to it if he were here long enough, but he had no intention of that being the case.

Are all Verity creations this similar? he mused, thinking of the brief vision he'd had of Battgjald, and the members of Balavad's own retinue, who had been alike to the people of Vinnr in most ways he could see. *Why would that be? Reality to my kind is fixed, it seems, but the makers can create any form and any function, can't they?* Like his body had earlier, his mind, his understanding of reality, felt disjointed. He'd never imagined traveling beyond his own realm. Why would he? He served Vaka Aster; his duty lay in Vinnr.

A crushing sense of insignificance suddenly filled him. His devotion now was only to Vaka Aster's shell, an inert statue that still, for all its coldness and distance, held his world's fate in its stone. What good was long life when what he lived for had all but abandoned the world of Vinnr? What was he to a Verity? What were any of them? Motes in their realities, hardly the greatest of their creations, barely worth their brief lifetimes, a few turns for a commoner, or a few centuries for someone like him who'd pledged everything to serve. A being that was capable of creating everything could hardly be blamed for paying little of it any mind, for lacking devotion or even a sense of responsibility to the small, fleeting human breed, which had... what purpose exactly?

To amuse. That's what Balavad had said.

Bardgrim pointed to a chair, and silently, still lost in thought, Ulfric sat. After rummaging inside a container, the Himmingazian returned with an item wrapped in cloth, containing presumably the Scrylle. "Here. I'll be back with the Fenestros."

Ulfric controlled his reflex to snatch the cylinder and took it solemnly instead. "I'm coming with you."

With an eye roll, Bardgrim strode to the rear of the cabin and past a heavy hatch leading to an alcove and another hatch. "We can't both fit inside the core, so you have to wait here."

He gave a single nod, and Bardgrim slid inside the smaller opening. Within moments, he returned with the Fenestros and held it out. At first Ulfric couldn't believe the Himmingazian could palm such a thing: a ball of yellow and white fire, like a sun shrunken to the size of a kórb fruit, ablaze with a heat that would turn even stone to ash. Then he realized it only appeared this way to his weirded eyes. He took it.

The Himmingazian added, "We won't get far until I put that back, so I suggest we do this quickly. No one is supposed to be on Isle Stonering, like I said, and we don't want to be here if the… anyone else shows up."

Back in the main cabin, Ulfric returned to the table and quickly removed the Scrylle cylinder from its cloth wrapping. The scepter, made of an identical celestial metal to both of the other Scrylle's he'd so recently held, comforted him with its sameness. Here, at least, was an artifact that was like home, and if all went well, would get him there.

He placed the scepter upright, preparing to set the Fenestros atop. But with a glance at Bardgrim on the opposite side of the table, he stopped. Despite the way the Himmingazian leaned casually on his hands over the tabletop, his shoulders were rigidly set, the muscles in his neck taut as stretched springs. For a moment Ulfric considered ignoring him, but the man had not done anything—yet—to cause Ulfric to mistrust him, and had even come to his aid. Their bargain was fair, though Ulfric was sure Bardgrim would be disappointed in his end anyway. The writing on the Scrylle's inner parchment was indeed a map to the other Fenestrii of this realm, the same map all Scrylles contained for their respective worlds, and it would not take Ulfric more than a moment to tell the commoner where they were.

He slid the parchment out of the Scrylle's inner core. The cold yet smooth material against his rough hand reassured him in a way he'd not been when seeing the Fenestros. The parchment was neither paper nor cloth nor hide, but something like all three, the color a pearlescent white. He'd held the parchment within the Vinnr Scrylle enough to know the material would never fray or tear, and its runes would never fade.

After he unrolled it and laid it flat on the table, the runic script covering it danced in front of his eyes, more a dream of words than words themselves. He knew the Himmingazian would be seeing nothing of the sort. This was the effect of his travel along celestial paths, and to a commoner the runes would simply be oddly difficult to focus on. In a flash of insight, he reached for his Mentalios chain.

Perhaps looking through the lens would mitigate some of his visual defect.

To his relief, it worked. The Verity runes solidified and revealed the locations of the Fenestros that sat before him on the table (Isle Stonering's name easily discernible on the map), as well as three of Lífs's others. Interestingly, one was not visible. *That means it's in another realm,* Ulfric thought. *Odd.* On a whim, he decided not to concern himself, or the Himmingazian, with this. Too many other things were more important.

"Bardgrim," he said, "your stones are scattered widely across your world. One remains unfixed. The Knight you met keeps it." To himself, he wondered, *What is Griggory doing with one of Lífs's Fenestrii?* His guess would be just as wild as his guess about why Griggory was here in the first place. "And the fifth… it's not here. It must be outside your realm."

Notes of giddiness infused Bardgrim's voice as he asked, "Well, four out of five is still three more than I have. Where—can you tell me where they are now?"

With one eye still shut, Ulfric raised his head, seeing the Himmingazian for the first time with normal sight. As he had thought, Bardgrim was tall like the Yorish and flaunted a carefully trimmed and styled mop of brown curls that stood high over his forehead, even when damp. His sharp nose and bright orange-brown eyes gave him the appearance of an attentive, scholarly type, reminding Ulfric again of Acolyte Irrick, but with a touch of rogue. He looked to be somewhere on the low side of his thirties, by Halla-turn reckoning. Yet his smooth skin was a pale, soft green—was the man ill, or was this normal for a Himmingazian?

Ulfric listed off the locations of the two other fixed stones, names and places that meant nothing to him, and Bardgrim watched him like a hungry bruhawk, repeating each place—though his own expression seemed puzzled. When he got to the last visible stone, Ulfric said, "I can see from the runes that the last Fenestros and Griggory are at," he had to let his mouth get used to the word before he could say it, "Bludghadda."

Bardgrim stood up straight and pushed his hand through his curls.

"I've had the Scrylle for almost a six deca-cycles. The places you named are a start, but the stones could be almost anywhere now."

"No, as I said, at the moment, these stones are where I told you, Griggory's included."

Bardgrim eyed him skeptically. "All the places you listed are cities that existed a long time ago, when Himmingaze still had land—and cities. Our cities are built on the water now, floating. It's not going to be an easy task to retrieve them."

"Ah," he remarked with disinterest. With the task done, his focus returned to the Scrylle. Concealing the Mentalios inside his armor and setting the celestial parchment aside, he grasped its cylinder. The time had come to, hopefully, return home.

As Bardgrim watched, he set the Fenestros atop the cylinder and spoke the Elder Veros words to see inside. The heart of the stone began to glow, and Bardgrim's eyes widened with wonder.

"Huh, I had no idea it did *that*," he murmured. "It is actually just like a kaleidoscope."

Ulfric leaned over the stone and gazed into it. Just before he made the mental leap into its streams of lore, he thought, *If Griggory had been keeping this, why didn't he ever return home? Will it show me the way to open a starpath well? If not, I must find Griggory. He may be my last hope.*

CHAPTER TWENTY-FOUR

I f praying hard to all the Verities to show mercy and spare your life were to ever become a tournament-worthy sport, Mylla would win every medal. Her panicked, beseeching litany forced itself past her clenched teeth as they plummeted from the *Vigilance*—and kept plummeting *long* after she was ready to stop. The launch had seemed to be going smoothly—right up until the moment they left the *Vigilance*'s deck and hit the air. Which really meant that the *prelaunch* had gone well, it was the *actual* launch that had caused her world to turn, literally, upside down.

Unlike the copilot seat in the Wing fighter, the cargo space in the modified scout did not afford Mylla a view of the outside. In the lifetimes that passed as Lock struggled to get control of the nose-down spiraling craft, she couldn't decide if this was an improvement or not. Her involuntary pleas to the Verities suggested it wasn't. When his frantic grappling with the ship's controls finally brought its wings and thrusters into harmony and smoothed out the ride, she, too, finally found some control and silenced her airless entreaties. The sudden jolt that brought the ship into a saner trajectory bounced her stomach back where it belonged, and she pulled her knees closer to her chest like a frightened child and willed her thoughts away from the here and now.

She didn't know how long they'd been flying before Havelock spoke. "If I'd known you had these in the Knights, I would have considered staying at the Conservatum. How are you doing back there?"

Peeling her tongue from the roof of her mouth, which now felt dryer than the burnt crust of Mount Omina, took some effort, but at last she succeeded. "Is there a word for feeling as if your guts are trying to shoot through your eyeballs? If so, that's how I'm doing."

"I'm sorry, love. I didn't realize how delicate this ship was at first. Should be smooth sailing from here. Promise." They were both silent for a bit before he said, "These dragørfly ships are supposed to have the same invisibility as the *Vigilance*, right?"

She grunted an affirmative.

"Then why could I see it while we were still aboard? And how do we know if it's working now?"

"The flint glass cloaks are activated by celestial light, either from Halla or from the reflection of the stars. They're always cloaked out of doors, but not inside unless celestial light can be focused on them."

"Then how do you see each other when you're flying?"

"They're visible to us when we look through our Mentalios lenses." She fingered the thick chain holding her Mentalios around her neck. Clasped in a certain way, the chain would hang around her head and allow the Mentalios to hang directly over her eye when holding it was impractical. Another of the Stallari's innovations that the Knights relied on.

Lock nodded and gently feathered the craft's wings, refining the flight with the precision of a master. "We'll be there soon."

For the first time, she detected a note of strain in his voice. What could he be thinking? What fears were he fighting to keep in check? The distance to Asteryss gave her more time than she really wanted to think about this, but the diversion was almost welcome. She understood his distress. The stakes were so much more personal for him, as he stood to lose his family and home. She hadn't had a family other than the Order in ages and had grown accustomed to her lack of attachment. And when Halla-turns were like days to you, a home could be anything that offered mere moments of comfort and respite from a duty that sometimes felt too much like a burden, and other times just a meaningless fancy. She reached for him, idly stroking his neck as they flew, wanting him to know that he wasn't as alone as he might feel.

Safran had been right. She loved Lock and always would. She didn't know a way to put this feeling behind the demands of her oath, no matter how important that oath was.

Soon enough, these thoughts pulled in another direction, to the last thing she'd seen before Lock had closed the dragørfly ship's hatch and they'd dived from the *Vigilance*'s launch deck. The Stallari Regent had appeared just as Mylla had settled in to the ship's cramped cargo seat. Her gaze locked on Mylla immediately. The ferocity, always boiling in the depths of Eisa's eyes, had been there, of course. But what *hadn't* been there was what stayed with Mylla, an absence more curdling than the anger she'd expected to see. There'd been no surprise in Eisa's expression, only a cold look of expectations fulfilled.

Now that coldness busily worked itself into Mylla's tenuous composure, seeping into the cracks of her conviction, making her doubt: *Am I worthy of the oath I took? Am I failing in my duty by pursuing what's right, or at least what I think is right?* Decisions and strategic plans of such great importance should come from those with the centuries of experience to make them wisely, shouldn't they? And what was Mylla but a novice Knight with a weakness for a man she would outlive by hundreds, perhaps thousands, of turns? A weakness for what was temporary in a life that was pledged to the eternal.

Further fueling these doubts was the memory of Eisa's words the night before, burning inside her: "Power is a living thing, novice. It needs to feed and it grows. Its ultimate end is more power. Why would a Verity be any different? A being of *all* power. What's left for it to gain but *more*..." Words she had said to explain their circumstances but which only served to cloud Mylla's understanding of all that had come to pass in the last two days. If Eisa truly believed Vaka Aster, and all Verities, existed with only one principle—to rule with absolute dominion and feed a need for more power, even at the cost of their own creations—how could she or any of them reconcile their honor with devotion to a being who didn't value it? Was Eisa's allegiance to a Verity she believed to be innately indifferent, at best, and outright malicious, at worst, what made her so endlessly bitter, almost cruel? Was it Mylla's fate, and the rest of the Knights' as well, to become the same?

She would lose heart if she thought about it any more. As luck would have it, or maybe wouldn't, she didn't get the chance.

Over Lock's shoulder, she could see a thin slice of the horizon beginning to darken with shadows, though the daystar glowed directly overhead. Fixating on the strange sight, she wondered if this was some kind of secondary shock and she was on the verge of passing out from the drop from the *Vigilance* after all. Then she realized what they were seeing, hundreds of the usurper's attack ships filling the sky surrounding the city of Asteryss. The sight dispelled her doubtful, anxious thoughts instantly. Which might have been nice, had they not been instantly replaced by new fear.

The hovering sickle-shaped ships had taken a defensive formation as they hung motionless in the sky like black crescent moons. Havelock eased the ship's engine down until they slid forward barely faster than a horse could trot. She guessed he didn't want to run the risk of being detected because of a draft as they flew unseen by the hovering ships, yet her instinct told her they should get past them as fast as possible. Regardless, airborne tactics, she had to admit, were not her strength. On this, she would defer to the Wing pilot.

Instead of aiming directly for the largest gap in the formation, as Mylla would have anticipated, Lock circled wide around the city until they flew past it and over the western sea, then doubled back. Did he suspect a trap? Eyes straight, lips pressed tight, she sat still as they penetrated a gap within the circle of attackers. Her dueling tensions about crashing and being detected kept her thoughts embattled until she realized they had moved past the circle undiscovered and now floated directly over the high steeple of Vigil Tower atop the city's seaward ring wall.

Occasional pillars of black smoke rose randomly throughout the city, meeting the seaward breeze and scattering before rising too high. From up here, the city seemed quiet, but the smoke belied the fact that things were not right. These were neither hearth nor forge fires but the smoldering remnants of buildings ablaze. Knowing Asteryss had been attacked and seeing it herself were two different things, and again her thoughts strayed to Lock. Asteryss, his home and where his family still lived, had stood for thousands of turns and had been peaceful since the Cataclysm seven hundred and some turns ago. Even for a soldier, such a sight would be rattling.

Nervously, she scanned ahead until spotting the corner bastions and flat roof of the Conservatum's expansive hall in the city's center. Mylla blew out her breath in relief—it was still intact—then gasped as something buzzed the glazed shield of the cockpit just in front of her eyes.

By Vaka Aster, they've found us! Frenzied signals from her brain prompted her to cry out a warning. But they were instantly overridden when she realized: *No, that wasn't one of the attackers, it was Yggo.*

The sentry's silver wings flapped ahead of them, reflecting the gleaming daystar's rays. The second hawk, Urgo, shot down from above moments later, and they flew side by side ahead of Mylla and Lock. Unlike whatever force controlled the usurper's attack ships, the bruhawks' wystic sight detected the dragørfly scout clearly, and Mylla's relief at their presence relaxed her tensed muscles. Safran was watching.

THE BRIEF RELIEF Mylla felt upon landing safely at the Conservatum lasted only as long as it took for her boots to hit the roof. They had a mission and no time for indulgences like relief. The open halls of the Resplendolent Conservatum, though lit brightly by Halla and unchanged, nevertheless pressed in forbiddingly on Mylla as she led Havelock to the last Fenestros in Vinnr.

On second thought, one thing was changed: all sounds, from the omnipresent drone of the lecture halls to the chatter of acolytes and teachers to the hurried footfalls and swishing robes of all who dwelled within, were hushed—or had been silenced. Though she and Lock made almost no noise, she worried even their own breathing might be enough to cause their discovery.

Moving with all the stealth of their respective training, they took just minutes to descend to the limestone catacombs below the ancient complex, where the smoke-tinged smell of the outside air gave way to the cooler, cleaner yet still musty odor of the tunnels. Only the highest order of Conservatum scholars, those known as the Resplendolent Prelates, and the Knights Corporealis knew of these underground passages, which eventually wound their way to other corridors, one to Vigil Tower and another to a cave mouth on the cliffside overlooking the brilliant beryl Verring Sea.

Once they reached the concealed doorway to the underground— locked, but Eisa had given Havelock a key—and entered its quiet and safe confines, Lock whispered, "I don't think I'd have found this so quickly without you, despite Stave and Eisa's directions. What is it with the Knights and caves?"

Mylla ignored the barb. "I'm glad we made it, but it was too easy. Where is everyone? The city and the Conservatum seem completely deserted."

"Hiding, maybe?"

She didn't like this. The Conservatum had too many dark corners, halls and rooms, points of egress and ingress. It hadn't been built to be a fortress, only an institution where those with both the hunger and aptitude for knowledge came to pursue either scholarship as a Prelate or priesthood as a Cyan or, for the rare few, acceptance into the Knights Corporealis and ordination by Vaka Aster. In Mylla's memory, the halls had been a place of peace and learning. And never once empty.

But it wasn't always so, Mylla, she reminded herself. *Don't let your experience cloud the history you know. There were times of unrest when the Knights Corporealis had to flee the Conservatum and even the cities and remain hidden from commoners. Being the servitors to a celestial maker marks us, and that mark isn't always understood.*

She touched the nine-pointed star on her chin thoughtfully as they stood inside the entryway to adjust to the dark they were about to enter. Through every tumult and historical uprising since its inception, the Conservatum had remained stalwart and unharrassed, the contributions made by those under its roof beyond suspicion and always too important to empires to challenge, even when others', and sometimes the Knights', deeds and intents were questioned. She recalled Arch Keeper Beatte's and Commander Brun's quick accusations beneath the keep the day prior and frowned. It seemed more than possible that the integrity and intent of the Knights would once again fall under scrutiny. All because of the actions of a marauding Verity. The taste in her mouth grew sour at the irony.

"Come on," she nudged Lock, "we've still got some distance to cover. Quietly now."

"Are there torches or illuminates? It's so dark."

Her klinkí stones rolled into her palm before he finished. With a gentle toss, she sent them airborne and blew a puff of breath in their direction. Each emitted a slowly pulsing blue glow and lit the skillfully hewn and decorated walls of the catacombs. "Follow me. Draw your sword. Stay close."

Forced to skulk, she mused at how like a low insect she felt. Being compelled to hide in her own childhood home, among the halls where she'd grown and learned and finally become worthy of the oath she'd taken to protect Vaka Aster, seemed a cruel twist of fate. As they neared the Fenestros chamber, a drawn-out shriek echoed toward them from the direction of the entrance.

Instantly, Mylla palmed her stones and snuffed their light. "Hold still," she said, though she knew it wasn't necessary to tell him.

A similar cry quickly followed the first, the noise so high-pitched it was more like pressure against the delicate membranes of her inner ear than sound. She couldn't identify it as human or animal, but it was most definitely not the hail of a welcoming party.

Lock dared a whisper. "I don't think we're alone in here."

"I concur."

"Do you have any idea what that is?"

Wind? Something large, scaly, and hungry risen from the sea? Perhaps… ghosts? "I don't, but we better hurry. Not far."

Now letting only a single klinkí stone light their way, Mylla gave up skulking and broke into a scurry. The sounds behind them drew farther apart from each other and at times closer to her and Lock, but they didn't seem to be moving intentionally toward them. Soon, she and Lock reached the simple wooden door to the celestial stone's chamber and she pushed it open. Her heart, heavy enough already, took its time on the next beat, as if laboring against the weight of boulders. "It's dark…" she muttered.

"Light it up," Lock suggested.

"No, you don't understand. The Fenestros creates its own light. It's not here."

He pushed past her into the chamber, able to make out a tabernacle carved into the far wall. An *empty* tabernacle. "Now what?" he said.

She gently closed the door behind her, careful to do it as quietly as possible. "Unroll this and hold it up for me," she said, handing him the Scrylle parchment—which she'd taken without Eisa's knowledge. Given their mission, it made sense for her to bring it, and she was glad she had listened to her instinct to snag it, as well as the instinct to do it on the sly. Her gut was telling her Eisa had an agenda that ran deeper than the one she said aloud, and Mylla never ignored her gut. "It's not far," she whispered. "Still in the catacombs, in fact." Upon closer inspection, she continued. "By Vaka Aster's light, this can't be!"

"Shh!" In the next moment, Lock's curiosity overcame his admonishment. "What do you see?"

"Brun. Commander Brun has the Fenestros."

"… This parchment even shows the name of who carries it?" He watched her face closely, looking for any sign she might have been joking. Seeing this wasn't the case, he offered, "That's good. Brun is a reasonable sort. She will likely be content to give it to the Knights when we explain why it's necessary."

"She thinks we're all traitors, Lock."

"Why?"

"I haven't got time to explain." She re-rolled the parchment and placed it back in a bandolier pouch. "We have to catch her before Balavad does."

Pacing back to the door, she drew it open—

—and looked into a dark oval of a face overshadowed by a deep hood. Yet the form was nearly as familiar as any of the Knights.

"Irrick?" she said after her throat overcame its paralysis. "Thank Vaka Aster it's you. Are you hurt?"

The acolyte, standing nose to nose with her, said nothing but reached up with white hands and pulled back the hood. His blank eyes chilled her. They seemed to be lit from within by a dull, sickly glow, and his usually umber skin carried the same pallor, corpse-blue in the light of her stones. His thin lips parted as if to speak. What came from between them, however, wasn't words.

The shrill keen he issued knocked her back. In pure reflex, she brought her fist, still gripped around the hilt of her sword, upward into his chin in a rapid undercut violent enough to sweep him from his feet. He came down hard, knocked unconscious by the weighted sucker punch. She gasped at what she'd done but couldn't deny that something was very, very wrong with her friend and Knights' ally.

Immediately, the catacombs filled with more of the screeches they'd been hearing, now moving in a direction that was undeniably directly toward them. Sheathing her sword and leaning down, she swept up one of Irrick's arms and looked to Lock. "Help me, grab his other arm. We'll lock him in the chamber. It might keep him safe." No matter what it took, she was not going to lose another friend, or leave another behind.

"Let's do this quick. We have to get out of here!"

But the day had other plans. From the far end of the corridor, seven black- and silver-clad forms appeared in the gloom, approaching on soundless feet. She and Lock froze in place, each with one of Irrick's forearms clenched in their grips. The members of the approaching party were tall, like the Yorish, and lanky, almost emaciated. *Like the priests from Battgjald,* Mylla realized. They walked bowed forward, almost as if hunchbacked, and each carried a sword with a crooked barb at the tip. The group contained both women and men, and their features were no different from hers or Havelock's. Except for one thing. Their skin, bloodlessly pale and grotesque-looking, seemed the very absence of color and heat, as if a rejection of life.

The group stopped and stood preternaturally still. Though one klinkí stone still hovered before Mylla casting its strong glow, the members of the group moved only their heads, turning them this way and that, looking or possibly *listening* for something. *They are blind*, she realized. Short chirrups and hoots came from them, as if they were querying someone. Querying Irrick, she was sure, for she couldn't deny that his eyes and flesh had taken on the same look as theirs. They had done something to him. But what? And could it be undone?

"Too many," Lock murmured. "Move back inside the chamber."

At the sound of his voice, the group of attackers' strange eyes fixed in their direction. The leader emitted another shriek, and the noise, unnatural and menacing, made Mylla's jaw tighten while her insides seemed to turn to water. They advanced forward, now with purpose, their strides jerky but able to swallow the distance between them with unexpected speed, their hooked swords raised for fighting. Jumping in front of Irrick's still form, she redrew her sword and opened her palm, already channeling the klinkí stones toward the onrushing peril.

The stones flew into the group, lighting up the ghastly, thin faces, and striking the attackers' shoulders, torsos, legs, arms. She wasn't trying to disarm them, not like she had the Dragør Marines beneath Aster Keep. She recognized a duel to the death when confronted by one. As they usually did, her klinkís created an explosion of chaos among the aggressors—but didn't stop them.

Why aren't they falling? Why aren't they bleeding?! her mind yammered. Aloud, she directed, "I'll hold them back. See to Irrick!"

Lock remained beside her, stubbornly refusing to retreat and leave her to fight alone. She continued to fling blow after blow into the group, slowing the onrush, yet they still pressed inexorably toward her and Lock. This fight would have to be won by blade-work, not by wystic stone.

The awful shrieking went on as they closed the gap. Mylla took her fighting stance, sword at the ready, and saw Lock do the same beside her.

"Direct assault, go for their heads. Forward!"

The voice caught Mylla by surprise—it hadn't come from Lock, but it didn't seem to have come from the attackers either. Then a curious thing: the light cast by the glowing stones showed new faces, familiar because they wore the helmets of the—

"Marines!" Lock said.

Someone hurled a torch into the center of the attackers. Now boxed in from in front and behind, the enemy force flailed and screeched as pandemonium took over. Some turned back, others continued forward, and Mylla let her blade have its fun. The danger of accidentally striking the troop of Marines forced her to retire her stones from the fight and leave them hovering near the ceiling, lighting up the battle. From the corner of her eye, she saw a short Marine swing a mace into the sneering visage of a marauder, caving in his skull. Instead of moving on to the next, the Marine stayed in place and swung her mace again and again, turning the obviously dead attacker's head into pudding. Only then did she rejoin the fray.

"That's it, Marines! Not a skull left intact!"

Brun?

Mylla and Lock stood back to back, parrying and gouging, thrusting and swinging, managing over and over to puncture and hack their attackers but without obvious effect. Even wounded, the pale fighters barely slowed. She heard a grunt behind her, and Lock's back shifted, catching her off guard with the sudden absence of a counterweight. She staggered back but would have kept her balance if not for Irrick's still form tripping her up. Even as she came down on top of him, an attacker brought his blade down over her in a wicked chop. She got her own sword up to ward off the blow and kicked out into the attacker's shins. He shrieked, then was spun halfway around as someone sliced into his flank. With a lunge, she was back on her feet, but in moments the Marines had finished off the rest of them and smashed the brains from the heads of the two opposing her and Lock.

She looked up and came eye to eye with Brun's steel. Again.

"Knight Evernal," the commander said from behind it. "You'll understand if I don't seem surprised to find you here."

With a blink, Mylla pulled her stones to her and set them into a shield pattern between her and the commander. Brun twitched, but she did not drop her sword.

CHAPTER TWENTY-FIVE

Jaemus studied Aldinhuus for a while as he stared into the sphere atop the thing called a Scrylle. Aldinhuus's reverence and concentration were written in the way the skin beside his strange eyes creased and his lips pressed together into thin lines. What in this world or any other could he be looking at? With a clammy tickle along his spine, he said, "What is it that you're doing now exactly?"

Barely sparing the breath it took to say it, Aldinhuus replied, "Quiet." A moment later, he whispered, "By the fates, so that's what's become of your maker."

Feeling his advantage rapidly slipping away, Jaemus employed his usual, arguably unwise, tenacity. "Listen, we need to have a discussion about what's going on here. That Scrylle is mine and—"

Before he could finish, the lights inside the ship suddenly went out, pitching them into darkness except for the glowing orb.

"What..." was all he had time to say before the angry buzz of overcharged power couplings filled the hold. Within seconds, the floor hatch slid open, and light from outside rose like a specter through the opening.

"Bardgrim, we have the ship surrounded," warned an amplified voice. "Come out, and do it without anything in your hands."

"Aaaand now this," he muttered.

Aldinhuus asked sharply, "Do you know who's out there? What they want?"

As he started to answer, he noticed another light, not the orb itself but a strange bluish glow—make that *two* strange glows. Aldinhuus's eyes, lit like the orb before him as if they shared the same inner spark. Unnerved, Jaemus still managed a response. "Yes, it's my former crew. The Glisternauts of the *Bounding Skate*, here to collect what they think is rightfully theirs."

"What did you steal?"

"Steal?" The very word offended him. "'Claimed' you mean. The *Octopod* is mine." As if to emphasize this, he patted the wall. "I designed it, I fly it, I created the power harness that gives it the juice to continue forever, thanks to the Verity stone. My crew didn't believe me when I said it was our ticket to the stars, and I was stripped of rank and station for the heresy of implying its power might actually come from the Creatress. So I decided to prove it before they could lock me up. You see, we Himmingazians have little tolerance for superstition or claims of divine beings and creators. We *require* proof."

Though the darkness shadowed the Knight's face, Jaemus could hear the light contempt in his voice. "You've seen the stone and what it can do for yourself. What more proof could be required?" Without giving him time to respond, Aldinhuus went on, "What will happen now?"

From outside: "Bardgrim, you have till the count of three. One…"

"They'll collect me, well, *us* I assume, and lock us in the brig."

"Two…"

"I won't be locked up, Bardgrim."

"Three."

"It's not as if they're giving you a—hey! Don't do that!"

The Knight had, unsurprisingly, let free his flying trove of kinky stones, and they hovered in a swarm above the hatch, ready for anyone or anything that might appear. Before someone entered and found their head filled with a few extra eye sockets, Jaemus took two long paces toward the hatch, ducked under the stones, and positioned himself on the ladder. "Coming out! Peacefully!" He shouted the last word at Aldinhuus, then said quietly before descending, "Let me handle this. Don't hurt anyone, Aldinhuus. These are my friends, even if we're on a bit of hiatus."

When his boots hit the slick stones below, he slowly turned with his hands out to the side and saw five Glisternauts lined up just outside the hull's protective shelter. Their flight uniforms repelled the constant rain, but Jaemus knew from experience the incessant drips would be finding their way inside the crew's collars and prickling their skin. The two 'Nauts on each flank held their right arms out, brandishing shelk-sies—wrist-borne shullet launchers. Captain Cote Illago stood in the center, the rain running down his face making his angry expression shift dynamically.

Jaemus spoke. "I suppose it wasn't hard to guess I'd come here."

Cote remained silent. Knowing the Glisternaut captain as Jaemus did proved to be unhelpful in this scenario. He couldn't decide if Cote was angrier about Jaemus's abduction—*reclamation*, he reminded himself—of the *Octopod* or about finding him at the forbidden temple. Their last argument had been loud enough to echo throughout the *Bounding Skate*'s corridors, and had probably been echoed a second time among the crew as they passed the story from one to another.

Two cycles prior, their argument had been raging long enough that it had become clear to them both a truce would not be reached—and Cote would have to arrest him. After a bellowed curse, Cote had slammed his hand on a tabletop in his cabin and growled, "You'll put this matter aside, once and for all, Jae, or I won't be able to stop the fallout you know is coming."

He'd responded, "You've seen what the stone can do. You think someone like me, someone with this much brilliance, could ignore the possibilities? Look outside, for the Glister Cloud's sake! How many more anni-cycles does Himmingaze have before everything is as sodden as your brain? And you won't even give me a chance? Couldn't there be some truth to the myths of the Creatress, even if those truths are buried under endless cycles of superstition and distortion?"

"I'll not have the word 'Creatress' spoken aboard the *Skate*. This is a serious matter, and you know it. You can't be heard giving credence to any of those lies. Not you, Jaemus, Glint Engineer. You *are* the standard of reason and rationalism in our fleet. What you're saying is… treason." With reluctance, even regret, he'd finished, "And it's my duty to stamp treason out before it flares."

Jaemus had stared into his stern face, looking for a crack in his visage, a softening that showed he hadn't meant it, but found nothing. "Slavery to tradition and ignorance may kill us faster than the Glister Cloud, *Captain*. Are you really a Glisternaut, or just a drudge?"

He knew he shouldn't have said it, but by that point it had been too late. He couldn't take it back.

"Get out." Cote's lips had gone colorless as he tightened them against whatever harsh words he might have said. His hands had hung clenched into fists at his side.

The fight had been the final push. Jaemus couldn't continue to waste his time trying to rally the Glisternauts to a cause they purposely chose to ignore, even at their peril. And fighting with Cote hurt more than the knock to his reputation. Win or lose, he didn't have the stomach, much less the patience, for it anymore. So Jaemus had left Cote's cabin and stolen the *Octopod* (*claimed!*—he again reminded himself) before the 'Nauts who'd been called to apprehend him could do it, then fought the storm for three full cycles to get here to Isle Stonering. For all his wits, however, he clearly hadn't thought his plan through well enough to evade his own crew. Maybe he'd wanted to get caught. Maybe he was tired of the dread, of feeling helpless against a Great Cosmos that cared nothing for the people who lived in it. Though, if what his new acquaintance said was true, his dread and helplessness were both prescient and well-founded. So what options did that leave him?

He looked over his shoulder to see if Aldinhuus had followed him, but he hadn't appeared. "Captain Illago, I am not here alone. I have someone with me I think you should meet. And, if you can find it in that stubborn—" He caught himself, stopped, restarted. "In your wisdom as a Glisternaut commander to listen to what he has to say and see what he might show you—"

Cote cut him off. "Search the ship and tie the traitor's hands. Former Glint Engineer Jaemus Bardgrim, you're being constrained and charged with treason and the theft of a Glisternaut craft. If you care to ever speak as a free man again, you'll shut your mouth until… until I can stand to listen to you."

Jaemus hesitated, if for no other reason than because he disliked either of his two options: resist or give up. The decision lost its meaning a moment later when, before anyone moved, a column of lightning so wide it seemed to immerse the entire island flared around them. Jaemus felt as if a base drum had been planted in his midsection and struck by a giant. Instead of a flash of white, the world flared brilliant blue for a moment before his eyes snapped closed and he clapped his hands over his ears… despite the pointlessness of it.

I'm not dead? he thought after a few ticks. The lightning, *it might have been lightning*, had dispersed without turning him to ash, or even singing him. He heard a man yell incoherently and another cry, "What it the Cloud are they?" and finally braved a peek.

The air surrounding him and the crew teemed with small flying *things*. Dozens, *hundreds*, of them darted around the discombobulated crew, speeding toward their eyes, then veering off before striking, apparently in some kind of coordinated attack. One of the crew members fired off his shelksie wildly, a shullet hitting the hull of the *Octopod* and ricocheting off into the heedless downpour. None of the swooping insectile things came at Jaemus, but he fell to his stomach anyway, more concerned with being accidentally shot than accidentally… flown into?

Behind him, he heard the crunch of boots landing on the rock. The Knight. He looked over his shoulder and saw the man appraising the melee, his klinkí stones floating above his palms. His face showed no hint of surprise—he seemed almost to be in a trance—and the strange deep-blue hue of his eyes swirled in a glowing miasma. Were these insects something else he'd brought from his own world? (Was he really starting to think the man had come from another world?) At the moment, Jaemus wouldn't have discounted anything, even if a Verity itself had ripped open the sky and peered through a gap in reality with the grin of madness on its face.

"What are you—" he started to ask, but there really wasn't a need, was there? It was obvious what the man was about to do. Attack his crew, maybe lethally. He'd already promised he wouldn't stand for being locked up.

"No, not today, Master Knight. Not any day."

Jaemus rolled to his back and kicked out. His boot heel struck Aldinhuus's shin, causing the Knight to yelp. Aldinhuus's eyes shimmered, enraged, and Jaemus knew what would come next—kinky stone oblivion. Well, it appeared he hadn't fully thought this through. Again. With wide eyes, he braced for the inevitable.

Instead, he got lucky. Suddenly, the Knight slapped a hand to the side of his neck, his own eyes widening in shock, then toppled backward as his kinky stones fell harmlessly to the ground and dimmed. His booted feet twitched once, twice, then he was still.

Almost as if called away, the flying things ceased their assault and disappeared in the Glister Dim sky, their glittering wings quickly lost in the ever-falling rain. Jaemus sat up and once more raised his arms. He leaned over Aldinhuus, who's eyes showed deep confusion at his sudden inability to move, and noted the finger-long shullet the Knight had yanked from his neck—too late to stop its paralyzing venom from taking effect. Feeling inexplicably bad for the stunned and disabled foreigner, even as he tamped down against dark hilarity wanting to bubble up from his core, he said, "Don't worry, Master Knight. It's only temporary. But let that be a lesson to you."

He stood and turned to face the Glisternauts. Cote remained with his feet planted and his shelksie arm still in position to take another shot should it require more than one to keep the frozen Knight down. The rest of the Glisternauts regathered their formation, and their dignity.

Hands held up, palms out, Jaemus said, "Cote, I have *a lot* to tell you. But first, don't the Glisternauts have a rule about giving a prisoner a stiff drink before throwing him into the brig? If not, I insist we start."

CHAPTER TWENTY-SIX

Mylla locked eyes with Brun, neither blinking, and cast about for what to say to break the impasse: *We're not your enemies. We fight for the same cause. ... By Vaka Aster's light, when was the last time you had that blade shined? It looks like you've been using it as a garden trowel!* She disregarded the last option out of hand.

Lock spoke. "Commander, Dragør Wing Pilot Havelock Rekkr, reporting in."

Brun's gaze shifted to him. "Wing? How did you get here?" She turned. "Owers! You told me your entire squad went down defending the city."

A bedraggled Marine pushed past the troop of twelve. His uniform differed from the others, first because it didn't include a helmet, and second because it was made of royal-blue leather instead of plate armor. A lavishly detailed red and green flying creature, the famed dragør of the Dragør Marines, was embossed on the leather suit's torso, the emblem of the Wings and a match to Lock's own uniform.

"Jimp!" Lock said, overjoyed.

"By my wings," the advancing Marine said, "you made it!"

The two embraced and gave each other's backs good-natured pats.

Mylla heard Owers whisper to Lock, "Don't worry, brother, I covered for you."

Lock drew up straight and said quickly, loudly enough for Brun to hear, "You should get your eyes checked, Jimp. You must have mistaken my ship for another's." He turned back to the commander: "There's a bit… more to the story."

Brun's hard glare stayed on him another moment, then she finally eased back and lowered her sword. "Is it a story, or is it intelligence, Wing? Because right now what we need is as much intelligence and information as we can get. What do you know about this attack force? Not a single other Wing lived to share a word about what we're up against—not that we haven't all seen it for ourselves."

Beside Mylla, Lock struggled to speak and looked at Jimp, who nodded gravely. So Safran and Stave's description of the usurper's massive airborne force hadn't been exaggerated. Mylla could only imagine the shock and despair Lock was experiencing right now. But deep within, she realized her own most prevalent feeling was something entirely different. Gratitude. He was only alive right now because he had chosen to aid her when she'd asked. Owers was alive because Symvalline had taken his ship. Once this sank in, the scope of the destruction of Asteryss staggered her.

Brun went on before Lock found words. "Let's not talk here. The Marines—those of us who are left—secured a safe room in the catacombs. It's only a matter of time until more Raveners find us, but we're regrouping down here and readying our next wave of attacks. Which" —her usually stern features sagged for a moment—"if things continue the way they have been, might be our last. Come with us."

With an inward sigh of relief, Mylla palmed her stones. An uneasy impasse was better than no impasse, she reasoned. "Brun, how did you know about the catacombs?"

"It's my job to know how to keep Asteryss safe. It may surprise you to learn that the Knights aren't nearly as much of a mystery to us commoners as you think."

The Marine commander spun around to dissuade further discussion, but Mylla reached out to stop her with a hand on her shoulder.

"Commander, wait. Do you have the Fenestros that was in this chamber?"

Brun faced her, but something at Mylla's feet caught her eyes and she said, "It looks like we have another live one. Furthsom, Gann, tie him up and gag him. He's coming with us."

Furthsom—Mylla recognized him from yesterday's fray beneath the keep—passed the still-burning torch that had been thrown amid the attackers to another Marine and stepped forward to bind Irrick. Before that could happen, Mylla put up a hand. "What are you doing? This is my friend. Acolyte Irrick, one of the members of the Conservatum. He's not an enemy."

"He's been converted, Mylla. Like everyone else in the Conservatum," Brun said coldly. "We need information, he may have it."

She could guess what Brun meant by "converted," but the implications of the commander's orders disturbed her more.

Before she could continue to argue, Lock said calmly, "Mylla, we're in the open here and the commander has a place to go that's more defensible. If more of these"—he looked to Brun—"what did you call them? Raveners? If more are roving around, we'd be better off with the Marines. Can we just go with them for now, find out what's happened in Asteryss?"

She hesitated, not trusting Brun's intentions for her friend.

Lock continued, now speaking to Brun. "Do you have a healer?"

Brun looked momentarily confused by the question, then nodded, blank-faced.

"We can get Irrick the help he needs," Lock finished.

Sighing, Mylla let herself be persuaded. But first she had to know: "The Fenestros, Brun, where is it?"

Brun regarded her darkly for a moment, then said: "Safe. Now come on."

"You're bleeding."

Soldiers, many wrapped in blood-stained bandages, filled the chamber Brun led them to, which made Lock's statement hard to follow at first.

"Your arm," he said with more urgency as he gently touched her elbow, "let me see it. How bad is it?"

She looked at her shoulder and realized what was causing him concern. "Ah, it's fine. See? Already clotting. The attacker just grazed me," she said and rolled her shoulder back and forth to show him the superficiality of the wound. In fact, the Ravener had struck deep enough she'd felt the vibration from the force shimmy down her spine. A commoner would spend weeks in recovery and possibly lose the arm. As a perk of being instilled by a Verity's spark, she'd be as good as new within moments and wouldn't even have a scar. Knights only retained the scars they'd acquired before ordination, and some, like Stave, wore theirs with pride, a memory of life before.

"You sure?" His eyes bounced between her arm and her face, the concern in them heartbreaking in its depth.

She put her free hand over his and promised, "Yes, love."

Brun broke free of a group of Marines and approached. "Evernal," she said, "we've got a few injured, as you can see. Our healer is over-worked. Can you… do anything for them?"

The request took Mylla by surprise. "I'm not sure. Do you mean can I heal them with my 'wystic magic'?" The words Brun had used to level accusations at the Knights beneath the keep yesterday still rankled her.

The commander scowled, then said, "That's exactly what I mean." She sighed heavily and reached up to remove her helmet. Her disheveled black hair, matted with sweat and dirt, spilled free of the knot she'd tied it in. These soldiers had been fighting nonstop for two days, Mylla realized. It was remarkable Brun was even still standing, much less able to continue mounting a resistance. "Look, yesterday I saw the sky open up and an army of winged phantom killers enter Vinnr. I've seen my soldiers, my own Arch Keeper, and countless people of Asteryss, maybe even all of Ivoryss, changed by some monstrous means into pale husks with no memory of themselves or with whom their loyalties lie. While these may not be the works of a celestial sprite, I'm willing to treat them as such until things are fixed and this Holiness desecrator is dead or banished back to wherever he came from. Word is already spreading through the mouths of the usurper's soldiers we've interrogated that you Knights Corporealis have bounties on your heads, so you're obviously not the enemies my blade wants to stick. Which makes us allies—until further notice."

Mylla's mind reeled at this news. A bounty? The Arch Keeper turned into a pale husk? And, most disconcerting of all, they were now *allies*? "Brun, slow down, I don't know what you're talking about. But to answer your question, no, I can't heal these soldiers. Rejuvenation only works for those sworn to Vaka Aster who've received her mark." She pointed to her chin star. "I would offer to help, but time and circumstance necessitate that you give me the Fenestros. Now. I have to get back to the Knights."

"If you'd not noticed, we have a war going on here," Brun responded.

"And giving me that stone is the only means of winning it." She was stretching the truth, but Brun didn't need to know that. "Why did you take it anyway? You don't believe in Vaka Aster and the power of her artifacts."

"To keep it out of the usurper's hands. Obviously, it was the right choice."

The commander spoke as gruffly as usual, but Mylla noticed how her eyes fell aside and her volume wavered. Brun *did* still believe in the Verities. And she was probably as shaken to realize it and by the cause that made her.

Brun went on. "What I can't help but wonder is why, if the Knights think it's important, you weren't here sooner to get it."

Mylla wasn't going to take the bait. Time was too short and Brun was showing her usual willingness to be reasoned with, which was to say, none. As Mylla considered her next words, the guards holding Irrick brushed past, pushing the acolyte toward the far end of the chamber. He walked on his own, unbalanced and lumbering as if drunk, with a torn bit of cloth in his mouth and knotted behind his head. She watched the soldiers urge him, none too gently into a group of four more Marines against the back wall. They stood in obvious sentry formation and parted when Irrick's group arrived, giving Mylla a look at what, or rather *whom*, they guarded.

"Wait," she demanded. "What's going on back there? Was that one of the usurper's forces?"

"They're called Raveners, Mylla, at least that's what they call themselves, according to our friend in the back. He's been a *fount* of information. We just had to find the right motivation."

If Brun had so much as twitched her mouth to smirk, Mylla might have given her the same treatment with the pommel of her sword as she had Irrick and not have regretted it. Torture—the thought turned her stomach. "So that's how you knew you had to strike them in the head to kill them…" she murmured.

"No, that we learned by experience. It'll be interesting to find out if the acolyte can tell us anything more than this one."

"Let Irrick go," she warned, anger frosting the edges of her voice.

"That's not going to happen."

Before she'd finished the statement, Mylla's wrist twisted, freeing her klinkí stones—but Lock's grip stayed her attack. "Mylla, wait. Please for the love of life, don't do anything rash."

The room grew still around them, all eyes on the confrontation, all hands on weapon hafts.

Lock made a sound as if clearing his throat, the noise a dry and strained croak. "Commander, could you and I speak in private? Let me explain things? I think I may be able to broker a more conducive arrangement—for all."

Mylla glared at him.

"Commander?" he said, refusing to meet her stare.

Brun nodded and gestured with her chin. "Over there."

"Mylla, perhaps you could join Irrick? Nothing will happen with you watching over him. Right, Commander?"

Brun grunted noncommittally and turned on her heels, pacing beneath a sconce on the nearby wall to wait.

Mylla pulled her arm free of his hand and snapped, "What are you going to tell her?"

"The truth, love, just the truth." His mouth twitched in an attempt at a reassuring smile. "She's obviously seen the usurper Verity for what he is. Perhaps I can reason with her enough to force her mind to believe what her guts are telling her is true. If she can accept the Verity is not just smoke and mirrors, she'll accept that the Knights are the ones with the best weapons to fight him. She is a practical person. She'll come around."

"Just get the Fenestros so we can get out of here," she said shortly, then spun and walked to Irrick, forcing herself to ignore the commander and Lock's huddle. The information he'd divulge about the Knights far surpassed anything Brun could suspect, and under ordinary circumstances Mylla would never let him speak of the things he'd seen—but these circumstances were not ordinary, and Brun would obviously not be swayed by the "smoke and mirrors" of Mylla's Order.

She eyed the sentries standing between her and the acolyte. The nearest, a smooth-faced younger man no taller than Stave but twice as broad, held up a hand to stop her advance. "Sorry, Knight, we got these 'uns under strict control. Not to be disturbed."

His proclamation came out more weary than confrontational, and Mylla found herself sympathizing with these Marines for the trials they must have experienced in the last day, were *still* experiencing. She stopped. "You've been in the fighting outside? Do you know what has happened in Asteryss?"

The four of them turned their eyes to her, each regarding her with the typical mix of apprehension and awe with which most commoners viewed the Knights. "Aye," said the first. "The word is no battle has been this bad since the three kingdoms' war." His eyes brightened. "Were you... did you fight in that war?"

She cut off a tired laugh. The War of Rivening had been over two millennia ago. None of the living Knights had seen it. "No, I'm only three hundred and forty-two turns a Knight. That was long before my time. Or even the Stall—" Her voice caught in her throat. Speaking of Ulfric unsettled her.

Now their eyes held more awe than apprehension, as if the truth of the Knights' longevity made sense for the first time. "But you don't look a minute older than me," the smooth-faced man said.

"How old are you?"

"Twenty-seven turns and a winter."

"I was thirty-three when I took the oath. Acolyte Irrick, whom you hold there, will be thirty-eight this turn. He will be a Knight someday —" *if Vaka Aster ever comes back to us*, she didn't add. "He has spent his entire life devoted to serving our Verity, and our world." Softly, she continued, "And he is a friend. Please, let me speak with him."

The first guard looked right and left at his compatriots, gauging their willingness to let the bonds of friendship and fraternity, a value that lived in the core of every soldier, overcome their orders. Then he lowered his hand and turned to let her pass. "Do us a favor, huh, and don't get us in trouble."

"I give my word," she said, her gratitude carried by her tone.

Stepping past them, her eyes fell first on the attacker called a Ravener. Like those they'd fought in the passageway, this one's wounds, of which there were many, did not seem to bleed. Gashes to his arms and face gaped, the white, lifeless-looking flesh making her queasy in a way the sight of blood never had. The Marines had lashed his oddly long hands with a heavy rope to a metal sconce overhead, forcing him to remain upright, hunched over and barely keeping his feet. As Mylla stood there, he raised his head and brought his eyes to her face. Though his eyes were clouded, he bore no expression but hate.

"What are you?" she whispered, not expecting a response.

The Ravener's throat tightened, as if he intended to scream, but the gag on his face stopped anything but a muffled gurgle from breaking through. Unnerved, Mylla turned away and knelt to Irrick, who'd been tied with his hands behind his back and pushed to sit on the floor. "Irrick? It's Mylla Evernal. Do you see me?"

When he did not respond, she reached her hand to his chin, strangely unmarked by the blow she'd landed, and lifted it so she could see into eyes. They gazed at nothing, their vacancy far more than surface deep. The scholar she knew as Irrick wasn't present in this body. Whatever had happened to him seemed to have drained anything of the man away and left this... husk. *Brun called this "converted." He's become more like a corpse than a person.*

"Marine," she said as she rose, "do you know what's happened to cause this?"

"No, not with any certainty. All any of us have seen are loads of people being taken at sword point inside the flying black fortress. When they're released, they're like your friend there. Like they've had the life drained right out of them but can still walk around. Worse, whatever the Raveners are doing to them is turning them against their own people. Everyone who's come back to Asteryss has taken up arms against us."

"How many people has this happened to?"

It took him a moment to put what he'd witnessed into words. "Nearly everyone, Knight. The whole city, at least those the Raveners didn't kill outright for opposing them. The usurper's forces breached Asteryss's wall and boundary defenses in less than two hours and took the city by nightfall. No one's seen or heard from the Arch Keeper either. We're assuming she's dead."

Not a coup, as Eisa predicted it would be, Mylla thought. *Balavad was in a hurry to take Asteryss, maybe all of Ivoryss. He must have believed his plan to cage Vaka Aster had succeeded and he had no more need to be discreet. But he was wrong; the vessel is still safe.* A new urgency rode the heels of this last thought: *I have to get the Fenestros back to the* Vigilance—*now.*

She murmured her thanks and started toward where Brun and Lock still stood. His hands waved in the air, the gestures of a man wielding every ounce of his powers of persuasion in his argument. Brun's staid position didn't change, and her lips pressed tightly together as if to smother the words behind them. Mylla didn't like what she saw.

Before she reached them, the chamber door resonated with three short knocks, and the entire room of soldiers froze. Two more quick raps, a pause, and a final series of three followed, and the nearest Marine finally pulled the bars holding the door closed. As Mylla continued to Brun and Lock, another soldier, after conferring with the one who'd opened the door, advanced toward the Marine commander too. They arrived at the same time.

"Commander—" the older Marine said.

"Brun—" Mylla said.

Brun's hand shot up to silence her, the Marine, and Lock in a single, commanding gesture. She turned to the new Marine, "What news?"

"Commander," the man repeated behind a thick gray mustache as bedraggled as his voice, "the city is done. We've only five squads, scattered, who can still fight. But worse—the desecrator's fortress has been seen once more in the sky. It will be unleashing a new swarm any moment."

Brun took in the news without a visible reaction, then said, "Captain, you know as well as I that we cannot hold back more than we've already done." The Marine didn't reply, and Brun's brows knit in a cascade of wrinkles as she scowled. "There's nothing left to do but retreat to Magdaster. If we get there before the usurper's forces, we'll join Nennus's legion and prepare to mount a solid fight."

"You believe the Raveners will take the fight there?" the Marine asked.

"It's where Ivoryss's second-largest force is. Their intention is to take over the kingdom. Where else would they go?" She grabbed a water jug from a nearby table and passed it to the captain, who drank deeply. "Return topside, send word to all the remaining forces you can find and bring them here to the tunnels. We'll escape by sea and make haste to Magdaster. This will have to be done by stealth. Fate forbid we have to fight our way through soldiers who used to be our own forces."

"And what of the remaining citizens, those who can't fight?"

"We can't help them if we're dead. They'll have to stay hidden until we can bring reinforcements."

"You know what will happen to them." The older Marine's words carried no hint of a wish to dissuade the commander, only weary resignation.

Brun put her hand on his pauldron. "We'll come back for them when this is over."

The Marine gave a curt nod, then turned sharply and was gone.

"Commander—" Mylla started again, knowing it was now or never to force Brun to turn over the Fenestros before the Dragør Marines retreated from Asteryss.

Once more, Brun stopped her. "Take it, Knight." Her hand went into a bandolier pouch and brought out the stone. "I don't know what good I can make of it."

Momentarily wrong-footed by this unexpected turn, Mylla cast about for words. "Thank you. You've done the right thing to put your trust in the Knights Corporealis."

"Trust?" She sneered. "Hardly. I don't trust anyone but other Marines." She glanced at Lock. "And Wings. But we've lost Asteryss and we're not far from losing Ivoryss completely. I don't know what your handful of wystics think they can do with these trinkets, but you're not worth the effort to fight over it. Go, leave. Abandon Ivoryss on your flying warship." Brun must have caught the look Mylla shot Lock. Did he have to reveal the *Vigilance*? "Yes, Mylla, it seems I am guilty of underestimating just how little fealty you Knights have to Ivoryss, the kingdom that's sheltered your kind for how many turns? What's it matter now?" With a look of dismissal, too final to even show further disgust, Brun turned on her heels and began rallying her remaining forces. After barking a few commands, she turned back to the still-silent Knight. "If your kind ever gives a damn enough to redeem yourselves, then figure out how to undo whatever vile desecration the usurper is doing to our people. Maybe your wysticism and your *Verity* stones can actually do some good."

Redeem themselves? From what? "What about Irrick?" Mylla said, unwilling to leave without him, though she hadn't yet figured out how to take him with her and Lock.

Instead of responding, Brun yelled to the sentries, "Kill the Ravener, we haven't room enough or any more time for him. The other one"— she finished the Order while staring at Mylla—"is the Knight's problem."

In a storm of precision chaos, the Marines gathered their equipment, their wounded, and their provisions. Before Mylla had more than blinked, they started through the tunnels, leaving the chamber eerily quiet. Only she, Lock, Irrick, and a handful of bloodied bandages on the floor and a single torch remained.

She placed the glowing Fenestros in a pouch, then looked to Lock. "I'm not sure how we're going to take Irrick with us, but we have to..." Something in his face as he stared through the open chamber door made her trail off. "Lock." After a moment without receiving a response, she tried again. "Lock?"

When he faced her, he wore an expression of sorrow so dark he was almost unrecognizable. "I think I understand now why you wanted to leave me behind."

A lump that tasted of fear and faltering courage formed in her throat. "What?"

"She's right, Vaka Aster help me, Commander Brun is right, Mylla. Why would the Knights keep such advantages like your ships and your weapons to yourselves? Do you know how many people might have been saved if Ivoryss had weapons that strong? The kingdom might have stood a chance."

His words hit like an uppercut. "You must understand, the Knights are sworn to serve Vaka Aster and protect her vessel. We aren't Marines, or soldiers, not for any kingdom. We protect the *world*, Lock. If the vessel were ever destroyed, the world would end with it. You see that, don't you?"

His eyes, still on her face, glazed as he fought a battle in his mind. Desperate, she grabbed the neck of his leather armor. *"Don't you?"* she repeated.

"What is a world without the people in it?" he murmured, stepping backward until her arms had to extend fully to maintain her grip. Gently, he took her hands and pulled them free. "I think... I think my place is here now. I am a Dragør Wing Marine. And after seeing the acolyte and hearing Brun... the things the usurper is doing to our people, or rather, to *my* people—it's worse than prison or death. My family... I can't leave them to this. If this is their fate, I need to know for myself what has become of them. There's nothing more I can do for the Knights." He struggled to force the next words free from his chest. "Like you said, I'm not one of you."

Wildly, she begged, "Then *become* one of us. I will vouch for you and solicit Vaka Aster for your ordination."

He released her hands, and with a frown, he said, "Even *if* Vaka Aster were here to swear allegiance to, how could I serve her when she allowed *this* to happen?"

Helplessly, Mylla balled her hands into fists. "I don't have an answer to that."

The remained silent for another moment. Finally, Lock turned his head to where Irrick, still vacant and motionless, slouched. "Take the acolyte and go back to the *Vigilance*, Mylla. And do what you can to put an end to this."

Her skin went cold, and from a throat that felt as if it were made of knotty wood, she managed to croak, "Don't forget that I love you, Lock. And I'll find you when this is over."

Without another word, he spun to the door and loped after the retreating Marines. Mylla's heart shivered, and she thought of calling after him. But didn't.

In a daze, she collected Irrick, still bound, and dragged him through the tunnels and the Conservatum above to the scout, uncaring who or what may have awaited her in the halls. But she saw and heard no one until she reached the ship. Over the city loomed a behemoth, it's hull blackened matte steel, its size so immense it almost appeared to be a small moon. She didn't need anyone to tell her it was the usurper's warship, but its presence didn't deter her from rushing Irrick to the imperceptible dragørfly scout and disembarking. It wasn't until she felt the dampness of her tunic collar as she approached the docking bay of the *Vigilance* that she realized how long she'd been crying.

CHAPTER TWENTY-SEVEN

Ulfric heard flittering noises, like dry leaves brushing against one another in a light breeze, but seemingly coming from inside his head rather than from outside. He lay prone on some kind of bench or table. He detected voices and so remained quiet, listening. There were two, definitely *not* in his head this time, underscored by a dull hum that reminded him of flying aboard the *Vigilance*.

One of the voices said, "Jaemus, you must have completely lost your mind. It's the only explanation."

"Every word of it's true, on my reputation as an engineer. I think this man can help the Glisternauts." That was the Himmingazian.

"A man who jumps from the ceiling of a temple to its stone floor is exactly the kind of man who would say he comes from another world. How can you believe such muddle-mindedness?"

"I was there! I saw it, Cote. I know I can't convince you—and I'm actually glad that's the case. Just talk to him, when he wakes up, just talk to him yourself."

He heard a sigh, the kind that said *Enough is enough* more plainly than words could. "We've locked up the artifacts that belonged to the old Verity cult. Maybe without them so readily available, you'll find your way to making sense again. I can only protect you so much, but if you continue to dabble in the forbidden, you're pushing me too far." The speaker sighed again. "We'll be at the capital in a bit under a full cycle. You and your friend can discuss it with the Crest Council. But I'm done listening to this. I'll have food brought."

The next thing Ulfric heard was a hiss—a door opening?—and receding footsteps.

"Tinnyrot and foolishness," Bardgrim said beneath his breath and, as far as Ulfric could tell, sat down heavily.

For his part, Ulfric stayed still with his eyes shut. After what had happened at Bardgrim's craft, he didn't yet feel ready to open them. When Bardgrim had exited, he'd remained inside, listening to the exchange between the Himmingazian and the same man who was just here—wherever *here* was—wishing just as strongly as any soldier prepping for a battle that had yet to begin that he could see what was happening on the ground outside the ship.

The next moment, the world had filled with the cerulean blue light he associated with Vaka Aster, and when it faded, he'd suddenly seemed to have the capacity to see—not with his own two eyes but with *hundreds*. The sensation of flying coupled with a view through optics that were nothing like his own, so completely un-human, had nearly bowled him over. Yet, oddly, he'd known what it was.

The dragørflies, Vaka Aster's favored sentries, had somehow come along the starpath at his wish and, as if sensing the danger the newcomers represented, they began to sow chaos. All the while, he'd seen what they saw, the same way Knight Glór could see through the bruhawks' eyes. Fascination and bumfuzzlement alike had taken over as he witnessed the assault, all prompted by his simple desire to know what was going on.

Presently, not quite idly, he wondered what else he was now capable of after coming so far through the stars and unfamiliar realities. First a new language, now the dragørflies. What else? Was Vaka Aster somehow with him, aiding him in some way?

In a spin that was becoming familiar, his thoughts snapped back to his pain. Did it matter what new qualities he possessed? His beloved heartmatch and daughter, lost now to him forever, were all that had ever really mattered.

They live, Stallari. Let me speak.

He clamped his mind against that voice, too strange to allow free rein, too dangerous to allow it to give him hope.

From Bardgrim, he heard, "Never fall in love, friend. Even if your heart doesn't end up in a virtual prison, you may very well end up in an actual one. Case in point."

He remained silent, wondering what the Himmingazian could be talking about.

"C'mon. I know you're awake. I can hear you, er, *listening.* Sorry about that kick. I just didn't want you going off half-cocked. The Glisternauts aren't bad people, just people in a bad situation. And Cote and I are in a spat to end them all."

Ah, his shin. He'd forgotten about Bardgrim sucker-kicking him. In any case, it hadn't even bruised. It wasn't that easy to stop a Knight. The dart that had penetrated his neck and dropped him like a hammerblow, however—he'd be glad to have the recipe for that toxin. Sending his heart into another tailspin, he thought, *Sym would know what it was made of. Or she'd figure it out before Halla went down.*

He cleared his throat and finally sat up. Cracking an eyelid, *carefully,* he peered in the direction of Bardgrim's voice. The world still wavered in its writhing hues and glowing depths, so he kept his eyes slitted. "It is never wrong for one to love their duty. It is, in fact, the deepest honor." His own voice, but blackened by bitterness, whispered in his head, *And your duty? What good has it done you?* He silenced it.

Eagerly the Himmingazian responded, "No hard feelings then, huh?" After a moment of silence, he went on. "Duty? No, no, I'm talking about Cote. Fourteen anni-cycles together, every holiday and celebration they could spent together, every single promotion ceremony celebrated together—and does he give me the benefit of the doubt? Does he even listen? Not that he ever has, but this one time… still, nope. All I get are bars and his clenched jaw. He prefers the dogma enforced by the Crest Council and the rest of the Himmingazians over the genius his own lifemate.

Which is me, by the way, both a genius and his lifemate." He sighed. "Love is prison, Master Knight. Best stick to your… I don't know… your duty. At least you can't have a knife poked in your duty like you can your heart."

A laugh flavored with acid bubbled up Ulfric's throat, but he choked it back. What this commoner didn't know was better for him. Ulfric's duty, always followed, seventeen hundred turns of it, and yet here he was. Behind bars, his family most likely dead, abandoned by his Verity. The Himmingazian could not even fathom the sour irony in his advice. "Fourteen anything is an eye blink," he muttered, lost in his dark thoughts.

"Yeah? You sound like a man who knows what I'm talking about. Are you married then?"

Tears burned and he squeezed his eyes tightly shut. "My adored and I have been together for nearly five hundred turns."

"Turns, huh? You mean like anni-cycles? Sure, sure," Bardgrim said. "After a certain amount of time, I can understand how it would seem that way." Ulfric heard him shift, then say, "Are… are you all right?"

No longer listening, he tilted his head back, willing the pain to a dark corner of his heart, feeling the poison slowly killing it.

Isemay…

Her hair was copper, his little daughter's, as bright as the berries of the lind tree at the peak of the Ivoryssian vernal season. He remembered the way light glinted from the billowing halo of her curls when he would spin her in the air, her giggling like a thrush, him laughing uproariously at the sound, their joy the only thing that mattered in any world. In his long, dreadfully long, life he'd never heard a song as beautiful as his daughter's voice. And he felt sure he never would again.

Symvalline…

He'd fallen in love with her the moment they'd met in the Resplendolent Conservatum. Her brilliance outshone even the sparkle of her laughing gray eyes, and though her head barely reached his chin, no eye ever failed to notice her when she entered a room. Her presence filled every space, as captivating as a Verity itself. At least to Ulfric. Already eight centuries old at that point, he'd developed the foresight to recognize a future Knight Corporealis when he met one, and he'd promised himself to honor her commitment to the school and training, and later to her oath, and never let her know his feelings. But she had seen through him like a window and loved him back, and together they'd discovered love to be the one thing in the Great Cosmos that was more powerful, and more fulfilling, than duty.

Until Isemay came along, showing them both that there was a power even greater than their love for each other, and that was their love for their daughter.

Before Symvalline had given birth, they'd prepared themselves to leave the Order. What did any of their duty matter if they could not be a family together and enjoy those simple things that brought true meaning to living? And how could they stay ever young and watch their child age? The fear of that happening could have diverted them from their choice if they'd let it, but they'd thrown the fear aside and brought Isemay into their lives. For the last sixteen turns, they'd searched for a way to be released from their oath, to bring Vaka Aster back to Vinnr long enough to emancipate them and let them return to their mortality and commoner lives. To be a family, to raise their child, to grow old, and, eventually, to follow the habit of all people, from the most important to the least, and die. After so long, death no longer seemed a threat or a curse, but a reward of eternal peace after a lifetime of love and family and parenthood. After serving Vaka Aster for over two millennia combined, hadn't they earned something for themselves?

Yet, he reflected, the moment he'd achieved their goal and called Vaka Aster back, it had killed Symvalline and Isemay. And though he still drew breath, he had died along with them.

Your family lives, Stallari...

No, he'd seen the Raveners, seen Symvalline's struggle just to keep the mountain from collapsing on her and Isemay. He'd heard Balavad's command. *Kill them all!*

Ulfric paid no mind to the warm tears now streaming from beneath his closed eyelids. Their heat barely held a flame to the inferno erupting inside him. Hate was not simply hot, it was molten, and it consumed both itself and him, a curse of lava swirling, oozing, destroying. Though his heart felt as frozen as the glaciers of Ivoryss's arctic, his spirit burned. And in that black moment he took a new vow: before he died from heartsickness for his lost beloved Symvalline and the light of his heart, his darling Isemay, he would get his vengeance. On Vaka Aster, and if he could, on all Verities, for ripping his life from him.

Contemptible, monstrous beings, he thought. *All of them. I built a cage to hold Vaka Aster once, I can do it again. First Vaka Aster, the* Vigil Star, *then Balavad and the rest. This is a promise I will never, ever forget, like the scars I bear from life before the Knights Corporealis. And when I chain them, then... then I will find out if a Verity can die.*

You would destroy Vinnr too.

Sweeping his mind clear and wishing for a more permanent oblivion, he took the hem of his tunic and wiped his face dry. The newcomers Bardgrim had called Glisternauts had removed his armor and taken his klinkí stones while he'd been knocked cold, though he found he still wore his Mentalios. Holding it up, he looked through and was relieved to be able to clearly see his cell, which was barely wider than his arms if he stood and spread them open. Bardgrim's identical unit lay adjacent on the other side of metal bars. They each had a cot and nothing else. Ulfric had been a "guest" in more intimidating holding pens, but given that they were most likely aboard some kind of flying craft, the reality was that it would do him little good to escape the enclosure. He needed that Scrylle, which had been apprehended before he could open the starpath last time. To get it, he needed a plan, and that plan began with the Himmingazian, who could pilot them clear of their jailers.

He stood and dropped his one-eyed gaze on his neighbor. "Bardgrim." The man tensed a bit but stayed seated, watching him closely. "If I can get us free of these cells and promise to help you retrieve the rest of the Creatress's Fenestrii, can you get us off this craft?"

"Well that depends. You were looking suspiciously like a man who was about to stone his way through my friends on Isle Stonering. I know they've got us locked up, but it's just a matter of a misunderstanding, and I'd still prefer none of the Glisternauts—or any Himmingazian for that matter—is hurt. If you agree no one will get hurt, then I could be persuaded." He rubbed his chin thoughtfully. "Why do you want these Verity stones anyway?"

"It is your own Verity who created the world-eater you call the Glister Cloud. It will wipe away this realm and all within it, your maker becoming your unmaker." Ulfric recalled what he'd seen when he looked into the Creatress's Scrylle. What Lífs's own Order of protectors called Mystae had done. And what Eisa had done to them…

He pushed it aside. This realm's dark fate was not his concern. And he suspected Bardgrim wouldn't believe him if he told him. But he had to tell him something.

He plunged on: "The reasons why are too complex for a commoner to understand, and I've no interest in explaining anyway. With the stones and the Scrylle, I can… stop this from happening, and then find a way back to my own world." This wasn't truly his plan, more of an inversion of it, but Bardgrim, clever though he seemed, might not be clever enough to pick up on that.

And now Ulfric had snared the man's full attention.

Bardgrim's eyebrows rose cagily. "Or—and just bear with me for a moment while I break down the option that suggests perhaps myths and superstitions aren't the probable cause—because you cannot simply *stop* the Cosmos, which is where the Glister Cloud comes from. Maybe we can use the Fenestros stones to get beyond the Cloud. Like I've been trying to tell you *and* Cote *and* the rest of Himmingaze." Under his breath, he uttered, "You'd think the demonstrably smartest man in the Glisternauts would have an easier time convincing people of something this simple."

"No," Ulfric declared, "it's impossible to 'get beyond the Cloud.' There is *nothing* beyond the Cloud. I'm not saying *stop* the Cosmos. I'm saying beyond your realm, there is no Cosmos." He let the words hang, like a cloud themselves in the confinement, observing Bardgrim take this news in, mentally spin it around to consider every angle, and perhaps not quite reject it. "This is the nature of our celestial makers," he finished. "They create. And once their amusement wanes, they destroy."

Bardgrim's sandstone-colored eyes held his, assessing. "Look," he said, "I'm going to be straight with you. I'm skeptical of your, er, theories about makers and destroyers and this Verity pantheon business. I can see that you can see that. You're a bit saltier, or maybe just outright more unhinged, than anyone I've ever met, and, no offense, I don't think you know more about the Cosmos than I do. However, I'm willing to entertain your ideas for the sake of what I've already seen the Fenestros on the *Octopod* do. My ship is without a doubt the best machine the Glisternauts have and that I've ever designed. But after I installed that stone, it turned into a marvel, as if it was powered by the stars themselves. Stronger too. The hull integrity, I don't know how it's possible, but it somehow increased. It could withstand direct lightning strikes without losing power or even losing its trajectory. With no damage. So, the long and short of it is, I know I can't explain what it does or how it does it, but I also know what I've seen. And I know there's a reason. Until I find out what that is for myself, I'll take your, er... theory into consideration." He approached the partition. "If you're sincere, Aldinhuus, and if you swear you won't hurt anyone, then I think we can definitely help one another."

Despite the way Bardgrim tended to rub against the grain of his nerves, like an old splinter wedged under a fingernail that has stopped festering but still reminds you it's there when bumped, Ulfric liked what he heard. In his time, Ulfric had met a few skeptics in Vinnr, so he knew how obtuse and obstinate their minds could be. But this man had a good brain and wits that weren't mired in canon or doctrine. He'd have made a good Resplendolent acolyte if he'd been one of Vaka Aster's creations. Stepping up to the bars, he touched his chin with his right hand, then held it up, palm facing forward, for Bardgrim to acknowledge with his own gesture.

He merely stared at Ulfric. "Are you testing the weather or something?"

"No, Himmingazian, this is how we seal an accord. With noble intent, shown by the touch of one's chin, then we grasp palms."

"Ah." Bardgrim copied the movement, then awkwardly clasped Ulfric's hand. "Noble intent. Naturally. Friend, you really are from out of this world, aren't you?"

/ CHAPTER TWENTY-EIGHT

Mylla and Irrick reached the *Vigilance* with the bruhawks flying as her entourage. Safran was the first to greet her in the docking bay, with Eisa and Roi immediately behind.

As Mylla swung open the cockpit hatch, she could see the hesitation in Safran's expression, but she finally asked, *Havelock?*

"He chose to stay and fight for Ivoryss," she said, using what felt like the last of her strength to keep her voice from failing her.

Oh, Mylla, I'm so sorry. She reached out to assist Mylla as she disembarked, concern painted across her features.

"Did you get it?" Eisa asked before Mylla could step clear.

She pulled the Verity stone free and held it out. Eisa took it without comment.

Safran said, *Would you like a cup of tea before you tell us what you've—Irrick!* She pulled herself up the fuselage struts to peer into the cockpit at the well-trussed acolyte, then turned back to Mylla with a questioning look.

"I knew no other way to get him to stay still. He's been... changed."

Irrick's complacency as they walked the halls of the Conservatum had been a stroke of luck, but it had taken the persuasive end of her sword to get him inside the dragørfly scout. Unable to predict and afraid of what his change might move him to do, she'd trussed him so securely that he now resembled a spider's prey. During the flight, she'd had time to tuck away the guilt of treating a friend like a prisoner. But she knew better than to trust him.

"Safran, Roi, can you help me get him down? He needs to remain tied up until we can learn how to remedy what ails him. His behavior is unpredictable." *And unaccountable,* she thought.

The Knights settled Irrick in a midship storage closet with a stout door. He roused from his odd stupor enough to hiss at them in his strange new way, unsettling both Safran and Roi, but Mylla was too spent to be bothered by it now. Upon returning to the launch bay, the Knights listened as she told her tale both audibly and channeled using her Mentalios for Stave's sake, who was watching the helm.

"Asteryss has completely fallen…"

By the end of it, late evening bruised the skies. With her back rigid, she faced the Stallari Regent, readying herself for the rebuke for her brazen and unsanctioned leave that she knew was coming.

But Eisa surprised her. "I'll look into the Scrylle to see if it can tell us anything about what's happened to Irrick and how to cure him of Balavad's curse. Go to the hold and get something to eat, Mylla, then catch a few hours of sleep. You'll be on helm watch later. I'll speak to Stave and have him direct the *Vigilance* south."

Without another word, she exited the docking bay. Speechless, Mylla watched her go before turning to Roi and Safran. "Did I miss something?"

Roi twitched an eyebrow and offered the old expression, "Don't question a gift given by a shadow, for it can never reclaim it." He was right; it was probably best to just forget the whole thing and move on. They would soon be facing an even more unpredictable situation: the people of the Empire of Dyrrakium.

With their help, Mylla set about securing the dragørfly scout, and they all retired to the hold together, Safran and Roi seeming to realize that comfort from friends at the moment would nourish her better than any food could.

Did he say why he chose to stay? Safran asked as she set out cups and shook tea leaves into strainers. There was no need to say who "he" was.

Collapsing into one of the seats, Mylla said tonelessly, "His family is there. The city is his home. And he's not a Knight. He felt his contributions would better suit those with whom he is closest."

She was punishing herself, and she knew it, by minimizing the connection, and the commitment, she and Lock had made to each other by speaking of herself as his lowest priority. They'd met when he was twenty-three, a fresh inductee into Wing training, seven turns ago now. Though filled with youth's usual bravado, his eyes had held a quality that had drawn Mylla, a recognition of kindred spirits, perhaps. No other person in all her turns had made her feel as… *herself*… as he did. Lock had awoken her to the notion that there was more than being a Knight. Because she'd been too young to know her parents or her past, her life in the Conservatum had been her only identity. By virtue of who he was, someone who'd rejected the Conservatum to pursue goals of his own, she'd considered what it might have meant for herself to choose a life beyond the Knights. Just imagining it was a freedom she'd never known she was missing. And now he was gone. It seemed easier to pretend none of the past seven turns had happened. Maybe if she pretended long enough, she would come to believe it. She had a very, very long time to find out.

Safran placed a steaming mug in front of her, and Mylla automatically wrapped her hands around the warm crockery. She wasn't cold, but the heat soothed her. "All things being equal," she went on, straining to hide the bitterness in her voice, "I suppose I'm lucky. Eisa might have shredded me for going against her orders."

You accomplished the mission. There is nothing for her to be quarrelsome about, Safran said protectively. *The* Vigilance *and the vessel are safer for now. In the morning, we'll decide our next gambit.*

"What do you think she'll want to do with Irrick—if we can't find a way to cure him?"

"If he is cursed by a Verity, we may have no hope of countering such a thing. Eisa will likely recommend we free him from this unnatural torment." Roi's words dropped like stones on Mylla's chest.

"No," she argued. "He has been nothing but loyal to the Conservatum, and to us. We can't reward that with an… execution."

Roi chose to fall silent on the matter, but Safran frowned. *We'll keep faith in that fight, for now and always. He was a good friend and a stalwart servant of Vaka Aster. We'll find a way to help him.*

Mylla tried to ignore her reference to Irrick in the past tense. After a moment of contemplating her cooling tea, and finding no hidden hope there, she voiced her fear, "Eisa has served the Order too long. She's forgotten how to care about anyone, to feel anything for others. She only knows how to be dutiful. She's just… heartless."

Roi set down his own cup. "It isn't that she's forgotten. She had a heart, but it betrayed her. And she killed it."

She and Safran eyed him, trying to make sense of his cryptic words. Mylla asked, "What do you mean?"

"She is bound to protect the vessel. Her feelings for another put that charge to the test, and she was forced to make a choice. You can't understand because you didn't know her in days past, when her oath was still in its spring and her duty had not yet been tested."

Combat, wysticism, Verity lore: most of Mylla's skills came from Eisa's tireless and grueling—sometimes cruel—training, endured both while Mylla had still been an acolyte at the Conservatum and after she'd taken her oath to Vaka Aster. The older Knight had spared no trial or test to ensure Mylla more than earned her right to be asked to join the Order. And though Mylla had spent endless hours under Eisa's yoke, Eisa had never said a word about herself beyond the indirect telling of the grandness of their shared heritage, the Empire of Dyrrakium. And even those few moments of insight had been delivered with the subtle implication that Mylla didn't deserve to call herself a Dyrrak, and never would. All of which had resulted in Mylla never even considering asking Eisa about her own past.

Safran said, *Roibeard, tell us what you know. If Eisa is to lead us, we deserve to understand who she is. And who she was.*

Roi leaned back in his seat, his aged leather breeches sighing at the motion, still as stiff in places as their wearer was. Looking toward the ceiling, he thoughtfully rubbed the mark on his chin. "You know she is a Dyrrak," he finally began. "For five centuries, some thousand turns after the War of Rivening, before the kingdom was exiled, the Dyrraks once again tried to mend their bonds with Yor and Ivoryss. Eisa came to the Conservatum then. It wasn't until after the Dyrraks murdered the old Arch Keeper of Yor—if you believe the common history—that she renounced her heritage. At least as far as commoners were concerned. It was the only way to keep them from turning on the Knights, knowing we had a Dyrrak among us."

The way he blinked when his gaze fell back on them made it appear as if he'd forgotten they were near. "This was shortly after I swore my oath to the Order, when she turned away from all the kingdoms and stamped out any final loyalties she still had to commoners, all commoners."

He stood and walked to the kettle, leaving Safran and Mylla to share their surprise in silence. Mylla hadn't known any of this. Carrying the kettle—not by the handle, but holding it with both hands wrapped around the piping-hot body—Roi returned and placed the pot before them. Lifting his hands, whose palms were as red as the fires that had scorched Omina, he pondered the lesions for a moment. "If you live long enough, no matter who you are, you begin to forget the feeling of pain. You grow so tolerant of it that it no longer has much effect on you." To illustrate his point, he held his palms out so Mylla and Safran could see them. The burns were already gone. Mylla thought back to her wounded shoulder of yesterday, a gash that should have stopped her. But she'd merely noted it and continued to fight until it healed. "Pain of the body, anyway. Pain of the heart, it seems, does not ever become tolerable."

He poured more water into his teacup and stirred it with a finger. "Before the Cataclysm, she fell in love with a commoner. The commoner betrayed her, and the Knights, so Eisa killed her. And that was the last time Eisa acknowledged Dyrrakium publicly, or, as you have observed, Mylla, acknowledged her own heart. But trust me, she still has one."

His story finished so abruptly, Mylla wasn't sure if she understood. "She loved a commoner? But she holds them in so much contempt." It made a stark, perverse sense, but it was the last reason for Eisa's attitude toward the people of Vinnr she'd have thought of.

"Come here, novice. Let me show you." He withdrew his Mentalios and waved at them to hold theirs up. "Clear your minds and listen to my memories."

She had to fight down discomfort at the overwhelming intimacy of looking at another's memory, but curiosity compelled her to do as he directed. With Roi holding their wystic lenses in a stack, she and Safran stared into their centers while he closed his eyes and took a long breath. Mylla focused on nothing, as she'd been trained, and for a moment her mind clouded as if filling with fog. What could only be described as a powerful wind pushed through this, unnerving her with its intensity—but then she was somewhere else.

With a blink that was only in her head, she found herself in an unfamiliar pub, sitting at a long table with several others beside a roaring hearth fire. Laughter and the sounds of a poorly but enthusiastically played lyre and flute flooded her ears, but it was the woman who sat across from her who grabbed her attention. She looked young and carefree in the way she was dressed in a low-cut flaxen smock that draped off one shoulder, with her hair, long, black, and curly, left to flow unbraided down her back. As Mylla watched, the woman let out a raucous laugh at something the clearly Yorish ginger-headed woman next to her said, and the laugh wrinkles beside her steel-gray eyes showed her real age.

Eisa?

It was clearly her. The shaved sides of her head, the Dyrrak fashion, the black, already fading tattoos made this obvious. But her as a vigorous woman full of joy, utterly unlike the Eisa Mylla knew and could barely believe had ever existed.

A moment later the redhead leaned in and whispered something in Eisa's ear, and she looked directly at Mylla—or it seemed she did— with a look of mock surprise. Then she turned and grabbed the woman's cheeks and kissed her long and full, not caring that those at the table laughed at their zesty display.

A hand that seemed disembodied rose before Mylla and held out a bowlful of bread. "Bread, Eisa? Lillias? By the looks of things, you'll need your energy this evening."

The voice belonged to Roi and carried an amused lilt that was also unfamiliar. Mylla realized this was the past, and she was seeing a night they'd dined together at a public house through Roi's eyes. Eisa disengaged from the kiss and took the basket, saying, "Even a Knight Corporealis needs a night free of duty on occasion. Consider that a lesson, novice." She smiled impishly but kindly at Roi, not in the acerbic and biting way Mylla was used to.

She mused at how strange it was to hear one of her elders being referred to as "novice" as the fog blew back inside her mind. She waited in the stillness, her only companion a sense of foreboding. For Eisa to have been capable of so much happiness, whatever the betrayal was that had changed her and robbed her of anything but the stoic, merciless warrior aspect, it must have been unthinkable.

When the wind blew her mental sight clear again, Mylla stood in a quiet night-darkened hallway. The only sounds were breathing and muffled voices coming from a door in front of Roi's eyes. Eisa's back was to him, and in the stillness, a pulsing blue glow came from her hands. She took a backward step, raised an armored leg, and kicked the door open. Roi rushed into the room behind her, and Mylla sensed the form of another Knight at their backs. Roi's arm rose, but his great blade clenched in both hands never swung. There wasn't time before the six men and two women within had jumped to their feet preparing to defend themselves but been downed by Eisa's klinkí stones.

All but one.

The ginger-haired woman, whom Roi had called Lillias, faced them with an unwavering glare, though fear and more than a hint of resignation blanketed her face. Eisa's stones formed a ring around her torso, leaving the redhead no option for advance or retreat.

"Betrayer," Eisa said, the word sounding forced through a locked throat.

Lillias looked pointedly at the stones, then at Roi and the other Knight, then back to Eisa. "I am the betrayer? Hah. People of Lœdyrrak, your homeland, attacked my Arch Keeper, killed him. And you, obviously part of the scheme, killed acolytes of the Conservatum! Who is the betrayer here, Eisa?"

"Slag your lies, Lillias! I've read your letters. Every word you just said is false. Every word."

"Are they? The evidence is everywhere. The Lœyrrak ambassador's own knife is in Connaugh's belly, and witnesses heard the fight. You may have killed everyone here, Eisa, but did you think it was just us? We've been trying for so long to get you and your Order to make Yor the seat of Vaka Aster's reign. If you'd listened to us, to me, this could have been avoided. Yor doesn't bow to you, Eisa, your Order, or to any kingdom. Yor has stood aside too long while Ivoryss pretends it's Vaka Aster's chosen, holding the vessel hostage like some kind of prize. And you Lœdyrraks, ha! Pretending your devotion is pure. Zealots! If Vaka Aster favors the Lœdyrraks so much, why has she never stepped foot in your lands?"

The orange glow of wall lamps embedded around the room in small alcoves illuminated Eisa's face. Mylla saw her eyes sparkling with heavy but unspilled tears and her lips trembling. She seemed incapable of speaking, but she opened the stone circle just enough for Lillias to pass. The woman remained where she was, the full measure of accusation in her eyes lit by the stones' cerulean hearts. Then her voice softened. "Perhaps, it isn't too late, my love," she said, and went on to speak of some long-forgotten conspiracy. A moment later, Mylla heard Roi speaking to Eisa.

We need her alive, Eisa. The letters will prove Dyrrakium's innocence, and justice will be served, but keeping her alive will help ensure it. The Yorish court will need her to identify the other conspirators, as well.

Lillias still spoke as Eisa stood motionless, not acknowledging Roi. "And with Vaka Aster's sanctuary here, the Knights must relocate to Yor as well. Their longevity and strength can benefit Yor, too. If you persuade them to come, it will be enough to show where your fealty truly lies."

"Truly," Eisa said, "lies are all you're capable of, Lillias. The Knights' fealty is not a bargaining chip for fickle commoners to play with. Our duty is not to weak-minded chookters like you without loyalty or faith." Over her shoulder, she said to Roibeard and the third Knight, standing in the doorway, "Wait outside."

Roi and the other Knight backed through the doorway. An ominous tick of the clock passed, then Eisa came out. In the lamplight, Mylla saw a strange curved blade in her hand and her sleeve saturated with blood.

"Eisa?" Roi said.

She walked by him, never slowing, and repeated Roi's words: "She's no more threat to us."

The fog descended, and once more Mylla blinked into the present in the *Vigilance*'s hold. She looked at Safran, and her friend's troubled return glance told her she'd seen the same thing. "Why?" she asked Roi. "Why did she kill them? Why did the Yorish people make those accusations against the Knights?" What she knew of from history was the same as what this memory had shown: the Dyrraks attempted to overthrow Yor by killing their Arch Keeper. They'd unleashed what had been called the Cataclysm, a worldwide expulsion of Dyrrakium from the rest. They had not immediately given in, and the short war had been bloody.

Roi draped his Mentalios over his neck and tipped back his cup to finish his tea. Mylla remembered hers, now cold and unappealing waiting at her fingertips. She drank it anyway, trying to wash away the bitter taste Roi's shared memories had left in her mouth.

"Their folly isn't their fault. It's the cycle."

"Cycle?"

"If you are a Knight long enough, you will understand. People, the common people, don't have the advantage of knowing history the way we do. For them, it is a shadow of a past they are left to remember, and memory fades. For us, it lives on and never fades. War, civilization, life, and death. These are the cycles that continuously govern them. Things come and go for them, and they forget.

"We Knights are caught in the repetition, even though we live apart. First we are feared and resented, and they blame us for troubles that they cause but can't control. Then we leave them behind for a time and come back later to find we are tolerated once more, even sometimes welcomed. And if we let them, commoners will eventually come to revere us, or worse, to worship us. Letting them has come close to the undoing of the Knights in times past. Then a war or a sickness or a disaster happens once again, and we are the first to be blamed, and again, feared and resented—we become their target because we are flesh and blood like them, unlike Vaka Aster, whom they're afraid of and who is untouchable. It's happened dozens of times in Vinnric history. Temporality is all commoners' chief frailty. They just can't help themselves."

Maybe they don't want to, Safran put in. She stood, seemingly shaken by the experience. *I'm going to look in on Stave.*

Mylla and Roi nodded goodbye and remained at the table. After a time, she asked, "Why, Roi? Why does this cycle repeat? Vaka Aster could intervene, couldn't she?" She thought back to Lock's words in the catacombs. *Even if Vaka Aster were here to swear allegiance to, how could I serve her when she allowed this to happen?* "Why let people repeat mistakes that could be avoided?"

Roi's honey-colored eyes looked sympathetically into hers, and Mylla sensed he had glimpsed her thought in the Mentalios lenses. "Vaka Aster is a Verity, Mylla. Why should she intervene? We, 'we' being people, are our *own* race. We must rely on our *own* selves. If we let our maker mold our entire journey throughout eternity, then what good to ourselves are we?"

She leaned back, taking in his words. Eventually she decided: "That sounds like an excuse."

"That's all I can offer you as an answer," he responded. "As for the cycle, we Knights have learned to stay on the fringes, to stay true to our duty to the world—"

"You mean to Vaka Aster and the vessel."

"Which represent the world. We keep more than just passing kingdoms secure. We keep existence secure. That is a noble cause, even if commoners don't, or can't, grasp it."

She wanted to, it was a part of her nature, but Mylla couldn't find any reason to be contrary this time. There were no chinks in the armor of his level-headed reasoning to disagree with.

He went on, "Our duty to the world must be our only concern. Eisa has made her peace with that. Eventually you will too. You'll see it's the way it has to be."

"But we aren't always on the fringes. We maintain Vigil Tower. We share knowledge, tools, and so many other things with them that the common Vinnrics wouldn't have otherwise. Why not all of them?" she asked.

"You know the answer to that."

Of course she did. After understanding and seeing from Roi's memory how swiftly and decisively commoners could turn on them, it was no mystery. What defenses would the Knights, and therefore the vessel, have if they granted access to all of their wystic tools? If—or *when*—the cycle he spoke of again turned the people against the Knights, fleets of ships like the *Vigilance*, crewed by armies of commoners, against a handful of them would lead to a total extermination of the Order. And who but they had such unwavering devotion to the vessel? Who but they had the unbroken line of history and comprehension that created such devotion, and the understanding of what would happen if the vessel were threatened? Only the Knights could claim this.

She asked, "But we assist at the Conservatum. Why do we bother at all?"

Roi stood and carried the dishes to the washing area. "The Order must be replenished by a very specific type of person, those with great minds and great resilience, and recruiting them is the Conservatum's primary purpose. Through it, we do what we can to keep the goals of the people and the Knights aligned. And, ultimately, being in league with the doings of the Conservatum fills our turns. It is our only meaningful reprieve from duty."

She grew quiet as he rinsed the cups, seeing the role of the Knights, and the role she played, in a new way. His footsteps as he paced toward the far door grabbed her attention. "Roi, one more question, if I may. In your memory just now, there was a third Knight. I didn't recognize him. Who was he?"

"His name is Griggory Dondrin, the oldest of the Knights." He smiled, a bit wistfully. "You'd have liked him, Mylla. He was always curious and sometimes a bit reckless, like you, with a taste for wandering. He was always more of a philosopher than a fighter, and a good friend."

"What happened to him?"

The smile dissolved, and Roi looked to the floor. "I will tell you if I ever learn. It's been seven hundred turns since anyone has seen Griggory."

"Did he abandon his oath?"

He reached the open door and stood in the arch. Without giving her an answer, he said, "Your mind is unsettled, and it's late. Your path in the last few days has been all sharp rock and hard climbing. Get some rest before your watch. This is just a day, and like all days it will pass."

CHAPTER TWENTY-NINE

Ulfric spent a couple of hours describing to Bardgrim the rudiments of a Verity cage and how it would stop Lífs from ending Himmingaze—despite the fact that he now knew there was no Verity to stop. The Scrylle had indeed been in Griggory's possession, for some time, and what he'd recorded in it was truly surprising and troubling. But not Ulfric's current concern, and Bardgrim didn't need to know it. It was more convenient for Ulfric to spin tales to get Bardgrim to cooperate than to explain there was no hope for his realm. As long as Bardgrim believed what he wanted him to believe, the Himmingazian would help him get the Scrylle and escape.

"So, we get out of our holding cells, get the Scrylle and Fenestros, retrieve the rest of the Verity stones, then create some kind of cage that will entrap the Creatress, and then you'll head home? I have the plan right?" Bardgrim was asking.

Ulfric could see Bardgrim was already beyond dubious, but, wisely, was choosing to play along with his charade. To fulfill his own goals, the Himmingazian needed Ulfric's help. And because their priorities started with the same need—get away from the Glisternauts—Bardgrim was planning to cooperate. At least for now. Ulfric sensed they both expected nothing short of a double-cross from the other. Which of them achieved that first would be the surprise.

His own list of priorities was simple: getting back to Vinnr and, if Symvalline and Isemay had truly been lost, permanently caging Vaka Aster. Then, all that would be left to achieve in his life would be to do the same to Balavad. He would hunt the Verity with all the tenaciousness and skill his many hundreds of turns of service had instilled in him.

A Glisternaut delivered food in the midst of his and Bardgrim's discussion, and Ulfric realized he was somewhat spent. Though much of his vitality had been drained from him while summoning Vaka Aster back to Vinnr and then cage her, to his surprise, he didn't feel as weak as he might have expected. Still, hunger prompted him to dig into the strange food, not caring if it might be poisonous or inedible to his foreign composition. When he asked what it was, Jaemus gave him a finicky "Never Sea surprise" in response, and proceeded to pick less enthusiastically at his own tray.

As a man of Ivoryss, where the majority of people lived seaside and mostly subsisted on the sea's bounty, Ulfric's appetite for seafood spanned a wide selection. His favorite for centuries had been pit-smoked chelbiefin shark. Even though the Feast of Five Seasons celebration was the most common time to fix the delicacy, Ulfric had built a pit to smoke it any time the desire struck in the yards inside Vigil Tower's walls. But this... "food" of the Himmingazian' tasted like weeds boiled in seawater, though the consistency and density reminded him of a sawdust cake. However, it didn't kill him, and after several drafts of fresh water—which at least tasted close enough the Vinnric water—to clear as much of the flavor from his mouth as he could, he felt somewhat revived in flesh if not in heart. It was enough.

During the conversation, Bardgrim, to his credit, rarely interrupted and never gainsaid a word of Ulfric's. Whether this was just to humor him or more a matter of trying to, as the Himmingazian had put it, take Ulfric's theory into consideration until he found the truth for himself, he didn't know. And didn't care. Ulfric needed cooperation more than he needed a commoner's embrace of facts that may be too profound for him to even grasp, in the end. This was the reason acolytes studied for countless, sometimes tedious, turns at the Conservatum before being chosen to be and then ordained a Knight. Many truths, particularly those concerning the makers, did not come easily to the human mind without time to reflect and put it all into a comprehensible order.

Near the end of his account, Bardgrim inquired, "Two things I have to know. Tell me why you're holding that lens over your eye, and what in the Never Sea's many monsters were those flying bugs? Where did they come from?"

Out of the wonders the Himmingazian had just learned, these were his questions? Ulfric supposed he could take a turn at humoring him. "On my voyage through the celestial rift between realities, something happened to my vision. I can't see normally now without looking through my Mentalios. The 'bugs,' as you call them, must have come with me, and when they appeared on the island, I was able to use their eyes to expand my own sight."

"I'm not sure I understand."

"Like a bruhawk ally." He looked for a sign of comprehension from Bardgrim. Nothing. "You haven't got bruhawks, I'm guessing. Put simply, I can see using the dragørflies' eyes."

"You can? ... Okay, that's a trick I have to learn."

What he decided not to share was that, even now, he could still do it when he dropped the Mentalios. He had finally recognized that the rustling he'd heard upon first awakening aboard this ship was coming from the dragørflies themselves, who were hiding in the crevices of the craft like stowaways waiting to be called back into service. Had Vaka Aster sent them through the celestial well to serve him? If so, for what purpose? Was his Verity present as well but had not revealed herself? Too many questions, and regardless, he did not want the dragørflies near him, skulking like a snake in his head and bearing witness to any of his plans—if that were even possible.

Besides, he didn't need to know why the dragørflies were here to take advantage of their presence, and during the lull in the conversation while he and Bardgrim had eaten, he'd sent them on a hunt for the

Scrylle and Fenestros. As they slipped on quiet wings throughout the capacious ship, they fed the layout and directions to his mind. He now knew the inside of this craft as well as he knew the inside of the *Vigilance.*

Handy, that.

"The last question for you, Aldinhuus, is how you're going to spring us. These holding cells are no joke, but your confidence makes me wonder what other tricks you have up your sleeve."

In lieu of telling him, Ulfric responded with a demonstration. Now fed and rested, he held up a hand to silence Bardgrim and summon the klinkí stones. Though he could not see where they'd been taken, he could feel their wystic resonance, attuned to his own, nonetheless. Latching on to them using the Mentalios lens, he pulled them toward him along the ship's passages, the dragørflies still acting as his eyes while he used his new understanding of the layout to guide them.

It took very little time for the stones to reach them. At his command, they punched neat holes through the hatch separating the holding cells from the corridor beyond—eliciting a surprised breath from Bardgrim—then Ulfric directed one into each of the locking mechanisms in the cell doors. As he let the remainder hover, he concentrated on turning the wystic spark in the two embedded in the locks into burning energy, slowly melting them. In moments, he and Bardgrim heard soft *chinks,* and the doors shifted on their hinges, open at last.

Wonder bathed Bardgrim's words as he asked, "Where do I get—"

The sound of running boots from the hallway cut him off, though Ulfric had expected them. He pushed past his cell door and stood in the foyer, klinkí stones lingering above his open palm, which was drawn back in readiness to lob them at whoever entered.

"No!" Bardgrim slammed past his own door and placed himself between the stones and the hatch. "I won't help you if you harm any one of them. I told you. I swear by... by the Creatress."

Ulfric clenched his teeth against a curse. "We may have no other choice."

"Yes, we do. We can choose to surrender and try to convince the

Crest Council later to let me try my plans with the Fenestrii—and all that other stuff you said. But if you kill someone, you'll be executed. Your only choice will be how: be either drowned or turned into a living lightning rod."

While Jaemus rambled, the hatch fell open and three Glisternauts blocked it. They were all dressed similarly to Bardgrim in one-piece full-bodied uniforms with high collars that rose to cover their chins and lower parts of their ears. They differed by color and the addition or subtraction of minor ornaments.

One was dressed singularly, the captain Bardgrim had called Cote. He eyed the two escapees and said, "How did you... doesn't matter. Jaemus—Engineer Bardgrim—you and your conspirator must know there's nowhere to go from here but into the storm. Even if you could, which you know you can't, we'd just find you again, and things will go even worse with the Council than they already will."

With his back toward Ulfric, Bardgrim spoke up. "It was a mistake, Cote. Aldinhuus isn't quite right in the head, true, but if you'll just listen to *erfff*—"

Under other circumstances, the sound the engineer made as Ulfric's free arm tightened around his throat in a chokehold would have been funny. But today was not a day for laughter. Immediately, the three Glisternauts leaned toward Ulfric as if to pounce, but he dissuaded them with a demonstration of the stones' abilities. Before any of them even knew a reaction would be necessary, the lightning-fast projectiles smashed their shelksies into useless baubles dangling from their wrists, and left each of them staring into the blue heart of a klinkí stone hovering just before their eyes.

"Don't struggle, Bardgrim," Ulfric muttered. Then louder: "You people of Himmingaze can be forgiven your ignorance, but try to stop me from fulfilling what I must do, and not only you but Bardgrim also will suffer the ultimate consequence." The calm in his voice carried an unignorable promise. With a nod toward the right-flanking Glisternaut, Ulfric continued, "You, retrieve the Scrylle and Fenestros you took from Bardgrim's craft. If you're not back before I've counted to fifty, your captain will be the first to fall."

The Glisternaut said, "I don't know what you're talking about."

"The metal scepter and the silver sphere that were on the common room table in the *Octopod*," Bardgrim blurted.

The Glisternaut looked to her captain, who nodded permission, and she sped off. As they waited, Ulfric hoped Bardgrim was smart enough not to make any reference to their deal. His choice to use him as a bargaining chip—and be the first to double-cross the other—was in part to spare the Himmingazian any more suspicion than he was already victim of, warranted or not. Ulfric had chosen not to inform him of the plan for the simple reason that an authentic reaction was always more believable than even a well-acted false one.

"So much for goodwill," Bardgrim said. He'd wrapped his hands around Ulfric's forearm, tugging to no effect, though Ulfric didn't squeeze harder than was necessary to keep him still. "I thought you were better than this, Master Knight. Where's that nobility you spoke of now?"

Ulfric merely repeated, "Don't struggle and you'll be fine."

Pulling Bardgrim along, he moved closer to the hatch guarded by the Glisternauts, who obliged with a step backward. They were cautious but confident, a combination that on any other day Ulfric would have approved of. Today, their duty was in his way, and he would do what he had to do to overcome it. Bardgrim may not be willing to make sacrifices for his goals, but Ulfric was a man of will, and each moment that passed between him and the vengeance he sought only deepened his resolve. He had nothing to lose now, not even honor. What had fealty to duty done for him?

The captain spoke. "Stranger, what you've done, what you're doing, will not go unpunished. If you cause Engineer Bardgrim any harm, I promise you, I will deliver that punishment personally. You still have a chance to reconsider your actions. You can't get off the ship, and even if you could, we're far from any Himmingaze city. There's nowhere to go but into the Never Sea, and you know as well as I what creatures lurk there and how much they'd enjoy a change in their usual diet."

In point of fact, Ulfric did not know what monsters lurked there, though he understood these people still believed he was from their realm. Nevertheless, he could guess. "You'd thank me and escort me to my destination, Captain, if you knew what gift I will soon bestow on Himmingaze."

The leader looked to Bardgrim, who was finding Ulfric's grip growing tighter around his throat with every tug or twist he made, and said, "I'm having more than a little trouble understanding why you wanted me to speak to this madman, Jaemus, and it certainly hasn't seemed to benefit you any."

Bardgrim replied with a strangled, "*Chrrrk.*"

To Ulfric's sight, the corona of color around the captain shifted as he spoke, from a light orange to a feverish crimson, his emotions made visible. His glimmering sea-green eyes never left Ulfric's own. It was obvious to him, if not to Bardgrim, that the captain's feelings for the engineer ran deep. In an insight more prescient than his usual understanding of human nature, he could see that the captain's quarrel with Bardgrim was not based on anger but fear for his partner's choice to pursue heretical means to solving their world's issues, and the consequences that would be laid on him.

And because of his new view through his dragørfly allies' eyes, he now witnessed the Glisternaut sent to retrieve the artifacts as she flew along the ship's corridors. "Ah, blargin' rot," he grunted. "She's sent out the alarm."

CHAPTER THIRTY

Mylla didn't want to rest, couldn't have if she tried. How could she, knowing the world outside was falling apart, and with its passing so would the man she loved? She paced the now-empty hold, feeling drained and miserable yet restless. It didn't take long for her to recognize the unfamiliar emotion riding her back like a mountain intent on crushing her: helplessness.

Her thoughts returned to Asteryss City again and again, worrying it like a loose tooth, and she imagined what would be occurring there. Brun had ordered the city's desertion and led the Marines to seafaring ships docked under the cliff on which Vigil Tower stood. A cove cut deep into the rock hid the city's last-chance ships in case of the need for a stealthy sea voyage, usually reached by bringing dories and rowboats out of the nearby southern coastal town of Gethbrond. But there was another way, down among the catacombs, and Brun had known of it. *Thank Vaka Aster, Brun had known of it.* At least that one revealed secret of the Knights could benefit the people of Asteryss.

The ships, barely spacious enough to hold more than a dozen companies, but more than what it seemed the remaining Marines in Asteryss would need, would make good speed. Driven by sun-powered engines based on designs shared by the Knights, the chance existed that they could reach Magdaster within a couple of days. That was if they escaped the notice of the Raveners, or if their armaments were capable of defeating them should concealment and speed fail. Despite being formidable, the Dragør Marines' munitions had nothing on the *Vigilance*'s emberflare cannons. Just as she'd so lately come to discover, the Knights wanted it.

Would Lock's fate be to die at sea?

She paced some more.

What could the Knights do to stop the usurper from wreaking more havoc on the people of not only Ivoryss but all of Vinnr? And the much harder question: Should they? What could *she* do to save Havelock from the bleak fate suffered by Irrick and so many others? He may have chosen to step out of her life—*and isn't that what you wanted, Mylla. Of course, yes, but... no*— but that didn't mean she couldn't do everything in her power to protect his. So long as it didn't threaten or impede her duty…

From the corner of her eye, she saw movement and faced it. "Eisa."

"Novice, still up?"

"It seems we both are." Despite Mylla's fatigue, her muscles tensed automatically, and her eyes locked on the Stallari Regent, waiting for the inevitable censure that still hadn't come.

But a distracted "Hmm…" was her only reply as Eisa stepped to the vessel's dais and peered up at the stone figure, seemingly deep in thought.

It struck Mylla that Eisa, in a long shift and leggings, with her braid loosed and her armor put away for the night, looked more like the woman she'd seen in Roi's first shared memory—collected but not hostile, possibly even warm and amiable. Was it just a trick of the mind that made her think this? Or had Eisa's enduring coldness clouded Mylla's ability to ever see her as anything but?

She cleared her throat. "I expected you to be angry at me."

Eisa looked at her, the deep lines at her mouth's edges hinting at nothing. "Your departure wasn't unexpected. But I was surprised at your cheekiness regarding the Fenestros map—which I expect you to return."

With a bloom of chagrin in her cheeks that only someone more than three times her age could elicit, Mylla dug out the map and carried it to the Scrylle resting on the vessel's dais, still where it had been when she'd first taken the parchment. For no reason she could put her finger on, the Stallari Regent's lack of disciplinary action unbalanced her more than a rebuke would have, and she found herself speaking in her own defense.

"You should understand that I did what I thought was right. I serve—"

Eisa cut her off. "You ignored orders."

Ah, here was the woman she knew. "I serve Vaka Aster. Not you."

Instead of striking out, Eisa smirked, looking almost pleased. "And don't ever let your allegiance to duty change, Mylla. Never. That is the most important lesson there is to learn, one that even I can't teach, but experience, turns, and wisdom will, if you let them."

Mylla faced the vessel, twirling the Scrylle in her hands thoughtfully. When Eisa spoke again, her words cut.

"Your Wing friend, what was his name? It was inevitable, you know. The commoner did you a favor by leaving the way he did. I did you a favor by sending him back to Asteryss where he belonged."

She faced the older Knight sharply. "A favor? How?"

"He would have betrayed you eventually. Believe me. Commoners are simple. First they admire you, then they love you, then they resent you and fear you. It always ends in betrayal." Eisa paused, as if considering a new thought. "Unless you kill them first, I suppose."

"You're wrong. Lock loved me, *loves* me. He would never betray—"

"What did you think was going to happen? Tell me. Him a commoner, you a Knight. Him Ivoryssian, you Dyrrak." Eisa's eyes once more shone with their usual cold-forged ire. "That you would grow old, become heartmatches, live like royalty atop Vigil Tower? He's a commoner, novice, who turned away from the Conservatum. He's destined to do little but die. You are a Knight! Your duty and devotion to your own kind is your only consideration."

Silently, Mylla fought back her own fury. Arguing with the woman, who had killed her own lover to spare herself from ever feeling anything, good or bad, again would get her nowhere. Eisa was… ice, frozen in her own rigid, eternal, lonely numbness.

The Stallari Regent looked away from her, a struggle playing out in her face as she tried to smooth the angry wrinkles across her brow. "I want you to try to see my point, novice. You are just an infant still for all your turns around Halla, and you know so little about the human spirit. It, more than anything else, is fallible. You can disagree with me because you don't understand, and you may even hate me. But someday you will hate that I'm right more. And you'll learn you must either accept that truth or succumb to it as most do. There is nothing special about you. There is only doing your duty."

Roi had called Mylla reckless, and he wasn't wrong. Her next words illustrated this perfectly. "Just because you were betrayed doesn't mean all commoners are corruptible. Your prejudice only makes you bitter, not right, not about everything. And not about Lock."

Eisa's eyes widened, then she blinked and released a resigned sigh. "Roi told you about… the uprising against the Knights before the Cataclysm."

"Yes, Roi told me." Eisa's wound was so deep she wouldn't even acknowledge the woman she'd loved, even when Mylla had all but spoken her name. She marveled at the will it took to maintain such denial.

Eisa's silence dragged out as she stared thoughtfully at the vessel, using her fingers to brush off more of the grit that still covered it. Mylla decided it was prudent to leave her be. She placed the Scrylle back on the dais and took a light step backward—but didn't escape in time.

When Eisa spoke, her voice was quiet and far off, as if she were talking to someone from a dream. Or from the past. "The only thing that's 'right' is staying true to your duty."

Unable to resist the bait, Mylla responded, "Even if it means relinquishing your honor?"

She didn't get time to regret her words. Eisa moved like a crack of lightning, grabbing the hilt of Star Spark on Mylla's belt with one hand and pushing Mylla to the ground. She landed on her back with an "oof," then scrambled to get her arms beneath her and rise up. But the sight of her blade being swung back over Eisa's shoulder for a full-bodied strike that would sever a man in two—Mylla had seen it done—dissuaded her from anything but a cautious: "Knight Nazaria—?"

With a wild look in her eyes that could freeze Halla, Eisa growled, "Right now, novice, we have greater concerns."

Changing direction with the agility of a shark, Eisa pivoted on her feet and swung Star Spark at the vessel as if trying to fell an oak tree in a single blow.

Mylla pivoted as well, from disbelief to horror, and covered her eyes with her arm. "NO!"

The crash of metal on stone echoed throughout the hold, a strike that would raze the vessel and the realm. Clenching her jaw (how else does one prepare for the end of all existence?), Mylla fleetingly wondered if she would feel the world end or simply wink out of existence—but everything remained as it was. The *world* remained as it was. When the echo subsided, she dropped her arm and cracked first one eyelid, then the next. Eisa stood in the same position, breathing heavily, gazing at the vessel. The sword drooped from one hand, and she gripped the arm holding it as if the blow had injured her.

Mylla collapsed flat on her back as relief galloped through her. When she could speak again, she squeaked out, "What in the name of sanity did you do that for? Furious fates, are you trying to kill the world?" But the words were a reflex, and under them confusion skewered her.

A laugh so scathing it could have scoured paint from walls came from the older Knight. Mylla looked up to see Eisa standing over her, glaring madly. With a toss, she released Star Spark to clatter beside her. "This vessel has been abandoned," she said. "We are its protectors no longer."

As Mylla scrambled to understand what was happening, Eisa staggered and fell to her knees, a groan that sounded animalistic and tortured welling from her throat.

"Eisa?" Shaken to her core, she cried through her Mentalios: *Everyone, come to the hold! Quickly!*

With a shake of her head to force her rattling thoughts into some kind of sense, she grasped her sword and used it to help her to her feet. "Eisa?" she tried again and clasped the Stallari Regent's elbow to help her up.

It was like grasping wet rope. Eisa showed no sign of knowing Mylla was even beside her as her arm dangled limply from Mylla's hand. At a loss for what to do, she looked around the chamber as if the answer could be found written on the walls. She caught sight of the deep notch Eisa had made in the statue's carved robes. It was the only blemish on the smooth white stone. As a weapon of war, Star Spark could cleave most things in half with ease, but it had failed to mar the statue more than superficially. Wind and time could do worse damage. But Star Spark was more than a weapon of war. It was Knight-made and Knight-wielded, hallowed by Vaka Aster, imbued with the power to destroy the vessel. A commoner with a strong swing and a large ax could do it over time, but a Knight's hallowed weapon should have shattered the vessel with one strike. None of them and *nothing* should be here anymore.

Abandoned? she thought and reached out to touch the statue. It felt as cold as the goose flesh rippling across her arms and neck. Yesterday, she had known it, just as Eisa had. Something was different about the vessel, something was *wrong*. But she'd shoved that knowledge aside. Too many pressing matters at once had forced her to triage information into an order she could act on. And this *inconceivable* thing had drawn the short straw. But Eisa couldn't ignore it. Duty had mastered her, and now duty had apparently deserted her.

The urgency in Mylla's summons drew the rest quickly. Roi fought to assemble his clothes and Safran to tame her waist-length hair as they lurched in from the bunk chamber, clearly pulled out of sleep. Stave, his brown hair corkscrewed and disheveled not from sleep but because he was Stave, tramped in from the helm like an agitated bear, a cigar jutting from his lips.

What's going on? Are we under attack? Safran asked, then noticed Eisa. The alarming milk-white pall of the Stallari Regent's usually sepia skin gave her the cast of a fresh corpse. *Eisa, are you well?*

"Great Verities, what's wrong with her?" Stave asked.

Mylla's mouth worked silently as she looked around at the others. Each stared at her expectantly, awaiting some kind of explanation that would make sense. Eisa was, without doubt, the hardest among them. Whatever could shake her, could, and surely would, shake them all.

"Vaka Aster's vessel is deserted," she blurted. "Eisa struck it with Star Spark and nothing happened."

"With Star Spark?" Stave said. "That's impossible. I forged that sword myself and Vaka Aster hallowed it. A hallowed weapon would destroy the vessel, it would destroy it!"

"I know, Stave."

He flinched at her flat agreement as if she'd slapped him and looked back at Eisa, who stared at the floor with eyes as empty as Mylla knew the vessel's to be. Safran stood still, her expression halfway between stunned and disbelieving, but Roi crouched next to Eisa and reached out to rest a hand on her shoulder. Whatever he said to her must have been through a guarded Mentalios link, but even that failed to get a reaction from her. After a moment, he glanced up, catching Mylla's stare. Something uncomfortably similar to fear darkened his eyes. Without comment, he stood and moved to the vessel, exploring the cleft made by Star Spark with his fingers. After a moment, he picked up the Scrylle and turned to the others.

"She speaks the truth."

Silently, they stared at each other, the bedlam of their thoughts creating a buzz that passed through all the Mentalios lenses. One by one, the Knights lumbered dazedly to the table and took seats. Safran tried to coax Eisa up from the floor. Resistant at first, the Stallari Regent pulled her wrist free from Safran's hand and stood on her own. With one last look at the vessel, she paced out of the hold without looking back, without speaking.

Should I go after her? Safran questioned.

Roi shook his head. "That wouldn't be wise right now."

All eyes fell on the senior Knight. "I don't understand what's happening," said Mylla. "How could the vessel be deserted? Where is Vaka Aster?"

Roi pulled at his pale-wheat sideburns thoughtfully. "It is only stone, the vessel, at least now. Vaka Aster can instill any object with her celestial spark. She hasn't done so in living memory, but something must have caused her to shift."

"This has happened before?" Mylla said. "How?"

"How? How does a Verity do anything? They take forms their creations understand to give us a reason to keep faith in them, and perhaps to keep their own faith in us. If Vaka Aster moved to a new form and excluded us, perhaps that means *she's* lost hers," Roi answered in clipped phrases, uncustomarily short-tempered.

Mylla blinked.

Safran said, *What did the Stallari do? Has he doomed us all?*

"The Stallari?" Mylla said.

No doubt he caused this when he crafted the Verity cage.

"I think we've already covered this ground—" she started.

Stave cut off Mylla's reflexive protest. "Whatever it means or doesn't, we need to decide what we're going to do. The Order is falling apart, it is. Our Stallari, gone. Our Stallari Regent, useless. We have no Verity to protect. But we still have a Verity intent on taking Vinnr and all Vaka Aster's creation. We should stop the usurper. That's what we should do."

"Why?" asked Roi flatly, causing Mylla's heart, and everyone else's, she was sure, to stutter.

First to recover, she spoke with slow care. "I think I know what you mean, Roi. Without the task we took oaths to fulfill, to protect the vessel, we are adrift in purpose. Why should we do anything to save Vinnr if Vaka Aster isn't willing to stop the usurping Verity herself?"

The others stared at her, considering, until she went on. "But you already answered that question. Earlier tonight when you told me that our troubles as people of Vinnr are our own. If we rely on our Verity to decide for us and control our actions, we are merely mindless, like schools of fish that startle at nothing and react to everything. So why should we try to stop Balavad? Because that is our choice and the right one to make. Maybe this is a test. Vaka Aster wants us to prove our worthiness as Knights by seeing which path we choose for ourselves."

She had just talked herself out of her own doubts, she realized. Yet she questioned, as she was learning to do, if this was really true. Was it a matter of saving Vinnr, or just a matter of wanting to save the only sense of purpose she'd ever known?

Or was it something else? In the face of this final desertion by their maker, where, or with whom, did her loyalty truly lie? *If we brought the* Vigilance *and our skills into a fight against Balavad, we could save so many. We could save Havelock.*

You want us to volunteer to fight the usurper? Safran asked, watching her keenly.

"Yes. We should travel to Magdaster. We can assume he's going there. And we know the city has a legion of fighters. We might have a chance at ending this."

And Havelock is heading there, too, I think we can assume, her friend sent softly. Had she heard Mylla's thoughts, or was it simply a guess?

Mylla asked, "What other alternatives are there?"

Roi put in: "We could seek out the new vessel. The vessel is our duty."

Dropping Mylla's eyes, Safran said, *Or we could seek out the Stallari. He may know what's happened. He* must.

Mylla looked at Roi. "What do you think Eisa will recommend?"

Instead of a response, a shade of gloom darkened his eyes once again and his chin fell against his chest. She started to repeat her question, but a cold draft blew into the hold, silencing her.

The docking bay, Safran said, alarm widening her eyes.

As one, they jumped from their seats, but Roi spoke through the Mentalios: *She is already gone.* They ran to the hold anyway, and Mylla felt the wash of a dragørfly ship taking flight past the gaping hatch, though she could not see it due to its flint-glass cloak.

As they stared beyond the hatch, speechless, the stillness of the night sky folded over the final four Knights Corporealis, leaving them alone, without a leader and without a purpose.

CHAPTER THIRTY-ONE

A slow, reverberating tone carried through the ship, repeating every few moments. Sensing Aldinhuus's increased anxiety, Jaemus quit struggling. By the Glister Cloud's gasses, did the stranger have a grip! It was as intractable as a feeding fleech's. Antagonizing this cretin was sure to lead to unpleasant outcomes the likes of which he didn't want to imagine—or experience.

And secondly, there'd been something in his voice when he'd warned Jaemus not to struggle. Was he perhaps cleverer than his crude stone-happy aggression seemed to suggest? Was he trying to give Jaemus the excuse of plausible deniability and make him look a victim rather than a conspirator?

What a twist that would be.

Yet the menace slithering in Aldinhuus's next words turned the skin on Jaemus's cheek as cold as the Never Sea, despite the Knight's hot breath. "I gave you and your crew a chance, Captain, but it was clearly a waste of my time. I'll likewise have no time to regret what I must do next, but if you're lucky, you will. Nothing is going to stand between me and that Scrylle."

With a gesture of the Knight's free arm that had become all too familiar to Jaemus, the aggregate of blue stones gathered in a tight, portentous group just in front of them.

"Stop!" he managed to yell as the Knight focused on the stones and relaxed his chokehold a bit. "I know where to find another of your Scrylles!"

For a moment, Aldinhuus's grip grew so tight Jaemus could almost feel the walls of his throat touch, then it loosened and Aldinhuus growled in his ear, "What did you say? I warn you not to lie."

Helplessly, Jaemus's eyes tracked from the louring stones to Cote's face, then to the face of each Glisternaut nearby, all of whom he knew and had flown with for anni-cycles. He could gamble his own safety on a whim and a hope, but not theirs. Especially Cote's. Never.

"When you landed in the shrine," he continued, quietly so they could not hear, "four more of your Verity stones landed with you, along with another Scrylle. Remember the bag I left behind? They're in it. If we can make it to the *Octopod* and launch, we can return to Isle Stonering. If we outrun and outsmart the *Skate*, they'll never find us, and you'll have what you want."

"I told you not to lie."

One of the kinky stones broke formation and hovered a lash from Jaemus's eye. He blurted, "Two are blue and yellow, swirling in a pattern that's nearly watery, and two are as black as the ocean floor with strange silvery details." How was that for proof? Surely Aldinhuus's capacity for sense wasn't so far gone that he'd disregard Jaemus's precise description of the Fenestrii in the Creatress's temple.

"They've taken the Fenestros you used to power your ship. I heard your captain with my own ears. We can't leave on it."

"Yes, but—" The grip on his neck tightened and he sputtered and yanked helplessly on Aldinhuus's arm. It released a fraction. "But the original engine is intact. We can't fly as fast or as far, not without topping off with more seawater, but we can still fly."

After a pause that seemed a lifetime, Aldinhuus's arm dropped from his throat, and he was shoved from behind toward the doorway. "Lead the way to the *Octopod*, Himmingazian."

Tentatively, he paced forward. Watching Cote's expression ripple from expectation to confusion to frustration—and potentially some relief now that he wasn't being choked to death?—Jaemus noted his face nonetheless never lost the sharp edges of leadership. He could only hope Cote would eventually understand his reasons. His life-mate's safety was more important to Jaemus at this point than their companionship itself. It had to be. The chance of Jaemus ever proving his theories about the capacity for the celestial stones to take them beyond the Cloud had receded to barely more than wishful thinking at this point, he realized dolefully.

But he was, despite this setback, an expert at wishes, as well as thinking. So...

They passed through the doorway and Aldinhuus pushed him once more. This might not have bothered him so much if it hadn't been directly toward the throng of advancing Glisternauts, all aiming shelksies. If he had one wish that was greater than his simple wish to save Himmingaze, it was that people *would stop pointing weapons at him.* Before Aldinhuus could return the gesture, he said, "Now, hold on, Master Knight, just give me a ch—"

But before he finished the statement, Aldinhuus had done his thing and dispersed the kinky stones—yet they weren't sent to attack the Glisternauts. Several fell into a square pattern surrounding his and the Knight's feet, and one flew directly centered above their heads. As if a robe were thrown over them, a pyramid of blue translucent light rose from the stones below and fell from the one above, enveloping them inside.

Which would be great theatrics if not for the *tat-tat-tat* sound of shelksies being fired, a misleadingly benign sound, as if delicate seashells were being stomped on by hard, heavy boots. Jaemus closed his eyes, waiting for the sting followed by paralysis to hit him. And kept waiting.

"Move, Bardgrim."

Aldinhuus slammed a palm into his back hard, forcing him forward once more before he'd had time to adjust to the realization he was still conscious. He stumbled as his eyes flew open. *How could they have missed at this range?*

The troop of four Glisternauts blocking the passage fired again. This time, his eyes stayed open enough to witness sparks pop from the light envelope surrounding them as, it seemed, the shullets struck it. Struck it… and did not penetrate.

"I swear my life will not be complete until I get a set of these kinky stones," he said, awed. "How does—"

"Move," Aldinhuus said again, louder.

"As you please," he mumbled, and somehow, against the hollering of his instincts, began to walk toward the crew, one step at a time. Aldinhuus's blue shield of light kept pace with them, but his nerves still twanged each time a shullet struck it.

The Glisternauts, quickly recognizing their ineffectiveness, stopped firing. Without an apparent alternative, they retreated as the two men drew close enough to touch. Their confusion was obvious, but none was brave enough to actually try to reach inside the blue shield. Jaemus didn't look behind him to see who was following, not because it wasn't important, but because the Knight would undoubtedly use his none-to-gentle tactics to keep him moving forward. Jaemus would never be accused of being slow to learn.

Impossibly, they reached the docking bay. It only took a few too-close-for-comfort strikes of Aldinhuus's other kinky stones to persuade the 'Nauts guarding the *Octopod* to retreat. Once they were aboard and the hatch locked up tight, Jaemus started the power-up tasks to get the ship ready. "We're about to launch, Master Knight," he said as he settled at the *Octopod*'s controls and cycled the thrusters into potential. "You may want to sit. When I design things to go fast, they go *fast*."

Aldinhuus, for once, complied without question, figuring out the seat harness with relative ease, as if no stranger to flying ships. Noting this, Jaemus considered it evidence that the man was more likely to be a muddlemind than from another world. But if he was crazy, what did that make Jaemus for trusting to his schemes?

"No time like the present to run from our troubles, right?" he said aloud, though his words were not for his passenger. Depressing the hangar door opening sequence on his control panel, he prepared for launch.

"Jaemus, are you okay?" It was Cote, speaking to him via the wave-speaker.

"What's that?" Aldinhuus said, the slightest upward lilt in his question the only sign he was flustered by the voice coming from nowhere.

Distracted that the hangar doors were not opening, he mumbled, "It's Cote," and tried the opening sequence again.

"How is he speaking to us?"

Pulling his attention from the stubbornly still-shut hangar doors beyond the craft's view screen, he glanced at Aldinhuus. He didn't know what a wave-speaker was? So much for his familiarity with ships as evidence of his delusions. "Through this device." He pointed. "It transmits sound from one place to another."

Aldinhuus gave him a look that was equal parts incredulous and impressed. "Commoners in your realm have an adaptation of a Mentalios. Unexpected."

Again, that "commoner" reference. He'd ask about it later. If there was one. "Still in one piece, Cote," he answered through the wave-speaker. "Just having a bit of trouble with the hangar bay door."

"You know we can't let you leave," Cote said shortly.

Raising an eyebrow, he looked to Aldinhuus for guidance on what to do next.

"Get them to release us," the Knight said.

"My, erm, *tourist* would like to go now, Cote."

"You know that won't happen."

"Show me how to speak to him," Aldinhuus pressed.

Once Jaemus demonstrated the controls, Aldinhuus unstrapped his harness and stood so that he was visible to those outside the ship's view screen. "My mercy is reaching its limits, Captain Illago. I understand you are a man of duty, as I am." He paused for a long enough moment that Jaemus wondered if he was about to abandon this crazy scheme. "But you are also a man who is no more capable of sacrificing those he loves for his duty than any other."

Cote's response came quickly, decisively. "You've already shown that you're unwilling to forfeit your own life by hurting Jaemus or any of my crew."

"You are misreading the situation, Captain. I've shown I am not reckless, but as I said, there are limits. You don't know anything about me, but I'm not lying when I tell you that I have already forsaken my duty. And my family is dead. What do you think I have left to stop me from pursuing the course I'm on? Do you think I'll let your crew stand in my way?" As those words died, he turned to Jaemus. "Does this craft carry weapons?"

Jaemus shook his head. "Himmingazians haven't fought each other since the early days of the Glister Cloud. You're the only one threatening violence here." He let bitterness suffuse his words, ensuring Aldinhuus wouldn't miss his disapproval. For all the good that would do.

Cote didn't respond, and the time began to draw out. Aldinhuus grew still, his gaze taking on that faraway look Jaemus had now witnessed a couple of times. It usually preceded—

On cue, the troupe of winged dragørflies swarmed into the hangar.

CHAPTER THIRTY-TWO

Gathered at the open bay, the Knights received nothing but a fog of grim silence in return when they sent an amplified plea to Eisa using their Mentalios lenses. Below them, starlight glanced from the crest from the occasional breaking wave in the Verring Sea. Mylla noted the colder air, their northward journey bringing them farther away from the more temperate climate of Asteryss.

"Of all the things we've lost since this began, she's the one I won't miss, not a scratch," said Stave.

Stave, she's one of us, Safran accused. With a trill, she mustered the bruhawks, who swooped from their perches and gave chase to the dragørfly scout. *Hopefully Urgo and Yggo will be able to tell us where she's going.* Stepping closer to the bay's opening, she ran her fingers along the frame of her Mentalios and concentrated on the bruhawks' sight.

Stave grumbled, "Never trusted her. Never will. She's always talking about duty, but she seems blargin' eager to turn her back on it."

"Don't assume that," said Roi. "We—"

"Look, Roibeard, I know you and she've been together for a bit. But she's not trustworthy, she's not. She sows chaos. It's in her breeding, her bones. Dyrrak, through and through. It's why I never wanted her to be Stallari in the first place. Don't even know why she's a Knight, I don't."

"That isn't and never was your choice to make. Aldinhuus trusted her. Vaka Aster ordained her. She is next in line."

"She's no kind of leader, and she just proved it." Stave dragged his black curls behind his neck and eyed Roi. "Can't trust a woman who kills when she don't need to. And runs when it's time to fight."

Mylla captured the disbelieving laugh about to squirm from her throat. "Eisa? Run from a fight? No way, that isn't her."

Stave eyed her. "What d'you think she just did?"

She had no response to that and moved her gaze out over the landscape, troubled.

Safran cut in: *The bruhawks are coming back.*

The silver-winged birds swooped inside the open bay door and glided to their perches. As the others waited for her report, Safran approached a rabbit pen kept on deck, grasped one before it could escape her reach, and cracked its neck. She tossed it to the birds and turned back.

With stoic reluctance, she looked to the others. *She flew too fast. They couldn't keep up.*

"Any idea where she's headed?" asked Stave.

Dyrrakium.

"Or maybe to Magdaster," Mylla added. "She seemed to be flying northwest. Scouting it for us?"

Thorvíl's eyes suddenly widened. "The blargin' Fenestros!"

He shot out of the bay toward the sleeping berths, leaving them to the dread of their own realizations. Safran followed a moment later, and Mylla could hear the echoes throughout the ship as they tore through Eisa's belongings in search of the celestial stone. They returned shortly.

Launching a kick at one of the blocks that held the dragørfly ships in place, Stave cursed violently, using words few outside the seedier streets of Ivoryss would even understand. The bruhawks fluttered their wings, annoyed at the disturbance, then continued their meal. Safran said simply, *Gone. The Scrylle too.*

Expletives notwithstanding, Thorvíl's claims regarding Eisa's character were quickly losing their mystery. Now more than ever, Mylla wanted the full story. They all seemed to know much more about her mentor and their leader than she, and it was time that changed. "I know I'm the novice in the Order," she said, "but if I'm to contribute as I'm meant to, you have to stop hiding things from me." Noting Thorvíl's vexed scowl, she continued before he could interrupt. "Or *omitting* things, if you prefer. What did you mean by Eisa kills people she doesn't need to? Did you mean the commoner she killed in Yor?" She glanced at Roi, not sure she should be speaking of the tale he'd told her earlier. "Her lover?"

With a grunt of reluctant assent, Stave came clean. "Aye, Mylla. That's what I'm talking about. That woman, and none of her companions, needed to die. I wasn't with the Order yet when that happened, but I heard the story. She didn't do it to protect us or the vessel, and after that, she went on a blargin' berserker rage. Revenge is all she cared about. Not duty. You didn't know this, did you, but it was she who pushed Dyrrakium into exile. Not because she thought they weren't good enough to mix with the other kingdoms, but because the rest of us weren't good enough for *them*. Dyrrak zealots, all of 'em. She took their Fenestros and convinced them they didn't need to be part of this world anymore. It wasn't *worthy* of them."

"But... why would she?" She couldn't imagine doing something so pivotal, that changed the course of history in ways the realm would never even grasp. After the War of Rivening, each of the three remaining kingdoms was granted its own Fenestros, guarded and administered by a Knight guardian, and the Order itself kept the final two. The Fenestrii became a symbol of peace and neutrality, a link between all kingdoms. Any that called the others to an Armistice of the Stones would be granted it, and any open hostilities would be halted during these peace talks. If a kingdom refused, it lost not only the promise of peace but its honor. A denial of the Armistice was considered a breach of fealty to Vaka Aster, the worst, most disgraceful crime.

Seeming to know what Mylla was pondering, Stave picked up her thread of thought. "But after the Dyrraks murdered the Arch Keeper of

Yor—if you believe the common history—Eisa went back to her homeland and reclaimed their Fenestros, ensuring Dyrakkium could never again seek, or honor, neutrality. It's what led to the Cataclysm. And now you see why I claim she's a chaos-sower, she is." With the sheen of fury still in his eyes, he peered around the hold as if looking for more things to kick.

Roi spoke up. "The time was too unsettled. Eisa believed she had to do what she did to protect the vessel. The instability among the three kingdoms was becoming too dangerous. They might have united against us."

Stave took the brown stub of his cigar, now dead, and pitched it outside the hatch, much harder than was necessary to clear the deck. "Why do you always protect her, Mallich? She's rogue. She didn't consult the Knights and she broke faith. She's just one of us. She doesn't decide fate for all of us. And she most definitely has no place deciding the affairs of commoners, she doesn't. Not with the kind of hate for them that she bears. She doesn't deserve our trust or your protection, man. You must see that by now, you *must*."

The eldest Knight gazed down at him, unflinching, saying nothing.

Stave went on, harsh words rolling like bile from his throat: "And now she's doing it again. But what's she doing, huh? What's her plan, and if it isn't her intent to create more chaos, why has she acted without the rest of us? Where is she meddling now? Where, I ask you?"

Safran stepped up to him and placed an arm around his waist calmly, but her face mirrored the tension they all felt.

"If Vaka Aster deserted us," he finished, "it's more than likely due to Eisa and her feeble delusions, her personal vendettas." With a derisive bark that may have been a laugh but more closely resembled a frog choking, he added, "The only thing she's done that *does* surprise me is writing off Ulfric so quickly. I always thought they were friends. Not surprising she'd betray us after turning so quickly on him, it's not."

He'd said what he was thinking, and deep down, maybe it was what they were all thinking. Mylla had no response, instead looking to their de facto leader. Anyone who hadn't spent a few hundred turns with Roi wouldn't have been able to discern the shift in his composure, the flash in his eyes, the subtle tightening of his jaw. But Mylla knew him, and she recognized the anger he held back. As usual, he kept everything in check, drowned under water too deep for any of them to reach.

Safran broke the lull. *We cannot fight among ourselves. We are the last of Vaka Aster's Knights.*

Her clear conviction, even though silent to the ears, cleared away some of their cloying unease and suspicion. Safran reached out to Roi and to Stave, taking his hand despite his reluctance. Mylla mimicked her, and the four stood in a close circle, only the cold wind making a sound until Stave sighed along with it, releasing the last of his temper.

"Roi, I had to get that out, I did. But I'm done now, brother. We haven't got a star to guide us, but we have you, we have. I'll go along with whatever you think we should do. We all will." He caught Safran's and Mylla's eyes in turn, calling upon their agreement.

Safran nodded, and though still troubled, she looked as if she felt some relief. Mylla, less certain, gave one brief dip of her chin.

Roi looked around at them, jaw still taut but no longer with anger. To Mylla, he seemed unaccountably sad. Dropping their hands, he walked to the edge of the hatch, saying aloud but not to them, "I understand now why Griggory refused to lead the Order."

Refused to lead? thought Mylla. *What is this about?* So many secrets, so many things she didn't yet know about the Order. What else had been kept from her?

Still looking outside, Roi said more loudly, "We go to the northern stronghold."

But that meant… run? Hide? No, she was not going to do that. Not when the fists of a world-killer were clenched around Vinnr, *her* world too, after all. "Roi, we can't simply retreat and hide like cowards. We must stop the usurper. We have a duty!"

Roi turned and spoke words made of bricks: "No, Mylla. Until we once more guard the vessel of our maker, survival is our duty. Our only victory."

"But what about the people of Ivoryss? What about their survival? Their victory? We can *help* them."

Stave said in a voice that was meant to soothe but rasped on her ears like a hairshirt, "You're young still, novice, and you've not yet had time to get the... the *distance* you need from the common people. It's easy for you to understand their suffering, to feel as if they mat—" He stopped and looked at Safran, as if seeking help finding the words.

Matter, Mylla thought. *He was going to say "matter." Do all Knights lose their humanity? Will I?*

Safran understood his need for assistance and continued, *But we can't, Mylla. That isn't our mandate. We have a purpose that lies beyond their fates.*

"Not anymore," Mylla stated.

Silence met her words; the others couldn't dredge up an argument to counter them.

Desperately, she sought a reason to make them see that the people of Ivoryss, of Vinnr, *did* matter, that the Knights faced a deeper choice in this moment than to run or to fight—the choice to care or not, a choice that would be burned into their spirits for eternity if they made the wrong one.

And then a reason came to her. She hated herself for saying it, but she could think of no other way to push them over the cliff with her instead of just to the edge. She felt like a vile traitor, like an ungrateful turncoat, but she said: "And what if Eisa plans to join the usurper?"

Safran gripped her Mentalios tightly, as if to hold it together. *Mylla! How can you say that?*

Push made, now to plunge. Drawing a breath, she went on. "It makes sense, doesn't it? She's taken the Scrylle, the Fenestros. She has everything she needs to win Balavad's favor. Is it so hard to believe? Stave?" He'd be the easiest to convince, so, feeling tarnished by her own actions, she sought his collusion, or *complicity*, first. "For so many turns around Halla, her entire long life practically, she's been devoted to a Verity. Now that Verity is... gone. Eisa may seek to ally with the usurper because she has no other purpose to guide her. She is a Verity's tool." Her thoughts added, *And a broken one.*

The others considered, leaving her holding her breath and grasping for anything more she could say to persuade them. She was manipulating them with the dexterity she'd only seen practiced by a politician like Safran, but she wasn't proud of this newly discovered ability. If anything, she recoiled at her own cunning. "Even if I'm wrong," *please, let me be wrong,* "what if she is captured? The Verity artifacts are our last advantage. We have to retrieve those if we can, at the very least."

The beat of Urgo's and Yggo's wings as the birds retreated to their perches, all signs but the bones of the rabbit vanished, made them all jump. Then Stave said, "She has a good point, a couple of them, she does."

The topaz in Roi's eyes glittered as if on fire. "If we do this, all of us could die and nary a one will be left to carry on. The Order will end with us."

"If the Order no longer serves any purpose, perhaps that will be for the best," Mylla said softly, swallowing hard against the dread bubbling in her throat.

She counted ten heartbeats before Roi finally spoke again:

"To Magdaster."

CHAPTER THIRTY-THREE

As Captain Illago spoke to Bardgrim, Ulfric could hear the man's resolve. He thought he was safe, and men who thought they were safe were the easiest to attack. He asked Bardgrim if the ship had any weapons, and as the Himmingazian responded, that voice spoke once more in Ulfric's head.

Spare the Himmingazians your wrath, Stallari. You are a being of compassion and wisdom. It is why the others follow you. Rage and violence are not your way.

The voice felt more than sounded like a stranger's, and it was growing louder each time it spoke. He had never called himself "Stallari," which would have been odd. But it seemed he did now, and it didn't settle well with him. The distraction alone annoyed him. What was worse was how much harder it was becoming to ignore it.

"Himmingazians haven't warred since the early days of the Glister Cloud," Bardgrim accused. "You're the only one threatening violence here."

Bloodshed as a first resort wasn't his way, this was true. Of the Knights, only Eisa had ever been—how could he put it? Persuaded on a whim to resort to force? That was about right.

You would not hurt others for your own gain. You never have. This is why you were chosen as the Stallari.

People change. For further proof, once more all one had to do was look at what had become of Eisa after the Dyrrakium uprising.

The dragørflies can find a way to free you.

Now why hadn't he thought… ? But it *was* he who thought that. Wasn't it?

Reaching out once more with his mind, much like he did through his Mentalios, he called to the troupe of dragørflies and was instantly rewarded with proliferative ommatidial vision. The sights before him moved and whirled at speeds he could never travel on his own feet as the servants of Vaka Aster flew along the corridors of the *Skate*. It should have been disorienting and overwhelming, yet somehow he simply understood what he was seeing as if each sight came from his own two eyes in an orderly, human fashion. It was amazing.

The creatures swooped throughout the ship, once more following his mental command: *Find a way to open this hatch so we may escape.*

A set of them blew into the oval cabin inhabited by Captain Illago and a half-dozen other Glisternauts. They stood around a bank of metal and glass machines that looked nothing like those inside the *Vigilance*, but which he recognized nonetheless as the apparatus of controlling this ship. One of the Glisternauts caught sight of the hand-sized dragørfly closing in on her and began swatting at it. This clownish act might have amused Ulfric on another day, or in another life, but at the moment it served as an aggravation. He sent several more winged sentries toward the Glisternaut to harry her to distraction, and eventually she simply ducked beneath the console before her. The other Glisternauts scattered, presumably looking for a way to either capture or kill the pests without damaging their own equipment. He had a limited amount of time before that could happen.

"Bardgrim, I'm looking at a bank of lights and flat glass panels that show words in your language and other images."

"You're looking at what?"

He seemed mystified, and Ulfric belatedly recognized that he hadn't truly grasped Ulfric's dragørfly-sight ability. "Understand this, I am able to see inside the chamber this ship is operated from. I can see the devices and mechanisms by which it's done, but I don't know what's required to open this hatch. You do, correct?"

The Himmingazian stared at him as if he had once more spoken in Elder Veros, and this time from a mouth that wasn't where you'd ordinarily find it. Perhaps on his forehead or near his ear.

"Bardgrim! Do you know this ship well enough to know its controls if I describe them to you?"

At last, Bardgrim blinked, nodded.

"Good. Now pay attention." Ulfric described the console quickly, keeping a few sets of wystically empowered insect eyes out for the returning Glisternauts.

Holding his expression carefully still, Bardgrim said, "You see the round image of a dial on the far left screen?"

He nodded.

"Of course you do," Bardgrim muttered, then more loudly: "It has to be spun right a quarter turn, which will open a number pad."

"How is it spun?"

"You just touch it and drag your fingers in the direction you want to spin it."

Ulfric sent this message to the dragørflies, but their appendages were all too light to create enough pressure to turn the dial. "Is there another way?" he grumbled.

"Sure, I can do it from here, except they've disabled my frequency."

Ulfric drew a frustrated spurt of air into his nose, letting it blow out slowly between his clenched teeth. The Himmingazian would have to answer for his lies about the Fenestros and Balavad's Scrylle, but Ulfric had to keep his temper in check at the moment if he was to get any cooperation from him. "Another way that is *useful* to us."

"No."

This time his fists clenched, but then he had an idea. One dragørfly may not have the weight, but many…

Quickly, he sent the thought to his new pets. Heeding his orders, a cadre of about two dozen flew into formation one above another, letting their legs rest on the body segments of the one below until they'd created a tower almost as tall as a human. Then, on command, they all began to oscillate their wings in such a way as to create downward pressure. The lowest, poised on the image of the dial, lit up as the color of the dial changed from white to green.

Holding his excitement in check, he directed them to shift in a carefully calibrated motion to drag the bottommost creature in an arc, pulling the dial a quarter turn. And like Bardgrim had described, images of a series of numbers suddenly radiated out in a circle from the dial. "The number code, Bardgrim," he demanded, marveling again that he somehow had been bestowed not only with the ability to speak the Himmingazian tongue, but to read it.

As Bardgrim said the numbers, he sent them to the dragørflies. As if they were his own fingers, the creatures worked in harmony. Outside the *Octopod*, amber lights began flashing, a warning to those within the hangar that the hatchway would soon be unbarred.

So focused on the exit inside the control room and the dragørflies at the console, he was caught by surprise when some kind of metallic bar suddenly waved through his tower of insects, destroying it. The creatures took to wing instantly, dispersing to safety and leaving just one—the lowest dragørfly still standing over the final number.

"No," he growled.

Whack!

A hand came down atop the last creature, splattering its body across the glass screen. Darting pain shot through Ulfric's eyes into the core of his brain, and his hands flew up reflexively to cover them. "Mongrel-toothed slackface!" he growled. "Where did that come from?"

But then he saw. The Glisternaut who'd hidden beneath the console now stood, wiping her insect-gut-besmeared hand on her leg and swinging the bar frantically with the other at the remaining dragørflies like a blind amateur swordswoman.

"Hold on to something, Knight. I don't know how you did that, but we're off the *Skate* in three… two… ONE!"

He opened his eyes and saw that, despite the troupe of dragørflies' dispersal, the hidden Glisternaut had herself triggered the hatch to open by smashing the last creature into the final number in the code. With a speed so abrupt that Ulfric had no time to brace, the *Octopod* shot from the *Bounding Skate*'s docking hatchway into the glitter-in-the-dark rain of Himmingaze's sky and was far beyond the *Skate*'s sight within a beat of his heart.

CHAPTER THIRTY-FOUR

After the tarnished, smoke-filled atmospheres of both Omina and Asteryss, the clear starlit sky overhead and flickers of city lights below as they approached Magdaster prompted a sense in Mylla that took her a moment to recognize: hope. Maybe the usurper had taken all he wanted and left.

And maybe she shouldn't fool herself.

Halla had risen and set once since they started the journey to Magdaster, and the timing on their arrival was just as they'd hoped. The Knights preferred to arrive after dark, when fewer troops would be alert and the chance of battle slimmer. After the stories of the siege and swift subjugation of Asteryss, they hadn't expected such calm. Not a single Ravener ship nor the storied usurper's warship had harried them anytime during the journey, and none now hovered over Magdaster.

The helm's long-range spyglass, wystically enhanced to provide clarity even in the dark, gave Mylla a commanding perspective on the heavy contingent of guards at intervals atop the city's high walls. It seemed they'd at least received warning about Balavad and his forces. *Brun's last Marines must have arrived safely,* she thought, and that increasingly foreign sensation of hope washed over her again.

The legion here was at least ten thousand fighters strong, but Asteryss had had nearly double that and had fallen in less than a day. Her mind, seemingly bent on actively strangling her tenuous hope, latched on to this fact. *If Balavad wants to conquer Magdaster,* she thought, *is there really anything that can stop him?*

But she shucked that thought. She'd persuaded the Knights to come here on the chance there was a way. Therefore, she had to put faith in the belief they would figure it out. One Knight, with their training, Verity-hallowed weapons, and klinkí stones, was easily equal to a dozen or more commoners in a fight, and with the advantages of the *Vigilance*'s and remaining dragørfly scout's invisibility and the unmatched potency of the emberflare and emberspark cannons, they could sweep the skies free of Ravener ships with deadly stealth.

With an eye on searching out the best place to bring in the *Vigilance*, Mylla scanned the city. Like barnacles on a reef, the granite and timber buildings and towers of Magdaster stretched along the inland hills that spilled down to the northern coastline. The forbidding wall running opposite the sea along the city's flank and enveloping it from north to south served as a final impediment to any ground invaders, but its real defenses were its hilltop and seaside artillery. As Ivoryss's last large port city in the remote north before the land gave way to ancient and unsettled forests, the Magdastervians' hardy self-sufficiency gave them an edge of fierceness that only the foolish could fail to appreciate.

Though the city, like Asteryss, had been built long before the Vinnrics had developed flying ships, the wall and its defensive armaments stood steady against the living dragørs of the Howling Weald, and were thus always maintained to their peak strength. The endless weald itself created a need in the Magdastervians to remain ever-vigilant and ever-fierce.

She wasn't looking forward to appearing among them out of nowhere, especially now that they were on alert. Sharing a common enemy, she hoped, would make convincing them the Knights came to help an easier task.

Now floating above the city, she chose the spot where they would hover while they made contact with the Marines, just as Stave joined her on deck.

"How does it look to you, novice?"

"Our intention is to offer aid, so we may as well announce ourselves right off to the highest number of Magdastervians as we can. City center." She pointed to it beyond the wind screen.

Clicking his Mentalios into the housing on the deck's main spyglass, he peered through and swiveled the mount to where she indicated. "Aye. Looks to be quiet, it does, but there are a few lights. Guard houses, I'd say, with troops catching sleep and sharpening knives while they're off duty. Dropping right into their midst'll be exciting."

"You wouldn't have joined the Knights if you didn't crave a bit of excitement, eh?"

He cocked a thick eyebrow curiously at her, then grinned. "Mylla, you and I should find some time to compare ideas on what 'exciting' means." With a good-natured slap on her back, he started toward the hatch. "Let us know when we're there."

They'd discussed leaving someone aboard the *Vigilance* as the rest met up with Commander Nennus's legion and elected Safran. She would bring up the ladder to safeguard access to the ship and keep watch over them using the optics and the bruhawks. Splitting up would further weaken them, and it wasn't as if they would retaliate against any aggression by the Marines by using something as catastrophic as the emberflare cannon—that would kill Knight and soldier alike, for hundreds of paces. But leaving the *Vigilance* unguarded with the ladder down invited its capture. And no one would be safe with it in the hands of commoners. Until they had a pact with Nennus, they would not reveal all of their assets. And if they could find and enlist Havelock and Brun to speak for them, it could hasten their hoped-for collaboration.

With a final tug and tightening, Mylla ensured her armor was ready, then placed her hands around the yoke that controlled the *Vigilance*, steering them silently and invisibly into place. The *Vigilance*'s momentum shifted slightly beneath her feet when they arrived, and she released the yoke.

On her way through the hold to join the others, she had a fleeting thought. *If only Lock and I could speak to each other through Mentalios lenses.* She sensed the deeper part of the anticipation she was feeling was about seeing him again. Aloud, she whispered, "He should become a Knight. It is the only way we can be together."

A quieter part of her mind, however, questioned: *But is being a Knight still what you truly wish?*

Stepping onto the deck with the others, she told herself now was not the time for such considerations.

Ready? Safran asked.

Seeing Stave and Roi standing abreast of Safran sent a jolt of pride through Mylla. The imperial sight of the Knights Corporealis in full fighting regalia would make even the most decorated Dragør Marine pause in admiration. Scholars in spirit and warriors down to their very marrow, the Knights manifested a nobility that was nearly venerable, as if they were more than human, splinters of Vaka Aster incarnate. For a moment, she was transported to her childhood and the first time she'd seen the Knights like this, uniformed for a procession of state to coronate the new Arch Keeper. She'd been at the knees of her guardians, and though the memory of their faces was blurred by the passage of time, the image of these three regal celestially marked Knights before her, along with Symvalline, Eisa, and Aldinhuus and others who'd since been lost to the Order, had never dulled or faded.

With a mute nod, she pulled open the hatch.

CHAPTER THIRTY-FIVE

In the dark, only two things were known to Ravener Irrick. The first was a pull, a draw, a *straining* of his mind to... something beyond. Some light or heat, or both, called to him, burning like oil in his thoughts. He knew that light for what it was. The wystic spark of Vaka Aster, as potent as the darkness cloaking him but opposite in every way. It was infuriatingly near, he knew, but he could only see it if he got closer—if his new sense could still be called "seeing."

The second was a voice. The voice of His Holiness, Balavad the Verity and creator of Battgjald, a realm of which Irrick was now a servitor. His Holiness whispered at the base of his skull, always present, always aware of him, of his perceptions, of what he might think or do. A Ravener's mind, Irrick understood—in as much as he was conscious of understanding—served the Verity. A part of the maker, to be controlled and know all that the Ravener did.

In the darkness, Irrick's fate was slavery.

His Holiness's voice slid inside Irrick's mind. *Speak to me, Ravener. Where are you now?*

Holiness, I am a captive aboard the ship of the Knights Corporealis.

Where?

Irrick sensed an impatience in the tone, and it sent needles of fear into his flesh. *I cannot say, Holiness. But they are near. I can feel the Verity spark they carry.*

Moments of silence passed and the dark closed back in, shrouding Irrick and draining all sense, even of fear, from him once more. A Ravener, first a slave, was also a shell, a space waiting to be filled with his maker's aspirations. Soon, one came.

You must get free and kill the Knights. This is your anointed purpose, your reason for existing. Achieve this, and you will be exalted among all Raveners. As reward, I will give you all the knowledge of all the realities.

A new sensation tingled at the fringes of his mind: profound joy. No reward could possibly mean more to him than to be the recipient of this gift, this wealth of cognition—a treasure so immense only the Verities could claim it and choose to share it. This *was* his anointed purpose, and it had been since... before. Before he became a Ravener.

But that before *is inconsequent,* the Verity whispered to him. *Now, serving me, the zenith of all the Verities, is all that matters. I have already gifted you with much that you previously desired. Immortality, as well as strength far beyond your frail form. Use these now to escape.*

Irrick reached out, using his hands to understand his confinement because his eyes were blind. Intuitively, he hissed, his vibrating tongue no longer in pain. The noise echoed, and combined with what his fingers felt, they created a picture in his mind that was as clear as, or clearer than, his eyesight had previously been. The door to his small closet was made of wood, and wood could be broken. But the Knights who confined him had left nothing in the room but a wooden pail, a loaf of seedy bread, and a carafe of water. The carafe was made of clay.

It was enough.

From the helm of the *Vigilance*, Safran waited expectantly, her poise statue-still. Her eyes swirled with colors that flowed outside the borders of visibility to normal human sight as she gazed past the confines of the ship, seeing the world outside. Yggo and Urgo soared in loops around Magdaster's center square, keenly alert to the plight of the Knights below them. Wystic optics had their place, but the eyes of a bruhawk missed nothing.

It took the Dragør Marines on watch a few moments to understand, or at least react to, the sight of her fellow Knights descending inside a sphere of transparent blue light from what appeared to them to be thin air. Their warning shouts reverberated furiously between the granite walls of the town—sounds so urgent they came to Safran from both the bruhawks' ears and through the *Vigilance*'s hull. Her fellow Knights' thoughts channeled softly along the Mentalios link to her mind. They hoped the Marines' surprise didn't evoke such fear and hostility toward the Knights that they would be forced to fight in self-defense. They did not want to hurt these people.

Mylla, Stave, and Roibeard readied themselves as the soldiers quickly surrounded them. Words she couldn't hear were exchanged, though the stiffness and menace of their figures—both Knights' and Marines'—in the square told their own story.

Stave, she sent, *tell me what is happening.*

Just basic negotiations, my beautiful bloom of embers. The breed of these hinter regions have extra-small brains, they do. May take us a few more moments to convince them of our intentions.

She snickered at his tactlessness, reminded of the reasons Stave was so rarely selected as spokesperson for the Knights. Long turns past, he'd come from these hinter regions himself, which made his brazen insult that much more amusing.

Yggo swooped low as a gate to the square's capital building rolled open, sending Safran glimpses of a squad of heavily armored Marines as they formed up and stepped past it. She recognized Commander Brun but knew none of the others. Their leader, a stout dark-skinned man of middling commoner age, wore a breastplate bearing the red and green Dragør, wingless to show his membership in the ground and sea forces rather than the Wings. The emblem on his pauldrons proclaimed his rank as commander as well.

He must be Nennus. It didn't take the watch long to summon him. But is this a good sign? They are either very efficient or very uneasy.

Of course, both descriptions fit, and upon hearing Mylla's

recounting of Brun's tales of Asteryss, the local legion was right to be on edge.

Snippets of the conversation below came to her through the bruhawks. *Join in this fight... the Knights have a weapon that can wither the Ravener's forces... time is short before the usurper arrives...*

... Eisa was never here...

Safran tensed. So, they had guessed incorrectly. Eisa must have taken the Fenestros to Dyrrakium.

Leaning forward unwittingly, she strained to hear more, forcing herself not to interrupt as they parleyed, yet chafing against the restriction of staying behind.

A shriek sliced into the air, so shrill she felt it seemingly cut into her ears. Startled, she dropped her Mentalios and blinked, losing her connection to the bruhawks' sight. Within a breath, the shriek came again. It sounded inhuman and tortured, coming from Acolyte Irrick's direction.

A moment passed as she considered whether to leave her post here and see to him or continue her watch over those below. That scream, filled with daggers of affliction, decided for her. The Knights and the Marines' discussion, though tense and metered, did not appear to be on the verge of combat, and Irrick sounded as if he were dying. She had to check on him.

Pacing down the passageway to the locked closet, she noted the water seeping from beneath the door. Leaning against it, she listened and heard the ragged bellows-like sound of Irrick breathing in snatches that testified of pain or illness.

Quickly, she unlatched the door and pulled it open.

Limbs flailed at her, one hand striking her cheek and sending her into a half-turn. Before she could react, a gash seared along her neck and blood began pouring down her chest, then a shard was stabbed into her heart, hitting her with an icy agony so stifling that her lungs could not draw a breath.

With arms that felt made of lead, she reached for the hands holding whatever was lodged in her chest, unable to believe she'd been attacked. Irrick emerged from the darkness of the closet, his sightless eyes wandering, his bloodless lips hanging slack. She looked down and saw the sheet of blood covering her tunic, too much of it, more than any mortal could bear to lose. A shard of crockery bloomed from her heart. Her knees buckled, and she fell back against the passageway wall. Numbness spread throughout her body, and she used the last of her will to look back into the acolyte's looming white face.

A mask of undeath, she thought and blackness consumed her.

CHAPTER THIRTY-SIX

Jaemus stared past the ship's view screen into the miasma of color and storm outside. The only difference between the sky and the Never Sea underneath them was that beneath the fractured and glistening lights of the Glister Cloud the Never Sea remained the same ichor-dark indigo.

Sometimes during Glister Dim if the Never Sea was very calm, the Cloud's reflection could not be teased from the Glister Cloud itself, and he worried he'd simply fly straight into the camouflaged sea. He never had, yet, but in the recesses of his mind, he wondered what a death trapped beneath both the glittering envelope of Cloud and layers of leaden water would feel like. If the cold sea filled the *Octopod* and crushed the hatches shut with relentless pressure, would his last thoughts be of his lonely, frigid fear or simply acceptance of the futility of it all? A certain peace could be found in acceptance, he knew. He'd held his mother's hand as she'd slipped away from a wasting disease anni-cycles before. Too young and still so many things she'd wanted to do. And though the days leading up to her death had been painful for her, in the end, she'd looked into his eyes and smiled, comforting *him* instead of the other way around. "It's all right, son. This is where my suffering ends. There's nothing more to be sad about." And then she'd been gone, leaving him with the knowledge that she'd come to terms with the life she would miss, and finally accepting that inevitability had freed her from fear and replaced it with serenity. Her last lesson to him.

His father, proud of Jaemus though he was, remained skeptical of the Glisternauts' pursuit, and Jaemus's career kept him away from Jovus's city more often than not. Now, Cote was his closest family. And, yes, the Glisternauts as well, to a degree, though he knew they thought him eccentric and undisciplined. Two traits that were rarely enviable or respected in Himmingaze, where the values of order and predictability held sway. But in his own case, he thought they mixed well.

He'd solved many riddles on how to make Himmingaze's airborne existence safer and more productive, to improve the hydrofoil lifts that kept their cities' afloat above the roiling and unforgiving Never Sea, and make life under the looming Glister Cloud more comfortable, as much as it could be. And now he was integral into designing ships that might even get them beyond the Cloud and escape its terrible beauty and danger for good.

Unless, of course, what this stranger from, he claimed, a strange land said was true: there was no "beyond" the Cloud.

But that was absurd. Of course it was. Wasn't it?

In need of an escape from these thoughts, he glanced aside at Aldin-huus and startled at the man's striking luminescent eyes. Like the Never Sea below, they reflected the Cloud, with pinpoint beams and motes dancing and swirling against a shadowy cerulean cornea. The Knight didn't notice his reaction and seemed as deep in thought as Jaemus was. What could he be thinking of? This man, teetering so clearly on the edge of lunacy, who nonetheless possessed abilities unlike anything Jaemus had ever seen or could explain, what grim thoughts held his focus so completely?

He cleared his throat as he rose from his seat. "Shouldn't be more than a half-cycle before we get back to the island. I've set our coordinates and the skies are calm. Well, calm for Himmingaze. The ship should be fine getting us there on its own. I'm just going to run to the hold and see what kind of supplies are left."

The Knight responded without moving a muscle, eerily resembling a statue with gemstone eyes. "Sit."

Jaemus's legs took the command seriously and spilled him back down. *Traitors,* he mused. *I'm the one in charge here.* But that was a laugh. It hadn't been true for some time now.

"That's the second time you've tried to leave my sight, Himmingazian," Aldinhuus continued. "You've already proved you're not trustworthy. You may live in a world where your wits have always served you, but your wits have met their match, I assure you. Even without my turns of wisdom, far more than yours, I too am a man of many wiles."

Who talked like this? It was like speaking to a man who'd jumped from the pages of one of Gramsirene Vreyja's forbidden lore books. The only one he'd ever met with similar diction was, well, the man who'd indirectly heaped all this strangeness on him in the first place, the Knight called Griggory.

Accepting that he wasn't going to be allowed out of Aldinhuus's weird sight, Jaemus settled back in his chair. "A simple, 'please have a seat,' would have sufficed," he grumbled. A thought came to mind. "Let me ask you something. You said you and this Griggory fellow are from the same place, but your skin is dark where his is pale, I might even say sickly looking. I'll give you that neither of you fit in with the usual Himmingazian, but you look almost nothing like each other either."

"Griggory is a northerner. The kingdom he came from is now called Yor, but in his time it was still part of the one empire, before the War of Rivening, when commoners split the kingdoms into three. Ivoryss, Yor, Dyrakkium."

"And did you fight in this war?"

"It was over seven hundred turns of Halla before I was born, but I know much of it and have fought enough battles since to wish for no more."

"... I have a feeling you're going to tell me a 'turn of Halla' is similar to an anni-cycle here in Himmingaze."

For the first time in the conversation, Aldinhuus looked at him. "I have no idea what an 'anni-cycle' is, commoner."

By his tone, Jaemus judged Aldinhuus's words to mean something closer to, *Speak again, and I'll sew your lips shut.* He didn't need to be told twice and fell silent. At least for a moment. One attribute of his admittedly stupendous intellect was a tendency to fidget. And if he couldn't fidget, to speak. Which, as was once more the case, led his mouth to engage before his brain did. "I suppose we're lucky, then. With all your, ahem, 'battle' experience, at least you didn't kill anyone on the *Skate.*"

Once he realized what he'd said, he braced himself for the blowback that was certainly coming. But Aldinhuus simply turned to him and glowered darkly. Jaemus tried on a shrinking smile and began nervously fiddling with the goggles still hanging around his neck.

"What is that optical apparatus?"

"They're lenses to help me see better in the dark, especially during Glister Dim. They—"

"Give them to me."

"... All right then." He pulled them over his stack of curls, which now leaned lazily to one side from the few hours of astonishingly refreshing sleep he'd gotten while in the *Bounding Skate*'s brig.

Aldinhuus let the strap hang and held the lenses over his eyes, then twisted his head this way and that to look around the pilot's compartment. With a satisfied grunt, he took a moment to figure out the adjustable strap, then fit the goggles over his face and tightened them.

"What's mine is yours," Jaemus offered, only just managing to conceal his sarcasm.

"These are not unlike the eye shields I wear when I'm working in my craftery. Now I can look upon you and see just a man instead of... more than I can explain." He fell silent again, then asked with what Jaemus liked to think might have been a hint of admiration in his tone, "Did you create these?"

"I did."

"You are a lens maker, too, as am I, among other things."

He quirked an eyebrow at the Knight, waiting to see if he would say more, perhaps elaborate on why their shared inventiveness interested him, but Aldinhuus had returned to his laconic state. "You're sitting in the most marvelous ship in the Glisternaut fleet, one that I designed, and it's the goggles that impress you," Jaemus said, then sighed and looked back out into the storm.

Finally, he couldn't hold back any longer. "Aldinhuus, give it to me straight. I know our agreement relied on our cooperative effort to retrieve the rest of the Creatress's Verity stones. But now that we've left the map behind, it doesn't seem like that's possible. Does this other Scrylle back at the shrine have the same kind of map?" And the question buzzing in his head that he chose not to ask, at least not yet: *And if not, what do you need me for?* He was afraid he wasn't going to like the answer to that.

"Doesn't matter. If you're telling the truth this time"—he swiveled to burden Jaemus with his weighty scowl, felt if not seen through the opaque lenses—"I'll have Balavad's Scrylle and stones that I need to spin a new cage. Then I will put a stop to the two desecrators who killed my family. Forever, if I am lucky." His voice was so bitter it would have made chuffee grounds left to fester for weeks taste sweet.

This was news to Jaemus, and he spent a few moments letting it sink in. Was this story true or simply a new layer of the man's craziness? He cleared his throat. "Who exactly killed your family?" He wasn't intentionally being insensitive, but the wandering threads of Aldinhuus's story increased every time he spoke. It was both fascinating and a little like watching an explosion in slow motion. And as with any explosion, he worried the final outcome would be messy, at best.

Aldinhuus, apparently having exposed something he hadn't meant to, said abruptly, "Never mind."

The tickle of his intuition, something Jaemus always paid attention to, became a hard rub. "So that's what this is, isn't it? A... a vendetta. You never planned on aiding me at all, did you?"

Aldinhuus's silence answered for him.

Fine foggy mess you've gotten yourself into, you fool, Jaemus told himself. *This guy has you over a cistern. You know you can't fight him.* He glanced sideways at the Knight, taking in the full girth of the heftier man's arms and thick neck. *No way, nuh-uh. And you can't disarm him, unless you catch him by surprise. And if you just stop the ship and wait for the 'Nauts, you're putting them in danger too. No, this is your puzzle; you figure it out. And that apology you were hoping to get from Cote—you can bet the entire humble pie those tables have turned. Damn the skies and sea.*

The hold contained a locker stocked with shelksies that he could easily access if he had a moment to himself. But because he couldn't even leave his seat without arousing Aldinhuus's suspicions, as well as paint himself as a target for the man's remarkably well-aimed kinky stones, what options did he have?

Distraction.

Overcoming the urge to glance guiltily at the Knight became his sole objective in life as he, as casually as he could, reached for the control spheres that managed the *Octopod*'s pitch, yaw, and roll.

"What are you doing?" the Knight asked.

"Storm's getting worse," he responded after what he hoped wasn't a suspicious pause. "Need to adjust the..." *Just do it now, idiot!* his intuition commanded.

His left hand flew to his harness, unlocking the buckle as his right abruptly spun one of the control spheres, forcing the *Octopod* into a jarring half roll. He flew sideways from his seat, fortunately away from Aldinhuus, but unfortunately still caught partway in the over-the-shoulders harness. He now hung from the side of his chair like a fish in a net, struggling to extricate himself.

The Knight grunted, but Jaemus did himself the favor of not looking at him. His legs flailed as he tried to find footing, busting his shin painfully against the seat mount for his trouble. As tall as he was, his feet found purchase and he locked his legs, stood, and frantically extricated himself from the buckle.

"Right this ship now, Bardgrim!" the Knight roared.

For the moment, Aldinhuus struggled to unlock his own harness, now fastened tight because of his weight hanging against it. The

Octopod, being the precision machine Jaemus had designed it to be, would hold its course at this angle until either he corrected it or some unfortunate element of the storm made its own "correction," so he had a bit of time. But only a bit. The Knight had already stopped attacking the seat harness with brute strength and begun a cunning string of contortions that would get him clear in no time. Shambling against the ship's unnatural cant, Jaemus made for the hold and the shelksies that may now be his only chance at stopping a display of wrath he preferred never to witness.

He made it clear of the hatch and dogged it shut behind him, wishing he'd thought to build locks on both sides. Too late for wishes and dreams. The weapon locker, now on the ceiling—*water and lightning! why didn't I think of that!?*—taunted him. Scrambling to the table that was welded to the floor, he used what little grace nature had given him to climb to its narrow edge and place both feet along it as if standing on a tightrope. The *Octopod*'s constant speed made holding that position easier, but even a tiny jounce would send him flying. The hold had nothing but hard walls, sharp corners, and metal edges. Ignoring this, he reached over his head, and his fingertips just brushed the locker door handle. Drawing the deepest breath he could manage in an effort to increase his length even a bit, he swiped again, just managing to hook two fingers along the handle's edge and hold it. With a triumphant yank, he pulled it free and the door swung down. The shelksies remained wedged in their cradles, not locked, merely requiring a yank to come free. If he jumped, he could grab one.

It occurred to him that the Knight had had plenty of time to free himself from the harness by now. Why hadn't he come roaring through the hatch like a water spout through a hurricane? Shrugging internally, not one to question luck when it was good, he crouched as much as he could without losing his footing and sprang for the locker.

His luck turned inside out at that moment, and the ship suddenly leveled, sending Jaemus flying through the hold in an arc that was far from what he'd intended. He managed to make contact with the weapon locker, but with his temple instead of his hands, and seemingly all the lights of the Glister Cloud rushed inside his head, then dimmed rapidly as he lost consciousness.

"I KNOW what you're thinking, Himmingazian, but I will not harm you."

For the last few moments, Jaemus's eyelids had been fluttering as his thoughts jumped undecidedly from one side of the veil of consciousness to the other. The voice was the Knight's, so he must be watching. This thought, which was the awake sort, creeped him out just enough for him to open his eyes completely. The Knight's blocky, stubbled chin and its odd blue nine-pointed star marking, along with a perfect view of the tangle of wiry hair inside Aldinhuus's nose, filled his sight as the Knight leaned down to speak closely.

"I need you to fly this ship."

Jaemus started to speak, found his throat uncooperative, cleared it, and croaked, "And I thought I was just good company." After a pause, he added, "It seems you're able enough to fly the *Octopod* on your own, in any case."

Now fully lucid, his senses were telling him that the ship was level and flying smoothly. Obviously the Knight had, instead of chasing Jaemus as Jaemus had assumed he would, taken to the ship's controls and put things to rights. Despite being the oddest human being he had ever met, this man had more tricks up his sleeve than Jaemus was prepared to guess at. *Mixing unhinged with genius is never going to turn out well*, he mused. *At least not for me.*

"True," Aldinhuus said, straightening up to provide Jaemus, who still lay on the floor where he must have landed, a better view of the hold. "I've learned a bit about this craft and its capabilities while you've been out cold. Not terribly different than the *Vigilance* herself when it comes down to the mechanics of flying. But I've yet to understand your navigational optics. So I still need you."

These words struck like a frigid wind. *Still need you.* As in, *But I won't at some point.* Gingerly exploring the bump on his temple, tender to the touch, he griped, "You've threatened me, my crew, and me again, Aldinhuus. I can see quite clearly you're not sound-minded. As much as I'd like to help you accomplish this vendetta you're plainly on, I'm really not seeing a good reason to do so. If you're going to kill me, or steal my ship, or juggle some fancy space rocks, fine. Get on with it, then. I'm not enjoying being your lackey or your puppet, and, to put it simply, I'm not going to do it anymore."

Well done, Jaemus. That's your death warrant sealed. He sighed audibly, unwilling to look into Aldinhuus's face and read whatever wrath or revenge was written there. *At least you've gotten him far away from Cote and the Glisternauts. Hopefully they remember you fondly, or at least, remember the good you've done Himmingaze.*

Without warning, Aldinhuus rocketed up from his crouch, hauling Jaemus by the collar with him. Expecting the worst, Jaemus did the last thing he'd ever considered doing to another person: he swung his fist as hard as he could and, amazingly, connected precisely with the star on the Knight's chin.

"OUCH!" Jaemus yelled, his fingers screaming as if he'd just slammed them into a rock.

The Knight, still gripping his shoulders, sagged backward, pulling Jaemus over with him. Flailing his hands to try to maintain his balance, he unintentionally hooked the goggles Aldinhuus still wore and pulled them up to his forehead. They hit the floor together, Aldinhuus soundlessly, Jaemus with a heavy "oof." His face was merely a nose away from the Knight's. Aldinhuus's eyes were half-closed, but slits of his cornea that were visible blazed with liquid color that Jaemus could not look away from. He rose to his knees slowly, as if moving in a dream, but he had no desire to move or turn his eyes aside from that flashing chromaticism.

"Look. Listen." The words slid from Aldinhuus's throat, but Jaemus could have sworn it wasn't his voice.

And that's when things got *really interesting.*

Mist-like cerulean tendrils filled the hold, darkening and thickening the air inside, closing in all around him until he was wrapped in a dense cocoon. It grew dim until all he could see were shifting blue streamers all around. The only source of light were the two glowing beacons of Aldinhuus's weirded eyes. They grew both closer and distant at once, disorienting Jaemus even more than the blanket of mist now filling his ship.

Still, he had no impulse to panic. For some reason, he felt only a deep curiosity similar to when he became immersed in exploring a new apparatus or machine. He felt, almost, as if he verged on a great discovery that waited on the tip of his brain, beckoning him inexorably until he reached out and grasped it.

Jaemus, he told himself, *you should be worried. Your ship is filling with smoke... or something like it. Maybe you crashed and hit your head harder than you think. You might be sinking to the bottom of the Never Sea right now. Wake up!*

You aren't dreaming, creature of Lifs.

The voice was like crystal in his ears, but it wasn't in his ears. It was in his head. He didn't have a chance to ponder this before Aldinhuus's eyes flared like blue fire. Jaemus should have blinked. Instead his own eyes grew wider, wider—or so he assumed. All his physical sensations seemed disembodied and beyond him now—and he was pulled into the blaze, now shining with the luminosity of a thousand stars, shifting, glittering, growing, as if seen through a pool of water—

—was he drowning?

At a complete loss, he found himself asking the crystal voice the same question, *If I'm not asleep, then am I drowning?*

Look. It repeated itself. *Listen.*

He reasoned that if he was being asked to do something that required being not dead—looking and listening—he must not be drowning. Unless this was a moment of lunacy before he died in some other horrible way, but he was certain he'd find out eventually. Hesitantly, he told the voice, *I'm all... ears?*

I cannot hold him away too long or it will break his mind.

Him? You mean Aldinhuus? He guessed he knew where this conversation was going. Which was confirmation that he was indeed falling off sanity's edge, just as his strange new confederate had. Who knew lunacy was contagious?

Yes. I brought him to this realm to keep him safe, but the Knight Corporealis has wrapped chains around his mind that detain me, and he has barred himself from hearing me. I see through his eyes when they are not veiled. This distracts him, but it's temporary. You must speak to him for me, creature of my quin Lifs.

Oh indeed, this was getting good. *So, if I'm a creature of Lifs, and Lifs's your quin, that means you're a Verity too? Are you the one Aldinhuus calls Vaka Aster?*

Yes. Now heed. You must tell Aldinhuus this: I made him my vessel because he is the strongest of my creations, but he made his mind a cage to hold me. If he dies, Vinnr dies with him.

But you're some sort of celestial being. Can't you just, er, decamp from him, whatever it's called?

Only the maker of this cage can unmake it.

Uh-huh, sure, I understand, but he calls you *the maker. If you made him, can't you... ?* He stopped himself, realizing the implications of a maker reversing the making. The crystal voice's next words confirmed this uncomfortable truth.

Yes, I can unmake him. And then Vinnr, a realm that you do not know, but one with as many creatures and marvels as your own, would be unmade as well.

If one could squirm in their own thoughts, Jaemus did now. After sitting with this news for a moment, he realized, in the off, *off* chance that he wasn't going crazy, this might be his opportunity to achieve what he'd been hoping to all along. Maybe he couldn't get the Himmingazian people clear of the Glister Cloud, but what if he could clear the Glister Cloud from Himmingaze? If this was a Verity, it might know. So he asked, *Aldinhuus told me that's what's happening to Himmingaze, that the Creatress is slowly unmaking it. Can you tell me how to save it?*

Ulfric is fighting. I have to release him now. No creature's mind can withstand a Verity's control of it for long. Creations must be free to be their own masters. It is one of the rules we five Verities agreed on when we created all. This was our purpose for creation. Tell him of Vinnr: it will be the loss of his world if he dies. Tell him. Make him believe. His duty is to protect my vessel, which is now himself.

All right, definitely, I'll tell him. But can't you at least show me how to find or reach out to the Creatress? he pleaded.

The five cannot see each other.

Can't see... ? What kind of tinnyrot—

Tell him, Himmingazian. Tell him not to destroy his world.

CHAPTER THIRTY-SEVEN

Once the tumult had settled and Commander Nennus was summoned, Mylla unclenched her hand around her klinkí stones, noting sharp twinges in the divots they left in her palm. The squadron coming through the gates looked every bit as serious as she and the Knights felt, and she knew their negotiations would be no less strained than she had expected.

As their new leader, Roi was the most temperamentally suited for the task of convincing the city and Dragør Marine commander of the Knights' intentions, and she assured herself she would hold her tongue unless absolutely necessary. She hoped Stave was capable of the same.

Searching the faces of the soldiers accompanying Nennus, she noted Brun was there, as was the older captain with whom Brun had spoken in the tunnels beneath Ivoryss. She continued scanning the group, hoping to spot Lock among them, but a different face, one almost as familiar as Lock's but far less expected, arrested her attention instead. Henrick, Lock's father.

As Roi and Nennus spoke, Henrick stared back at her with the same green-brown eyes as Lock's. She could barely focus on the discussion, wanting more than anything she could recall wanting in all her turns to ask Henrick what had happened to the rest of his family—his heartmatch, Elinora, his five daughters—and where Lock was. Once a city guard and protector, he now wore the robes of a politician and traveled as one of the Arch Keeper's advisory council throughout the kingdom. Yet here he stood bedecked in armor, with a sword and bandolier of petards hung on crossed baldrics over his shoulders. In Asteryss's desperation, it appeared even the noncombatant citizens had been called to take up arms against the usurper's forces.

But, still, where was Lock? Had he found his mum and sisters? If so, surely he'd be here now. Colder inside and out than the crisp northern winds could account for, Mylla glanced again at Henrick. What did that glint in his eyes mean? Excitement? Or sorrow? He stared back at her without reservation. Was there something he wanted her to know?

"We didn't expect to find Magdaster still unmolested by the usurper's forces, and came to offer our assistance while fulfilling our own obligations to Vaka Aster," Roi was saying. "You're fortunate too. Magdaster may remain overlooked by Balavad. But our first need is to know if one of our Order has come this way, the Knight called Eisa."

Nennus spoke in a voice that sounded like boulders rolling along the bottom of a great river. "Commander Brun tells me the Knights Corporealis are fewer than ten in number. I see but three. And you say one has gone missing. How, then, did you intend to offer assistance in stopping the usurper? What wystic tricks and contrivances are you hiding?" He glanced meaningfully toward the heavens, where the *Vigilance* remained unseen but the bruhawks lingered in tight circles unlike any bird of prey's ordinary behavior. "And what, do tell me, Knight of Yor, do you expect in return?"

A twitch from Stave beside her drew a glance from Mylla. He remained silent, though his bird's-nest brows drew together in a furious scowl. Where Brun's gruffness stemmed from her outspoken disbelief in and distrust of Verity lore and the Knights themselves, Nennus's own harsh demeanor was more an innate product of the lands he and the Magdastervians inhabited. Even inside the heavy walls, the Howling Weald pressed against her mind as strongly as it did the city's borders, like a leafed and needled shroud of creeping darkness. It was said the trees roared and the forest itself fought back when people tried to thin out the edges. She didn't believe the silly story—obviously the timbers used to help build Magdaster came from nearby—but the dragørs that remained shrouded by those woods awed and frightened her as much as any living human. With these flying beasts at their gates, it was no wonder Magdastervians treated everything that came from outside their walls with cold suspicion.

His demeanor unchanged, Roi said, "Our ship can destroy more of the usurper's forces than any armaments your walls bear, and aye, our Verity tools and contrivances may help us learn what we can do to deflect this threat. You may know as well as we do that no other Verity besides Vaka Aster has ever visited this realm—or at least been known to visit it. We don't claim to have the power to stop Balavad the Usurper, though Knight Nazaria carries artifacts that may protect us. *All* of us. I ask again, Commander, is she here?"

Mylla was certain Roi intentionally chose to avoid implying Eisa might be here as a prisoner. Surely Brun had shared all that had occurred between the Knights and the people of Asteryss, including her initial suspicions roused beneath Aster Keep when Ulfric looked to be in league with Balavad, and it would not have escaped Brun's notice that Mylla had visited Asteryss right before the usurper's warship arrived for its last cleansing of the city that had forced them to retreat for good. Would these events seem yoked together enough to prompt them to capture Eisa if she'd come this way?

Staring at Roi like a man judging between two evils, Nennus sucked air between his teeth. "This man's son," he said, turning half-aside and waving a hand at Havelock's father, who obeyed the gesture and stepped forward to stand beside the commander, "says he has seen this ship of yours, been inside and flown in it, and you admit it exists, yet you still feel the need to hide it from those with whom you wish to collaborate. You can understand, Knight, why I retain my doubts."

Roi stood silently, weighing his response before saying it aloud, as was his way. Before he could, though, Nennus continued. "Knight Nazaria was never here, unless she, too, came unseen and in secrecy as your ilk seems to prefer. So if she has the tools you claim may aid us…" He let the statement hang, the implications too varied to be certain of.

"I see," stated Roi. "A moment, then." He took a step backward and beckoned to draw Mylla and Stave into a huddle.

She noted as he did the tightening of hands on sword hilts around her and the way the soldiers pressed closer. It was clear; whatever the Knights did, they would not be free to leave. Ignoring the jab to her pride—how wrong she'd been to believe she could understand Eisa's mind—she channeled to the others, *I think it may have been a mistake to come here.*

I sense it too, novice, Stave imputed. *Their fear is too strong now to think they'll act reasonably, it is. Time to get on. Roi?*

The elder Knight dipped his chin slightly, and Mylla noted that sag around his eyes again, a shadow of sadness. He sent, *Ready your klinkís.*

She no sooner opened her palm to release her stones when a sharp… not sound, exactly, but a *feeling* of sound, like a cry that has been transformed into a spear point, drilled into her brain. She staggered, then blinked and realized the others had felt it too.

"Safran!" Stave yelled, flinging his stones hastily up.

As soon as he said her name, Mylla realized Safran was in trouble. Something terrible was happening (had happened?) aboard the *Vigilance* while they stood in this courtyard. Her stones and Roi's instantly followed Thorvíl's, forming up into a circlet around them.

"Stop them!" shouted Commander Nennus, and the ring of guards began to close, with their weapons raised, on the Knights from all sides.

They may as well have been carrying wet wheat stalks for the damage their swords did to the bubble of blue light that encapsulated the three of them. No common weapon had power against the klinkí stones and the protection of Vaka Aster's spark. They rose into the air, concentrating on Safran, trying to learn what had caused the shock through their Mentalios lenses.

In her fear for Safran, Mylla didn't fail to realize that she was losing the chance, maybe her last, to ask Lock's father what had become of him. It seemed fate was determined to mock her, maybe all of them.

UsING his forked tongue and desiccated windpipe to generate shrill hoots and shrieks, Acolyte Irrick shambled along passages in the empty *Vigilance*, finding that these sounds were his new eyes. As the noise bounced from stem to stern throughout the ship, images emerged as if from fog in his mind's eye, gray and faint at first but sharper and clearer the higher he keened. The void contained no color, but he barely recalled color anyway. Instead, the scents of things accosted him, a sensory storm stronger and more arresting than any color had ever been. Between these qualities, he navigated quite easily, in harmony with his new mode of engagement with the world.

The voice of His Holiness never left his mind. *What are you seeing now, Ravener?*

A hallway, Holiness, and a room, a large open hall. And here, a dais bearing the statue of a woman, but many hands taller. She is—

Vaka Aster's vessel... The voice went silent for long enough that Irrick stilled completely, awaiting his next order. Then: *You've done very well, Ravener, very well. Now take control of that ship and learn its location. Once you do, you will reveal it to me. I am coming for it.*

WITH THE ENRAGED SHOUTING of the Dragør Marines clamoring from below, Mylla drew the *Vigilance* hatch closed to cut off the bulk of the noise, though the faint *dink dink* of spears being thrown against the hull still reached them. Stave sped away like a cyclone, hollering Safran's name. Roi bore a sanguine look, the expression he wore when using his Mentalios, and Mylla joined him.

Safran? they called. *Where are you? What has happened?*

No response.

Roi sent, *Mylla, to the bridge. I feel danger closing, from within and without.*

Together, they sped through the ship and found Stave already hammering against the stout metal hatch that led to the *Vigilance's* bridge, cursing with such ferocity that it was a wonder his words didn't burn it down. But it wasn't to be. The hatch was shut and locked from within.

"Klinkís!" Stave cried.

Still attempting to locate Safran and discover her plight—though by now Mylla had suspicions—they began an onslaught with the klinkí stones that, eventually, would break through, but it would take time. And they didn't know how much they had.

Two of us are nearly as good as one, Roi sent. *I'll search the rest of the ship.* Through the Mentalios, even more quietly than a whisper, she heard his next thought and learned his suspicions matched her own. *Irrick.* Whatever had befallen Safran had been caused by the Conservatum acolyte.

What have I done? she thought, renewing the fury of her attack on the hatch.

In moments, Roi sent, *I've found her. The acolyte is free.*

Stave grew still for a moment, his stones dancing at his fingertips like little blue flames. *How is she?*

Gravely injured, but she'll survive.

The knots of Mylla's insides released a touch at the news. Then Stave was saying, "Mylla, you stay here and guard this hatch. Keep working on opening it, but if that blargin' commoner comes out, I want him for myself, I do. Understand?"

She raised a scornful eyebrow but nodded, and Stave loped off. She wouldn't let him kill Irrick in cold blood. The man was clearly not acting from a place of intent but from some hold or force the usurping Verity now had over him. He could not be blamed, no matter the damage he did, or could, cause. There was no way Irrick would betray them unless his will had been stolen from him.

Moments later, she heard Stave wail, "Ah, no, Safran! I'll kill him, the boggin' slag!"

Hurriedly, Mylla pressed herself against the hatch and spoke in a voice she hoped only carried to Irrick and not back to the others. "Irrick, Irrick, can you hear me? Listen, you need to come out of there now. I know what you've done isn't your fault. But you have to open this hatch. I can protect you, but you have to let me show them there's a reason to."

Her words seemed to be useless. Not a sound came from the bridge, but she did hear something else…

With a start, she realized it was the *Vigilance's* engines coming to life with a low whirr. Was he trying to fly the ship? He'd never even seen it, much less been aboard. It wasn't possible.

Nevertheless, the *Vigilance* was flying. But to where?

Dread slimed through her, and she renewed the attack on the hatch. *Do you feel that?* she asked the others, wanting to confirm it was not her imagination.

A discomfiting silence came in response, and she was about to repeat herself, when Roi sent: *The bruhawks have sighted something… Verities curses, I can't believe it…*

Then Stave: *What in the realms of the five Verities is that?*

What's going on? she cried, ceasing her hammering with the stones.

Another moment of silence followed, and she turned to retreat back through the ship to find them, and find out what new catastrophe was about to hit, when Roi spoke. *Mylla, you must escape. Take the dragørfly scout and go.*

Stopping dead in her tracks, she said slowly, *Escape? What—*

Safran has shown us through the bruhawks' eyes… the ship, the usurper's warship—it's too big, we can't fight this thing, and it is getting closer. You must go, find the Stallari or Eisa. They'll know what to do.

I won't leave, she resolved and picked up her pace, now almost running. *We fight together, keep the faith—*

Listen to me. If Balavad takes the Vigilance, *no one will be left to stand against him, and no one left to keep faith in this fight. Save yourself, save what's left of the Order, live to fight on. Remember, Mylla, survival is our victory.* Just as she attempted another protest, his voice, now harder than Eisa's heart, commanded, *Get out now!*

As if at the end of a whip, she hurtled through the ship toward the launch bay, her feet carrying her but Roi's words the force that drove her. *I can't leave them, I can't do this, I am a Knight, my duty is to Vaka Aster, I am breaking my oath if I go…*

On and on her mind yammered, but not loudly enough to stop her. She reached the launch bay and opened the hatch, the bite of the outside air sharper than normal against her panic-hot skin. They had gained more than a little altitude, but Magdaster still sprawled beneath the ship, though her view was too limited to see the approaching warship.

For the second time in so few days, she launched the small scout with her mind whirling in a cyclone of fear and dread. As soon as she cleared the *Vigilance*, she brought the craft high enough to see in all directions—and there it was.

A monster, like something from the depths of a sea, a kraken plated with pure-black metal and gleaming onyx ports in the hull. It filled the sky with its blankness, no lights emitting from the massive shape. Iit seemed to have the power to reverse light, to suck all ambient glow from the ether and twist it into something dead and poisonous. Shaped like a manta ray the size of a city, it glided toward the *Vigilance*.

Oh Vaka Aster, she couldn't watch it destroy the people she cared about. Without thinking, she fired the emberspark cannons, once, twice, their liquid-light projectiles rocketing into the warship's hull with the force of storms. They flared explosively on impact, then dissipated into the air as if they'd never been. The enemy ship absorbed each strike with barely a mark left on its hide.

But her shots did not go unnoticed. As the gap between the warship and the *Vigilance* closed inexorably, dozens of shining black ports speckling the hull began scissoring open. Mylla knew the Ravener attack ships would be coming forth. Simultaneously, a seam split lengthwise along its blunt bow and spread wider with the slickness of a treacherous smile. She recognized the seam as a hatch, a yawning mouth to swallow the *Vigilance*.

Her mind cycled rapidly among many options. Stay, for they could not see her. Go, for she had no chance against so many. Or...

No. *You would have to be more than insane,* she told herself as her mind tentatively explored this third choice.

Why not? Infiltration was an option, wasn't it? If she snuck inside the warship, she might remain undetected, she might be able to rescue her friends. Mightn't she? She began to steer the dragørfly scout toward the warship's opening hatch. If she was brave enough—

A force struck the scout hard enough to pitch it into a sideways dive, like a leaf blown from a tree by a strong gust. *What... ?* But the question remained unfinished as she scrambled to get control. Whatever struck her hadn't come from the warship, and the Magdastervian artillery could never reach this high.

The falling sensation, the thing even her nightmares' monsters feared, grew worse as the scout gained speed toward the earth. Her training, all the endless repetition of it, kicked in. She gripped the steering yoke as her feet feathered the pitch and yaw controls with something best described as panicked luck. Above her, the oscillating insectile wings that gave the dragørfly ships their name hitched in their out-of-sync frenzy, two on opposing sides stopping briefly. Then, by some miracle, all four resumed in a harmonious buzz that brought the craft back to parallel with the ground.

Not a moment too soon. The high limbs of the Howling Weald reached out not a sword's length below, trying, it seemed, to yank her down. Three heartbeats later, she knew the worst of the danger was behind her, and the ship was still aloft. Whatever had hit it had not damaged much.

What *had* hit it?

All that training did you some good, I see.

Eisa! At the sound of the Knight's voice along the Mentalios link, Mylla flicked her wystic lens over one eye and scanned the area wildly. Through the bulbous cockpit cover, she finally spotted Eisa hovering overhead in the other scout.

Consider that a warning shot, novice. Your Mentalios discipline has never been your strongest skill. I could hear from here what you're thinking about doing. Don't even try to get aboard that warship. Unless you want to die with them.

Skimming the boundary of the forest, she tilted the craft to rise and meet Eisa, asking, *And what is it you're thinking of doing, Eisa?*

Stay away, novice. You may yet find a fate that serves you. Or that you'll eventually—perhaps willingly—serve. Eisa's scout executed a nimble turn-around and began flying directly away from the usurper's warship, which had now swallowed the *Vigilance*, sending the parting words: *You've been warned.*

Of all the treachery and deceit she had witnessed in the last days, even in her full three hundred and some odd turns combined, this one hurt like no pain ever had. Eisa was running, leaving her companions to a fate none of them could guess, betraying them and everything they'd all sworn as an Order, almost as a family, to protect. And only Mylla, the youngest of the Knights, the greenest and most novice, stood a chance at stopping her.

With all the haste the scout's engines could make, she flew toward Eisa.

Knight Nazaria, you can't abandon the Knights, or your oath. If you don't come back and help them, I swear to Vaka Aster I will make you.

The gap closed between the two scouts, and Eisa brought hers around so they hovered nose to nose. Mylla could see her clearly, and the intensity of the elder Knight's glare felt like it would burn her. *You don't know what you're doing, novice. You're no good to them dead. Come with me, if you have it in you. Back to Dyrrakium where we can rally the worthy people of Vinnr against the war you know is coming.*

A murmur began to rise from deep in the center of Mylla's mind. In her hands, Eisa held the Scrylle and Fenestros linked together, and the celestial stone blazed in an iridescent swirl that glinted from Eisa's eyes.

Mylla sent: *They are traitors to this world, and you'll be one too if you forsake your oath.*

Her words were like oil thrown onto fire. Eisa's face morphed into a mask of rage. From her vantage, Mylla saw her reach for something, and she suspected Eisa meant to fire on her again.

Mylla slammed her palm against the emberspark trigger. A beam of energy like lightning flew from the barrel mounted beneath the engine.

Direct hit.

Eisa's dragørfly scout flared in an iridescent explosion comprising hundreds of hues of blues, reds, greens—which just as quickly faded to nothing.

You stupid, young, naive novice. Eisa's fury turned her tone, even through the Mentalios, into hot embers that seared Mylla's mind. *Did you forget? Nothing can kill one who bears a celestial stone, not one who learned its powers from Vaka Aster herself. Maybe in a few hundred more turns you'll learn something. But they won't be turns of Halla.*

The murmuring in Mylla's mind suddenly grew louder, and she realized what it was: Eisa speaking an incantation, something she was pulling from the Scrylle.

Sensing a threat more terrible than the warship, Mylla jerked the scout's yoke, meaning to run, to escape. Before she could, beryl radiance split the world, so bright and sudden even her eyelids were useless against it. It was a light she'd seen before, when Lock had broken into Vaka Aster's chamber on Mount Omina. When the Stallari had disappeared.

A surge of fire or... something... went by her, *into* her. Was she screaming? Was she dying?

The surge redoubled and pushed her into a vastness as broad as the night sky and just as studded with stars. Distant shining bodies flashed and erupted around her, beyond her. Every glittering shard of their light pierced her like the points of a billion needles. She felt no pain, only a sensation as if she were disintegrating, spreading across oceans of stars, her body fragmenting and transforming into... she didn't know. Her mind, unable to grasp what her being was experiencing, simply stopped struggling. Her final thought was a memory of the day she'd sworn her oath to Vaka Aster, of looking into the face of her creator for the last time, and of how the glittering spark within Vaka Aster's eyes had been as beautiful as the eternal sea of stars spreading around her.

CHAPTER THIRTY-EIGHT

Shrill wind whistled through the scout and interrupted Mylla's dimensionless dream. Her eyes, no longer seeing stars, darted around and then fixed on the view beyond the cockpit—a storm of lightning and vapor. The windscreen was shattered, leaving ragged edges in the metal frame, and water slammed inside and drummed into her in painful spatters. All was speed and chaos interspersed with the storm's crackling strobes. She caught glimpses of an ocean beneath her reflecting the lightning—an ocean she'd never seen before. There could be no question. She was no longer in Ivoryss above the Howling Weald. Had Eisa done this?

Driving wind slammed into the dragørfly scout and pushed it off course, partly shearing the oscillating wings from its body. Heart beating in a symphony of fright, she pulled hard on the yoke to regain control. The ferocious buckling and bouncing of the storm would surely crash the ship before she could bring it to heel. No pandemonium had ever felt this intimate or this bent on destroying her.

As she battled against the elements and the scout's own quickly unraveling integrity, the water closed in on what was no longer a safe distance below. At her speed, diving into it couldn't be a worse idea, but the doomed scout clearly had no more intention of staying aloft. It headed toward the sea at a speed that sent her stomach into the roof of her mouth.

Wrenching the craft's controls with every muscle in her warrior's frame, she brought it level at the last moment before it slammed into the waves. Its landing skids skipped across the water, sending her flurrying upward once more. The port wings snapped away with a final screech of metal, but the starboard ones still responded. Mylla forced them into braking position, sending the craft into a sideways airborne spin that immediately began to rotate like a barrel in water, and then *was* a barrel in water as it touched down on the wave tops once more and commenced rolling. Her body, held fast in the pilot's seat, already accepted what her mind did not—there was nothing she could do now —and she released the yoke, pulling herself into a tight ball.

The momentum was enough to keep her bouncing over the ocean's surface, sending gouts of freezing water into her face again and again. She wondered if she'd drown before she ever sank, but then, with a hard lurch that vibrated her bones like a lute string, the ship jolted to a stop. Her teeth slammed shut on her tongue, the instant agony overriding everything else, even thankfully her sheer terror. She'd somehow, unbelievably, reached a shoreline.

Everything stilled. Except her heart, which slammed against her ribs hard enough that it seemed to be trying to escape. She couldn't blame it. This punishment was beyond what she deserved. It took her a moment to realize that by a stroke of luck the lightweight craft had landed midbounce above the waterline and pushed into a gap between large jagged blackish rocks, where it was now stuck fast. She hung from her seat upside down, close enough to reach out and touch the water with her fingers but at least protected from the punishing spray by what remained of the scout's fuselage. No matter how much time and muscle Stave put into trying to set it right, this ship would never again be airborne. It was scrap at best.

Her struggle to get free of the seat's harness left her partially immersed in the frigid, beating waves. Before abandoning the ship completely, she braced her feet on the underwater stones and rummaged among the remains of the interior, hoping with all her strength that the Mentalios, which she'd instantly realized was no longer around her neck, hadn't fallen out. She found it snagged in lashings in the rear compartment and gratefully strung it back around her neck. Star Spark, too, remained firmly in its dedicated case next to the pilot's seat, and her klinkí stones remained within her vambrace, where they belonged. If nothing else, she was armed, and therefore prepared for... whatever she had to be.

After pulling herself up the slippery, rocky beachhead, cursing first Eisa, then every star, Verity, and whims of fate she could think of for the trouble, she looked around. An island, small, forbidding-looking, and as inhospitable as one could imagine except for the crumbling temple that rose in ruins from the center.

But it was the sky that drew most of her attention—the iridescent, amaranthine sky filled with rain and a myriad of swirling vapors of varying colors and hues. It was at once beautiful and awesome. Equally captivating and menacing. No, this was definitely, definitively not Ivoryss.

Nor was it even Vinnr.

It seemed she had her answer to what Eisa had done. The errant Knight had banished her, sent her to some distant realm by a starpath well. Though Mylla had never experienced a journey like it, the incantation Eisa had been weaving, the artifacts she held and whose powers she was master of, and the light that had struck Mylla's ship and her feeling of being launched through the skyways of the Great Cosmos clearly pointed to a jaunt through a well.

So then, where was she?

Chilled now to the point that her teeth chattered, she picked her way over the rocky ground toward the temple. It appeared deserted, but she drew her klinkí stones anyway. As she climbed the three steps toward the once-grand entryway, a nearby movement flickered in the corner of her eye. She turned quickly in that direction, but there was nothing there—if you can call a sky full of lightning and strange, glittering purple ether and unknown stars *nothing*.

The gloom of the interior instantly made her feel unwelcome, but the space appeared empty. The seal inlaid in aubergine and green stone in the center of the pitted marble floor told her whose shrine it was: Lífs, the Creatress. *So I am in Himmingaze.*

She knelt and traced a finger over the nearest part of the symbol, a simple pattern of three circles that when marking a Knight's face would be arranged with one over each eye and one slightly higher, centered on the forehead. The realization of the temple's shoddy condition sank in slowly. If the people of this realm had so little regard for their Verity that they would allow the creator's sacred places to fall into ruin… well, that said all it needed to about how they perceived their maker, and perhaps, how their maker perceived them.

Have all the Verities discarded their worlds? Is this true of every realm? The Syzycki Elementum marks the end of all existence?

She shuddered, not even a little from the cold, and stood abruptly to continue her sweep of the interior space. Light from her klinki stones and outside provided enough to see, but everything bore a shadowy, spooky pall. Near one of the main support pillars, she made out something lumpy that didn't appear to belong. When she got closer, she saw it was a satchel.

Strange, did someone leave this here by accident? She couldn't know, but she could at least see what it might carry and learn if it would help her.

When she opened it, she nearly fainted.

CHAPTER THIRTY-NINE

Ulfric blinked rapidly. His mind seemed to have wandered, and he remembered a strange vision. After correcting the *Octopod*'s flight, he'd been about to force Bardgrim back to the cockpit and hold him there, tie him to the seat if he had to, but the next moment he was in the stars, walking across a glowing horizon, the Great Cosmos bursting around him with living color and swirling light—the same sensation as when he'd slipped along the starpath well from Vinnr into Himmingaze. He'd wondered where he would awaken this time.

Yet he'd known, somewhere deep in his mind, that he wasn't among the stars and ether of the Cosmos by his own choice. Something had tugged him here this time, maybe both times, and it could only be Vaka Aster herself. Toying with him, careless and void of all human qualities. How could he ever have given his life for such a monstrosity? He'd struggled then between the dark and the light, tugging against the veils of the Cosmos and reaching inside himself to find those things that made him Ulfric Aldinhuus, companion of Symvalline Lutair, father to Isemay, Stallari of the Knights Corporealis, and a man. It had been like wading neck-deep through star-spotted mud, and each time he came close to himself, something had blocked him, pushed him away, and he'd felt as if he were losing himself to infinity.

The voice spoke again: *The Himmingazian has something to tell you.*

"Aldinhuus. Master Knight?"

Ulfric jerked, blinked again, and pulled himself—or was released—from whatever this trance was. Unexpectedly, he found Bardgrim still gripped tightly in his hands but not fighting him. *What is going on with you, old man?* he asked himself. *It is unlike you to suffer from a weak and wandering mind.*

He released Bardgrim and pushed him back enough to free his klinkí stones from a pocket in his tunic. "You're going to fly this ship, Bardgrim, or Vaka Aster help you—"

"I know. I know, and I'm on it." The Himmingazian pivoted and started back for the cockpit.

"Stop!" he yelled, unsure of what Bardgrim was planning this time.

Bardgrim complied, oddly easily, and turned to him. "No more tricks, Aldinhuus, I promise. I'm on your side now. I believe you."

He had to blink again to absorb this surprise.

The engineer continued, "You wouldn't believe… well maybe you would. But anyway, the most incredible thing just happened, and I was told to tell you—"

"So you speak Elder Veros after all." He said the words flatly, no longer bothering to accuse Bardgrim of lying.

"I… what?"

Astonishingly, the Himmingazian managed to look genuinely surprised, probably at his unintentional failure to maintain his charade of ignorance any longer. Every word he'd spoken since Ulfric had released his shoulders was in perfect Elder Veros. "You'll forgive me, Bardgrim, if I refuse to believe a single word you say."

Bardgrim remained, mercifully, speechless for a moment, clearly stuck in mid-fluster.

"Now get in there and ensure our course is still set for the shrine."

Eyes still wide, Bardgrim nodded and stepped past the hatch to the cockpit. Ulfric stayed right behind him and heard the man muttering, "I can't believe this. I can even think in Vertasian, or Elder Whatever. Talk about being starstruck."

He made for the pilot's seat, but Ulfric stopped him. "No. You take that chair. I'm flying now."

"You're… ?" He chuckled, as if he assumed Ulfric was joking. Then he saw the look in Ulfric's face, and his own expression drooped. Making for the copilot seat, he said under his breath once more, "Of all the indignities… You sure about this, Aldinhuus?" he finished more loudly.

Without answering, Ulfric pulled the eye shields that had been knocked askew back into place and snugged the strap. Instantly, his mind cleared, along with his eyesight. "Utterly," he answered and placed his hand heavily on the engineer's shoulder to illustrate how sure he was.

Bardgrim sank into the copilot chair, and Ulfric pocketed his klinkí stones. Taking the pilot seat, he pushed away its harness and turned to face the engineer. "Now show me what to do."

"First, let me tell you—"

"Anything you say besides how to control this craft will earn you lessons in pain that you'll forever carry scars to remind you."

"… Okay, then. You see that sphere in front of you?"

It took less time for Ulfric to feel comfortable with the rudiments of the *Octopod*'s controls than the typical first-time pilot. Over a thousand turns of existence had an accelerative effect on mental acuity, and he'd always enjoyed, thrived on even, the study of how contraptions and mechanicals functioned. He could see the Himmingazian and himself had this in common, same with lens-crafting. Of his many insufferable qualities, he at least had two that were tolerable.

Once Bardgrim had ensured their course was set, he told Ulfric they'd reach the island by Glister Dim, which, through a bit of question and answer, he interpreted to be equal to a bit less than a quarter spin around Halla by Vinnr measure. Once Bardgrim had delivered this information, Ulfric's threat to batter him if he kept talking finally won the reward he craved: silence. This gave him time, more than he wanted, to think, to grieve the loss of his family, and to feel the already deep roots of acrimony and anguish splitting apart his spirit. What would come after vengeance? He didn't even have death to look forward to, not with certainty.

A sudden interruption pierced his fretting: *Stallari, where are you?*

Jerking upright in the pilot's seat, he said aloud, "Mylla?"

"What?" Bardgrim asked, but Ulfric ignored him.

The moment dragged out, and he started to believe this new voice was a furtherance of the many he'd been imagining in the recent past. Then it came again.

Stallari?

It seemed impossible, but there was no doubt: this was Knight Evernal's voice channeled through the Mentalios. The difference between it and the continuous garbling of his own thoughts was absolute. Without a thought to why, he yanked the engineer's eye shields from his head and lifted his Mentalios, feeling his thoughts project stronger than they'd ever done in Vinnr.

Mylla, do you hear me?

Stallari! Her reply was instantaneous. *Where are you?*

Where was *she*? That was the real question—but he had a guess. When he'd passed into Himmingaze, he'd come through the old, crumbling shrine of their creator. If Mylla had come through the same well as he, she was there too. The shrine itself was a starpath gateway.

We are both in Himmingaze, the realm of the Verity called Lifs, he answered. *Are you in a ruin of white stone with a soaring archway overhead?*

Her voice when she responded carried emotion like an anvil, heavy with relief. *Yes, yes! Lifs's temple. On an island. Oh Verity's stars, what—*

As if hacked in half with an ax, her channeling went silent.

He called out to her several times, without response. Turning, he found Bardgrim watching him curiously. "Faster, Himmingazian. Even if it means turning this craft inside out, you must get us to the shrine *now*."

CHAPTER FORTY

Mylla had been sitting cross-legged with her back against a pillar for an unknown amount of time. In the circle of her legs, she'd arranged the contents of the satchel: the foreign Scrylle and the set of six Fenestrii, two of Balavad's, four of Vaka Aster's. Beside these sat her klinkí stones, glowing a deep blue. She'd been concentrating energy into the klinkí stones to warm them up and help her dry out. Enough time had passed that she was now barely damp, yet she still hadn't found the courage, or overcome the shock enough, to do more than look at the Fenestrii.

The Stallari had been here. He must have, given that he was the last to possess these artifacts. But she'd never seen this bag, which meant someone else, whoever's bag it was, had been here too. Why would they leave it behind? What had become of Aldinhuus? What did it mean that both he and she had come to the same realm? And without her dragørfly scout, what would she do?

And there was something more, a temptation that, while she fought against it, hindered her from thinking coherently about her options.

She had the usurping Verity's Scrylle and a Fenestros to view inside it in her possession. What things could she learn from them that would help her rescue the Knights, maybe even save Vinnr from the usurper?

She only needed to look inside to discover how to summon the Verity cage, and if she ever found a chance to use it, she would be so enabled.

Still, she hesitated. Being a novice with limited turns in the Knights meant she was not yet as strong, her Verity spark not yet as robust, as her elders'. If she fixed her mind too long on the contents of a Scrylle, even Vaka Aster's, or tried an incantation that took more skill and stalwartness than she had yet cultivated, she could drain that spark, and she could die. Alone and in this dreadful, dark place in a realm she'd only vaguely heard of, where apparently Verities were forgotten. This was a fate she'd never considered and that now made her mouth dry and her heart flutter like a bird's.

She knew Ulfric, under ordinary circumstances, would dissuade her, maybe forbid her, from looking into the usurper's Scrylle. But these were not ordinary circumstances, and Ulfric wasn't here. Who knew if he would, or even could, return. Hers was the only counsel she had.

Outside, it had grown darker. Warmer now, and completely dry, she let her klinkí stones abate and tucked them away. A new thought came to her: *The Scrylle may show me how to create a starpath well and get home, just as Vaka Aster's does.*

And that did it. She couldn't just sit here and wonder what her options were. She knew what they were. It was up to her to have the fortitude, and the willingness to risk everything, to take them. *You may yet be able to save the Knights, and the Stallari.*

Getting to her knees, she grasped the usurper's Scrylle tentatively, at once uncertain of herself and almost dangerously thrilled at the prospect. The closest thing to being in the presence of Verities themselves was immersing in their lore. She carefully stood the cylinder on the floor. After picking up Balavad's onyx Fenestros, she allowed herself one last moment of hesitation. Once she placed this stone in its mount, she would be pulled inside a lore that was only somewhat familiar to her, most of which she could not even guess at. The wystic incantations, the knowledge, the history, and so much more of a people and a realm she knew only by name and now by dint of its Verity's aggressions in Vinnr; all would be unleashed at once. She was without the guidance and presence of a more experienced Knight to shepherd her. Only her caution and Knight's training would give her any control of how this lore transferred to her mind. If she could not attenuate its flow using her own will...

She dropped the Fenestros into its mount.

With the same gentle ease of blowing out a candle, her mind floated free from its corporeal tether, pulled into a black-and-silver miasma of the archaeology of Battgjald and the Verity Balavad.

The buffeting started immediately. Oceans of lore poured into her with a tidal wave's relentlessness, stretching her mind until its borders thinned like a bubble threatening to pop. Explosions of incredible, unimaginable things: tools, cities, lands and oceans, devices, flying ships, medicines, histories of events and people, incantations and the wysticism of a place and people foreign to her. She flailed to gain some kind of mindhold on the barrage of alien minds whose knowledge had created this Scrylle. This was the lore of people who were both different and obscurely familiar. The people of Battgjald, fundamentally, were like those of Vinnr.

But it came so fast, deluging her, her mind creaking against the strain, snapping at its moorings. The experience of looking into Vaka Aster's Scrylle, created by those with whom she shared a common legacy and primordial birthright, was not like this, not crushing like this. Even as she struggled, she marveled at all there was to learn, to see, to know—but it was too much. She couldn't stanch the flow. Desperately, she fought, yet slowly felt herself being lost, drained at her core as the struggle sapped her strength and the celestial spark that sustained her.

Then, with no notice, the spout of archaeology cut off, leaving behind ethereal stillness.

With a rush, she felt she was herself again, still disembodied but back in control of her mind. Just Mylla. Though her eyes saw nothing, an echoing emptiness seemed to surround her. Uncertain what was happening—perhaps this was the final spark leaving her body?—she attempted to speak. When the words came, she didn't know if she spoke them aloud or only in her mind, but it hardly seemed to matter.

Hello? An indefinable shift in the void signaled to her that she wasn't alone, another presence had joined her. *Vaka Aster?*

A Knight. A Knight whom I know. You were at Aster Keep. You are... Knight Evernal.

The voice, unmistakably Balavad's, roiled inside her mind like a serpent. *No,* she whispered.

From the still void, a deeper blackness swept over her thoughts, seeming to steal the air along with all sound and sensation, leaving nothing but emptiness.

So you have my Scrylle, Knight, the Verity said. *Where have you taken it? Let me see.* And as if she'd fallen asleep and by some enchantment awoken in another's body, Mylla's vision changed.

Of all the strange sensations she'd experienced in the last few hours, this was the most bizarre. Her body remained distant, something she knew was hers on a cerebral level but which she felt no physical connection to at the moment. This in and of itself wasn't totally unknown. Knights trained for many kinds of rituals, and learning to part thought from flesh in order to attain clarity was just one of them that she'd done many times. When she found that she could see again through her own eyes, it seemed they were covered with a film of some sort. Instead of plain vision, she perceived the world as deep swirling, flashing color that illuminated more than any human eyes had ever seen, she was sure. It was as if her vision were alive, or the lights it saw were. Everything breathed and pulsed chromatically. It was breathtaking, like discovering a world covered over by this one, but made visible. Every part of the perception was so strong, she felt she could almost taste the colors, smell the lights. Despite the alienness of the sensation, the experience captivated her.

But, like the wash of wystic lore from the Scrylle, she could not control it. And this vision did not seem to be her own. She knew she was under the sway of the usurper, like a puppet. He had taken her sight to use for his own purposes.

As if a witness to a crime she could do nothing to stop, she observed from the void as her own eyes swept the interior of the ruin. In moments, they fixed on the seal of Lífs on the floor.

Himmingaze, Balavad intoned. *It would be wise of you, Knight, to remain there until I arrive.*

Abruptly, she was blind again as the Verity abandoned her mind. For half a heartbeat, all was the blackest black inside her head, then with the violence of a thunderclap, she was flung back inside her skin. The sensation jarred her so roughly that she fell forward, knocking the Scrylle over and the Fenestros free of its mount.

The cold of the chamber washed over her hands and face. She rolled faceup, grateful to be back to herself, back in her body, and free from the deluge of the Scrylle lore.

But what have I done?

Looking into the Scrylle had made her defenseless and opened her weak mind to the enemy. Now he knew—*he knew.* She had hoped to find something that would help her and the rest of the Knights, but instead she had led their enemy to more weapons against them.

The thought made her sick. Climbing woozily to her knees, she reached for the pillar to pull herself to her feet. Rising made her head swim, partly from the aftereffects of having just been assaulted by a maelstrom of foreign lore, partly from having been vandalized by a Verity, and partly from simple horror at her own ignominious, destructive feats.

Frantically, she lurched outside, craving the sharpness of the cold rain to slap her out of the panicked paralysis. At the base of the steps to the temple, she looked upward into the strange, foreign sky, the light now dimming toward full night. Without thinking, she channeled an anguished cry through her Mentalios, a cry for help, a cry for the one person she knew who might.

Stallari, where are you?

Expecting no response, she hung her head, letting the frigid rain seep into her collar and once again dampen her skin, as well as her spirit.

Mylla, do you hear me?

The sound of Ulfric's voice through the Mentalios washed over her head like a warm breeze. It had to be her imagination, didn't it? Wishful thinking? But it had been so… usual. His voice as she'd known it now for hundreds of turns around Halla.

Stallari? she tried, hoping her hopes were not shattered. Another trial of her spirit at this moment would utterly defeat her.

Then her vision blurred for a moment and her knees buckled, dropping her onto the sharp, unforgiving rocks. *I've used too much strength. First looking into the Scrylle, and now channeling thoughts so far. It's taking too much of a toll. If I continue, I'll weaken too much.*

But she couldn't simply remain silent, not now, not after finally hearing Ulfric again. This was her last chance to help Ivoryss and Vinnr. To help the Knights. And possibly, if she wasn't too late, to help Lock.

The pain of knowing she could fail tore into her.

Mylla, do you hear me?

Stallari! Where are you? She gasped as dots danced before her eyes.

He responded immediately. *We are both in Himmingaze, the realm of the Verity called Lifs. Are you in a ruin of white stone with a soaring archway overhead?*

Yes, yes! Lifs's temple. On an island. The effort it took to say that much forced her to crumble forward, and she caught herself on her hands before pitching face-first into the ground. The dots danced in front of her eyes again, and she blinked several times to clear them. As she was doing so, she caught sight of something in the air near her. Straightening back up, she looked to her right. Within the swirling dark violet sky, broken by fat raindrops that struck her head and ran into her eyes, she thought she could see something floating in the air over the water. It moved swiftly, undulating like a pennant in a calm but steady breeze, but much larger. Even as it rippled through the rain, she could see it was very long, at least three times her height. She squinted to try and see it better, but the dastardly rain only got in the way.

Lightning flashed. And she saw…

Oh Verity's stars, what—

CHAPTER FORTY-ONE

The Knight and Jaemus had switched seats to allow Jaemus full control as they approached Isle Stonering. He landed the *Octopod* at the single flat space at the north end, the same place he'd originally set down. Despite Aldinhuus's obvious urgency, distress even, Jaemus found himself with little to say. The encounter with the Verity had left him too rattled to maintain his normal streaming monologue or dialogue, depending on the availability of another with whom to chat.

A celestial being. A real celestial, a skywalking star sprite. He rolled this thought in his mind, twisting the description, changing the tone with which he said it to himself, trying every permutation of the idea he could think of. Because the truth was, it was impossible that a celestial power beyond that of nature itself existed and created, well, everything. But the truer truth was, he'd just met said power—and he actually believed it was real.

A maker of everything that is or that can be thought of. Not just nature, but nature's creator.

And the funny thing was, every new description he came up with seemed equally correct. They all fit because *everything*, by definition, was part of a Verity's milieu.

"Open the hatch, Bardgrim. We can't waste a moment."

The Knight's fraught tone cut through his reverie. That was another thing. Something had agitated the spit out of the man just a short while ago, and they'd come close to burning out the *Octopod*'s engines to get here. He hadn't shared what it might be, and Jaemus, admittedly, had reached his maximum tolerance for weirdness for the time being. He was willing to let it go.

They ring-shaped exit hatch retracted and the ladder automatically began unfolding. Before it finished, however, Aldinhuus jumped down and ran off into the dark rain—leaving Jaemus alone.

"Watch out for the—" he began before it struck him. After all Aldinhuus's threats and bluster, he'd just left the door wide open for Jaemus to escape.

It only took him a breath to realize, however, that he wasn't going anywhere, not after what he'd experienced. He had too many questions, which may as well be chains tethering him to the Knight. No way could he leave without answers. No way.

Climbing down more cautiously than Aldinhuus had, he stood with his back to the ladder for a moment, squinting into the glittering dark. Fleeches inhabited the waters around here. And now without his goggles, they would be ten times harder to see.

Despite his caution, he could barely make anything out past the *Octopod*'s muted lights. The only sound was the steady wet patter of water on hard rock. Aldinhuus had disappeared into the miasma.

He spared a thought for the shelksies aboard but didn't bother going back for one. The projectiles had no effect whatsoever on a fleech, and they were too fast to target anyway. Picking his steps carefully, he paced toward the temple's entryway, calculating how much time they had before Cote and the Glisternauts would arrive.

This concern was wiped from his mind the moment he rounded the front of the temple and saw what had been his worst fear since childhood lying before him.

"What is it?" Aldinhuus asked, his tone almost conversational.

They stood before what was clearly a woman's body, though she seemed bulkier than was common in Himmingaze. Where in the

Cloud could she have come from? It wasn't at her body, however, that the Knight's question was directed. It was the layers upon layers of iridescent fleech scales wrapped around her.

"Oh, water and lightning…" Jaemus managed to whisper before his stomach did a violent flip-flop, half from revulsion, half from fear. The fleech's mouthpart had attached to the woman's neck, leaving her head exposed. Her open eyes were rolled back, rainwater collecting in their whites and leaking over the edges, as if her corpse still cried.

Aldinhuus had him by the collar with one hand before Jaemus was even aware he'd moved. "What is that thing, Bardgrim?" he demanded.

"It's a fleech. If you knew that woman, forget her. She's already dead. They attach to their victims and digest them from the inside out. Almost impossible to kill. And where there's one, there's others. We have to get inside."

The goggles remained fixed on his face for a moment as Aldinhuus read his expression for the truth, then he released him. "Stand watch," he commanded and released his kinky stones.

"Stand watch, yes, I'll just…" he heard himself saying, but his feet had other ideas. He slowly began backing toward the steps to the temple, hoping but doubting that Aldinhuus would either follow or forget him. He had the intestinal fortitude to withstand threats by otherworldly warriors, conversations with celestial beings who weren't supposed to exist, even breakups with his beloved, but he could not handle a fleech. He just couldn't.

His heels struck the bottom stair as the Knight unleashed his bombardment of glowing cerulean stones. They moved so swiftly that their lights left trails that stayed aglow after the stones' passage, turning the entire area around the fleech and its prey into a bright-blue enclosure. Most left divots in the creature's thick scales, but it didn't move, seeming not to notice. Aldinhuus controlled how hard he struck, obviously not wanting to perforate both the monster and the woman it held. But Jaemus knew their resilience. He also knew that half of their strength came not from resilience but from quantity. He stared wildly about, knowing that more were coming, or maybe were already—

"Here!" he screeched, toppling onto his hind end as a pale ribbon streaked directly toward him from the sky.

He watched, frozen, as the mouthpart of this second fleech widened on its approach to his throat. Frantically, he squirmed backward up the steps, smelling the rot escaping the thing's maw just before it struck. *Couldn't have just kept my mouth shut and not told Aldinhuus about the other Verity stones, could I?*

Reflexively, he flung his arms up in front of his face in a futile attempt to protect himself, his eyes squeezing shut. Just before the strike, something wet but much slimier and heavier than the rain drenched his arms, some splattering onto his cheek. He opened his eyes. Aldinhuus now stood with arms and legs wide, waving his hands in two directions, one toward the fleech he'd just diverted but which was now coming in for another attack on Jaemus, the other sending stones into the hide of the one eating the woman. The airborne fleech dove and writhed, but each time it got near him, a kinky stone would pierce it and divert it from a direct course. It wouldn't survive that for long.

Jaemus's gratitude lasted only a breath before he spotted one, two, maybe five more coming out of the Glister Dim sky. "Friend, if you've got any more of those up your sleeves, now would be the time to use them!" he yelled, pointing into the approaching barrage.

The Knight followed his gesture and let out a grunt at the sight. "Bardgrim, grab her and pull her inside. I'll hold these off."

"... Uh. Grab her? With that thing wrapped around her? She'd dead!"

"No, she isn't. Do it! Now!"

Even had he not been terrified almost into paralysis, he wasn't the strongest man in the world, and she looked heavy, though he knew fleeches themselves to be deceptively light. But he also knew fear had a way of giving people strength, and he could hardly leave the poor woman—the poor *Vinnric* woman, for what else could she possibly be? —to die horribly in the never-ending Himmingazian rain.

He rushed to her body, refusing to look into the sky and watch the approaching murder monsters. Unwilling to get near the fleech's mouthparts, though he knew it would not unlatch until it was full, he grabbed the woman's boots extending from the bottom of the tight coils. In the process, he also got a handful of the thing's scaly hide, and his stomach lurched with disgust.

As he began dragging the woman—and Cosmos clutter she was indeed heavy—he yelled, "Come on, Aldinhuus, use that light shield to protect us!"

Aldinhuus did not seem to hear him. Jaemus could see the man had his hands full, but he absolutely did not want to be left alone with a fleech and what was most assuredly a dead woman inside the temple while the Knight met his doom outside. Because, he had to be realistic, that's exactly what was about to happen.

Just as he twisted his head aside to see how much farther he had to go, something slammed into him from behind. No, not *something*. He knew what it was. The fleech whipped its coils around him faster than lightning, and its mouthpart would have attached to his neck, but he dropped the woman's legs and got his arms up just in time.

Did he scream? Did it matter? This was the end. He smelled the dank scent of the remnants of the hundreds, maybe thousands, of dead sea animals that had been the monster's last meals, and his brain decided against taking a deep breath for another scream. Not that it would have helped. Despite the monster's lightness, it was too strong for him. The mouthpart strained against his upraised forearms, making a squishy sucking sound, and its scaly body tensed around him, squeezing harder the harder he fought.

With his last bit of air, he offered a guttural roar to the fates that had forced this fine mess on him and squeezed his eyes shut. He'd seen all he wanted to.

CHAPTER FORTY-TWO

The flying maggot-like fish continued their onslaught in such numbers that Ulfric was having trouble keeping them at bay. He flung a formation of stones just in time to knock one away from his face before it latched on, but more followed. And more. There had to be a dozen in the air, and they were tough. Tougher than a full-grown chelbiefin shark.

Risking the quickest of glances rearward, he saw the engineer dragging Mylla toward the shrine at an agonizingly slow rate. It was a good thing he turned when he did—just in time to ward off another of the things that had been aiming directly at Bardgrim's back. But the next instant, a scaled tail snaked past Ulfric's defenses and wrapped around one of his ankles, yanking hard. His stance, as hardy and unrelenting as a mountain, barely budged, and he stoned the thing liberally before it let go.

A few had lost the fight, and their corpses plunked to the rocky ground. But more came. From behind him, the engineer yelled out, and Ulfric knew it as the sound of defeat.

I can't beat an ocean of these. I need assistance.

Where were his dragørfly allies? What had he done to call them before that he wasn't doing now? And then it came to him.

Ripping free the eye shields, his vision instantly morphed into the otherworldly sight he was barely getting used to, and his mind again loosened, as if more than he was present. Just as it had the first time he'd needed aid, a stroke of blue light blossomed in the air around him, and when it cleared, a legion of his dragørfly allies abounded. Assistance had arrived.

The flying soldiers glowed with a piercing spark that lit the area all around them. As a single formation and with almost mechanical precision, they swarmed the attacking sea monsters and clasped on to them. The fleeches writhed and twisted in whip-crack contortions, looking as if they were being gashed by daggers from whatever the dragørflies were doing to them. With their assault diverted for the moment, Ulfric turned just as a fleech attached itself to the engineer's neck and pulled him to the ground. Ulfric loped to his aid and directed the klinkí stones in a concentrated onslaught just below the thing's mouthpart. Mylla might be able to survive whatever these creatures did to their victims, but Ulfric had a feeling the Himmingazian was made of less stern stuff. Within moments, the fleech was in two pieces, and Ulfric gripped the head and yanked the mouthpart free.

"Are you all right, Bardgrim?" he yelled, keeping his defenses focused on the writhing mob surrounding them.

There was no response for a moment, then: "I think I'm ruined from eating fish for the rest of my life."

He glanced back and saw the engineer extracting himself from the dead fleech's loosened coils. "Help me. Grab her other foot," he commanded, squatting and taking one of Mylla's boots. "Quickly!"

Holding back the diminished fleech attacks with one klinkí-stone-wielding hand, Ulfric tugged Mylla with the other. With Bardgrim's help, they entered the shrine and slammed the heavy doors closed.

Bardgrim released a boot and fell back against the wall beside the entryway, breathing hard. Ulfric quickly performed the same beheading on the fleech attached to Mylla and soon had the thing free. Bending down, he slid his arms beneath her armpits and dragged her free of the dead monster.

"Mylla," he muttered, looking into her lifeless face. To his weirded sight, her eyes seemed to gleam with a white-gold light, and the air immediately surrounding her skin, as cold as the rain, shimmered with minute flashes of the same light. Oddly, a color he'd never seen before, and for which he had no name, something that was gold and silver and purple all at the same time, sparked from the aura surrounding her too. He couldn't identify it, or what caused it, but chose not to dwell on what it might be. The important thing was, she wasn't dead, her Verity spark sustained her. But it was weak, and it would take time for it to renew itself and grow stronger.

But she was here. *Somehow*, she was here. For a moment, his pride at her strength and resilience swelled, much as it did when Isemay showed him one of her many accomplishments. The sharp pain in his heart was unexpected.

The interior suddenly lit up brightly, stunning him for a moment. He blinked and pulled the eye shields back over his eyes. "What are you doing, Bardgrim?" he asked after turning and seeing the source of the light in the engineer's hand.

"It's an illuminator. I can barely see in here. And for you…" He pointed the light beam so it shined on the floor near a pillar—and on the set of artifacts Ulfric had last touched in Vaka Aster's sanctuary at Mount Omina.

Ulfric paced to the artifacts and knelt beside them, barely believing they were here. The engineer had surprised him with the truth. Bardgrim's satchel lay nearby. It was about this size of a folded cloak and would serve to carry the objects. He swept everything but one of Vaka Aster's Fenestrii inside, barely sparing a glance at Bardgrim to assess what new trick he might be playing, and returned at once to Mylla.

"I'm sorry about your friend," he heard Bardgrim say but ignored him.

Removing the eye shields once more, he lowered onto one knee beside her, set Vaka Aster's Fenestros in the center of her chest over her armor, and pulled her hands so they lay atop it. Pressing his own hand down to keep hers from falling, he closed his eyes and channeled a simple invocation using his Mentalios. Ambient energy from within the chamber slipped by him, collected by the Fenestros. Beneath his hand, the celestial stone glowed, growing warmer, and soon the heat spread into her body, past her hands through his own. He continued chanting, absorbing without intending to part of the charge's vitality. With the Fenestros serving as a healing dynamo, it would not take long to rejuvenate his fellow Knight Corporealis.

Her chest rose and Ulfric opened his eyes, continuing the chant. The color had returned to her pale flesh, light umber with a touch of red rose, just a shade more like fire than his own earthen hue. A beat later, she blinked then coughed.

"Havelock," she whispered as she turned to see his face. After a moment, she was able to focus. "By the Verities, Stallari. Is it really you?"

He ceased chanting and pulled down the eye shields, leaving her hands over the Fenestros. "Yes, Mylla, it's me."

Her eyes closed again in relief. When she opened them, she looked down at the stone beneath her hands, grasping it tighter. "I thought it was Ba—"

But she cut herself off and looked at him with a plea in her dark eyes.

"You thought it was what?" he asked.

He couldn't tell if she hesitated because he'd just stolen her back from the brink of rejoining the Great Cosmos or because of something else. She licked her lips, dropped her eyes. Pulling herself up to a sitting position, she said, "I can't believe I found you. And—who's that?"

She'd spied Bardgrim, who stared at them with his mouth gaping in speechless surprise.

"A Himmingazian," Ulfric responded. "He found me when I came through the starpath well, and now he's aiding me to..."

He stopped. To what? He had Balavad's Scrylle, but more importantly, he had a trove of Fenestrii, the keys to creating the Verity cage once more. He only required their vessels now to imprison them and stop their reigns of suffering amid the realms. It was time, wasn't it, time to get back to Vinnr and fulfill the promise he'd made himself.

Exact vengeance on the monsters—the *real* monsters, not those pestilent water maggots outside—who'd killed his family, stolen his life.

Mylla, too rattled to comment on his pause, spoke. "Stallari, so much has gone awry. We have to get back to Vinnr at once. Reopen the well quickly and take us."

That was a curious statement, and one that filled him with dread. He rose and lent her a hand, helping her to stand as well. Speaking slowly, deliberately, he asked, "Did you not use the Scrylle of Vinnr to create the starpath and bring yourself here? You must have the Scrylle still, yes?"

Sorrow hardened her expression. "No. I didn't come here by choice. Eisa… Eisa has betrayed us all. She took the Scrylle."

The blood drained from his face. Eisa would never…

Would she? So much suffering had been heaped on the Knight in her turns, so much loss. But she would never, *never* betray her oath. Her resolve to serve Vaka Aster and protect the vessel was the strongest of any living being he'd ever met.

But wasn't betraying his oath what he planned to do? Was it so hard to believe she would fall from faith and quit the fight as well?

No. After all, it wasn't.

Through numb lips, he asked, "Where is Vaka Aster's vessel? What's happened in Vinnr?"

CHAPTER FORTY-THREE

*W*here is Vaka Aster's vessel? The question nearly doused the renewed Verity spark within Mylla. "What do you mean? We all thought, *hoped*, you... don't you know?" she asked.

Ulfric took a step backward. Planting his feet, he said, "I do not," then repeated, "Tell me everything that's happened."

In clipped phrases, she quickly told the tale of all that had come to pass since Ulfric had disappeared. At her question, he explained how he'd reached this realm purely by accident, somehow inadvertently opening a starpath well and going through when he'd destroyed the Verity cage, and that he didn't know how to reopen it. She might have sped through her explanation quicker if she'd used the Mentalios, but she didn't trust herself to be able to hide certain things from his keener mind. Things like the fact that she'd shown Balavad exactly where to find them. Things like what had become of Symvalline and Isemay, a calamity, she assumed he didn't yet know of.

As she came to the end of the story, he asked, "Why did Eisa send you here?"

"I don't know." And she didn't, *couldn't*. The older Knight's reasons had become a wall of shrouds and deception by the time Mylla had clashed with her.

He thought for a moment, then said, "Perhaps it was to protect you. I don't doubt your words, Knight, but they are hard to swallow. Eisa has always been true to the Order, even at great cost to herself." He paused, then added, seemingly to himself, "There is a strong link between the two realms for Eisa, and Griggory as well."

Surprised to hear him speak of the other Knight, whom she'd only recently learned had existed, she asked, "Griggory? Why've you never spoken of him?"

He hedged, looking away from her before answering. "That is a story for another time. First, we must get back to Vinnr." He retrieved the Scrylle of Battgjald from the satchel near him.

"No," she blurted and reached out to grasp his hand.

At first taken aback, he grew grave—*graver*—at her expression. "What is it?"

No choice now. She dove into her confession. "There's something worse, something much worse, I have to tell you. I have made such a misstep, Stallari. When I arrived here, I attempted to look in Balavad's Scrylle. I was trying to find a way to conjure a well on my own. But somehow, when I gazed inside, Balavad was there. He took over my thoughts, my very being. The usurper... knows we're here."

A flash glimmered behind the strange eye shield Ulfric wore, as if his eyes themselves glowed, then he began sweeping the celestial artifacts into the satchel she'd found them in, saying, oddly, in Elder Veros, "Come, Bardgrim, we must get back to your ship and depart with all haste."

"But those fleeches outside..." the kórb-fruit-colored foreigner protested, also in Elder Veros.

"We'll get past them," Ulfric said, pulling one of Vaka Aster's Fenestrii from the bag and holding it in his palm. "With this, I can weave a shield that would hold off a dragør."

She could see the Himmingazian hesitate, afraid of facing the fleeches, as he called them. Or perhaps he feared something else. Her own skin broke out in gooseflesh at the memory of the water monster that had attacked her unawares. She'd have preferred not to meet another of those creatures, but it sounded as if the means to escape this forsaken island and its resident life-suckers awaited them.

"Look, Aldinhuus," the Himmingazian tried, "there's something important you need to know. I'm supposed to tell you—"

"Later. Mylla, gather your klinkí stones and anything else you brough with you."

"Where are we going?"

"As far from here as we can get."

Without another word, he pushed past the doors, letting hard rain pelt the white stones of the temple's floor. Holding the Fenestros out with a single hand, he flung his own klinkí stones into the storm with the other. He murmured some words, and lines of white-gold light from the Fenestros shot out to connect with each of his smaller stones.

"Come," he commanded and stepped outside.

Mylla glanced back at the Himmingazian. His eyes bounced from the entryway to her. *His eyes, their color is so similar to Havelock's,* she thought, and the pang that accompanied the observation struck deep. "It's okay. We'll protect you," she told him, speaking Elder Veros too, apparently their common language.

After what appeared to be a contentious internal debate, he paced to her left shoulder, and they followed the Stallari.

CHAPTER FORTY-FOUR

Things were moving almost too fast for Jaemus to keep up. It was one thing to break the rules of your own fleet just to try saving a world (proving your own engineering brilliance while you were at it). It was another to join ranks with a madman who threatened to harm said fleet, and it was quite another still to learn that myth was fact, and madmen, and now possibly mad*women*, from another world were the only ones who might stand between the end of the world and, well, *not* the end of it, instead of you and your brilliance after all.

There were limits to how many brain-bursting realizations one man could withstand over the course of just a couple of Brights and Dims. Consequently, he reeled behind the two Vinnric Knights as Aldinhuus, as promised, made quick work of the current wave of fleeches. Somehow the Fenestros and his own kinky stones created an envelope that, unlike the one aboard the *Skate*, instantly turned every fleech that dared try to penetrate it into a smoking husk of hideous, rank flesh. The two hundred or so steps to the safety of the *Octopod* went by in flashes and bursts, and the three made it aboard the craft before he'd had time to do more than acknowledge his woeful lack of preparedness for this current predicament.

There was still one thing he could do, and that was fly, at least better than Aldinhuus. "I'll take us up," he said as soon as the hatch had closed, "and get us some distance as quickly as I can."

Surprising him, Aldinhuus held up the Fenestros. "Would this help?"

Recovering immediately, he said, "Master Knight, it can't hurt," and reached for the stone.

"Wait," the new Knight said, and put her hand over the stone before he could grasp it. "You trust this man, Stallari?"

Now he was more than a pinch curious about the answer to that question, and he froze to wait for it. Though this new Knight seemed a bit less… grumpy, she still looked dangerous. Armor like Aldinhuus had originally worn, kinky stones, *and* an intensely long and sharp sword hanging in a belt across her back. A fine silvery patina gilded the delicate but heavy-looking hilt, and its pommel bore a star with nine points. The craftsmanship of this bizarre weapon could not have been finer, and Jaemus didn't doubt its blade would be as sharp as its maker was skilled. What this woman lacked in Aldinhuus's brawn, she made up for in the kind of military bearing Cote had.

He looked to Aldinhuus, awaiting what felt like judgment.

With a single curt nod, the Knight gruffed, "I do."

The new Knight shifted her eyes to Jaemus once more, then dropped her hand. "As you were," she said.

With all the haste he could manage, he placed the foreign Fenestros in the *Octopod*'s unique harness and returned to the cockpit to prepare for takeoff. As he did, he heard the new Knight question Aldinhuus about the dragørflies, which had dispersed once more after the last fleech fell, using a word he didn't understand. Aldinhuus gave a brief explanation, saying they'd come through the well with him. Though Jaemus couldn't articulate to himself why he didn't think that was the full truth—how could the things just appear out of thin air, even if they had originally traveled along the starpathway with Aldinhuus?—he chose not to offer any of his own thoughts on the matter.

When he returned from the Fenestros compartment, Aldinhuus quirked a questioning eyebrow and asked, "Are there any weapons besides those tiny arm apparatuses on your ship, Bardgrim?"

"Shelksies?" he offered. "No, but we wouldn't need them. Like I said, Himmingazian ships don't bear weapons. The *Skate*'s not going to attack us." *At least not in the way I think you're implying,* he admitted but only to himself.

"It isn't the *Skate* we need to worry about."

This caught him off guard. He opened his mouth to ask what Aldinhuus meant, then decided he didn't really want to know. "Then off we go," he said lightly, though the tone was feigned, and eased into his seat. "Should be just a few moments until the thrusters are suitably powered."

"Mylla," Aldinhuus said, "you take the second seat up here. I'm going to take a closer look at those weapons the Himmingazians carry. There are some in the hold."

Jaemus focused on getting them in the air while the Knight called Mylla sat beside him. Feeling her stare as he followed launch procedures, he eventually turned to her. While Aldinhuus was a mellow brown with brown hair, she was darker but with a hint of red and her hair was black. A goodly height, her eyes were almost level with his, and were the largest, darkest eyes he'd ever seen. They shone so brightly they seemed to be lit from within by a shadowy lamp. Her smallish nose reminded him so much of a button he had to tell himself not to press it.

She seemed to be staring at him with the same fascination, but eventually asked, "How long is what you're doing going to take?"

"Just another minute or two." He tried a smile. "I'm Bardgrim. Jaemus Bardgrim, Glint Engineer." The last two words were in Himm, as there didn't seem to be an equivalent in Elder Veros. Remembering the gesture Aldinhuus had made inside the *Bounding Skate*'s holding cell when they'd agreed to assist each other, he made a guess that it might also be some kind of universal greeting, and touched his chin with his right hand, then held it out palm forward for her to grasp.

One of her eyebrows, a thin horizontal black line, arched. "What are you doing?" she asked in a tone that made him feel quite silly indeed.

"Oh, uh, I just thought... I'm trying to say it's nice to meet you, Master... ?"

"Knight Evernal. Should I just call you Glunt?"

"Heh, no, it's Glint. That's my title, my job."

"I cannot press upon you strongly enough how important it is that we leave here instantly."

"Right. Master Knight," he called through the hold, "you should sit down and brace yourself."

"Go," Aldinhuus called back.

With smooth efficiency, he accelerated, letting the same ascension technology that allowed Himmingazian cities to hover over the waves of the Never Sea rather than on them. The *Octopod* rose straight up before engaging the forward thrust. Though they'd discussed no course thus far, instinctively Jaemus spun the bow toward the west, away from Himmingaze's most populated floating city-state. He was about to accelerate but gave Mylla one last glance, noticing her safety belt wasn't buckled.

"Let me just show you how to..."

The way her eyes suddenly widened made him stop. Jerking his head back to look past the windshield, he spotted what she had.

"Water and lightning, what in the Glister Cloud is that?" he cried.

In his forty anni-cycles, he'd never seen the glistering sky completely black. But it was now. Everything outside of the *Octopod* was simply gone, replaced by a massive shape seemingly composed of complete darkness.

"It's the usurper's warship," Mylla said. "Turn us around. Now! Get us out of here."

After the word "warship," no other words had ever been less necessary to say aloud. Dipping the port side, he spun the *Octopod* on its axis, allowing himself the brief elation of knowing nothing could catch them once he activated the harness and drew power from the celestial stone.

But like all the wonderful bouts of enormous luck he'd had in the last couple of cycles, this one, too, flamed and died like the fleeches against Aldinhuus's Fenestros-fueled shield. The *Bounding Skate*, having caught up at last, hovered before them.

"Come on, Glunt," Mylla cried. "If that warship takes us, more than our own doom awaits. Go!"

But he couldn't. Cote and the Glisternauts were here. And after seeing how much the encroaching warship frightened this stalwart-looking Knight, even if Jaemus could escape with the *Octopod*'s celestially charged speed, what would happen to Cote?

"I can't," he said simply. "I can't leave them at the mercy of that. Whatever *that* is."

CHAPTER FORTY-FIVE

The ship had stopped its erratic tilt, and though Ulfric had a firm grip on the shelksie locker, the anticipated shock of speed hadn't yet come.

"What are you doing, Glunt?" Evernal's voice, pitched high with alarm, broke from the cockpit. "We must flee!"

No further prompting needed, Ulfric shot through the hatch to intercept whatever new calamity the Himmingazian was about to attempt. And just when he'd finally begun to trust him…

But there wasn't time, or need, to explain what had caused their aborted escape. He looked beyond the windshield and saw for himself what the issue was. The *Bounding Skate* had arrived. "Bardgrim, go around—"

Mylla spun around and cut him off. "Stallari, the usurper's warship has found us."

A memory flashed in his mind with a jolt. Balavad's voice in his head saying, *A starship, Stallari. You are looking at the flagship of a great people… This starship brings the bearers of my gift: preservation from needless destruction.* And with this, a view of the behemoth ship as it had risen over Vinnr in front of his eyes.

"Balavad's ship—" she started, but it was his turn to cut in.

"I know the ship."

"… How?"

"Knights," Bardgrim interjected. "If you've got some kind of magic-rock power you plan to wield against that comet of catastrophe, no time like the present." The wisp of hope in the engineer's voice, so tiny, couldn't have moved a feather.

"We have to run," Mylla pressed.

"No." Both of them looked at Ulfric with eyes bigger than his shrinking heart. "We must stay," he ruled.

Mylla stared at Ulfric as if he were mad. "If the Verity catches us with the artifacts, we will be defenseless. Vinnr will be defenseless. The only thing we can do is run!"

"No."

As the words left his mouth, a shadow oozed over the *Bounding Skate* from behind them. The warship drawing closer.

Mylla rose from her seat. "Then we fling them into the sea. If he seizes us, we mustn't still have the Fenestrii or Scrylle. They are all he needs to overtake Vinnr completely."

A voice came out of the wave-speaker, stopping Mylla just as she started toward the hold. "Jaemus." It was Illago, the captain of the Glisternaut ship. "Glister Cloud's lights, are you seeing that? What is that thing?"

The engineer scrambled to respond. "Cote, run, do it now, as fast as the *Skate* can go. It's a warship. It's come for the Knights."

"Knight-*s*?" Illago questioned. "You have more than one muddle-mind with you now?" Jaemus shot a look over his shoulder at Ulfric, his eyebrows arched as if to say *I'm not the one who said it.* Illago continued, "We've taken control of the *Octopod*, Jae. A little trick you showed me. Did you forget? None of us leaves until you stop this sense-lessness."

Looking surprised, Bardgrim began jostling the various controlling dials and spheres along the ship's console, but quickly gave up. Defeated, he turned to Mylla. "We're not going anywhere now. They've got the *'Pod.*" He leaned his head back to look through the top of the windscreen, no doubt assessing how long they had until the warship struck.

Watching Mylla carefully lest she attempt to dispense with the celestial artifacts as she'd threatened, Ulfric asked, "Is there some kind of grappling hook? I don't see how. They're not that close."

"Yes, in a way."

Bardgrim looked as if he was going to launch into a complicated explanation, but Ulfric jumped in before he could and stepped to the controls. "Show me how to speak to Illago."

The engineer touched symbols on his glass screen and said, "Go ahead. You try and make him see sense. The Cloud knows I can't."

"Captain Illago, this is Stallari Aldinhuus. You are in more danger than you can comprehend. If you value your lives, you should escape before it's too late. But first release the *Octopod*. We've business with this warship that no one else can see to."

"Oh, Verities…"

Mylla's breathless utterance pulled his attention away from the wave-speaker, then he saw it too. A swarm of sickle-like flying craft was spreading around and above them, a fleet more numerous than any formation of the Dragør Wing fighters he'd ever witnessed.

She said one word: "Raveners."

They filled the sky like bats, forming a barrier too thick to fly through. Without weapons, the *Octopod* may as well have already been captured.

"They are made for war, Ulfric, and they fire projectiles that can take out a Wing fighter. They'll blow us into pieces in no time."

The sheer, unbelievable number of them held him transfixed—until the sound of Mylla's boots made him spin around as she lunged into the hold. He raced after her and caught her by the shoulder just as she grabbed the satchel.

"Drop it," he warned.

She did, but only to swing a fist into his nose and another into his gut. He parried her next blow as his eyes began to water, making the eye shields difficult to see through. Knowing her fighting skills intrinsically—he'd helped train her, after all—he continued to block and reroute every attack she flung at him. Vaguely, he heard the Himmingazian yelling something.

Before she wore herself out, he gripped Mylla by the throat and squeezed. She reached up to break his hold, and he clasped both her wrists with his free hand. Using his larger body, he pinned her arms against her armor and shoved her against the wall. "You cannot toss them into the sea, Mylla. I won't let you."

"Stallari, what is wrong with you?! Will you betray the Knights and Vinnr the way Eisa has? We cannot let Balavad have them!"

"No, what we cannot do is get rid of them! I need them. Don't you understand, novice? They killed my family. Symvalline and Isemay are dead because of Verities. Our makers are nothing but monsters. I will have vengeance on this celestial deceiver and all of them if I can. You can't stop me. The only master who can control me now is death."

Mylla ceased struggling and fell completely still. Her expression—sorrow, regret, and a bloom of red in her cheeks and drop of her eyes that confessed a hint of shame—told him she knew the truth also: his beloved and his daughter were dead.

"Don't fight me to serve *them*, to serve monsters," he uttered, his voice breaking.

Her eyes were wide, her face flushed. He eased his grip on her throat. Behind him, the engineer was breathing quickly, fearfully, as Mylla searched for something to say.

"Ulfric, please. You cannot believe you can win some kind of war against Verities, can you?"

Releasing her completely, he stepped back. "All I need are their vessels. I have many Fenestrii and time to find the rest, and I know the incantation to create the cage. One by one, I'll stop them. Then Vinnr will be free. All the realms will. Will you help me?"

"But it's you," Bardgrim said. At Ulfric's sudden glare, the engineer reached out to touch the wall, grabbing something stable as if in need of reassurance. "That's what I've been trying to tell you, Aldinhuus. You're this vessel whats-it—Vaka Aster's vessel. She told me herself. When I, erm, *accidentally* slugged you in the chin and knocked off the goggles you're wearing—really, really sorry about that, by the way—

she somehow got into my head... or something. It's how I gained this sudden and amazing fluency in Elder Veros, I think. Neat trick, by the way..." Ulfric's stare promised violence if the engineer didn't quit yammering. With a clearing of his throat, he continued, "I don't know quite how to explain it. This voice, it was just a voice, came out of stars... or maybe I was in stars... like I said, hard to explain. But she told me she'd chosen you as her vessel and that you'd thrown her in a cage in your mind. Something to that effect, anyway. So, if it wasn't just me suffering from bad fish and vapors, it looks like your mission is already accomplished. You're the vessel *and* the cage."

Ulfric felt his mouth form the word "absurd," but he didn't say it. He looked at Mylla, whose eyes jumped from his to Bardgrim's and back, disbelief and shock fighting for control of her face.

"This isn't..." he finally said but trailed off. But it *was* possible: the voice in his head that wasn't his, that knew more than he knew. The dragørflies, the unaccountable absence of his thoughts, the loss of time.

Stallari, listen. Let me speak.

"NO!" he yelled, and gripped his ears, backing up until the backs of his legs struck the table.

Mylla rushed forward as if to help him but stopped short in confusion, or fear.

From the cockpit, he could hear Captain Illago yelling in distress. It was too much, too much to take in. It couldn't be true, but it was the only thing that made all of it make sense. Vaka Aster had embodied many vessels, many forms, over the thousands of turns that had preceded his existence. It was all there in the Scrylle. He'd just never expected to witness their maker do such a thing in his term of service. She'd been in the Nazaria Dyrrak for so long.

Until now, it seemed.

"There's more," Bardgrim continued, his voice graver than Ulfric had yet heard it. "She told me that only the maker can unmake the cage. And if you die, your world, Vinnr, does too."

CHAPTER FORTY-SIX

I f not for the voice coming from the ship's cockpit, Mylla and Ulfric might have remained in stunned silence at the implications of the Glunt's revelation for hours. She could think of thousands of reasons to believe he was either crazy or lying, but none harmonized with what her instincts told her. The Stallari himself did not refute the Himmingazian; how could she?

"And one last thing," the Glunt said. "The Verity said she'd break your mind if she tried to control it. So I guess that means you have to work out some sort of time-share arrangement?"

His tone was difficult to interpret, but she struggled more with his meaning. "Stallari," she finally managed, "please help me understand what the Himmingazian is saying. Is this true?"

Ulfric stood rigid, his gaze through the dark-lensed eye shields appearing fixed on nothing. The other ship's captain continued to channel his voice to them, and Mylla finally caught the words. "Jaemus, Jaemus, are you hearing me? We can't escape. There's no way past these enemy craft, and they're forcing us toward the giant ship."

The Himmingazian turned back into the cockpit. She heard him respond, "I'm sorry, Cote. Sorry to get you involved. On the bright side of the Cloud, I'm sure we'll be joining you soon."

Though his tone held a desperate kind of sarcasm, Mylla could not imagine what "on the bright side of the cloud" meant. The sky here was nothing but glittering murk and ether interspersed with lightning, rain, and monstrous flying water worms. She could see no cloud, bright or otherwise, amid all of that.

The ship rocked to port suddenly, making her scramble to keep her footing, followed a moment later by a loud *pop* coming from outside the hull. Then another jolt came, and another.

"Knights, Knights! The little ships are firing at us!" the Himmingazian cried.

But she already knew this. She'd heard the sound before, above Mount Omina when she and Havelock had been pursued by the Ravener attackers. And she also knew Balavad's plan was not to kill but to capture them.

"They aren't trying to shoot us down," she said hollowly.

"Is that the good news or the bad?" the Glunt asked.

"They want you to come about. Follow that other ship. They're taking us captive."

"Ah, so it's the bad." With a worried rake of his hand through his thick tower of brown curls, he settled at the helm.

"Mylla," Ulfric finally said, "listen to me. Don't do anything unless I tell you. I will handle this."

"How?" she asked. "What are you—and Vaka Aster—planning?"

"To finish this. If I am a vessel, then the form Balavad has taken is one, too." He lifted the Battgjald Scrylle from the satchel, holding it as if it were something slimy yet essential, like a half-rotted apple in the hands of a starving man. After a moment, he returned it to the satchel and slung it over his neck so that it hung beneath one arm.

Mylla's thoughts buzzed chaotically, but she did her best to rein them in. "Call Vaka Aster, then. Our creator can end this on our behalf."

"Don't you think our *Vigil Star*," he sneered the words, "would have come to our aid already if she intended to?"

"But we must try, *you must try!*" She couldn't fathom this obstinacy in her leader, with so much at risk. "What if you're wrong, Stallari? You are risking all of Vinnr. What if Balavad kills you? Just—"

He clasped her shoulder, not gently, but in control, the lines of his face tight and certain. "All I need is to be near him. I can cage him in his vessel using the Vinnr Fenestrii. I can end this myself. You, novice, must for one last time keep your faith in this fight. Keep your faith in *me*. I have never failed the Order or our maker."

"But if you fail now..." she breathed.

He released her and stepped back. "Then pray you see your family and Wing pilot again in forever death."

Another blast from the Ravener ships rocked the *Octopod*, and the Glunt yelled to them, "The *Skate* no longer has a lock on us, so I'm just going to steer us inside the giant doom-ship if no one has any other ideas, all right?" When neither of them answered, he muttered something else, then went quiet.

"I hope..."

She couldn't finish the sentence. What did she hope? That the Stallari was wrong, that Verities weren't monsters, that her life's purpose had been for good not evil? Yet, did the fact that Balavad had invaded their realm and Vaka Aster had done nothing to stop him prove only that Ulfric was right? If so, what was there to hope for? What allegiance did a Knight Corporealis have, what purpose to defend, if not to protect and serve their maker? And to do so without reward, without acknowledgment, without friends or family to spend the ages of their prolonged lives with.

With nothing left to say, she stepped into the hatchway and turned her back to Ulfric. Shame for her thoughts wormed amid her insides, and she didn't want him to see it or catch hints of it in their Mentalios link. Looking beyond the windscreen, she saw the larger native ship was all but devoured by the usurper's warship, the *Octopod* within throwing distance behind. She stared into Balavad's warship's massive hold, just a giant maw of dimness hiding in the torrent of rain outside, and thought of Havelock. A man of Vinnr. A man she loved. The only one she ever truly had.

Like a piece being laid into a puzzle, or a Fenestros dropped into a Scrylle's setting, she suddenly understood her true purpose, and it bathed her with a cold sort of relief. This was it then. Havelock, and all commoners, were her purpose. She had these many "gifts" endowed her by Vaka Aster, which she could, she *would*, from this day forward redirect to benefit her fellow people. She would renounce her oath to her Verity. Whether or not she was stripped of her Verity spark, she would continue to serve only the people, no longer the Verities and their fey caprices.

Provided she didn't die today, of course.

CHAPTER FORTY-SEVEN

As the shadow of the warship consumed them, Ulfric's thoughts darkened as well. What was the truth, he wondered, and how much of it now mattered? If Vaka Aster had somehow changed his fabric from man to vessel, not only transferring the responsibility of Vinnr from his care but forcing it upon his very existence, did that in any way change what he'd decided to do? Should it? To be first *abandoned* by one's maker, then *merged* with her—it was just another betrayal, an attempt to wrest his will from him and make him lower than a servant, make him a puppet.

But he'd gotten the better of Vaka Aster, hadn't he?

Yes, and now he would do the same with Balavad. If Vaka Aster wanted freedom, the Verity would have to kill him and take it. He had nothing left to lose but life, and that had become a withered, bloomless rose already.

The moment they landed inside the warship, Ulfric opened the outer hatch, ready to face an army. Dropping to the hangar floor, he retrieved his klinkí stones from a pouch he'd found on Bardgrim's ship and sent Mylla a warning through the Mentalios: *Ready your sword!* But the message seemed to go nowhere. Had their lenses failed?

Mylla tossed her klinkí stones in the air—but they clattered to the ground, like regular stones. Wide-eyed, she whispered, "It seems hope has abandoned us."

Immediately, Ulfric tried to animate his own stones, to the same effect. Through the eye shields, he watched a horde of ghastly pale and hunched Raveners array themselves before them, carrying hooked swords raised in readiness. But they did not attack.

The Himmingazian dropped down and stood behind him and Mylla. Ulfric spared him a measure of sorrow. Even the foreigner had been betrayed by the Verities, first Vinnr's and now Battgjald's. He wondered if Bardgrim felt fear or something closer to the same rage pulsing through Ulfric. A rage so strong he had to stifle a reflex to yell at the enemy mass, *Get on with it!* They would. When they were ready.

A hissing noise, sibilants instead of words, rose from the rear of the formation, slowly working its way forward as the echelon parted like water. A Flesh Caster, wearing robes similar to the one Ulfric had smashed to paste in Vaka Aster's sanctuary, made her way through the crowd and stopped before them.

Speaking in Elder Veros, she said, "Creatures of Vaka Aster and Lífs, His Holiness will privilege you with an audience in his consecration chamber shortly. There, you will be given a chance to redeem your faithlessness and tell him where the true vessel of Vaka Aster lies, for he has learned of your deceit. And you will be offered forgiveness once you've declared your contrition, as is his way. First, however, return His Holiness's sacred objects." She held out a fish-belly white hand.

"I'm thinking that's a bad idea," Bardgrim whispered.

"Take them yourself, betrayer, if you're able," Ulfric spat.

The Flesh Caster's eyes narrowed. "Betrayer?" she hissed. "I still serve my Verity. You built a cage for yours, Knight, and then hid it away from even your own Order. Who is the betrayer here?"

Cold uncertainty wormed down his spine. From Mylla, he knew the rest of the Knights had been taken by Balavad. What had the Verity and his Flesh Casters done to them? How much did Balavad know? What, if any, advantages did they have? The warrior in him prodded the situation from all angles, finding none to be smooth and none to be sure.

Let me see, Stallari. Free me.

That voice—Vaka Aster's voice—blew through his thoughts, insistent. Pain lanced into his forehead, making him suck air quickly between his teeth. Then it was gone, leaving behind a dull ache like a tooth loosened by a boxer's blow. As he had since the first time he'd heard the maker's voice, he refused to listen. Refused to let it take over his mind. Refused, once more, to be a pawn in her games.

"Cote!" Bardgrim yelled and turned as if to run. Before he could, several Raveners pointed their weapons at him, prompting him to rethink his actions. The misery on his face could have made the dead weep.

Ulfric glanced aside and spotted the crew of the nearby *Bounding Skate* being turned out by more Raveners. The Himmingazian folk were receiving rough treatment at the hordes' hands. In the massive hangar, easily the size of five of Asteryss's city blocks, the only advantages Ulfric could see were space and distance. But even if anyone tried to run, there was no escape. And with Vaka Aster's Fenestrii and his and Evernal's own Verity-spark weapons and devices useless, the only path remaining was to face Balavad. Ulfric was ready.

The Flesh Caster reached out once more to take the satchel, and Ulfric angled it aside to refuse her. "Take us to Balavad, usurper that he is, and I will give him his artifacts myself. Or kill me. Because you will have to if you wish to have these."

The enemy priest's lips parted in a smirk around her pointed grayish teeth. "Do you think you can deny me, against this?" She swept her hands out on both sides, gesturing to the hundred or more Raveners spread throughout the hangar. "My master told me you were clever, but it seems he may have been mistaken."

"Was he?" Ulfric taunted.

Without responding, the Flesh Caster grew rigid suddenly, her eyes losing focus. After a moment, her slack expression went tight and she said, "His Holiness has agreed." Turning to the horde, she emitted what appeared to be instructions in that same sibilant language, and the assembly quickly drew a tight circle around Ulfric, Mylla, and Bardgrim.

"Wait," Bardgrim pressed. "I'm just a Glint Engineer from Himmingaze, not a Knight. I'm sure I would be much less of a bother if you just … uh, tossed me in a cell with the others over there." He tilted his head toward the *Skate*'s crew, every one of them looking shocked, horrified, and totally outside their element.

The Flesh Caster hissed again and spun around to look at him.

"Leave this one, slave," Ulfric demanded of her. "He's not part of this."

Bardgrim shot him a grateful look but flinched when the Flesh Caster took a stride toward him. She reached out and grabbed both of his cheeks suddenly, yanking his head toward hers. Her height allowed her to look directly into his eyes, which widened anxiously as she peered into them. Again, her body stiffened, but this time when she spoke her voice thickened and deepened, becoming another's. The voice of Balavad.

"A Himmingazian, creature of Lífs." She drew his face closer.

Mylla's hand went to the hilt of her sword, but Ulfric stopped her with a quick shake of his head. She couldn't protect Bardgrim. Neither could he.

The Flesh Caster continued, "My quin's realm is filled with fascinating creatures, much like my own. I will be back for your kind soon. But not now." The priest licked her dry lips with a pale forked tongue, keeping her grip on Bardgrim's face as she gazed at him with her dull eyes. "You... there is something about you. You'll come to the consecration chamber, too."

So the enemy can see through his subjects' eyes and speak through their flesh, Ulfric realized. *The same way Vaka Aster can through me*. It seemed there was no end to the violations their makers would subject them to.

The Flesh Caster jerked slightly, then dropped her hands. "Don't struggle, creature of Lífs," she warned in her own voice. "Or any of you." Following another hiss, the horde pointed their weapons on the trio and began forcing them toward the far end of the hangar.

As they walked, Captain Illago's frightened cry echoed behind them. "Jaemus. Jaemus, whatever they do, resist them!"

CHAPTER FORTY-EIGHT

The way to the usurper's consecration chamber unrolled beneath legs that felt like wet cloth to Ulfric. Mylla's sword had been stripped from her, without bloodshed by some miracle, and she plodded next to his right shoulder with a stiff, heavy gait that screamed defiance and rage. The Raveners hadn't even bound their hands, unconcerned the three of them could mount any meaningful resistance. And without access to their klinkí stones or the power to draw upon Vaka Aster's spark, which seemed to be blocked inside this Balavad's domain, they couldn't.

Behind them, Bardgrim muttered, "I'm beginning to think this Verity business is bad for everyone, Himmingaze and your own home. Scratch that, I'm well beyond beginning and right in the middle of being certain of it."

Ulfric couldn't miss the heartsickness underlying his voice. "I can offer no consolation, other than that it will end soon."

As they walked, his thoughts turned to the artifacts in his satchel. He quelled a desire to look into the Battgjald Scrylle again and ensure he knew every syllable of the incantation to create the Verity cage and force one into it. If he did not speak it precisely, all of this would be meaningless. But the danger would be a thousand times worse if he looked into the celestial tome, enabling Balavad to see his thoughts. He'd seen the usurper's ability to occupy and control his own minions' minds, but he'd not been able to breach Ulfric's—except when he'd opened it to the Scrylle. Some vital link Balavad had with his realm's people seemed to be missing between him and Ulfric, perhaps all Vinnrics. Perhaps that was achieved through this "consecration" ritual, whatever that was. Ulfric was counting on that barrier to keep his plan secret.

Stallari, Vaka Aster whispered, *you need my aid. Release your mind to me. Remove the shields that cover your eyes and let me see.*

His skin grew hot, tingling. For the first time, he chose to respond. *You betrayed me once. I am not fool enough to let you do it again, Vaka Aster.*

A Verity cannot betray its creations. You *are because* we *are.* Her tone, so fluid and sincere, did not sound menacing to him, nor did it sound compassionate. It sounded nothing but alien. She went on: *Vinnr now depends on—*

Enough! Like a fist, he clenched his mind against her invasion as tightly as he'd ever clenched a sword in battle. The pang he'd felt earlier, like an icicle being driven into his forehead, struck again. Deeper this time, and harder. A spike rather than a nail. He dropped his head and pressed a palm against it.

"Are you okay, Ulfric?" Mylla said.

He said nothing, focusing on the pain, willing it to dissipate. The Verity would *never* rule his mind. Never.

They passed into a new section of the ship and the walls opened up into a taller, wider tunnel, large enough for an army to walk through, ten abreast. He raised his head again and saw dark metal rising in giant plates on each side, with rivets holding the structure together that were as wide and thick as a person's thighs. They passed several entryways yawning with blackness, but Ulfric didn't glance down any of them. His focus was born not from courage but from wrath. Today, he would either win or die.

When they reached a set of imposing iron-like doors at the end of the corridor, the mass of Raveners pressed them through. A sickly yellow light coming from within pulsed strongly, and Ulfric's eyesight dimmed as he struggled inwardly against the urge to remove the eye shields and give Vaka Aster what she wanted.

The troop halted as one, sending the three of them stumbling into the backs of the nearest Raveners, but they were paid no heed. The horde broke apart slowly, like oil over a mirror's surface, and slunk toward the edges of the vast hall they had entered.

Ulfric took in everything around them. The chamber was as massive as the courtyard outside of Aster Keep, and the yellow glow came from lights set into recesses in the walls. Shadows swallowed the spaces between the lights, yet he could still see figures keeping a vigil within them. These were different than the Ravener horde. Though they had the same pale, lifeless countenance, their eyes were more alert, more sentient. Somehow, more terrible. They wore crimson ceremonial robes, and on the forehead of each was the chevron pattern of Balavad's Flesh Caster Order.

The thought of their corruption disturbed Ulfric deeply. But the sight of his fellow Knights, Stave, Mallich, and Safran, was much, much worse.

The three were bent to their knees side by side before white stone pillars, just three of many pillars lined up through the chamber's center, their hands bound behind them. Mallich's head was raised, and Ulfric saw his eyes widen at the sight of him and Mylla. Safran slumped against Stave, clearly in great pain. All bore wounds and gashes innumerable, their faces and clothing bloody and torn. They were not healing as normal, another indication that their gifts from Vaka Aster waned here. Upon catching sight of Ulfric, the expression on Mallich's drawn face flattened, becoming unreadable and inscrutable. Stave, ever unwilling to concede defeat, used the hand not clutching Safran to give him the Knights' salute.

Like a voice in a nightmare, Balavad seethed from the far end of the chamber. "Stallari Aldinhuus, again you are subject to me. Your craftiness has only prolonged Vinnr's foreordination, not thwarted it. You will not deceive me again."

The Verity glided forward. His black robes scraped the floor behind him, the rasp of the ragged hem along metal making Ulfric's teeth ache.

Balavad observed him closely as he approached, and Ulfric saw the malignant intelligence behind his black eyes, taking him in, considering him, planning his doom. He had never felt so exposed.

Be strong, Ulfric, he told himself. *For the memory of your family. For Symvalline and Isemay.*

The Verity flicked a wrist toward Mylla and Bardgrim, and Raveners pushed them aside toward the other Knights, then made them kneel as well. Ulfric noted relief in their eyes at the reunion. They were together again, friends still bonded. He had been with them all for so many turns, grown to love them with a fierceness only time and bonds of fellowship can nurture. What he was about to do might seem to them an abomination, or worse, an abandonment. Their Stallari, turning his back on duty and caging the Verities, both the usurper and Vaka Aster, for he had no intention of releasing her. Ever.

So be it. He would learn to endure his fellows' judgment while he also learned to endure the loss of his family. If he could not save Symvalline and Isemay, at least he might save his companions.

"Your trinkets," he growled. And without ceremony, he pulled the satchel over his head and dumped the artifacts before him. Around him, Raveners hissed menacingly at the sacrilege. He didn't care.

Then he realized his folly. He had intended to call up the Verity cage through his Mentalios, using the wystic lens link to hide his words so Balavad wouldn't be able to hear or stop him. But the Mentalios link was broken in this place. He could not silently channel the words to cage the Verity without it.

Aloud it would be. Feigning concession to his certain fate, he too knelt and bowed his head—letting the Verity think he had at last accepted defeat, but really to hide his lips—and began whispering the words to imprison Balavad within the net of Fenestrii.

CHAPTER FORTY-NINE

"*Now* you kneel, Stallari," Balavad taunted. "You should have been doing so all along."

Ignoring him, Ulfric continued speaking, the words rolling from his tongue as fast as he could utter them. As before, the energy poured from him, pulled unrelentingly into the stones that lay before him.

"What are you—" Balavad paused. For a moment, he seemed to freeze in place, silent and senseless.

Ulfric dared to hope.

It was a mistake.

Still staring intently at the artifacts as the incantation tumbled from him, he heard seething laughter, then Balavad spoke.

"Creature of Vaka Aster, you disappoint me. You cannot cage me. Not with another Verity's Fenestrii. So many eons of wisdom in you, yet you are still so foolish." His voice darkened. "I warned you."

He didn't look up, wasn't willing yet to concede to this final defeat, and kept whispering the cage incantation. From beside him, Ulfric hear Mallich yelling, "By the doom of Verities—Ulfric!"

At the alarm in his voice, Ulfric looked up in time to see a wall of fumes rumbling toward him. He grimaced, then screamed as it enveloped him, or more accurately *suffused* him, the experience like a sponge absorbing pure agony. Every muscle, every shred of skin, even his hair filled with pain, pushed to a point of bursting as he absorbed more and more of the poisonous miasma. Rigid with pain, he could neither writhe nor speak. All he could do was scream.

Balavad's voice overrode the cacophony, speaking directly in his ear. "If you want this suffering to end, there is only one task left before you: tell me where my quin's vessel is. Tell me, and I will grant the rest of your Knights peace. Life among my Flesh Casters rather than the death, slow though it might be, that your refusal to tell me will bring them."

For a moment, the miasma lessened, giving Ulfric a moment of sweet relief that was so tempting a respite that he almost considered Balavad's proposal. Shame nearly drowned him, then more screams filled his hearing, not his own this time, but Mallich's, Stave's, Mylla's, Safran's, and even the Himmingazian's. Forcing his eyes open, he saw them swallowed by the malignant vapor. Suffering. Dying.

"They won't last as long as you might, but their suffering will still feel an eternity to them. It will break their minds and their bodies before I release them," Balavad promised.

Through a throat that felt lined with broken glass, Ulfric cried, "You wish to know where the vessel is? It's me! I am the vessel!" He ripped his lenses from his head, revealing the cerulean swirl of Vaka Aster's light in his eyes.

Balavad's arms lifted and crossed in front of his chest, and his grim vapor left its victims and surrounded him instantly, thickening to pitch-black like a shield. Ulfric felt skeins of it ripped from his body, like fingernails, leaving behind a merciful emptiness. He slumped forward with a grunt, but his relief was momentary as he realized what he'd done. Vaka Aster now gazed out through his eyes, as Balavad did those of his slaves, her own will widening the cracks in Ulfric's, which weakened more every time he removed the eye shields.

Release me, Ulfric.

Never.

Release me or all is lost.

"No!" he raged, and with unknown reserves of strength, he stood and faced Balavad. "I am the vessel, usurper. I am that which you seek. Destroy me, and you will destroy Vinnr. You will lose your own game. There will be no victory, you pathetic sack of swill."

The hall had fallen silent, Raveners, Knights, and Bardgrim all staring at Ulfric, struck dumb by his brazenness.

Balavad could barely be seen inside the roiling miasma encircling him. In the stillness, the sounds of hundreds of minute wisps of wind rose, the noise coming from above. One by one, all heads but Balavad's and Ulfric's tilted to locate the source of the noise, a collective sense of either wonder or foreboding sweeping through Raveners and Knights alike.

From within the inky morass, Balavad's eyes glittered, his focus on Ulfric. Slowly, like melting candle wax, the Verity's expression shifted from alarm to dark and sinister amusement.

"You *are* Vaka Aster's new form, yes. But you are more than that, aren't you?" The pale lines of his lips split over his teeth like a slug squashed by a sudden weight. "Oh so clever. So *clever!* You have indeed caged my quin as I required. The only way she can free herself is to break you. My quin, my transcendent quin. You have given your realm to me yourself. If Vinnr is destroyed, it is *you* who will destroy it."

The cloud began sliding across the floor with Balavad at its center, his flaming red mane the color of congealing blood within the vapor. His feet no longer touched the ground, and when he reached Ulfric he loomed over the Knight like a malevolent specter of fate. Again, his expression shifted, becoming a mockery of compassion, and he said peaceably, "You are the savior of your world after all, Stallari. A true hero, dutiful, and wise. You have served me better than any creation in all my endless existence. I make this offer one last time. You will be rewarded, if you accept. I can give you anything. I can remove your pain, I can create a new family for you, I can even make you believe they have been your family all along. You will have back *everything* you think you lost—for loss is temporary. I can make you whole again. I can do this, because I am the Verity who only creates, not destroys."

The Verity raised his hands and held them apart. The space between sucked a vortex of the dark vapor into a swirling, hypnotic mass, and then it cleared completely. An image formed in the middle, and Ulfric's torment gave way to recognition. This was a memory, *his* memory, and one from not long past, perhaps plucked from his mind when he'd opened it to Balavad through the Scrylle. Isemay stood before him, staring into the memory keeper he'd given her just days ago, though it felt like lifetimes. He stood beside her, gazing at her face adoringly, a smile on his lips. That had been the last time he'd felt joy. In its place, all he had now was longing, emptiness, an endless life of sickness of heart and spirit.

"You can have this again," Balavad promised. "Any version of it you wish. We can decide on another vessel to hold my quin so that you may join my ranks. And then, I can clear your mind and memory of all pain and suffering and spin you new thoughts, any you wish, if you choose it. But if you do not, you will be caged like my quin, forever enslaved with nothing but memories of the dead for comfort or company. The choice is yours."

It would seem a simple choice. No more suffering, all he had to do was ask. All he had to do...

Abruptly, the ceiling lit up in a storm of blue-green radiance, revealing a myriad host of dragørflies, glittering in a hovering mass over the entire chamber. Balavad looked up, and the vision between his hands disappeared.

At some silent command, the mass dived as one into the inky darkness surrounding the Verity. Wrath drove them, an intention to attack, to burn, to destroy. They struck the black vapor, penetrating it, and a storm of light and dark commenced within.

I cannot distract my quin forever. RELEASE ME, Stallari.

The vice suddenly squeezing his mind made him cry out, the potency of Vaka Aster's command stronger than ever. He wrapped his hands around his head, trying to block what he could not—because she was inside, there was no more barring her if she didn't want to be barred. Once more, he fell to his knees, the pain driving him down like an anvil. He wanted to abdicate, to do as she asked and let go of the chains he used to grip his own thoughts. But he would never do it.

Why? he cried. *Why do anything you ask? You let my family die! After all my service, all Symvalline's service, you let them die as though our sacrifices meant nothing.*

Your family lives. They are preserved and secure.

Why would I believe you?

I will show you.

He was thrust into a bright emptiness, millions and billions of tiny specks of light moving past him too fast to discern. Then, just as abruptly, he came to a stop. His vision coalesced down to a small area, as if he stared through a monocle. Unlike a monocle, however, the lens he seemed to be peering through was faceted. Through it, he saw the beloved face of his daughter staring back at him.

"Isemay?" he whispered.

"Da! Is that you?" she cried. "Is it really you? Not a memory? How… where are you? I was so worried you were—"

He felt his hand reaching for her, though he could see nothing but the image of her face and a background of tall stone-like towers. He yearned to touch her soft cheek. "Are you safe, Crumb? Where is Symvalline?"

She seemed as shocked to see him as he was her and stammered, "I-I don't know. Mum and I are in Arc Rheunos. There are people here who've helped me, but Da, Mum was… she was taken."

His inner sight began to grow cloudy, obscuring her. "Da!" she cried.

But the vision misted away and was gone like smoke on a stiff breeze. "Isemay! Symvalline!" Ulfric wailed.

As the words left his lips, a blasting hot wind carrying hundreds of dead dragørflies battered his body, pushing him onto his back.

Urgently, Vaka Aster said, *Ulfric, you must open your mind to me and allow me to stand against Balavad—*

"They're alive!" he cried aloud. "You did spare them! Take me to them!"

We cannot go to Arc Rheunos while we are vulnerable and I am bound to you. It was a mistake that brought us to Himmingaze to begin with. But I can return us to Vinnr and end my quin's onslaught. Just let go the shackles on your mind.

But all Ulfric heard was that he could not go to his family while Vaka Aster remained caged. Fighting against the blasting furnace of Balavad's and the dragørflies' battle, he rolled to his side and reached out for the usurper's Scrylle. His thoughts oozed like mud in his head, murky, sucking at him like quicksand. All he knew was that he had to look inside Balavad's Scrylle, find a way to unmake the cage. Once he freed his maker, surely he could go to Symvalline and his child. Surely there was mercy in Vaka Aster, and she would let him do this.

He grabbed the celestial scepter, but neither of Balavad's Fenestrii remained in the pile he'd dumped them in. Frantically, he scanned the floor. There—he'd kicked them aside when he'd fallen, and one had rolled toward the Knights, unnoticed by the Raveners.

"Mylla," he commanded, "bring me that Fenestros."

CHAPTER FIFTY

I t was said that Knights could not go crazy, that their minds were stolid and toughened by Vaka Aster's celestial gifts. But what Mylla was witnessing in the Stallari could be described in no other way. She too saw the vision held between the usurper's hands, the Stallari's daughter holding a finely crafted pendant. The way Ulfric stared—it was like watching a dying man drawing his last gasping breath before surrendering to eternity.

Then the dragørfly legion struck, the Stallari cried out, and his hands flew to his head. The next moment, he fell and his eyes rolled back as if he were having a fit. Mylla and the remaining Knights watched in shock and horror as their leader mumbled incoherently, alternately writhing in place and growing rigid like a corpse. In his paroxysm, he scattered the celestial artifacts. One came toward her, but she feared to reach for it, despite the Raveners' distraction. The four Knights present had heard Ulfric declare he was the vessel, but she didn't know if they had been able to fully grasp that truth yet, and what was at stake. She was almost glad they couldn't communicate through their Mentalios lenses. She wasn't sure she could bear it as they all realized they were witnessing their last hope to save Vinnr and preserve their Verity's dominion splinter into lunacy.

At Ulfric's heart-rending cry of, "They're alive! You did spare them! Take me to them!" and his conversation with his surely dead daughter, Mylla's last doubt died. Balavad had won. The Stallari's mind was broken. Their leader could lead no longer.

Ulfric looked at her then. "Mylla, bring me that Fenestros."

Her many turns of responding to his commands had her reaching for Balavad's Fenestros before she realized she was doing it. But she stopped herself. Desperation lurked like a dangerous beast in the deep lines of his face and belied the tone of his voice, a tone that rang of hope and, even more tragically, of belief. But she no longer believed, she *couldn't* believe, his intentions were true. Their Stallari was gone, reduced to a fractured, hollow, unpredictable shell. It gutted her, even more than watching Havelock turn his back to her, for she'd had so much longer to learn to admire and love Ulfric, as a mentor, as family. Now nothing could save them.

Unless...

She jerked her head to look at the Glunt, who stared at the dragørfly-and-Verity battle glassy-eyed and dumbfounded, and the memory of something he'd said rang through her mind. *When I slugged you in the chin and knocked off the goggles you're wearing, she somehow stepped into my head.*

"Mylla, the stone!" Ulfric demanded.

Still, she didn't move. Rattling the Stallari's mind had given Vaka Aster a moment of liberty, at least the Himmingazian's description had made it sound that way. Could Mylla perhaps do the same? Free Vaka Aster by knocking Ulfric senseless?

One thing she was almost certain of: she could punch much harder than the Glunt.

With the speed of a bruhawk, she swept up the Fenestros and lunged toward Ulfric. The fuming edges of the usurper's inky cloud roasted her, and she caught the sound of wrathful screeches and hissing—the Ravener horde alerted by her actions readying to attack. Ulfric jumped up to meet her and reached out for the Fenestros. Grasping it tightly, she bypassed his arm and swung with all her warrior strength, connecting squarely with his temple.

She expected him to topple instantly. No one could have remained upright with the strength she put into her swing. But he merely lurched a step as his head rocked aside. At that moment, a tendril of the black vapor surrounding Balavad whipped out, wrapping around her much as the flying sea worm had earlier. It crushed her, the pressure agonizing, squeezing the air from her. From behind her, Safran cried, "Mylla!" as she was jerked around to face Balavad, his sooty eyes ablaze with rage.

"That's mine," the Verity rumbled, his voice corrosive in her ears. "Release it."

The pressure increased, as did the pain, and she cried out and dropped the Fenestros. She tried to draw a breath, but the vapor choked her. Around her, the last of the dragørflies burst into smoke and ash, their battle all but lost.

"Now you will see what happens when you or your Knights cross me, creature of Vaka Aster," Balavad said and sent the tendril still locked around her whipping toward Ulfric, preparing to rip her apart before his eyes.

She blinked at the jolt, and when her eyes focused she was face-to-face with—

Vaka Aster.

"Help us," Mylla breathed.

And then she released one final scream as what felt like a million daggers tore through her flesh.

CHAPTER FIFTY-ONE

Jaemus's one regret was that he wasn't going to live to have any more. As he watched Mylla bash Ulfric with the Fenestros, he reflected that, though he'd never been one for fisticuffs, he certainly wished the old hermit Griggory had done the same to him before he'd ever stolen the celestial artifacts from his Gram. Maybe then he wouldn't have ended up where he was now, nor would Cote and the Glisternauts. They all could have died a peaceful death under the, by comparison, *delightful* effluvium of the Glister Cloud.

And things continued to get worse.

A writhing branch of vapor extended from the terrifying Verity's bubble of shadow and fastened Knight Evernal in a grip that practically shrieked *This is what agony looks like.* From where he knelt, he could see her teeth gritted against a scream and the muscles in her neck straining hard enough they looked ready to snap.

The Verity ordered her to release the Verity stone and flung Evernal around to face Ulfric. He saw her eyes widen, then she did scream. The wail sounded wrenched from the depths of her spirit, a wracked, excruciating cry. By the way it cut off abruptly and her body tumbled bonelessly to the chamber floor, he knew she was once again dead. This time *really* dead, surely.

And despite that she kept calling him "Glunt," her passing saddened him. With an unexpected lump in his throat, he turned his eyes back to Ulfric.

Who was acting quite strangely indeed.

No, *acting* wasn't the right word. *Glowing.* As Jaemus watched, the ends of Aldinhuus's hair lit up, as if filled with the same bioluminescent chemicals that many of the creatures in the Never Sea hosted, each strand turning into a blue-green rope of radiance. And the star on his chin practically *blazed.* In moments, the rest of the man's skin joined in the transformation and began incandescing like pure blue fire. Jaemus fleetingly wondered why the Knight had never done *that* before, then the thought fled as the light suddenly erupted, like the heart of a star, and filled the chamber with the power of a sun.

In sheer disbelieving terror, Jaemus squeezed his eyes shut, even clapped his hands over his ears, though there was no sound. A painless wave of pressure hit him, seemed to sink into his chest, and then the dread, terror, horror—every emotion he should have been feeling—all disappeared, as if consumed in the impossibly bright pulse of blue. He didn't know if it was death itself that was squashing his natural responses, or if knowing death was inevitable had simply made him accept it. The frightening Verity was terrible and was probably going to kill them all in some unique and horrible way, but this explosion would at least be quick.

But, then, if it was going to be so quick, why did he have so much time to think it over? And if death was this slow, he certainly wasn't complaining about how little it hurt. Which was to say, it didn't.

For being such a brilliant engineer, Jaemus, he thought, *lately you've only excelled in misjudging things. If you live through this—ha, ha—you may need to rethink your high opinion of yourself.*

He heard clattering and thumping around him and, oh so slowly began to peel open his eyes, steeling himself for whatever attack would come next. For the moment, however, this looked to be an unnecessary concern. The entirety of the Ravener horde lay stunned on the chamber floor, still enough that he wondered if they, unlike him, had been killed by the eruption of light, which had mercifully subsided. What remained was a cerulean-white halo around Aldinhuus, surrounding him, yet somehow coming from *within* him.

Of course, Jaemus realized, this wasn't the Knight he knew, not strictly anyway. This was their Verity herself, Vaka Aster. Mylla had somehow released the celestial sprite from whatever cage Aldinhuus had erected, and the being now practically oozed through Aldinhuus's skin.

He didn't need to warn himself not to misjudge what to expect next —there was no doubt that whatever happened, things were about to get *very* interesting.

"Release my creations from the influence of your spark, Balavad, and desist from your assault on Vinnr." The voice carried the same crystalline resonance Jaemus remembered from when Vaka Aster had spoken inside his mind, but was now deepened by Aldinhuus's own bass.

"My quin," the scary Verity said. "I would not have expected you to meddle with the will of your own Knight."

Vaka Aster refused to be baited. "Why do you seek to control Vinnr? You are master of your own realm."

Balavad settled to the floor, still cloaked by his miasma, and drew closer to the Vinnr Verity. Where Vaka Aster's ring of light and his dark cloud touched, sparks like shooting stars flew hither and yon. Jaemus detected a sharp, though not unpleasant, odor, like lightning-struck stone. The Knights to his right had not been affected, as he hadn't, by the sudden surge of radiance from Vaka Aster, and they bowed their heads in reverence, though their eyes followed the two Verities raptly. Amazingly, they appeared calm, almost serene. Jaemus realized his own face must look comical to them, arranged, it felt, into a wobbly rictus of shock and terror.

For no reason at all, he thought, *I am representing Himmingaze here. A little dignity isn't too much to ask for.* The absurdity of this almost made him chuckle, but he doubted he'd ever get over this superlative fright enough to chuckle again. Nonetheless, he forced his expression into one he hoped was a little less like a man about to piss or pass out, maybe both, and more like one on the verge of the greatest discovery in Himmingazian history.

"The Syzycki Elementum requires singularity and a singular dominion," Balavad said. "Because of us, the Five, it is broken, but I will restore it. I will become the Elementum."

"No," replied Vaka Aster. "The Syzycki Elementum is all things, united or sundered. It cannot be broken. Nothing that exists does so outside the Elementum. Has our sundering so corrupted you that you've forgotten?"

"Then my ambitions are part of the Elementum as well," the monstrous one reasoned, and Jaemus had to agree with the sense of his words—if everything was part of one thing, then nothing was an outlier; it was basic logic—as little as he understood what in the name of Himmingaze and the Never Sea's black waters they were talking about. "And I will be its master," Balavad finished.

"From One unified to Five sundered Verities, each with our own realm over which we have unchallenged dominion—this is what we as the Elementum decided," Vaka Aster said. "If you break with the Elementum, you forfeit your rights within it."

Vaka Aster held both arms out, and a blue-green wave of light flowed from Ulfric's open palms, splashing as many as half the assembled Raveners. Many had begun to stir sluggishly and reach for their weapons, their expressions reflecting confusion, disorientation, and in some, a dawning dread. As Jaemus stared, awestruck by the rippling light, he realized some of the horde were changed. Their garb was the same, but their skin now glowed with color that appeared more alive than dead, and their eyes had cleared, varying in hues from blues to browns to greens. Though their features ranged from fair to dark, to the last they all looked very like Aldinhuus and Evernal, in short, like people of Vinnr. They must have been mutated and absorbed into Balavad's army, but were being reclaimed by Vaka Aster.

Yet it seemed as if the usurper wasn't willing to give them up. "Accept your losses," he snarled, "and leave these creatures to me. You abandoned them. I offer them what you taunt them with and then take away. *Their lives.* I will spare them and allow them to continue eternally under my sway."

"Corrupted, twisted lives. I have taken back my own creations. The first, the most fundamental rule of the Elementum was to set the realms in motion and permit our creations to unfold on their own, to follow their own wills, without influence beyond what is necessary to preserve our realms. Do you think they would choose eternity as your puppets? That is not life as the Elementum intends it."

Balavad's acid voice carried throughout the chamber. "Your own corruption, Vaka Aster, is that you believe their wills matter." He laughed. "You speak of rules, yet here you are, having yourself forced your will on one of your own."

"I have stepped forward in his absence."

"You stole his form."

"To preserve my realm."

"*Your realm,*" Balavad sneered, waving a long-fingered hand dismissively. Then, in a tone as smooth and dark as warm oil, he crooned, "Perhaps you would be easier to persuade if you no longer had one. To arms, Raveners!"

Balavad's hand chopped downward and his miasma billowed, enveloping Vaka Aster in a cloud of black. For a moment, it looked to Jaemus as if he was staring into an absence of matter and light, as if a hole to the eternal emptiness beyond the Great Cosmos had opened where Vaka Aster stood. Then biting pain pierced his chest, the same as the first time Balavad's poison fog shot through them. As Jaemus cringed and clutched at his torso, barely keeping his eyes at a squint, he saw the people of Vinnr gripping their own bodies, some groaning, some stumbling back down to their knees. In terrifying synchronicity, the Raveners of Balavad's realm swept up their hooked swords and readied to attack.

"You were outwitted by your own Knight, Vaka Aster, and have become trapped in a cage you cannot escape. I can see this wound I inflict on you spreading to your creations. As your vessel dies, they will too. Your weakness for your lesser creations has decided their fate, as it has your realm's." With a nightmarish grin, he called, "Raveners, destroy them."

A new spike of pain shot through Jaemus's gut, and a guttural cry escaped the pale golden-haired Knight beside him. Beyond him, the swarthy Knight and the injured one clutched each other tightly, their eyes squeezed shut in torment. The pain grew agonizing, mounting in a pressure that he felt would burst him to pieces, and he wanted to beg fate to just kill him outright.

"Then let it be your realm's fate as well," came Vaka Aster's voice, thin and echoing as if traveling from a great distance. "One vessel is as assailable as another."

From the center of the dark circle, a glow began to burn, igniting the black ether into curling flames.

Lightning-fast, the glow formed into blue flames in the shape of Ulfric's body, then shot toward the usurper, colliding with an impact that made the air roil throughout the chamber like a hard ocean current. Jaemus's pain dulled, allowing him to draw a full breath that smelled of an unlikely mix of brimstone and sea breezes. The fallen Vinnrics scattered among the Raveners seemed to recover too, and they dove for weapons. The chamber erupted into hand-to-hand combat as some defended themselves against the Raveners, and others attacked first. Ghastly shrieks and screams, grunts and cries of rage flowed throughout, a spectacle beyond any Jaemus had ever seen—or wanted to.

So he did what seemed appropriate. He remained tucked up on the chamber floor, hoping not to be killed.

A hand grasped his shoulder and shook him, breaking through the fear he very much wanted to surrender to. The pale Knight loomed over him, speaking, but Jaemus couldn't understand. "What?" he yelled over the din.

"Are you all right?" the man asked, speaking in Elder Veros.

"Er, I'm not dead," was all he could think to say, because in this situation, "all right" hardly seemed the term that fit.

"Come with me. You can't stay—"

A Ravener launched himself at the Knight, forcing him to release

Jaemus's shoulder and defend himself. In stunningly fast movements the Knight jumped aside, swinging fists, dodging strikes, and was soon grappling with the Ravener. The shorter Knight had risen as well and provided an arm to assist the wounded Knight. These two fought as one body, their combat skills remarkable despite having no weapons and one being injured.

The having-no-weapons situation, however, did not last long for any of the Vinnric Knights. The first Raveners to attack them had been felled into bloodless heaps, and their wickedly sharp blades claimed and used against them. The sight of the pale Knight cleaving through the neck of his next foe made Jaemus light-headed and nauseous. He had to look away, struggling to clear his mind of a picture *that* hideousness. The Knights and Raveners alike seemed to have forgotten him anyway, and it appeared that if he remained lying motionless where he was, he might be mistaken for dead. As strategies went, he could think of none better.

The two Verities seemed to be locked in combat, becoming a vortex of flashing and pulsing in a chaotic crescendo that rhythmically swelled and ebbed throughout the chamber, as if Jaemus had fallen into the heart of the Glister Cloud. If the beings were equal in power, they could not destroy each other. But, if he understood it right, they could destroy each other's vessels and thus end their worlds and everything that was part of them.

Helplessly, he scanned the immediate area, debating with himself whether he preferred to die standing on his feet or cringing on his belly. Through slitted eyes, he spied Evernal's body and the mound of celestial Fenestrii, Balavad's Scrylle, and satchel Ulfric had dropped nearby. Such simple objects had started this whole inter-Cosmos war. Perhaps they could be used to prevent another—if anyone survived, that was. Like him, for instance. The Verities fighting here weren't his own, after all, and if they destroyed their realms, Himmingaze wasn't going anywhere—at least not right away.

Decided, he scrambled to his knees. A sickly pale Ravener spotted him immediately and lunged with blade raised. Before Jaemus could so much as force out a cry, the golden-haired Knight had removed the Ravener's head. The felled creature didn't bleed.

Jaemus decided it would be best to stay on his belly and writhed and inched the last few paces to the artifacts. Hastily sweeping them into the satchel and slinging the long strap over his neck, he looked toward the chamber's entryway and calculated how fast he could get there and back to the hold he'd last seen Cote and the Glisternauts in. Wishful thoughts were in abundance today, it seemed, and he began to suspect he could make it if the furor here kept the Raveners and Vinnrics occupied.

Fate dealt him another slap, reminding him wishes were rarely reality, when his movements attracted yet another Ravener. Jaemus turned to spot the approaching enemy, close enough for him to realize, *That's unusual. Their tongues are forked like the mythical slangarook*—idiotic last thoughts, but he hadn't exactly had time to plan them out...

The Ravener loomed and Jaemus sucked in a breath and closed his eyes, felt warmth jet over him, which he assumed to be the swing of the hooked blade coming at his neck, then smelled that pungent sea-breeze scent again. Notably, however, he did not feel the cut of a sword.

Opening his eyes, he realized what had happened. The two Verities had parted once more, and only Vaka Aster still stood. The ghastly Verity's body lay on the floor, withered and smoking putridly. The Ravener that had been about to strike Jaemus lay nearby. Dead or stunned, Jaemus didn't know, but diminishing sparks from whatever Vaka Aster had done to him bounced from his carapace like hot grease.

Around the chamber, Raveners and Vinnrics alike stood utterly still and stared at the two Verities, some with weapons held in midstroke. Disbelief dominated every face. Jaemus felt an urge to whoop with joy he could barely contain. It was over, right? Until he caught the eyes of the pale Knight, which, though a somber golden-brown, were locked in an expression that looked all wrong on that stern face. Fear.

"Unlike you, my quin, I am not caged in any form. I am free. How does it feel to be a slave to your own creation?" The voice of Balavad sounded wrung from the air like festering ooze from a bandage, coming from everywhere. "Yours is the nature most corrupted by this sundered existence. You will see this truth better without the distractions of your realm. I am patient, and I will help you."

As if commanded, the Raveners commenced their attacks, and the Vinnrics had no choice but to engage. Vaka Aster stood an arm's-length away, and the being glanced over Aldinhuus's shoulder at Jaemus as if to ensure his safety, then turned away and grew still. The halo surrounding Aldinhuus flared again, forcing Jaemus to lower his eyes.

As his vision adjusted to the glare, he noticed the body of Mylla at his knees. Her face looked so peaceful, and he took a moment to appreciate that. She'd died in horrible pain but had perhaps found rest after all. Wherever she was, it had to be better than here. *May you pass safely into whatever you Vinnrics consider the next phase*, he wished at her and prepared to stand. Now was his chance to run for the ship hangar and Cote.

Her eyes popped opened, scaring him almost to death.

Were these Knights impossible to kill? It certainly looked to be the case. Her head was turned to the side, looking at something behind him. She was... was she trying to speak? She caught his astonished stare, and her eyes pleaded with him.

"Glunt..." she whispered.

"It's not Glunt, it's—" He cut himself off and leaned closer to her. "Sorry, not important. What can I do?"

Her gaze snapped back behind him, and with a sudden certain fear that he knew what he'd see, he jerked around.

A Flesh Caster stalked toward Vaka Aster's back, pointing the sword taken from Evernal—but Jaemus saw the way the being's eyes blazed red and knew better than to believe he was *just* a Flesh Caster. It was Balavad, in a new vessel, and nothing stood between him and Vaka Aster except Jaemus and the downed Knight Evernal. With darting glances, he searched for someone close by who could help, but the melee was too fierce, the other Knights scattered amid it.

"I'm about to do something very heroic," he whispered—to Evernal, to himself, he wasn't sure. "And I already regret it. Preemptive regret. It's a thing."

The Flesh Caster-turned-vessel hadn't noticed him crouched over Evernal. Just as Balavad lunged, Jaemus sprang over Evernal's body into the blue halo at Vaka Aster's back, shoulders angled to shove the celestial being aside. He thought wildly, *Being incinerated by blue starlight will at least be more memorable than the dozens of other ways I've nearly died in the last few Glister cycles. Avoiding being swallowed alive by a fleech is at least some consolation.*

CHAPTER FIFTY-TWO

E NOUGH.

Vaka Aster's voice boomed, nearly shattering Jaemus's skull.

By the Glister Cloud's gleaming, he thought, *that was loud! I suppose being a celestial sprite lends one extra volume.*

He gazed around, taking in a view he couldn't quite make sense of

Oh my... the sky, it's so enormous. ... Where am I? I can see every star in the Great Cosmos. It's so... it's so...

Hold on, is that a sword sticking out of me?

CHAPTER FIFTY-THREE

"Wake. Wake now, Knight of Himmingaze."

Jaemus twitched at the voice, a gruff and unfamiliar one. *Is this another Verity? By the Cloud, I hope not. I can't take another one.* His eyes remained closed as he pondered how he might have come to be lying prone on the most uncomfortable bed he'd ever been on. *Wake? Does that mean what I hope it means? I'm not dead? Because I should be dead. I saw a sword—*

His eyes flew open. "—hairy haberdasher's dangling balls of yarn! Have I been stabbed?"

He remembered the explosion of light after he'd lunged at Vaka Aster—*What was I thinking? I'm not a hero!*—then the strange sensation of flying through the Cosmos, then, and this was really the main thing, the sword that had appeared to be growing from his stomach.

"Oh thank the water and lighting!"

Jaemus blinked, barely able to make out two hazy forms in front of him. After another blink, he had to force himself to believe that he was staring into the eyes of—

"Cote?" he sputtered. "Is that really you?"

"It's me, Jae. I'm here."

Still gripped by panic, Jaemus reached for his midsection, frantically running his hands along his belly. He expected to find cold steel but touched only the fabric of his flightsuit. "But I... I was skewered like a fish on a giant sword. I could swear it."

"Aye, 'Gazian. You were indeed."

His sight had mostly cleared, but he wasn't at all sure if that was a good thing. A man's head, as solid- and dense-looking as a battering ram, with thick black curly hair pulled back in a rope, loomed just above him on the opposite side of Cote. The man peered into his face, and Jaemus recognized him: one of the Knights aboard the warship. He was sure he'd witnessed him lop at least six whole Raveners into a collection of Ravener bits all on his own.

But that wasn't what held his attention. *Stabbed, dear Cloud, that's not how things were supposed to go.* Against the will of his stubborn, leaden tongue, he asked, "Am I... am I dying?"

Cote responded, "No, you're okay. Somehow, by a providence that I still can't fully believe is real, you're okay."

The black-haired Knight leaned back, scrutinizing him. Jaemus kept his eyes on the stranger's face as he waited for what looked like was going to be bad news, noting details he'd not been able to see on the warship. Like most people's, this Knight's eyebrows came in a set. Unlike most, instead of a gap midway over his nose, his brows connected in an unbroken line there, but were split neatly over the left eye in a long, deep scar that ended in brambly mutton chops. He was easily the hairiest being, man or beast, Jaemus had ever seen. The other thing that stood out on his face was the nine-pointed star in the center of his bouldery chin.

Finally, the Knight said, "Nay, you're not dying, you're not. Why would you be?" He grabbed one of Jaemus's hands in a grip that felt as strong as a mounting clamp for a Himmingazian shuttle, then stood, pulling Jaemus to his feet, too.

"Wait!" he yelled, preparing for the assault of agony that must surely be the side effect of being speared through the middle. But it didn't come.

Instead, he perched on legs he would have expected to start quaking and spill him back to the ground. When he realized they held him no less sturdily than ever, his curiosity quickly outgrew his alarm. A quick, cautious glance at his belly revealed his own blood, already dry, and—and now *this* was really the main thing—no marring of the skin visible through his suit. Why no gaping wound blossomed from his belly was a question he decided could wait until shock and a lingering suspicion he was in the throes of some kind of death hallucination could be either confirmed or denied.

The Knight was watching him bemusedly, and Cote rose beside him, putting a reassuring hand on his shoulder. Unsure what to say, Jaemus took in his surroundings.

They occupied a chamber of some sort that looked like it had been blasted to pieces, and the roof was caved in. *A bit like the Creatress's shrine,* he thought. Though this place looked battered by violence rather than time. A doorway with a broken timber door barely hanging from its hinges led toward another space beyond, but it was too gloomy to see much of it.

The space was filled with what seemed to be all or at least most of the Glisternauts who'd been aboard the *Bounding Skate* before it had been swallowed by the warship. They all looked well enough, if confounded and scared, and a few flashed him smiles when they saw he was able to stand. The impression he was left with, more than anything, was that he was among a group of refugees.

"Let's see if I have this right," he began shakily. "Not only have I survived being impaled, I've also miraculously healed completely, we are safely off the wicked sprite's ship, and we are now in... let me guess, Vinnr?"

The Knight said, "You've got that right. I pulled the sword out myself, I did. Star Spark, Mylla's sword. Would have destroyed Ulfric, and Vaka Aster, and all of Vinnr if you hadn't stepped in front of that Ravener before he could strike. Brave man, you are, brave and," he appraised Jaemus, "tougher than you look. What they say is true: thin skin knits quick, it does." With a lighthearted slap on Jaemus's shoulder that nearly sent him tumbling to the floor, the Knight asked, "What I most want to know is why the Knights of Lífs's Order bear Vaka Aster's mark." His misshapen eyebrows rose questioningly.

The entire monologue was so outside of Jaemus's scope of understanding that he could do nothing but remind himself to close his mouth, which he'd realized was agape. Then it began to dawn on him. "You think I'm a Knight, like you? Of Lífs? No, see, I'm no Knight of anything. I'm a Glint Engineer." Even as he spoke, his thoughts fixed on a very important question. *Healing? How could I be healing? That blade went all the way through me!*

The Knight's misshapen eyebrow bunched in a momentary scowl, then arched in a look that said *Have it your way*. "Strange jest. I think I may not be onto your people's humor, Knight—or should I call you Mystae? That's the Himmingazian Order, if I'm not mistaken, eh?" He reached out and grasped Jaemus's right elbow with his left hand and placed his right on the center of his chest. "Name is Stave Thorvíl, Knight Corporealis of Vaka Aster. Let me be the first to welcome you to Vinnr, Knight of Lífs Glunt Un-gee-nur."

"It's not Glunt, it's Jaemus, Jaemus Bardgrim." Ordinarily by this point, he might have been annoyed at how badly everyone garbled his name and title, but his mind was too awhirl with unbelievable notions to care. He had to repeat them, as if doing so was the only way he'd believe them: "This isn't Himmingaze and... just to reiterate, I'm not a Knight. And I'm definitely not a Mystae." To Cote, he said in Himm, "They think I'm one of them, a thing they call the Knights Corporealis, esteemed protectors of the Verities." He forced a chuckle and looked at Cote to back him up on his assertion he was no such thing, but his life-mate was looking... less than agreeable. In fact, the way his forehead was stepped with wrinkles showed he was toying with a thought he wasn't altogether comfortable with.

Stave went on. "Heh, all right then. You're trying to tell me the people of your realm, they're just quick healers, they are. I suppose I'll have some time to get used to you. No telling how long it'll be until Vaka Aster sends you back. You speak fair Elder Veros, though, for a man who's not a Knight, I'd say you do." He gave Jaemus a conspiratorial wink. "Suppose all Himmingazian folk do that too then, do they?"

"He was ordained by Vaka Aster, not Lífs."

They all looked toward the resonant, clear voice. The female Knight from the warship, who'd clearly been injured but seemed hale now, was approaching from the far side of the chamber. She wore a satchel —Jaemus saw it was *the* satchel, the one that had contained all the celestial artifacts—over one shoulder, and carried a Fenestros in her hand.

Stave paced to her and wrapped his arms, both bulking through the armholes of his sleeveless brown tunic with more muscles than Jaemus had in his entire body, around the woman. Her height almost matched his, but his width swallowed her frame completely. "Glad you're back, love. How was the hunting?"

She stepped out of his embrace, and said, "We captured enough for another day or two, and there are still two parties out. The commoners, and our Himmingazian guests, won't go hungry." Then she looked to Jaemus, kindness softening her middle-aged face. "You're something else, Master Himmingazian. A truly unique spirit. I don't think any language has the words to tell you how much gratitude we all have. You saved worlds." Her lips moved when she spoke, but her voice, he realized, seemed to be coming from the celestial stone. "I am Safran Glór."

The admiration in her eyes made his cheeks flush, and he stammered, "It... it wasn't anything—I mean, it *was*, but—"

He cut himself off as she poked curiously at the exposed flesh beneath his torn flight suit.

"Whoa, quit tickling," he said.

She removed her hand, then held the Fenestros up toward his face. Its surface shifted from a swirl of gold and white to a smooth, glasslike finish. He saw his reflection perfectly in it. The high collar of his flight suit had been torn and rumpled and now fell away from his face, exposing his chin and neck. In dark blue lines on his chin, as clear as his nose, was a nine-pointed star. His mouth fell open again.

"It's true," she said and lowered the celestial stone. "You've been ordained by Vaka Aster and gifted the Verity's celestial spark."

"Um—about that. I… I'm not sure I like the sound of it. What exactly does 'gifted with a celestial spark' mean?"

"It means Vaka Aster has chosen you to be one of us," answered a new voice, coming from the tallest and palest of the Knights from the warship. "I'm Mallich Roibeard, Stallari Regent, at least until Ulfric rejoins us. And I speak for us all when I say we will never be able to thank you enough."

Jaemus felt as though his mind was about to lift off on a jaunt into the Cosmos again and abandon the rest of him. "I think I need to sit down. Not feeling too sparky at the moment." His legs spilled him to his rear, but Cote held on to him, easing him down. He mumbled, "Can someone please explain what's happening?"

The Knights sat in a semicircle around him and described what had occurred between the moment he'd saved Vaka Aster's vessel, Ulfric, and now. The first thing he was told was that two days had passed. His not knowing the meaning of the word "day" meant the conversation stalled at first until he finally deciphered it—it was about as long as two cycles of Glister Dim and Bright. He'd been out for that long. As they explained, he translated into Himm for Cote, who grew paler and paler as the tale unfolded.

His vessel-saving jump in front of Evernal's sword had alerted Vaka Aster, and she'd simply… ignited. Stave described it: "Like an ember-flare cannon the size of Halla." In the explosion, a starpath had opened, and every person of both Vinnr and Himmingaze had been transported through it, arriving safely on the flanks of Mount Omina, the natural terminus of Vinnr's starpath well.

Almost immediately, Ivoryssian scouts who'd been watching the portal had found them and begun taking the Ivoryssians and other Vinnric survivors back to Asteryss. In the meantime, the Knights had barred all but the Himmingazians from entering the mountain sanctuary, as much to shield Ulfric and Vaka Aster from the stunned and frightened Vinnrics as to protect the foreigners. The people of Vinnr had just been invaded by a force from another realm. The Knights thought it prudent to circumvent any looming hostility they might retain for strangers by keeping the Himmingazians separated.

"We know only that the warship was destroyed. Beyond that, we're still waiting for Ulfric, or Vaka Aster, to tell us," Mallich said and looked meaningfully toward the far end of the chamber.

Jaemus peered in that direction, focusing closely for the first time, and realized a raised platform of stone sat there. A body lay supine atop it. "Is that Aldinhuus?" he asked.

The three Knights nodded. "Yes," Mallich confirmed. "And he has not yet awoken. Nor has the Vigil Star."

Jaemus watched a dark look pass among the three Knights. "Has anyone given him a shake?" he asked.

Stave chirruped out a laugh that sounded a bit like a Glisternaut ship's engine backfiring. But the mood was instantly snuffed when Jaemus artlessly blurted the next thought to cross his mind. "And where is Knight Evernal?" At the way their faces fell, he knew. "She's… gone?"

Safran answered using the Fenestros, "Gone, yes. We don't know if she's rejoined the Great Cosmos or not, however. Until Vaka Aster graces us, we can't say."

Silence fell over them, each thinking their own thoughts. For his part, Jaemus couldn't help but wonder at the meaning of Evernal's disappearance. She'd been awake, aware, and completely alive the moment before his act of heroism. So why wasn't she here with the rest of them?

With no answer available, his thoughts moved on to the idea that he had for some reason been converted into a super Himmingazian who could easily walk off a stab wound the size of a soup bowl. *When was I... "chosen"? Was it when I knocked Aldinhuus out, and Vaka Aster got into my head? Did the Verity zap me with her sprite spark then?* He wondered if he'd ever know what had truly happened, or why he'd been given a so-called gift he'd never really asked for. Finally, he said, "So, what now?"

Mallich answered. "We don't know if Balavad has been defeated, and we don't know what kind of circumstances have befallen Ulfric and Vaka Aster. So, we're going to wait until the last of the Ivoryssians has returned home, then rebuild the interrealm portal and go back to Vigil Tower. If fortune finds us, Ulfric will be conscious by then."

"... And if he isn't?"

One by one, they looked at him, but it was Safran who spoke. "Then we will mourn our lost sister and celebrate our new brother. You were ordained under... unusual circumstances, Jaemus Bardgrim, but we welcome you among us. You're one of us now. A Knight Corporealis."

CHAPTER FIFTY-FOUR

little sloth sleeps on a rock and dreams of ants and berries
A girl runs up and pets his ruff and slips the sloth some cherries
Ulfric heard Isemay's voice from far off, echoing inside a starscape as vast as the ache in his heart. He was remembering her singing that little tune to herself when she'd been very young, her child's voice so sweet and silly. If he was dying now—and he hoped he was—he was content that her voice would be the last thing he would hear. Why would he want to go on if Symvalline and Isemay were gone?

But that wasn't the truth. Was it? He'd just seen Isemay, heard her speaking through the memory keeper he'd given her. Before Vaka Aster had taken over his mind, his body. Before his maker had told him she could not set him free. Before he'd escaped into the void, trying to remember to forget. Because nothing his maker told him was the truth.

Was it?

How long had he been in this black? The tomb of exile?

They are in danger.

Her voice, Vaka Aster, crashing through the shield of grief he'd erected as if it were made of paper. He pushed back, tried to ignore her and her accursed presence. He felt her here with him, and he bent his full will on keeping her away. He would not tolerate her deceptions any longer. Better to remain untouched, uncorrupted, within the bitter pool of sorrow he had fled to.

If you do not come back, one way or another, you will be the doom of Vinnr.

Come back? To what? More death. No hope. He couldn't face endless eternity any longer. Wouldn't. Not without his beloved heart-match and child. He hated Vaka Aster for expecting this of him. Hated and reviled her and all she'd done to ruin his life, his happiness.

Return to yourself, Ulfric, and unmake the cage you've bound us both in. You must find a way to set us free. Look in Balavad's Scrylle, it will show you the way. Only then can you seek your family in Arc Rheunos, the realm of my quin Mithli.

She was taking it too far, his maker. The unchecked duplicity, the taunts.

His silence broke: *I'm finished with your deceptions, Vaka Aster. I am not the fool you must think. Balavad's Scrylle is unreachable.*

No, Stallari Aldinhuus, it is here, in Vinnr, where you are.

That was interesting. Had Balavad been defeated? Was it true they were back in Vinnr? *If I am in Vinnr, why is my family in Arc Rheunos? Bring them back to me, Vaka Aster, or let me go after them, and I might believe you.*

It cannot be done. It is too dangerous to travel the starpaths in this form. Endanger yourself and you endanger my realm.

He realized he'd been drawn into a debate with Vaka Aster once again, despite his unwillingness to do so, but he brushed this fact aside. *Why,* he asked, *did you send them there in the first place?*

The starpath opened to all the realms when you tied yourself into this knot we now occupy. At the moment I was caught between vessels, I became aware of Knight Lutair on the mountainside with the Raveners of Battgjald drawing near. When I took them into the starpath, it was only chance that sent you to Himmingaze and them to Arc Rheunos.

He remembered the moment clearly. Balavad had tortured him with the vision of Symvalline holding an avalanche at bay with her klinkí stones while she and his Crumb crouched beneath and a group of Battgjaldic warriors approached. He'd been so certain their deaths were imminent and had done the one thing he could think of: he'd pleaded with Vaka Aster to spare them and, hoping to release Vaka Aster, had thrown himself into the halo of circling Fenestrii that composed the Verity cage Balavad had tricked him into creating. And now he understood fully. He'd freed his maker from one cage, but by his will or fear or some wystic strength he hadn't known he possessed, he'd turned himself into the prison that now shackled them both.

Why did you do this to me? he thought, and wasn't sure whom he was asking—himself or his maker.

You are the strongest of my creations.

Once more, grief settled into the silence that drew out like eternity's river, and he pulled the veil of blackness between him and Vaka Aster to shut her out of his thoughts completely. Yet one statement she'd made tickled his mind. And soon it came to him.

You drew Sym and Isemay into the starpath? You intervened on their behalf? It was known, or assumed, the Verities did not interfere with the lives of their creations beyond what was necessary to keep their realms stable—if they chose to. If Vaka Aster had saved Symvalline and Isemay from the Raveners, she'd defied her own rules.

She did not respond to his questions, and the silence drew out. He tore the veil between them aside, demanding an answer. *Why?*

Finally, it came, but the answer did not satisfy him. *It is enough that I have. You are among the Knights again,* she went on. *They protect you, protect us. Balavad's Scrylle is the way to remedy this. You can be free. But you have to awaken from your despair. Your greatest power is hope. Use it and save everything you love.*

These words jolted him, triggered a memory. When he and Symvalline had first started discussing leaving the Order after Isemay had been born, she had said almost the same thing. "Ulfric, the most precious gift we have isn't our long lives, it is our love. Vaka Aster will release us from our oaths when we show her what our daughter means to us."

He'd responded, "Vaka Aster is not a being guided by reason. There is no way of knowing what she'll do if we ask for this."

She'd twined her hand into his and smiled in a way that always disarmed him, teasing, "Old man, your overlong dedication to your duty has made you forget freedom and having hopes for your own sake. It's understandable. But don't worry, my love, I remember, and I will hope for both of us. Our maker will release us. Trust me."

But now it was up to *him* to release their maker, wasn't it? Which meant, in a strange twist of fates, that it had become *his* choice whether he would see Symvalline and Isemay again.

I will do it, Vaka Aster. But you must swear to me you will not interfere. Once I return to my waking self, stay out of my way. No one but I will be master of my own will. He almost couldn't believe his own boldness, even insolence, to be making demands of a celestial being. But he had grown so tired of being a pawn. If Vaka Aster wanted freedom, then he would have it too. He would agree to nothing that didn't ensure his will would finally be truly, entirely his own.

Her response came without hesitation. *I leave your fate, and Vinnr's, in your hands, Stallari Aldinhuus.*

Ulfric opened his eyes.

EPILOGUE

The ancient citadels and minarets of Dyrrakium, even the humblest of them composed of red stone and decorated with the flashing iron-like puurite stone, blossomed in the haze of the arid coastal plain beneath Eisa's dragørfly scout like the flowers in a half-remembered dream. It had been hundreds of turns since she'd been back to her homeland, since the Cataclysm in fact, but far fewer since she'd last spoken with Domine Ecclesium Nazaria, ruler of the empire.

As she targeted the flat courtyard inside the Ecclesium's palace for landing, her eyes brushed over the blade lying beside her on her pilot seat. The length of a hatchet, it was too big to be considered simply a dagger, and though it was ceremonial, it was no less deadly. It had been given to her by the long-dead Domine Ecclesium over a thousand turns ago when she'd passed her Fifth and final Phase of the Lœdyrrak, a test for all half-agers in her home kingdom to gauge their worthiness and strength along their path to citizenry. "Lœdyrrak" meaning "flourishing land" no longer existed. The name of her home had been changed to Dyrrakium, "exiled land," or simply "exile," after the Cataclysm.

Many things had changed after the Cataclysm, so named for the events that had brought the kingdoms of Ivoryss and Yor to the brink of war against Dyrrakium. The empire had tried to usurp the Yor throne—or so commoners believed—and, failing that, Dyrrakium had closed their borders against all other kingdoms. But that was another story, and not quite the truth.

The Cataclysm had brought about many changes. For Eisa, they had been more personal, the losses sharper, most particularly the loss of her lover, Lillias, which in turn had nearly caused her the loss of her faith. To save them, she'd had to make sacrifices. And she'd made them willingly. Now, none but her own people, the Dyrraks, knew the truths buried at the heart of the Cataclysm. Not even the Knights knew the things she'd done.

One of those hidden truths adorned her Dyrrak dagger. The Stallari wasn't the only Knight who could glean secrets and spin wystic contraptions from the Scrylle. The weapon bore the distinct curve and greenish metal blade common to Dyrrakium. The haft, however, was singular. A broken, rough chunk of stone, about the size of a child's fist, served as the pommel nut. Only the top of the stone was polished, a half orb suggesting it may once have been part of a complete sphere —as it had been. The haft of this specific blade seemed a fitting setting for the stone, after what she'd used it on—or rather, whom. As for the stone fragment, two others existed, and when put together, the fifth Fenestrii of Lífs, Verity of Himmingaze, would again be whole. No one else but the current Domine Ecclesium—and of course, Griggory Dondrin—knew this truth.

The two other pieces of the Fenestros were in the hands of the Domine himself and the Speaker, who provided a conduit for the celestial power within the stone. The Speaker had once been a noble-woman of Yor, and she had not chosen her role. It had been forced on her. *What would it be like to see her again?* Eisa wondered. *After so long.*

With a sharp self-rebuke, she pulled her eyes away from the stone. Thinking of Lillias, the woman she'd loved and who had betrayed her, was an unacceptable distraction. *Has being away from the Dyrraks for so long made you soft, Eisa?*

As she landed the scout in the Citadel Suprima's courtyard, a consort of servitors wearing short tunics and sandals and the Domine Ecclesium were already waiting for her. They'd been expecting her. The fragment of Verity stone atop her dagger, which she'd used to notify the Ecclesium of her coming, had finally served the critical purpose she'd always known it would: Dyrrakium had needed to be warned of the usurping Verity's plans to give them time to prepare. The Knights may think her a traitor, but it wasn't true. No one had more faith in their maker than Eisa Nazaria. And no one had a better-trained army than the Dyrrak.

The fledgling Dyrrak warriors, bearing Fourth Phase rune badges, cut and healed into blackened scars on their chests and arms, stood in a circle with their heads bowed as the Domine Ecclesium approached the scout. As she disembarked from the scout, the crunch of red sand beneath her boots, a feeling as familiar and welcome to her as breathing, made her almost smile. But she didn't.

Ecclesium Nazaria stepped forward, crossed his arms over his chest, and bowed deeply.

"Domine Ecclesium," she said, "how keeps your faith?"

Straightening, he responded, "Eternal, unchanged, and pure, Nazarian Most High."

Nazarian Most High. It has been a long time since I've heard that title. She noted the resemblance between this leader and herself, the same clear gray eyes, pitch-black hair, and red-umber skin. As her descendent—her nephew, twelve generations removed—none was more fitted to lead both the Nazaria Line and the empire, for their family had taken over rule of Dyrrakium when Vaka Aster chose a Nazaria as her last vessel, over two thousand turns ago.

In that ancient age when all the kingdoms were still united as one, Vigil Tower was built on the mainland and taken as residence by Vaka Aster. In the years that followed, after the War of Rivening and Lœdyrrak's creation, Eisa had joined the Knights at the age of thirty-six turns instead of ascending as the next Domine Ecclesium. Her duty then had been easier, despite it meaning living her life among the lesser kingdoms as a Knight Corporealis.

The faith of the Dyrrakium people was stronger even than the

Knight Order, and it would stand against the greatest challenges facing their Verity after the Knights fell. Second to serving Vaka Aster, Eisa's other purpose had always been to ensure the Dyrraks would be prepared when that day came. As it had now.

"It is good," she said. "As I told you, I've come on urgent business. Another Verity has broken faith with its kind and is spreading its dominion throughout Vinnr. Yor and Ivoryss have already fallen."

"It is worse than we expected," the Dyrrak leader said.

Ah, this was good. If the Domine Ecclesium was aware of the outside world, it meant the Dyrraks were still maintaining spies in the lesser kingdoms. "What do you know?"

The Ecclesium beckoned to a nearby servitor, who came forward with a tray of fruit and a firkin of fermented syke liquor, a favorite Dyrrak drink. Eisa's mouth watered in anticipation of the bittersweet taste of her homeland, and the way it scoured the throat and mind.

"We have found foreign spies crawling through Dyrrakium," the Ecclesium said. "And have learned their purpose, then cleansed them like the vermin they were."

"It is good," she said again, approving. Strength was one of the Dyrraks' Six Aspects of Devotion to the Verities. If a person dared pit themselves against the Dyrraks, they would be pushed, mercilessly, to the edge of their own. "You must prepare yourselves," she went on. "Vinnr has reached a new age, and the Dyrraks may be the only people left by the time this Verity's plundering is stanched. The armies of Dyrrakium have had enough time to prepare. Send them in full force to Ivoryss, for that is where the battle is now."

"And you, Nazarian?"

"I believe I may know how to stop the desecrator, but I must travel the stars to learn more. I will leave you this." She retrieved a map from a pouch and handed it to him. "Keep it safe. Should you need to parlay with the Knights, this will let them know I've sent you."

The Ecclesium took the map, and Eisa enumerated the details of Balavad's forces and strategies.

When she finished, the Dyrrak leader asked, "And would you like to see the Speaker before you go?"

Your chance to see Lillias once more, perhaps for the last time. Eisa strangled that thought. "No. I leave forthwith. Keep your faith in this fight, and Vaka Aster willing, I will return soon."

"Faith eternal, Nazarian. May the lights of our celestial maker ever shine through your blades."

AFTERWORD

To my treasured reader, I'm deeply grateful for your readership your presence in my wordy world. If my book has touched your heart with magic or transported you to another realm, would you consider sharing your thoughts through a review on your favorite retailer? Your voice carries immense value and can guide fellow readers to a tale that resonates with them too. Together, we can build a community of kindred spirits, connected through the power of storytelling. Thank you for your kindness and support.

Don't forget to join my newsletter at www.tammysalyer.com/news letter to stay up to date on new releases and receive a free collection of stories. Cheers!

ABOUT THE AUTHOR

Tammy is an inveterate verbarian, who spends her days surrounded by the written word, both hers and others'. As an ex-paratrooper with the 82nd Airborne Division, her stories are often as gritty as a grunt's pile of three-week-old field gear. Her military science fiction Spectras Arise series debuted to acclaim in 2012, and her epic fantasy adventure series The Shackled Verities was launched in 2020. She's currently five books deep in a Weird West series called Otherworld Outlaws, featuring half-fae sawbones, a necromancer gnome, and a hoodoo cowgirl galavanting into mischief in the Old West.

When not hunched like a Morlock over her writing desk, Tammy runs and bikes silly miles with her super-cool weirdo partner in the Pacific Northwest playground and spends an inappropriate amount of time watching Henry Rollins videos on YouTube. Contrary to whatever ideas her last name might conjure, she's never really been much of a Slayer fan.

Fantasy, space opera, satire, and snark fans will feel right at home with Tammy. Learn more about her and her books by visiting www.tammysalyer.com. She hopes you enjoy reading her works and welcomes your reviews.